The Taxidermist's Catalog

THE TAXIDERMIST'S CATALOG

A NOVEL

JAMES BRUBAKER

BRADDOCK
AVENUE
BOOKS

UNCOMMON BOOKS · UNCOMMON READERS

Printed in the United States of America
10 9 8 7 6 5 4 3 2 1

FIRST EDITION, September 2019

ISBN 10: 1-7328956-4-5
ISBN 13: 978-1-7328956-4-5

Book design by Savannah Adams
Cover photo by Mick Haupt, Unsplash

Braddock Avenue Books
P.O. Box 502
Braddock, PA 15104

www.braddockavenuebooks.com

Braddock Avenue Books is distributed by Small Press Distribution.

For Jessica, always

THE
TAXIDERMIST'S
CATALOG

A NOVEL

I. NEW GHOSTS FOR AN OLD CITY

Jim Toop disappeared in 1977. He was twenty-seven years old. The first song on his first album, *New Ghosts for an Old City*, is called "New Ghosts for an Old City." Toop wrote the song in 1967 within months of moving to Los Angeles with his father. He was seventeen. It's always been one of my favorite of his songs. That's not to say it's one of his best. In fact, as an album, *New Ghosts for an Old City* is a middling collection of songs, known more for its raw production and off-the-cuff songwriting than its quality. The most raw and off-the-cuff song on the album, though, is the title track. That's why I like it. Across four albums released between 1969 and his disappearance in 1977—his last album was released in 1975— Jim Toop never sounded as pure and unfiltered as on that first song. In his fingerpicked guitar lines can be heard a rare restlessness, in his voice a bare uncertainty—he doesn't sound like a musician recording an album in a Los Angeles studio, but like a kid who had just moved from Ohio to New Mexico to California in the span of three years, and who might at any moment start crying through his low, vocal fry. The song is a mess, but it's an honest mess. Even the album's cover is messy: a man, presumably Toop, wearing nothing but white briefs and a Richard Nixon mask, years before Watergate, is leaning against Griffith Observatory, playing a guitar next to an upside down top hat into which a few coins have been tossed; Toop's name adorns the lower left hand corner in a sloppy, hand-written scrawl; the album title drips down across the top in an illegible, lime-green, psychedelic font. It's a miracle anyone found the album or knew what to call it when they did. But listeners found it, and despite its rough edges, they liked what they heard. When Toop begins the album singing, "Found you in a gold rush/pink-cheeked, face-flushed/Hushed beneath flickering lights on screens," the frayed edges of his voice are so ragged that he sounds ancient. Some Toop fans, myself included, believe that—though there is no clear textural evidence to support such a claim, save for the emotional intensity with which the lines are delivered—the lyric represents Toop's first reference to a key figure in the mythology surrounding his music: the beloved, mysterious Angela.

But I digress: Toop's work after *New Ghosts for an Old City* improved mightily on the skeletal songs and timid melodies that hobbled that album and, though he never achieved any sort of real commercial success, his work was adored by critics and earned a small but impassioned cult following, among whom I count myself a member. That's why when Richard Epps, Editor-in-Chief of *Folk! Magazine*, calls and says, "Dan, Daniel, Danny—I've got a job for you," and I say, "I'm contemplating retirement, for good—I mean, Jesus, I'm closing in on sixty," leading Dick to counter with, "It's about this new Jim Toop tape that just landed on my desk," the only thing I can do is ask how much he is paying, even though we both know already that it doesn't matter. Richard Epps doesn't answer my question about payment for the same reason that, instead of asking if he should send a car, he tells me one is already on the way.

*

Of course Richard Epps and *Folk! Magazine* have a car to send. And sure, it's a modest car, but the magazine shouldn't exist, period, what with the decline of print media and all. Technically, the car is Epps's, not the magazine's, and it's usually driven by his twenty-four year old son, Ronnie, who graduated from college a couple of years ago with a degree in journalism. Now he drives the "company" car for his dad. Were it not for Richard Epps's generous inheritance, I suspect the magazine would have shut down a decade ago, an early victim of the industry's decline. Thanks to the deaths of his wealthy parents, though, it lives on, albeit as little more than a vanity project—a glossy, eight and three-eighths by ten and three-quarters vanity project that boasts interviews with and articles on prominent contemporary folk artists. As for that modest car, it's a well-kept, maroon, 2000 Toyota Camry with about eight thousand miles on it, presumably all city, and a driver who talks to his passengers about the jobs he's applied for since finishing college, and how his driving is helpful since he can list an honest-to-god print magazine on his résumé. The first time I was ever in this car was when it was brand new and Dick Epps himself—Ronnie wasn't even old enough to drive yet, not by a longshot—drove across town to pick my puking-drunk-ass up at the bar. That was the day that my divorce from my second wife, Amanda, was finalized. I was belligerent and out of cash so the bartender asked me if he should call a cab or the police. I had one of Dick's new business cards in my pocket so I handed it to the guy and twenty minutes later I was sprawled out across the Camry's backseat, my head propped up beside the open window in case I needed to be sick again. Dick asked me why I was so upset over Amanda as, from what I'd told him previously, the divorce was amicable, necessary even. In response, I mumbled some shit about Betty, my first wife. I don't remember any of this, but Dick told me after the fact. He said, "I hadn't heard you talk about Betty like that in a while." I asked him, "Like what? What did I say?" He said," I'm not sure, but you were feeling it. This is why, when Ronnie Epps pulls up in the maroon Camry and opens the back door for me like he's some kind of real chauffer, I decline and sit in the front instead—too much baggage in that backseat. Also, up front I can probe Ronnie for information about this tape I'm on my way to find out about.

I'm a bit skeptical because I haven't heard anything about the tape. Even if its content is minor, though—which I strongly suspect is the case as Toop was known for not recording more songs than he intended to put on an album—as a follower of the Toop fan community, if a new tape had been discovered, people would know. Once settled in the car, I ask Epps's kid if he knows anything about the tape. I ask him, "You like Jim Toop?" Ronnie says, "Jim who?" I say, "The musician whose tape I'm going to talk to your dad about." He says, "Tape?" Then: "What tape?" I tell the kid never mind what tape and let him drive in peace.

*

Among his critics and fans, there are two main narratives about Toop's career. The one in which I'm most interested has to do with Toop's romantic involvement with a woman named Angela. I'm in the minority. Most of Toop's fandom is primarily interested in his disappearance. But there are enough of us—or were, anyway, before we started running out of songs to painstakingly analyze—interested in Angela to drive a comprehensive critical discourse rooted in seeking out and analyzing all of Toop's references to Angela, despite most of the songs' lack of concrete, textual evidence connecting them to her. Sometimes, though, that's what fans and critics have to do when an artist disappears leaving behind only a small and finite body of work.

For the uninitiated, Angela doesn't show up by name until Toop's final album, 1975's criminally underrated *Your Sunglasses are in the Junk Drawer*. Though Angela was only named in one of that album's songs—only one of Toop's songs, period—when she did show up, the singer's powerful romantic longing for her was clear. From that single appearance on Toop's "New Mexico" album, fans deduced that Angela lived in New Mexico, where Jim Toop had lived with his father for about a year, shortly before their move to Los Angeles and the beginning of his music career. This prompted a segment of fans and critics to look for Angela in every reference to every woman on all of Toop's albums. There was no way anyone could have known to look for Angela when Toop was releasing those earlier albums, but after that one reference, and in the growing vacuum left in the absence of new music, we've had plenty of time to find Angela in Toop's songs, to construct a Frankenstein's Monster of Angela from the stray lyrical hints and clues Toop left in his wake. Who knows if the Angela we've created has a real life counterpart at all, or, if she does, if that counterpart is anything like the fragmented mosaic that exists in our minds. Of course, the centrality of Angela's importance to Toop scholars and fans pales in comparison to interest in Toop's disappearance, all those conspiracy theories and sordid stories with which even some folks who have never heard a single note of Toop's music seem to have at least a passing familiarity. But I'm not interested in that scene. The reason I'm cautiously excited about this new tape is the possibility of learning more about Angela, to have new music to comb, pick apart, analyze—to feel, as fleeting as it will probably be, the way it felt to be a Toop fan ten, fifteen, twenty years ago, when we obsessed over Toop's Angela, grasping at straws in search of a clearer narrative and a greater emotional coherency in his work. Forget the fact that such coherency probably doesn't exist—the excitement was in the process, the search. Until today, my interest in Angela had waned, faded to the point that I questioned why I was ever interested in her at all as—after all, Angela, like discussions surrounding Toop's disappearance, is peripheral to the man's music, is merely a footnote that informs, rather than shapes Toop's musical legacy. Sometimes, over the past decade, or so, after everything that could be said about Angela had dried up, I thought that maybe my own interest in Angela never had anything to do with Toop at all, but with the *idea* of Angela. Or maybe it was something else altogether. I don't know. But now, today, with the promise of new-old music from Toop, even if the music in question is slight, I'm feeling some of that old excitement. Now, a confession: I'd be lying if I didn't begrudgingly admit that I'm slightly curious, too, to see if any of the new material feeds the ever burning flames of the UFO abduction stories and conspiracy theories that have, for decades, dogged discussions of Toop's disappearance.

Ronnie drops me off in front of the six-story building that houses the office of *Folk! Magazine*. Epps runs his operation out of a quarter of the fourth floor, impressive for a high quality, niche magazine with low circulation. He is outside smoking. I ask him for a cigarette. "You think I made it this far giving away cigarettes for free?" he says. "Give me a smoke or I'm leaving," I say, a hollow threat. Richard Epps fishes a cigarette out of his jacket pocket, tosses it to me. I ask for a light. "You're helpless," Richard Epps says. He strikes a match on one the building's bricks. The first couple of puffs make my head hum. I haven't smoked in months. When the buzz settles, I ask Epps about the new Jim Toop tape. He says, "It's a tape, alright." I ask if it's real, half joking, expecting an easy confirmation, because who would go to the trouble of faking new songs by Jim Toop? His response catches me off guard. "You tell me," he says. "We'll talk inside." My curiosity piqued, I finish my cigarette too quickly and feel a little bit nauseated as we head inside.

*

Epps pulls the tape out of a manila envelope. It's a 7" Ampex reel-to-reel. I ask if he has the original box; he doesn't. That's a shame. The tape is half-inch, eight track, 1,800 feet; if recorded at the industry standard of fifteen inches per second, it would contain just under fifty minutes of music. I ask if we're going to listen. "Do you have a machine, or what?" I ask. "Not here," Epps says. "So what am I supposed to do with it?" I ask. Epps tells me, "Take it with you." Reading the surprise on my face, Epps quickly adds, "Not to keep, but for as long as you need it."

I ask what he wants from me, what the tape even is, fully expecting a few half-finished melodies, maybe a discarded song from early in Toop's career, some guitar strumming and banter. Epps turns the envelope upside down and taps it. A hand scrawled list falls out, faded and written in pencil on a small sheet of yellowed paper. I hold the paper under Epps's desk lamp. Across the top are printed the words "The Taxidermist's Catalog." Beneath is a list of songs:

1. Frozen
2. Desert Birds
3. Sideways Glances
4. Forget Me Not
5. Paintings of Old Flowers
6. That Old Game Show
7. (Hideaway) Bed
8. Mark's Novel
9. Thirty Seconds
10. Weather
11. Nothing Truer
12. Cormac Bleeding

I recognize several titles from old rumors of Toop's final, unfinished project, long believed to have disappeared with its creator. This is not what I was expecting when Epps called. This is huge. "You're shitting me," I say. I ask him what else he knows about the tape. He says, "This is how it was sent to me. Just like this." I ask where it came from. Epps says he doesn't know, the tape was left in front of the *Folk! Magazine* offices last week. I ask who knows about it. "Nobody," he says, and I believe him. If Ronnie doesn't know, and the Toop fan community doesn't know, who else is worth telling? "So why are you giving this to me?" I ask. "You're going to find out if it's real," Epps says. Then: "You really thinking about retiring?" I say, "Something like that." I ask him if he's listened to the tape—he has. I ask, "What do you think?" He says, "I think it sounds like Toop, but you're the expert." I ask him if it's good. He grins, says, "Damn good," then we talk about money.

*

Just to be clear, we're not talking a lot of money here, but more than I expected: a grand up front, and two more upon reporting my findings, with an option, for two grand more, on writing the album's liner notes and/or a feature for *Folk!* when the album is released. Also: .15% in royalties for all copies sold of *The Taxidermist's Catalog* during its first three years of release, which won't amount to much. This was Epps's opening offer and I accepted it. I probably could have negotiated for more, but why bother?

*

See, Dick Epps and I both know that he didn't need to pay me much. Why? Because I've been a Jim Toop fan since I was a teenager, and an expert in Toop for my entire professional career as a writer. My first published and paid piece of writing was a retrospective on Toop's career. I was only nineteen when Toop disappeared, but in 1978, when his first album was brought back into print—the others never went out of print—I pitched an article to *Creem*, a profile of Toop, with an emphasis on his *Black Triangle* album and the mysteries surrounding his disappearance. I was young still, and *Creem* paid me seventy-five bucks for a heavily edited article that filled two pages. I'd arrived. A few months later, when the *New Ghosts for an Old City* re-issue hit the bins, I was hired to review it. I wrote two hundred words about the formative quality of the album, about how its songs paled in comparison to Toop's later works, but also about how it was an exciting album and a sensitive exploration of the modern mythology surrounding Los Angeles as seen through the eyes of a nineteen year old transplant. I wrote about how Toop's acoustic song sketches celebrating Hollywood's ghosts on songs such as "Charlie," about Chaplin of course, and "Lillian," about Gish, were wide-eyed and dewy, but also haunted. I compared the minimalist production to that of Nick Drake's *Pink Moon*, another artist and album that were just becoming light blips on popular music's radar thanks to a recently released box set. *Creem* paid me twenty-five bucks for the piece, slashed it to a hundred words and buried it in the reviews section. They could do to the piece what they wanted, I was just happy to consider myself a professional writer. After that, once or twice a year, publications started asking me to weigh in on new rumors surrounding Toop's disappearance, write new pieces about his work, and even to speak on the occasional panel about pop star mystique or artists who became more successful in death than in life. Through all of this, I've successfully kept my distance from the hard-line conspiracy theorists, while writing just enough to keep them interested.

There are other things that Richard Epps knows about me, too, from long gone days spent drinking, smoking, and jawing in bars, that tipped my interest in this particular assignment—for instance, he knows that the first dance at my first wedding, when I married Betty, was soundtracked by Toop's "Shapes Inside the Clouds," off of *Your Sunglasses are in the Junk Drawer*. He also knows that, during said dance, at the moment when Toop sings, "That point past forever where the sky meets the sand/is the end of my love, the strength of my hands," that I wept. Epps knows that Toop's third album, *Ohio Songs*, released in 1974, is my favorite album of all time, not because it is as good, or even as important as the albums right behind it on my list—rounding out my more or less predictable top five, on any given day, you'll find, in no particular order, Van Morrison's *Astral Weeks*, Dylan's *Blood on the Tracks*, The Beatles' *Rubber Soul*, and Springsteen's *Darkness on the Edge of Town*—but because Betty and I moved to Ohio shortly after our wedding when she accepted a job as a professor of Popular Culture at Bowling Green State University. We spent the late eighties and our early thirties together in Northwestern Ohio before something irreparable happened in our relationship and I had to leave. Those were good years, though. We listened to *Ohio Songs* every Sunday morning, and occasionally drove down I-75 to Dayton, where Toop grew up, and explored the city and its surrounding areas looking for the sites named in the album's songs—the Dayton Arcade, The Pine Club, Dixie Highway, the Witch's Tower up on Patterson Boulevard. Once, we drove to Washington D.C. just to visit the Arts and Industries Building of the Smithsonian to see the original Wright Flyer—it appears on the cover of *Ohio Songs*, an image from Kitty Hawk taken on the day that the Wright Brothers first showed the world how to fly—and wore out the dubbed tape I made of the album, playing it repeatedly in the car's tape deck. Later, the album came to mean something else to me. I'm not sure if Richard Epps knows this part or not, but after I had to leave Betty, so many of the songs contained such primal and lovely longing—presumably for Toop's mysterious Angela, even though Toop wouldn't have yet known Angela, assuming she's real, when he lived in Ohio (One of my favorite lyrics: "Ohio taught me how to fall in love/And you taught me how to fall, fall, fall apart")—that I'd listen to feel the ache for my own lost love. Here is the album's tracklist:

1. Base x Height and 6
2. We Learned to Fly
3. Flood
4. Huffman-Prairie
5. Hush, Hush (Leaves Change Slow)
6. Twelve
7. Here Come the Greys
8. Trains and their Cargo
9. Bike Shop
10. Dixie Highway

See, Dick Epps knows that Toop's music isn't just something I enjoy—it is inside me, is an immense and intangible part of me. Maybe he is exploiting that a little. Or maybe he thinks he's doing me a favor.

*

And, for sure—Richard Epps is doing me a bigger favor than he could possibly know. When I told him I was thinking of retiring for good, I meant it, and not in the way most folks do. I'm not going to come out and say it, though. It feels foolish, juvenile. But I'm old and tired and I've got nobody in my life—no family, no partner, nothing—and I sometimes think that maybe it's time, to borrow a phrase from Zeppelin, to ramble on. But now I've got this tape. That's something.

*

On the ride back to my apartment, I'm mostly silent. I'm already beginning to feel a bit uneasy about my task and I'm not sure why. About half way there, Ronnie Epps ask,

"What's in the envelope?" This startles me because I have forgotten that the envelope is sitting in plain view on my lap. I foolishly place a hand over it, as if I might be able to conceal it, and say, "Just something your dad asked me to listen to." I feel the weight of the tape on my lap for the rest of the ride.

*

But let's back up for a moment and take a closer look at the history of this tape, and why it even needs to be authenticated: when Jim Toop disappeared in April, 1977, he was on a solo tour through the South and Southwest. He'd been working on his fifth album and wanted a break from recording so he could tour and give his new songs a chance to breathe. He talked his label, the now defunct Ocean City, into letting him book a couple of festival gigs in New York and Pennsylvania, which would be followed by a promotional tour heading back west. He sold albums out of the trunk of his rental car and road tested new material. When Toop left, he took the tapes he'd been working on with him so that he could continue to record on the road if the opportunity presented itself. This is a bit odd, as most labels and studios would balk at the idea of an artist removing master tapes from a studio, especially without leaving a copy. As Toop was known to be private about his work, only he and his primary recording engineer, Steven Copass, knew exactly how much of the album had been recorded.

After the festival gigs, both at mid-sized universities, Toop's tour properly began in Memphis and was set to take him through Tupelo, Little Rock, Tulsa, Dallas, Albuquerque, Tucson, and San Diego before he was to arrive home in Los Angeles. Toop's Tucson gig was scheduled for three nights after Albuquerque, but he never showed. His rental car was found abandoned on I-25, a few miles outside of Truth or Consequences, New Mexico. Neither Toop nor his tapes were ever found. After the disappearance, Steven Copass was fired for letting the tapes go. He'd worked at Ocean City for twenty years. After he was fired, he got wasted and drove his car into the ocean. Or that's how the story goes. The story also goes: the reason Ocean City was so upset about the missing tapes was because they were struggling financially and Toop's album-in-progress was going to be his breakthrough, the big release they'd been waiting for—a collection of songs that married Toop's critical success with a broader commercial appeal. As far as Ocean City was concerned, Toop was recording his best collection of songs and they were going to sound great on the radio alongside popular musicians of the time—think James Taylor, Cat Stevens, Jim Croce. According to Ocean City's founder, Dillon Hawkins, Toop's new album was going to *save* Ocean City. When pressed, Hawkins copped to having heard only a few songs, but those songs, in conjunction with Copass's regular updates, were enough to convince Hawkins—and subsequently all of the fans who have long ached to hear the lost album—that Toop had been working on something truly special when he disappeared.

*

At home, I open the hall closet to dig out my old reel-to-reel. It is buried beneath piles of boxes—so much bullshit I don't want to deal with, but I try. I move the first two, straining my back on the second. I test my body on the third, but my back is too stiff, and then I start thinking about what's in these particular boxes, and so I leave the tape in my desk drawer, for now, make dinner, and watch some television. Some cable channel or another is showing a block of *Cheers* episodes, so I boil frozen ravioli, toss it with canned marinara, and watch a Halloween episode in which Cliff dresses as Ponce De Leon and falls in love with a woman dressed as Tinkerbell. At the episode's conclusion, they meet up the following night, sans costumes, and dance awkwardly to one of the songs they'd danced to before—"Moon River"; it's a sweet ending, and makes me want to check my online dating profile, see if I have any hits. Instead, I go back to the hall closet and look at all those boxes. I know that the reel-to-reel is somewhere on the bottom of the stack, probably next to similar boxes containing other heavy items, unused kitchen wares received as gifts for my second wedding—from her family and friends, not mine. The rest of the boxes are full of Amanda's books. When she left, I tried to get her to take all this junk with her but all she took was her suitcase. She promised to come back for the kitchen shit, which I knew I'd never use, and the books, which were hers to begin with, but she never did. This was all about twelve years ago. She went to stay with her sister in Minneapolis, and I haven't heard from her since. Even though I've come to terms with our divorce—we were married for less than two years—I'm not prepared to dig through these boxes tonight.

*

Three days have passed and I still haven't listened to one of the most significant and unexpected musical discoveries of the last thirty years. Though Toop was never as popular as the Beach Boys, he is revered enough in the critical community and has enough of a cult following that the discovery of *The Taxidermist's Catalog* is, or will be, bigger news than the release of *Smile*. More people were hungry for *Smile* for longer, but we knew that the album existed in fragments and demos. We heard much of that album when songs wound up on other albums. Jim Toop's album wasn't like that. It was just *gone*. There are people, some of Toop's biggest fans, who would probably pay thousands of dollars, right now, to listen to the tape in my desk drawer, but here I am, not listening to it so I can avoid having to confront a closet full of somebody else's boxes.

*

But maybe there's another reason, I tell myself, why I haven't listened to the tape yet. Maybe the tape is a burden. While I certainly find the prospect of the tape's contents exciting, I might be troubled by the very real implications of actually having it, of being responsible for verifying its legitimacy, for doing whatever it is that Epps has tasked me with doing. There will be controversy the moment word of this tape reaches the Toop fan community, which isn't by any means large, but which has grown steadily since the musician's disappearance. In fact, it's probably safe to assume that Toop's audience has grown *because of* his disappearance, thanks to the slew of conspiracy theories and UFO abduction stories that have taken root and grown in the public imagination over the years. When news of this tape hits, all of the conspiracy theorists, UFO-ologists, and amateur sleuths will come bubbling up from their secret lairs and parents' basements to analyze, dispute, discredit, assess, affirm, deny, and twist, twist, twist everything about the tape to fit their pet theories. I don't know that I want to deal with that. This tape has the potential to undo the theories and beliefs of thousands—maybe tens of thousands—of interested parties. If these songs disappeared with Toop, and they are on a tape in my desk drawer, how could Toop possibly have been abducted by UFOs? How could such a clean-sounding copy of these songs have been discovered if Toop had been kidnapped by a cult or wandered into the desert to die? This tape has the potential to shake the community to its foundations, to undo—or at least reconfigure—the mysteries at the heart of Toop's allure.

The more I consider the implications of the tape, the more they terrify me. Despite my love for Toop's music, I find myself suddenly resenting the responsibility with which Richard Epps has burdened me. Maybe I'll never dig through Amanda's boxes of junk. Or maybe I'll take the tape and put it in the microwave, or leave the fucker sitting next to a stack of powerful magnets. Maybe I'll listen to the tape ten thousand times until the ribbon begins to fray and warp and the music flakes off in tiny specks on the floor to be sucked up by my vacuum cleaner. Of course, I won't—can't—do any of those things for the very reason I'm tempted—this tape possesses a peculiar gravity. And, whether it is the sheer excitement of hearing new music thought to be lost forever, or the tape's ability to change, or even provide closure to Toop's story, its power is undeniable. And here, my chest begins to tighten, my breaths quicken, I feel my pulse behind my eyes, between my shoulder blades. I pop a Xanax and work to steady my breathing. I'll get to the tape, I will—because who doesn't love answers? Who doesn't love a good ending? Who doesn't love an ending, period?

*

Who doesn't love an ending? That's a foolish question when dealing with the cult of Toop. As much as I enjoy Toop's music, I'm not, nor have I ever been, particularly fond of his fans. The problem with the cult of Jim Toop is that it evolved slowly, over decades, allowing each layer to solidify, to become static and inflexible. The biggest piece of the Toop puzzle, as most fans and theorists know, is his 1971 album *Black Triangle*. The album was released to positive reviews, was treated as a strong sophomore effort that found Toop building on the songwriting promise of his debut while adding new textures to his arrangements and smoothing out the rough edges. Here is its tracklist:

1. Speed Limit
2. Just the Other Day
3. Black Triangle
4. Ransom
5. Desert Highway
6. Ascension
7. Sacrifice
8. Peyote Blues
9. Said the Cactus to the Cloud
10. On the Wind
11. Black Triangle (Reprise)
12. You were A Loan

The most peculiar thing about the album is its preoccupation with disappearances. The album title and corresponding song, of course, are believed to reference UFOs, which is supported by the album's mysterious cover: a black field with a single black triangle, subtly edged with white, in the center—when Pink Floyd released *Dark Side of the Moon* two years later, Toop's small fan base famously took note and called for a boycott of Floyd and the work of Storm Thorgerson. Back to the point: because Toop disappeared, many fans believe that the song "Black Triangle"—which tells the story of a lonely desert traveler who sees a large black triangle fall from the sky, and from which powerful "Beings of grey/their eyes ablaze" emerge to seize control of Earth's destiny before whisking the lonely human away in one of their black triangles—was somehow prophetic. They believe not only that Jim Toop was abducted by UFOs, but that he *knew* he would be abducted by UFOs, either because he had been in communication with the song's "Beings of grey," or because he had precognitive abilities. Fan speculation didn't stop with "Black Triangle," though. After Toop's disappearance, fans began to believe that *other* songs on the album contained the *actual* truth of the artist's disappearance. For instance: "Speed Limit" is about a man who drives his car off the road then walks into the desert, never to be heard from again; "Ransom" tells the story of a young musician who pulls over in the desert to urinate only to be kidnapped by men who ask for a ransom that is never paid because they were sending unaddressed ransom notes into the world by tying them to the backs of rattle snakes; In "Sacrificed," the protagonist winds up lost in the desert only to be found and sacrificed by a cult.

Most of the songs on *Black Triangle* tell stories like these, about men disappearing from or into deserts, and while each tale, and its accompanying theory, is quite different, all of the theories seem to agree on one thing: Toop somehow knew he was going to disappear and had some idea of how it would happen. Beyond that fact, though, there are disagreements aplenty. Some believe Toop was able to see the future, but not clearly—he knew he would disappear in the desert but didn't know how, resulting in the competing possibilities that comprise *Black Triangle*. Another faction believes that Toop could see clearly into not just his own future but the futures of several alternate universes—that he was destined to disappear in every universe, in each one a different way. Perhaps the most perplexing part of all of this is how few Toop fans take issue with these approaches to the man's career. The few rational fans that challenge these sensationalist theories do so on grounds ranging from close-readings of songs ("Black Triangle" never refers to its "powerful strangers" as aliens, leading some to read the lyrics as an interrogation of class and power in America), to the simple, pragmatic claim that, perhaps, Toop couldn't see the future at all, but self-fulfilled his own prophecy, orchestrated his own disappearance in the desert to stoke the flames of his fandom and construct an enduring legacy.

With regards to these theories, one thing is certain: in the thirty-odd years since Toop's disappearance, his cultural and musical legacy has grown, largely through the rampant speculation about his disappearance. If not for the crazies and deluded, it is quite likely that nobody would have bothered to unearth the mysterious tape that is sitting in my desk drawer, waiting for me to, for me to, for me to, what?

*

But let's forget about the conspiracy bullshit for now—important as they might be in fueling the cult of Toop's fandom, these theories and narratives are insufferably obtuse and far-fetched. Let's talk about the other narrative surrounding Toop's work, the one that kept me invested in his music long after he disappeared. Let's talk about Angela. While I've been avoiding the boxes in my closet and the tape in my drawer, I've been spending a great deal of time listening to Toop's other albums. Tonight, I'm listening to

Your Sunglasses are in the Junk Drawer, which includes Toop's first and only released song that mentions Angela by name. The song is called "Angela." Here are its lyrics:

> Angela and me, we met young
> Beneath a wild desert sun
> Having some wild desert fun
> Way out in old New Mexico
> Well Angie winked
> And she held my hand.
> We'd go walking, kicking sand,
> Falling into something like love.
> But then I packed my car and I hit the road
> Like a hungry wolf, like a lone Tom Joad
> I said, "Honey, I'll miss you. You know that's true
> But I won't look back."
> Oh, Angela, her red hair
> A waterfall down her back
> Oh, Angela, her eyes,
> How they closed when I touched her face
> Oh, Angela why'd we ever begin—
> When we were one
> I felt the warmth and the water of the world on my
>   skin
> When Angie drinks she
> Sips her beer with a widow's grace.
> When I pick lashes from her face
> She makes wishes and smiles
> Angela, she saw the wind
> And she stopped time
> When she was mine.
> Way back in old New Mexico.

Well she sent me pictures and a little note
The pictures, private and all she wrote
Was please come home. Well Angie I miss you
But you know I won't look back

With those lyrics in mind, it's easy to see how Angela captured the imagination of many of Toop's romantically minded fans. Toop's depiction of Angela gains much of its power in depicting her as the Platonic Ideal of a romantic partner, but that's not the only reason she has become the object of so much romantic fixation—no, it's the circumstances of the narrative, the speaker's longing for Angela, and the pangs of wistful desire woven into the song's sense of wanting and being wanted. The romance, the desire, the bitter-sweet passion that comes with losing a beatific love—this is what drove myself and others to comb through every single one of Toop's songs looking for more references to a woman who might not even really exist—that is, all anyone knows for sure, not counting rumors from those who have traveled to New Mexico and claim to have met her, is that Toop wrote a song about a character named Angela. But that was all we needed.

If anything is going to get me to clean the boxes out of the closet and listen to the tape, it's Angela, and every time I listen to one of Toop's old albums, I inch a little bit closer to listening.

*

But then I slide half way back. See, I've grown so accustomed to the existing canon of Toop songs and their depictions of Angela, that I'm not sure I want it to change. Maybe I'm not that different from the conspiracy theorists and mystery hounds after all.

It's been five days since my meeting with Epps and I still haven't moved the tape from my desk drawer. The boxes in my closet seem heavier every day, the burden of truth surrounding the tape more consequential. I spend my evenings reviewing albums for *Rolling Stone* and *Billboard*. I've been writing for these magazines long enough that reviews of albums that interest me have shrunk and been shuffled deeper into review sections. When McCartney or Dylan or Simon or Springsteen release a new album, I get a lead review, but otherwise, people don't want to read the shit I write about. Who needs to know if the new Richard Thompson album is any good? Those predisposed to buying it will. Nobody else cares.

Tonight, after writing a review of an uninspired anthology of previously unreleased Dylan minutiae, I visit some Jim Toop message boards to see what fans are talking about, to see if word of the new tape has started to trickle out—it hasn't. One of the smaller, fringe boards, *Toop's Triangle*, is ablaze with passionate conversations about a recent installment of a late night call-in show that dedicated a segment to Toop's disappearance in honor of a new book written by a prominent UFO-ologist. Most of the board's users are thrilled by the attention the interview heaped on their cause, but others are upset because the show didn't address alternative theories. Other Toop-dedicated forums are slow. I find nothing of note until I visit one of the smaller, newer fan communities. It's called *Sea Foam, Mean*, named after a lyric from *Your Sunglasses are in the Junk Drawer*. The most recent thread in the main Toop forum is six days old, is posted by a user named DesertBirds77. The thread is titled, "What if..." and the body of the message reads, "…Jim Toop's lost recordings were found. How much would they be worth? What would they mean to you?" This is the user's first and only post. Despite it being a title from Toop's "lost" album, the use of "Desert Birds" doesn't mean much as it is one of the titles fans have known about for decades thanks to old studio logs and setlists. The responses to DesertBirds77's query are dismissive, flippant. One poster says that the question is irrelevant as the missing recordings are on the other side of the universe in a black triangle, hovering over a dark desert road on some other planet. Other posters responded in kind, but placing the recordings instead in shacks or desert caves or buried with Toop's sacrificed body. Nobody participating in the thread is taking seriously the possibility that Jim Toop's final recordings might have actually been found. I wonder who DesertBirds77 might be, if he or she might have some connection to the tape. The obvious possibility is that it is Richard Epps. The post was made a week before he gave me the tape, so perhaps he had been trying to generate fresh interest in the missing songs, or had been trying to track down information. Something tells me that Epps is too smart for that, though. He knows that the Toop community is filled with conspiracy theorists who know how to track IP addresses, and that if anyone found his post suspicious, they'd find him.

Before I shut down my computer for the night, I log in to my *SilverDate* profile. I have two new messages since my last login three months ago. I started the profile a few weeks after Amanda left, when I was certain that our marriage had been undone by our age difference—she was fifteen years younger than me. After a handful of middling dates—two melancholy widows, three divorcees, two women in their thirties who lied about their age to gain access to *SilverDate* in search of a silver fox sugar daddy, and a couple of spinsters who'd never had the urge to settle down—I stopped updating my profile. I check in occasionally, but haven't answered a message in years. Still, sometimes when I'm feeling the right kind of lonely, I look, and sometimes I think about finding a companion, but it hardly seems worth it now. Who would want to be with a washed up, miserable old shit like me anyway?

*

I wake up in the night from a dream about Angela. This is a thing that sometimes happens. I don't know what she looks like, so I guess the dream is about the idea of Angela. In the dream, she touches me and I touch her back. I go to kiss her but she turns away.

*

I first found myself drawn to Toop's Angela around 1982. Toop had been gone for five years and I had just married Betty. My love for Betty felt huge, and in Toop's songs about Angela, I sensed a similar bigness of feeling. That's what compelled me to search Toop's lyrics for more references to his grand love. As much as I came to appreciate Toop's Angela as a romantic ideal, the roots of my interest were in my love for Betty. If I had any family and friends in my life now, they might suggest that this is why I've never been entirely able to shake my interest in Angela, but it's not, I don't think. No, my continued interest in Angela, even as that interest has waned without any new material, has more to do with my love of analysis, my desire to suss out theories from Toop's sometimes obscure lyrics. As such, over the years I have identified a number of passages from Toop's songs that I strongly believe to be about Angela, though she's not named in any of them.

On "New Ghosts for an Old City," from the album of the same name, Toop sings, "Found you in a gold rush/pink-cheeked, face-flushed./Hushed beneath flickering lights on high screens." Though the lines are layered with imagery related to Hollywood and California, *not* New Mexico where Toop would have met Angela, the ragged longing in the singer's voice speaks to a fraught love, a distant inaccessible love, as if he is singing across the desert to her. From the same album, and perhaps more clearly about Angela, comes the following verse from "Mulholland Drive":

> Girl, come to the West Coast
> We'll get high with the old frontier ghosts
> Girl, we'll be up over the skyline
> Looking down from Mulholland Drive
> Like when we were young,
> Just you and me and the silent, starry night

By imploring his lover to "come to the West Coast," Toop clearly signifies distance and the past. As the album was recorded not long after Toop and his father relocated to California, we can reasonably assume that this song is about Angela. At the same time, the universality of the song's longing, of wanting to get high with a lover and lie out beneath a starry sky, speaks to many young men, and I'd be lying if I said the line didn't remind me, personally, of many nights from early in my relationship with Betty.

Perhaps unsurprisingly, as it's Toop's "disappearance" album, *Black Triangle* includes no discernible references to Angela, or to any women for that matter. But the references returned, in force, with Toop's third album, *Ohio Songs*. On "We

Learned to Fly," Toop sings, "You and me we're broken voices/ sipping drinks and getting high," an echo of the sentiments in "Mulholland Drive," while on "Here, the Leaves Change Slow," Toop provides a detailed description of what we can assume was his early relationship with Angela:

> We kissed on your back porch
> The hot spark and the cooling torch
> But you're not fooling anyone
> This might be over but we're not done
> And at night we hear the leaves call
> As they shake and fall
> They were green in the spring
> Then turned red for a spell
> Now they're brown and falling down, down,
>   down...
> Until it all comes back to green
> That's when you'll come back to me
> That's what me and you do
> Or I'll come back to you

While the song's changing seasons (and leaves) can hardly be attributed to New Mexico, the song is clearly about a relationship nearing its end. In what can be read as a follow-up to this song, one verse and its corresponding chorus in "Down the Dixie Highway" calls for a reunion between separated lovers:

> There was a time when this strip was imagined
> Before the burger joints and drive in screens
> Before we knew what heartache really means
> Before I hit the road and headed west
> Even then I knew you were better than the rest

Meet me in Ohio
We'll drive down, down, down
The Dixie Highway

While these lyrics are fairly self-explanatory, they barely register when compared to what was yet to come on Toop's next, and final album, *Your Sunglasses are in the Junk Drawer*, which is widely acknowledged as his "New Mexico" album. Though the cover is a fairly literal representation of the title—a close-up shot of an open junk drawer in which a pair of plastic green sunglasses are half buried beneath rubber bands, a screw driver, a cigarette lighter, toothpicks, a bottle opener, and a sheet of paper on which Toop's name and the album's title have been written in all capital letters with a thick marker—the back of the sleeve features an image of Turtleback Mountain, which sits at the edge of Truth or Consequences, and which is known for a particular precipice that, when viewed from the appropriate angle, looks like a turtle. Of course, this is the album on which the song "Angela" appears, as well as a handful of other tracks that seem to reference Toop's romantic interest. The clearest reference of the bunch, outside of "Angela," appears in the song "New Mexico":

Whoa, whoa New Mexico
Met a sweet little girl down there
Flowers in her red hair
I want to go back, I want to go back
I'm going to go back
To New Mexico

Here, we can safely assume that Toop is singing about Angela due to the red hair. Elsewhere, we see less specific, but probable references to Angela in "Sea Foam" and "Kite Flyin'." "Sea Foam" finds Toop describing a conversation between himself and a romantic partner whose behavior seems consistent with Angela:

> The only theater in town is closed; it's painted sea
>   foam green
> She says, "Boy, I call that aqua, what does sea foam
>   even mean?"
> "Well girl, I'm headin' out real soon
> To live beneath the California moon."
> She says, "Sorry,
> But I've got no love for the silver screen."
> I say, "Forget the movies, we'll stay at the beach,
> And I'll show you what sea form even means."

Though somewhat convoluted, this exchange reinforces the idea that Toop wanted to continue a relationship with Angela after he moved to Los Angeles. On "Kite Flyin'," we're treated not to more drama of impending separation, but to the innocence and intimacy that comes with a new relationship:

> We flew kites
> In the day
> And found sites
> At night
> Where my fingers found their way
> Across my lover's starry face

Toop's voice, wistful and smooth, the melody delivered with a lilting swing, suffuses the lines with nostalgia for his long-lost, almost decade old (remember, *Sunglasses* wasn't released until a good eight years after Toop and his father left

New Mexico) romance. Of course, we don't know how things turned out for Toop and Angela after the young man moved to California, just like we don't know if any of my readings of Toop's songs are accurate—we're not likely to ever know. As much as I sometimes think I want to know those answers, I'm not sure I want to know if I'm wrong.

*

It's been a week since my first meeting with Richard Epps. I'm eating mac and cheese, the shitty orange kind, and watching a porn DVD from the 90's. It's night. I'm sitting in the dark, bathed in only the fleshy blue light from the television. I don't touch myself when I watch porn. I don't get hard anymore. I don't even particularly enjoy porn, but sometimes it helps numb the aches I contend with daily, reminds me that I was once a person who fucked and came. A tubby man with a huge cock is fucking a tiny blond woman when my phone rings. It's Epps.

He asks what I've learned about the tape. "Nothing," I tell him. "I'm working on it." He asks what I've done. I tell him I'm listening, analyzing lyrics, looking for clues in the production. Epps says, "And?" I say, "Be patient." He tells me he was hoping to have some answers by now. I say, "This might take a while." Epps pauses, then asks: "Are you watching porn?" The blond woman is kneeling in front of the tubby guy, pumping his huge cock with her tiny fist, looking up at him in anticipation. I lunge for the remote and mute the television, tell Epps that I'm channel surfing. I say, "I'll let you know when I find something conclusive." He says, "I can find someone else."

At first, I feel almost relieved at Epps's threat, but then I look back at the silent couple on my television, watch the tiny woman spit on the tubby man's cock. I look at the mac and cheese on my lap, and I look to the closet at the end of the short hallway and I begin, for a moment, to feel almost protective of the tape. This tape is *mine* and what am I doing? Watching porn and eating processed mac and cheese. Richard Epps can't have the tape back, can't give this assignment to anyone else. I resolve not to give up on Jim Toop, on Angela. I say, "I'll know something soon," and hang up the phone without giving Epps a chance to respond. I look at my closet, again. I have work to do.

*

As I move Amanda's boxes out of the closet, I feel a bit nostalgic. My time with Amanda wasn't bad—our lives and wants simply weren't compatible. I'm stirred from my nostalgic reverie when a cockroach scurries out from between box flaps. I don't have any roach spray so I squish the fucker then run down to the closest bodega to buy some. When I return, the door to my apartment is ajar. I check my pocket for my cell phone and remember it's charging on my desk. I think to knock on a neighbor's door and call for the police, but why bother? It's not like I have anything of value to steal. It's not like I'm worried for my safety. The lamps in my apartment are all off, but a small beam of light flutters across the wall of my front room. I pull the roach spray out of the plastic bag, pause, and take stock of my situation—the guy with the flashlight could be twice my size, could have a gun. I consider leaving, waiting for twenty minutes and coming back, let the guy take whatever he wants—maybe some books and CD's, an armful of records, my fourteen inch television, maybe my microwave. The TV and microwave are both old. The only thing in my apartment worth stealing is the tape.

The tape.

Only Richard Epps knows I have it. Odds are, a thief wouldn't even notice an old reel-to-reel tape in a desk drawer. But what if he knows? What if this thief is here *for* the tape? What if Richard Epps is up in his office, tied to a chair, having been beaten within an inch of his life until my name fell from his lips like so many broken teeth?

Knowing I have nothing to lose, I ease my way more fully into my apartment, roach spray ready. I flip on the lights and charge, discharging the roach spray in front of me, towards where I'd last seen the flashlight. The aerosol mist gets in my mouth, my eyes, makes me gag, and blurs my vision. Though my eyes are watering, I see a man in a black track suit and ball cap standing next to my desk. I point the roach spray at him and, sputtering through coughs, demand to know what he's doing. He breaks for the door but my apartment is too small. He can't get around me. I spray him in the face and pin him to the wall. We stand there, pressed against each other coughing, our eyes watering.

*

The perpetrator is sitting across from me, silent. The jacket of his track suit is unzipped, revealing a t-shirt that says, "I want to believe." He tells me his name is Fox Mulder. He looks young. "Fox Mulder was a character on a TV show," I say. "He was based on me," the young man says. This is clearly a lie. This guy can't be older than twenty-five. "You don't expect me to believe that," I say. "Believe what you want," the man says." I ask him for some ID, a driver's license maybe. He says, "Nobody carries ID on a search and seizure."

The absurdity of his rationale makes the man seem younger than I'd thought. I say, "I'll let the police sort it out." Adding, "Mr. Mulder," knowing full well how absurd it sounds, but not knowing what else to call him.

The guy who calls himself Fox Mulder is chewing his fingernails. I might have overestimated his age by a couple of years. He has mild acne running up his cheeks, a thin mustache, his hair is greasy. He's starting to look more like an awkward seventeen than twenty-five. He says, "There's no need to bring the police into this." Then: "It won't benefit either of us." I ask, "What *would* benefit us?" Fox Mulder says, "You have something that I want." I ask the kid what he's talking about, but I already know. The tape isn't even public knowledge yet and already this bullshit is starting. I briefly regret not just giving the tape back to Epps after our earlier conversation. "I'm looking for a tape," the kid says. I play dumb, say, "What tape?" I tell him I've got a lot of tapes, but I can tell he knows. He says, "The tape of Jim Toop's final, unreleased album that Richard Epps gave you." I try to change the subject, ask the kid how he got into my apartment. He says, "A tension wrench and a pick. These old locks are easy." Then, "The tape?"

I ask Fox Mulder how he knows about the tape and feel embarrassed that I've started thinking of him as Fox Mulder. He doesn't answer. I pick up my phone and tell him to start talking or I'll call the cops. He says that somebody told him about the tape. I ask him who, if it was Richard Epps. The kid says it wasn't, he doesn't think. He says he doesn't know who told him about the tape, that the information was passed on to him through an anonymous network of conspiracy theorists and computer specialists. "Hackers?" I ask. "Specialists," Fox Mulder says. I ask him what a bunch of hackers want with the tape. He says, "Specialists," again, clearly exasperated. Then: "We want to hear it. But more importantly, we want to know the truth." I ask him, "The truth about what?" Fox Mulder says, "The truth about Jim Toop."

I tell the boy, who seems more like a boy with each passing minute—he might be just old enough to have been the product of my first marriage, but is probably a bit young even for that—that this is what I want, too, but that I haven't even listened to the tape yet. He asks why not and I point to the closet. And here it occurs to me, if the kid knew about the tape, he might know more. He might be useful. I offer him five bucks and a chance to listen to the tape if he'll move the rest of the boxes out of the closet and promises not to tell anyone about what he hears.

*

Fox Mulder stacks boxes by my desk while I spray the roaches that scurry out. When the top layers are cleared away, he tries to move the reel-to-reel into my front room. He struggles, pushes it along the floor, moving one corner then the next. He seems weak. This is good to know if I need to fight him. I tell him to take the machine out of the box and put it on the floor next to the bookcase that houses my stereo. "You do it," he says. "You want the five bucks?" I ask. He says, "You can keep your five bucks. I just want to hear the tape." He pants when he talks.

I push the box the rest of the way to my stereo, reach inside and toss a handful of wires at the kid.

When Fox Mulder is done, I slide the Ampex reel onto the metal prong on the left side of the machine, run the lead-end of the tape into the empty spool on the right. Fox

Mulder asks me for a pen and paper so he can take notes. "No notes," I say. "Just listen."

I press play. We listen to *The Taxidermist's Catalog* in silence.

*

While the tape plays, I try to ignore emotional responses and focus on only my professional impressions. Those impressions: the tape is real; that is, the tape really seems to feature performances by Jim Toop; the arrangements are consistent with Toop's work and the songs' hooks are stronger and catchier than his previous work, corresponding with Ocean City's beliefs about the album's commercial viability; and there are multiple references to Angela—I scribble down as much as I can, but my ears are too old and my hand too slow to record anything of import. Though the performances sound very much like Toop, there are things about the recording that make me uneasy. The tape sounds too clean—it must have been stored in optimal conditions for all these years, a cool, dry place with a minimum of dust and debris. If the tape had been lying in the desert for close to forty years, it couldn't possibly sound so clean.

The bigger problem with the tape is that it sounds too finished. *The Taxidermist's Catalog* is, famously, an album that was never properly completed. We don't even have an account of how much of the album had been committed to tape when Toop disappeared, meaning it's entirely possible that every song here had been recorded, if not necessarily finished, before Toop vanished—but these songs, they feel utterly and completely polished, mixed and mastered. The levels are consistent from song to song, there is no evidence of splices, no audible tape hiss, and no white noise or studio chatter leading into or out of any of the tracks. In fact, two of the transitions on the album, from "Sideways Glances" into "Forget Me Not," and "Weather" into "Nothing Truer," find the later song in each pair slowly and seamlessly growing out of its predecessor's end matter. As this effect is usually achieved in mixing and mastering, I can only conclude that, before the tape made its way to Epps, someone else acquired, mixed, and mastered it.

*

A confession: I am glad, on first listen, that I am unable to pick out what Toop is saying about Angela. As much as I'm loath to admit it, my investment in Angela as an idea, or as a person, or as a symbol, or whatever, is still connected to whatever feelings about my marriage to Betty are still rattling around inside this old husk of a body. I don't want to deal with that shit right now, not with this kid here, this stranger.

*

When the album ends, Fox Mulder is crying, and maybe smiling a little. We sit silent, save for his quiet sobs, until the tape runs out and the loose end flicks around the reel. I pull a hanky from under a pile of old music magazines and throw it to him. I ask why he is crying. He blows his nose and tosses the hanky onto a ten year old copy of *Spin* with U2 on the cover. I can't tell if he's happy or sad. I don't understand what's happening, but whatever it is, this seems like a strange moment for crying. Once he composes himself a bit, Fox Mulder tells me that the cult of Jim Toop is over, that the tape clearly indicates that Toop neither died nor disappeared, at least in the sense that many of his fans believed, in 1977. I say, "That's a strange reason to cry," and ask him to explain himself. He begins to tell me that there are two things that he heard on the album that complicate many of the theories surrounding Toop's disappearance. I say, "I mean, I want to know why you're crying." He says, "Just let me talk." I shut up and listen. The first thing that struck him as odd was the broad, thematic sweep of the album's lyrics— as best as he can tell, the songs are all, or mostly, set in New Mexico, and they are all about isolation, secrecy, solitude; there is the sense that each song's protagonist, perhaps the artist himself, is hiding, has intentionally removed himself from the public eye, has gone underground. To Fox Mulder, this means Jim Toop enacted his own disappearance and wrote, or rewrote these songs after his disappearance. He tells me Jim Toop is probably still alive. "You know," I say, "Those themes aren't inconsistent with Toop's previous work." Adding: "He was always singing about alienation and fear and loneliness." Fox Mulder says, "But it's different now—he sounds angry." The young man's response doesn't sit well with me. Any true Toop conspiracy theorist would be quick to bend everything about the tape to fit his pet theories, would argue that the tape is additional proof that Toop was aware of his impending disappearance, that he wrote the songs in advance as a message to fans.

I try to ask Fox Mulder, again, about his crying. He ignores me and explains his second observation. He asks me to rewind the tape to the beginning of the last song, "Cormac Bleeding." I feed the tape back into the reel on the left and rewind, stop, rewind until I find the track's beginning. Before I press play, the kid asks me if the song was ever included on the lists of rumored tracks for the unfinished album. This seems strange as most Toop conspiracy theorists would know the answer to this. I tell him, no, the song was new. "That's what I thought," he answers. I press play. At the beginning of the second verse, he instructs me to pay attention to the lyrics. These are the lines Jim Toop is singing:

> The desert sand blows like sea-foam ocean crests
> Beneath the coming night
> The evening redness in the west

"So?" I say. Fox Mulder says, "It's a reference to *Blood Meridian*." Then: "That's part of its full title—*Blood Meridian or The Evening Redness in the West*." I know that a book of this name exists, and I know it was written by Cormac McCarthy, but that's all. Fox Mulder continues, "The novel was published eight years after Jim Toop disappeared." He tells me that this cannot be a coincidence. I suggest that maybe Cormac McCarthy somehow heard the song and used the line as the subtitle for his novel as an homage. Or, I suggest, maybe Toop and McCarthy knew each other, and McCarthy had used the phrase in conversation, prompting Toop to write it into a song. Fox Mulder is unsatisfied by my suggestions, and he's probably right. Such a meeting seems downright improbable, if not entirely impossible. Regardless, this bit of "evidence" will be difficult for even the most stubborn theorists to rationalize. I suggest something else that's possible, but maybe a little bit improbable: maybe it *is* a coincidence. I explain that, if this isn't a coincidence, there are only two practical conclusions I can draw: either all or part of the tape wasn't made by Jim Toop, or Jim Toop was alive, well, and still recording music at least as late as 1985. When I break it down like that for Fox Mulder, he says, "It's really Toop. I know it." I say, "How are you so sure?" He says, "You were listening. It sounds just like him." He's right, but the more I consider the McCarthy reference, the more I question what my ears thought they were hearing. I ask Fox Mulder, "Will you just tell me why you were crying?" Fox Mulder says, "I'm happy." I say, "I don't understand." He says, "That's okay." Then he asks me to make a copy of the tape for him. I tell him no way, then offer him a ride home because it is after midnight. He accepts. Before we leave, I ask him, "Were you happy just to hear the album—is that why you were crying?" Fox Mulder hesitates before answering, says, "Something like that."

*

In the car, Fox Mulder tells me he is eighteen. "Glad I didn't offer you a drink," I say. He says, "I wouldn't have taken it." I say, "Of course you wouldn't have." He says, "Really. I don't drink." I say, "Of course you don't. Why would you?"

Fox Mulder gives me directions to a townhouse in the East Village, not far from my apartment. It's a narrow, two story deal, belongs to his mom, or maybe they're renting. I don't know. I pull up to the curb and put the car in park. He digs through his pockets then hands me a small business card. Across the top in bold, red letters is printed the word Ambiguous, but it looks like this: @mbiguous. The ampersand is bright red, bold at the top and fading into a grainy, pointillist haze at the bottom. The card lists the kid's name as Fox Mulder. It also lists his "position" as "Minister of Historical Truth." I say, "You're one of those guys with the masks from that movie." Fox Mulder says, "That's Anonymous." He seems annoyed. I suspect this confusion is not uncommon. "If I were a member of Anonymous," he says, "I wouldn't be giving you a business card." I say, "Because you'd be anonymous." Instead of answering, he gets out of the car, then stops, leans in the open door, asks if he can hear the tape again. I tell him to stop by in two days. He says, "Wednesday?" I say, "Wednesday."

*

The next morning I wake up on the sofa. My back aches, and I've pissed myself, but only a little—not enough to soak through my jeans, but enough to make me smell and feel wet and worthless and alone. I don't move. A morning news show is on TV. I don't pay attention.

If it weren't for the tape, still fitted snuggly on the reel-to-reel, I don't know that I'd move today. Even that hardly seems like a particularly good reason. If I had kids, maybe my son would take me out to lunch and try to talk me into moving in with his family. That would be a good reason to get up. Or maybe my daughter would drag me to the doctor to look at my back, or to make sure my occasional incontinence isn't indicative of a more serious problem, of cancer or infection. I haven't been to a doctor in over a decade. What's the point? People with kids or wives go to the doctor. Not people like me.

A confession: I regret not having kids.

I guess that's not much of a confession.

When I finally get off the couch, I use Google to search for Cormac McCarthy scholars. I call the president of the Cormac McCarthy Society and am lucky to catch him between classes. I ask him if he's heard of Jim Toop. He hasn't. I'm glad. He won't understand the significance of what I'm about to ask him. I explain the situation, all about Toop's album, the perceived reference to *Blood Meridian*. I ask if there's any chance McCarthy might have known Toop. He laughs at me, but tries to be kind, says "McCarthy is notoriously reclusive. I doubt he'd pay attention to, or be inspired by a barely known folk singer."

After the call, I stay on the sofa and stare at the ceiling. I don't move to change my jeans or clean myself up. The more I think about my situation, the stranger it seems. That is, I understand why Richard Epps asked me to look into the tape, but I still don't understand what exactly he expects out of me, or how an eighteen year old kid found out that I have it. There is something here that I'm not privy to, and the more I try to figure it out, the less privy I feel.

*

Back on the sofa, still wearing my clothes from the day before, I call Richard Epps. I tell him that someone found out about the tape, but I don't tell him who. He asks how I know. I tell him that someone broke into my apartment. Before I can share any details, he says, "The tape?" I tell him it's safe, nothing was taken. "Did you call the cops?" he asks. I lie, tell him I did but they couldn't do anything. I ask him who knows about the tape. He tells me nobody. I ask, "Then how did someone know to come looking for it?" He asks, "How do you know they were looking for the tape?" I don't know how to answer. I didn't think this through. Clearly I know the would-be thief was looking for the tape because I talked to him, but I don't want Epps to know that part. I say, "I've lived here for almost twenty years and my place has never once been broken into. I have the tape for a week and that changes." Epps says, "Coincidence?" I say, "They didn't take a single thing. Not my booze, not my meds—nothing." I ask him, "What am I supposed to do?" Epps says, "I don't know—what do you want to do?"

And everything that comes to mind is absurd, over-the-top. I test Epps's investment in this tape to see if I can learn anything. I say, "I want to douse the tape in kerosene and light it on fire." He says, "Really now." I say, "Or buy an old microwave from the Salvation Army and put the tape in it and crank it to high, run it for five minutes." Epps says, "You're hysterical." I say, "I want to submerse the tape in liquid nitrogen then hit it with a hammer so it breaks into pieces. Then we'll freeze the pieces and hit *them* with a hammer so they break into smaller pieces. I want to do that over and over until the tape is dust." Epps says, "Fine. Whatever." I say, "You have a copy, don't you?" Epps says, "Of course." Then: "But you have the original." I say, "I want to auction the tape to the highest bidding record label so they can release the album and I can retire." Richard Epps doesn't say anything for a moment. I imagine him playing with an unlit cigarette, holding it between his lips and pretending to exhale smoke. He says, "Don't be rash." I ask Richard Epps why he *really* gave me the tape. He tells me the same thing he did before, that he wants to know if it's legitimate. "No secrets," he says. "No surprises." I tell him that, if that's all he wants, I'm fairly certain the tape contains music written and performed by Jim Toop, but that I'm not sure when and where it was recorded. I tell him there are some problems, that either Toop didn't record all of the music on the tape, or he recorded some of it after his disappearance. Epps says, "Well, that's interesting." Then: "I gave this tape to you because I knew you'd find the truth." I say, "Everybody wants to know the truth." Richard Epps says, "So find it." I say, "I'm trying, Dick." Then Richard Epps tells me to keep tabs on my expenses, that the magazine will cover as much as it can. I'm surprised that Epps has offered me more money. I ask him, "Are you doing that because you expect me to find out more about this tape than you're letting on, or because you want to buy my loyalty?" Epps says, "Those aren't mutually exclusive proposals."

*

So how does one begin to find the type of answers I'm seeking? Consult an expert. I dub a copy of *The Taxidermist's Catalog* onto a high bias cassette—Epps doesn't need to know about this—pack the original in my briefcase for safekeeping, and head downtown to see my friend Kyle. Kyle runs a recording studio called Wow and Flutter that specializes in analog gear. The studio was ready to close its doors fifteen years ago when Jack White romanticized and re-popularized vintage recording techniques. Through the eighties and into the early nineties, back when digital recording was dominating popular music, I was a luddite—I *swore* I could hear the difference, that analog sounded warmer, more real. With analog, unlike digital, we hear the sound as it's captured, the sound of the song and the room, not sound reduced to numerical data then reconstituted into a simulacra of the original. Anymore, I can't tell the difference. It's probably my age.

At Wow and Flutter, Kyle is eating a cheese steak on a TV tray in front of the mixing console. Someone is tuning a guitar through the playback speakers. I can't see the musician. Due to space and money constraints, the control room and performance areas are completely separate. There is no large window pane through which Kyle can watch his clients and make hand motions at them the way technicians and producers do in movies. If the band has a producer, he or she will go into the performance spaces when necessary, but otherwise stay out with Kyle. Kyle motions to the chair next to him at the mixing board. His mouth is full of cheese steak. He is tall, wearing a flannel and ripped jeans. His long hair falls down over his shoulders. I hand him the cassette dub of *The Taxidermist's Catalog*. He asks what it is. "Mixtape from your secret admirer," I say. "Really though," he says. I say, "It's a copy of Jim Toop's lost, final recordings." He says, "Really though." I say, "Really."

He asks where I got it so I tell him about Dick Epps and the reel-to-reel and how I didn't listen for a week, but after I did, I had some questions. While I'm talking, a skinny man with shoulder length, greasy hair sticks his head out of one of the performance rooms, says the band is ready. Kyle says, "Give me five."

When we are alone again, I tell Kyle I want to know when the music on the tape was recorded. I tell him I need to know if that's really Jim Toop. He says there's no real way to do either of those, but that he might be able to ballpark it. I ask him how long it will take. He tells me he's a bit behind schedule. Says, "I'm booked solid through the week, afternoons and evenings. I'll need some time." I tell him to be careful, to be discreet, that nobody really knows about the tape yet, and that Richard Epps would be furious if the tape wound up in the wrong hands. "I'm trusting you," I say. "I'll keep it safe," Kyle says.

*

And then I'm done for the day. For the rest of the afternoon and into the night, I feel lonely. This is not uncommon. I wish I'd told Fox Mulder to come back tonight instead of tomorrow. I drink cheap scotch and listen to *The Taxidermist's Catalog* three times, searching for references to Toop's Angela. Neither the scotch nor the references to Angela are particularly satisfying. The scotch is McClelland's Highland, fifteen bucks for a bottle, and the lines about Angela feel more disillusioned and resigned than love struck and heartbroken, as if maybe Toop had realized that Angela wasn't the great love he'd once thought her to be. Of course, maybe it isn't even Toop singing at all. But it *sounds* like Toop, feels like him. As I get drunker, I start thinking about Betty, the way she used to try to harmonize with me when I was singing along with Toop's songs, the way she'd tap her long, painted fingernails on the nearest hard surface when she was frustrated. Thinking about Betty hurts, so I try to think about Amanda instead. I don't think about Amanda much. She was too young for me and didn't want to have children. That's why she left. I told her we needed to have kids. She said we weren't the type of people that have kids. I told her we needed kids because we were going to get old and then we would die and who would mourn our deaths if not our kids. Amanda said she'd mourn my death. I asked if that meant she was planning on killing me, then I laughed. She didn't think it was funny. Amanda said, "Men die younger than women, and I'm fifteen years younger than you." I said, "Then why are you wasting your time with me?" That's when she packed her suitcase and left without taking her books or kitchen wares. We'd only been married for two years. Unless prompted by a closet full of boxes, I tend to not think about Amanda unless I'm trying to not think about Betty.

*

Fully drunk now, I realize I'm wearing the same pants from yesterday, that I went to Wow and Flutter in the pants I'd pissed in my sleep.

I don't do anything to rectify this—why bother when the same thing might happen tonight?

As I drift off to sleep, this line from "(Hideaway) Bed" on *The Taxidermist's Catalog* cycles through my head. It's a line about Angela, even calls her by name. It goes: "Angela and me we meet at dusk/I'm her dirty little secret and she's an empty husk of a dream, so red./Takin' up half of my bed." Typically, I sympathize with the speakers in Toop's songs. In this instance, though, the speaker is so bitter, so cruel, that I can only sympathize with Angela. I want to understand these songs, to understand this new, old Jim Toop. But I can't quite wrap my head around it, not because of the booze, I don't think, or even the songs themselves, but because of the way Toop seems to have changed between albums. Maybe I want to believe it isn't Toop singing, but I know better.

*

Something else I noticed about the tape: it contains a reference to New Coke, the Coca Cola brand's new recipe that debuted in 1985. The line, which I haven't quite worked out entirely thanks to Toop's unusual inflection, can be found on the song "Mark's Novel," and seems to compare a character in the song to New Coke, which, considering the soft drink's rapid public rejection, seems like a putdown. Combined with the Cormac McCarthy lyric, the possibility of coincidence is diminishing. Either Jim Toop was alive at least through 1985 or this tape is a fake. I'm not ready to share this latest discovery with anyone, not quite yet.

*

On Wednesday night, Fox Mulder shows up at ten. He is carrying a duffle bag and wearing the same track suit as before. He unzips his jacket, revealing a shirt with a math equation on the front. It looks like this:

$$\Delta t' = \gamma \left(\Delta t - \frac{v \, \Delta x}{c^2} \right)$$

I ask him what his shirt is and he tells me it's the equation for the Relativity of Simultaneity. "What the fuck is that?" I ask. He tells me it has to do with multiple events appearing to happen simultaneously, in two locations, to one observer, but not simultaneously to a second observer in a different location. He says, "It's about the problem of absolute simultaneity. Of our relative understandings of events in the universe." I don't have anything to say about this, so I just ask him, "Isn't it a little late to be out on a school night?" He says, "I'll be up until three anyway." While I set up the tape, I ask, "Is your name really Fox Mulder?" I say, "No bullshit. Tell me straight." He says, "That's what people call me." I ask him, "But is it your actual name?" Fox Mulder says, "Yes." I say, "I remember your street and address. I can look up your mother in the phone book and find out if you're lying." Fox Mulder says, "Phone book." I say, "I can Google it."

After a beat, Fox Mulder changes the subject, asks: "So are you going to make me a copy of this tape or what?" I ask him what he could possibly want with a copy were I to give it to him. He rubs at the acne on his face and tells me he would have the tape analyzed. "Like, by an expert," he says. I tell him I'm worried that if I give him a copy, he'll have it uploaded and all over the internet within an hour. Fox Mulder says, "You think us kids have a sense of entitlement, that we don't want to pay for anything, right?" I say, "I know you're interested in possessing a copy of this tape, and you haven't given me a compelling reason." He says, "I told you, I'm going to find out if it's real." I tell him I'm taking care of that. "It's my job," I say. Clearly exasperated, Fox Mulder says, "Can we just listen to it already?" I tell him yes and press play. When I sit down, I see him reaching into his duffle bag, fiddling with something. I ask him what's in the bag. He tells me it's his homework. I ask if I can see. He zips up the bag and holds it in his lap. "No bag, no album," I say, pausing the reel-to-reel. I grab the bag from the kid's lap. It's a little heavy. Inside, wrapped in a pair of pajamas, I find a small but sturdy DAT recorder with a built in microphone. "You were going to bootleg the tape," I say. He says, "You won't give me a copy." I say, "So you were going to make a shitty copy and use that to have the tape analyzed?" He nods. "What about the pajamas?" I ask. Fox Mulder tells me that he snuck out of his mom's house wearing his pajamas then changed behind their garage and took the bus to my apartment. I stop the DAT player and listen to what he's recorded, to our conversation up to the point when I found the player and shut it off. It sounds decent, but not great. I say, "You can use this to record one song for you to do with what you please." I tell him the quality won't be good. If he decides to share the song, it won't harm potential sales and maybe it will result in new information about the tape's origins. I make him promise that if he shares the song, he has to let me know if anyone contacts him for information.

*

Later, when I drive Fox Mulder home, we listen to the playback of the song he recorded—he went with "Cormac Bleeding," since it was the most likely to have been recorded after Toop's disappearance. The song sounds like it was recorded from two rooms away, is tinny and dull. The low end has been lost to the microphone, and the high end breaks with static at every crescendo. Fox Mulder says, "This doesn't sound so good." I say, "Sounds fine to me." He says, "You have the original." I say, "Yours is good enough." Then: "You'll be able to make out the lyrics." He says, I was hoping it would sound better." He sounds truly disappointed. I ask him, again, why he really wants a good copy of the tape. He says, "I just want to be able to listen to it." Then: "I like it." Something in his voice makes this seem almost sincere, but still, I suspect he's holding something back. I press, say, "Tell me why you really want the tape." Fox Mulder doesn't answer until we're almost at his house. Then he says, "I want the bounty for it on a torrent site." I ask him what that means. He explains how the torrent sites work, how users try to keep balanced ratios between how much they upload and download, how the sites offer "bounties" to improve a user's ratio if he or she is the first to upload a heavily sought after recording. I ask how a bounty could be set for something nobody knows exists, and he tells me that there isn't one, but he can negotiate a high one if he has a good quality recording.

I tell Fox Mulder I don't believe him. I say, "This isn't about any bounty."

Fox Mulder says, "Sure it is," in a way that convinces me that he's lying but that he's made up his mind not to tell me why he really wants a copy of the tape.

Before we reach his house, Fox Mulder tells me to stop a few houses down. The light in his mom's bedroom is on, so he'll need to sneak back in. "Worried she's going to bust your balls?" I ask, regretting the forced machismo before the words are even out of my mouth. "Something like that," he says. Then, "She doesn't really give a shit. I just don't want her to know what I'm doing." I say, "What, listening to music?" He says, "It's more than that." I shrug, put the car in park. Before Fox Mulder goes, I write my Gmail address on the crumpled up receipt from the roach spray I bought two nights ago. Shit: I'm *still* wearing the same pants that I'd pissed in two nights ago. I wonder if the boy can smell it on me. Maybe he thinks that's just how old people smell. I hand the receipt over. "In case you learn anything," I say. "I'll be in touch," Fox Mulder says. Before he can close the door, I stop him one last time, ask, "Have you ever posted online under the username DesertBirds77?" Fox Mulder says, "Desert what?" I repeat the name and he says he hasn't. I ask him if he can track a user name and IP address. He says sure, to send him a link. He tears the receipt in half, writes down his own email address and hands it to me. As soon as I get home, I find the thread on the message board and send it to Fox Mulder to see what he can find.

*

All I can do now is wait. I don't leave my apartment for four days. I send emails to editors at various magazines and pitch feature ideas. I receive an instant acceptance for a proposed interview with Pete Welch, who recently curated the release of a long-lost album by the long-forgotten band Arthur Cane Kills Moby Dick. A second pitch, an essay on Angela as the romantic ideal in Jim Toop's work is picked up quickly by *Rolling Stone*, not because I have anything new to say, but because nobody has written about it for a while and this is the last chance I'll have to write this specific version of this particular essay as—once *The Taxidermist's Catalog* is released—the narrative surrounding Angela is going to change.

When I'm not writing or listening, I research Jim Toop online. There isn't much I don't know about his career, but I've always worked with a certain set of assumptions that are now in flux—that he definitely disappeared, and probably died in 1977, that his lost tape would never be found. I'm mostly searching for information peripheral to Toop, for information that might help me get a better handle on the appearance of this tape. I've never been to Truth or Consequences, which is strange for a Toop scholar. Why haven't I been? Because the only people who go to Truth or Consequences for Jim Toop want to solve the mystery of his disappearance, are obsessed with conspiracy. Fuck those people. I look up the city on Wikipedia. It is a hot spa town. It changed its name from Hot Springs to Truth or Consequences in 1950 when Ralph Edwards, host of the game show Truth or Consequences, offered to broadcast an episode of his show from any city that changed its name to that of the show. I like this. It makes the name seem like something to laugh at. The city has two museums, a Historical Society Museum, and the Hamilton Military Museum. There is a movie called *Truth or Consequences, N.M.*, starring Kiefer Sutherland. The film was made in Utah and Nevada. I find a VHS copy on eBay and Buy It Now for ninety-nine cents, plus three ninety-nine for shipping, then I send an email to Fox Mulder, asking if he's heard anything about the song he uploaded, if he's learned anything about DesertBirds77. I get no reply.

*

Truth or Consequences, N.M. arrives in the mail within two days. The seller was close, over in Queens. I leave positive feedback on eBay due to the fast transaction and as-described condition of the item. The movie's box says, "When you're running on fear, don't stop for gas." The box also says, "...[A] gritty, effective crime drama..." The film is a bore, is all about stolen drugs and kidnapping. The film has nothing to do with Truth or Consequences, New Mexico. I contemplate changing the eBay seller's feedback to negative. But the movie was a gritty, effective crime drama so I let it go.

*

On my fourth day straight day without leaving my apartment, I receive an email from Fox Mulder. He tells me that DessertBirds77 was posting from an IP address in California. That's all he knows for sure. Then he tells me he's had a few inquiries from magazine editors about the leaked song, but none of them had information. Over the next few days, I receive three emails from editors at music blogs asking if I'd heard the new Jim Toop song that had surfaced and, if so, would I like to weigh in. I politely decline but check in on each blog to see what they are saying. Most are expressing doubt about the song's legitimacy, with two of the three positing that the newly unearthed song was recorded by one young up and comer or another trying to make a name for himself with a bit of viral marketing voodoo. In the comments sections and message boards, many commenters are skeptical as well. Some fans want desperately for the song to be real, but the skeptics raised good points, their most effective argument being that the song was clearly recorded on a handheld device. Nobody can quite wrap their heads around why the song would leak this way. For many, this is proof enough that the song is fake. Reading one thread on a Toop message board, I find myself getting nervous as users discuss their attempts to track down the source of the song's leak. I am relieved and impressed with

Fox Mulder's ingenuity as the closest the sleuths get is an IP address belonging to a donut shop just south of Dayton, Ohio, which leads some fans to speculate that it was Toop himself who leaked the song.

*

I am emailing edits of my review of the new Laurie Anderson album—bold and daring, rooted in her earlier successes but always looking forward—to *Rolling Stone* when I receive a Gchat message from a user named FWM93. The message says, "Hi." I ask who it is, though I have a hunch. The response is quick: "Fox Mulder." I ask, "Why the 'W'?" He says, "Fox William Mulder." I ask, "What do you want?" He responds: "Someone sent me a message about the tape." I ask who. My muscles tense. I am a little bit excited. Fox Mulder's next message says, 'The username was ToopFan." Then: "He says he knows where the tape came from." I type and send, "And?" He says, "I traced the IP address. It's out of Los Angeles." I say, "Where'd the tape come from?" Mulder says, "He hasn't told me yet." Then: "There's more." He says, "The IP Address is the same as DesertBirds77." I say, "So it's the same person?" He says, "The same computer anyway." I ask if he can learn more. He tells me some of his friends looked into it. Says, "They found a name attached to the IP address: William Toop." I say, "That's Toop's father." Mulder says, "I know." Then: "GTG." I type, "GTG?" He says, "Got to go," then logs off.

This news makes me uneasy. I begin to feel the familiar tightening in my chest, but before it takes over, I steady my breathing and focus on calming myself until the panic passes. Why would Jim Toop's father be inquiring about the tapes? Was it even him at all? Could this all be misdirection? None of it makes sense. I need answers. I text Richard Epps, tell him we need to talk, tell him I need to go to Los Angeles and he's going to pay for it. Epps responds, "We'll meet tomorrow."

I've never tried to talk to Toop's father before, not because I wasn't interested, but because he was known to turn down most requests, and the few interviews he did grant back in the early eighties weren't particularly fruitful. But now, if William Toop is asking questions about this tape, I *need* to talk to him. Could William Toop have been the source of the tape? If so, wouldn't that mean it's entirely authentic? Why would he send it to Richard Epps for verification instead of taking it to a label himself? None of this is adding up. I feel like I'm missing something, here.

*

The next day, Richard Epps texts me and arranges our meeting for right after lunch. When I arrive, he is drinking scotch—his is probably far more expensive than what I've been drinking at home. We exchange pleasantries then I tell him, without going into much detail, about DesertBirds77, ToopFan, and William Toop. I ask him who else might have known about the tape. "Nobody," he says, pauses. He's thinking about something but I don't know what. Then, "Not on my end anyway." I ask him if he's been in contact with anyone in Los Angeles about a leaked Toop song. He says, "What leaked Toop song?" I tell him all about Fox Mulder and the poorly recorded copy of the song and the message he got from ToopFan. I see an odd look cross Richard Epps's face when I mention Fox Mulder.

I say, "Do you know Fox Mulder?" Richard Epps ignores me, says, "You let a song from this leak?" I tell him, "I needed information." I say, "I'm surprised you hadn't heard—a number of blogs are talking about it." He asks, "Did you learn anything?" I say, "I told you what I learned." I say, "I need to go to Los Angeles." Then: "But you didn't answer my question—do you know Fox Mulder?" Richard Epps says, "That guy from the TV show." I say, "No, a real guy." Richard Epps says, "Yeah, I know the guy. He's one of Ronnie's friends." At least now I understand how maybe Fox Mulder knew I had tape, though I still don't know why he's so interested in it. I say, "So, Los Angeles." Epps says, "Why?" I say, "If William Toop, or anybody else out there knows about this tape, I need to talk to them." Epps ask, "Are you at all questioning this tape's authenticity?" I tell him I am. I tell him the tape sounds like Jim Toop, but there are inconsistencies. I tell him if I can learn more about where the tape came from, maybe I could verify its authenticity once and for all. I say, "Fly me to L.A. and I'll find out." Epps says, "I need more if I'm going to send you to L.A." I remind him about the anachronistic lyrics. He says that's not enough. I say, "There are at least two separate lyrics referencing things that didn't exist until eight years after Toop disappeared." Epps says, "It's not enough. It could be coincidence. Can you do this over the phone?" I say, "That won't be enough. I need to be there." He says, "I'll fly you to L.A. when you give me good reason to." I ask him what a good reason would be. He says, "Something concrete. Something irrefutable that calls the tape's origins into question." I tell him I'll be in touch and ask if Ronnie can give me a lift. He sends a text and tells me Ronnie will meet me downstairs.

A confession: I'm a little bit relieved that Epps doesn't want to send me to L.A. I don't like traveling. What will I do if I find something concrete to convince Epps to send me? I'll go to L.A., of course, but I'm not going to like it.

While I wait for Ronnie, I see that I missed a call from Kyle. I call him back and he tells me he's spent some time with the tape, that he has information for me, tells me he'll be available for the rest of the afternoon.

*

When Ronnie drops me off in front of Wow and Flutter, he asks, "What are you doing here?" I tell him I'm talking to a friend about the tape. He says, "What tape?" I say, "You know what tape." He says, "What are you expecting to find?" I tell him that I don't know then tell him I'll make my own way home. He says he can wait, but I tell him not to bother—I don't want to be in a position where he can ask questions after I have new information. I want to play this close to the vest.

Inside, a group of clean shaven young men dressed in black with hair to match are packing up their gear while Kyle puts microphones in padded cases. After the band loads out, I ask Kyle what he learned about the tape. He says, "Not much." I ask, "Anything?" He tells me the tape had been mastered digitally sometime in the last thirty years or so. He says: "Once a recording is converted into digital form, it loses sub harmonic information that might be useful." He adds, "If we had a pre-mastered copy, maybe I'd know more."

I ask Kyle if any of the music on the record sounded out of place, if there were instruments or sounds in the arrangements that couldn't have existed in California in 1976. He tells me that, for the most part, there aren't, that almost everything on the album existed in the seventies. I ask him what he means by "almost." Kyle pauses, looks a bit uncertain. He says, "What would it mean if there was an instrument on here that couldn't have possibly existed in California in 1976?" I tell him it could mean a few things. I tell him, at one extreme, it could mean the tape is completely fake. Kyle says, "This is Jim Toop. Without a doubt." I say, "I tend to agree." I present the other options: either someone who wasn't Toop came across the tape and added some tracks, fleshed out some arrangements, and prepared the songs for general consumption or Jim Toop survived beyond his disappearance and finished the recording himself, in secret. Kyle loads the tape into his console, cues to a specific time code. He hands me head phones, tells me to listen, then plays the very beginning of "That Old Game Show." He rewinds the tape, plays it again, says, "Do you hear that?" I shrug, say, "Hear what?' He says, "That synth." I tell him I don't hear a synth. "Listen again," he says. And there it is, buried in the mix, a gentle, burbling thrum. I nod, say, "I hear it." Kyle says, "Now, I'm not one-hundred percent sure, but I'm fairly confident in what I'm about to tell you." And then he starts talking about modulators and oscillators and tones and pitches. I cut him off, say, "I don't know shit about this shit." Kyle says, "All you need to know is this: if my ear is right, and it usually is, and if I'm hearing what I think I'm hearing, then that's a Korg Mono/Poly." Here, Kyle looks at me with his eyes wide, excited. He repeats, "A Korg Mono/Poly," as if I should understand what that means. I wait for Kyle to explain and I can see his excitement fade to disappointment, and probably annoyance as he realizes I don't understand. Finally, he says, "The Korg Mono/Poly didn't go on sale until 1981." I say, "Why didn't you say so?" Kyle says, "Fuck off." I ask him how sure he is. He says, "Ninety percent? Ninety-five?" Then he asks, "You think Toop's still alive?" I say, "Probably not, but now it'll be impossible to argue that Toop recorded all of this himself before his *disappearance*—if he made it at all." Kyle says, "That's definitely Jim Toop." I say, "It sure

sounds like him." Then Kyle says, "This is fucked up, man."
I say, "That's one way to put it."

*

When I get home, Fox Mulder is waiting outside of my apartment building. It is only three o'clock. "Shouldn't you be in school? I ask. He tells me the school day ends at two-thirty, asks if he can come in. I tell him I'm tired. He says it's important. This is the first time I've seen him during the day. In the sunlight, his acne is more apparent. I'd forgotten what acne was like. Fox Mulder appears to be in the midst of a severe flare up. "What's stressing you out?" I ask. "I'm not stressed out," he says. "Your face," I say. "That happens sometimes," he says. "Like when you're stressed out?" I say. He says, "Or I eat greasy food, or forget to wash my face, or spend too much time inside."

Fox Mulder follows me to my apartment. I ask him what is so urgent that he needs to talk to me immediately, though I'm fairly certain this is because Ronnie Epps told him where I'd been. Fox Mulder drops his book bag on the floor, flops down on the sofa. He pulls a bottle of Yoo-hoo out of his bag, takes a swig. With the back of his arm, he wipes a film of chocolate drink from his upper lip. "You drink a lot of that stuff?" I ask. "I have one most days," Fox Mulder says. "Chocolate is bad for acne," I say. He acts like he doesn't hear me, takes another sip from his bottle. He says, "You're not my mom." I say, "Obviously." Then Fox Mulder asks me what I learned about the tape. I decide to fuck with him, say, "You know what I learned about the tape." Fox Mulder says, "I mean from your friend at the studio." I ask Fox Mulder how he knows about that. He says, "If you want to keep secrets, be careful who you talk to." He says, "Ambiguous might not technically exist anymore, but our network is still bigger than you know." I say, "Ambiguous was bigger than anyone knew." Fox Mulder says, "What does that mean?" I say, "Nobody has heard of Ambiguous." He says, "The FBI investigated us." Then: "We shut down the internet." I say, "That was you?" He says, "Just tell me what you learned." I say, "One more thing." Fox Mulder says, "What?" I say, "I know Ronnie Epps told you." Fox Mulder says, "Whatever." I don't feel like dealing with the kid right now, am tempted to drag him downstairs and drive him to his mother's house, tell her I caught him breaking into my apartment, but that seems like more effort than it's worth so I decide to just get it over with and tell him what I learned. He seems disappointed through most of my explanation, but that's because I'm holding off on telling him about the Korg. Fox Mulder says, "I was hoping for something firmer." I say, "Firmer how?" Fox Mulder says, "Something to prove, without question, that Toop is still alive.

I tell him the tape could never prove that. Then I tell him about the Korg Mono/Poly. He says, "So?" I tell him it means that work on the tape was happening at least as late as 1981, which means we can safely assume the anachronistic lyrical references aren't mere coincidence. I say, "Toop, or someone, was working on these songs after he disappeared, at least as late as 1985." I say, "That's huge."

Fox Mulder says, "I just wanted something more." I say, "What more could you possibly want?" He says, "We need to find out if Jim Toop is still alive." I say, "If he's alive and hasn't been found yet, then there's no way in hell we're going to find him." Then I ask, "Why is this so important to you?" Fox Mulder says, "It just is." Before I have a chance to press further, a car honks from the street. "That's Ronnie," he says. "I've got to get home before my mom."

To be perfectly honest, I like—no, I *love* the idea of Toop being alive. I'd love to meet him and ask him about Angela, to find out he's been living happily under an assumed name with her all these years. Ask him if he's read any of my essays about his work. As improbable as it actually is, the possibility of talking to Toop excites me. But the odds of him still being alive are practically nil. It's not easy for a person, let alone one who is the object of interest for hordes of conspiracy theorists, to disappear, and stay disappeared, for decades. And that's why I'm fairly confident that Jim Toop is dead. I'm also growing increasingly certain, with each listen, that Jim Toop sang every word on *The Taxidermist's Catalog.* So what do I do with all of this? As much as I dislike traveling, the best way for me to learn what I want to learn is by talking to Toop's father. I wonder if word of the Korg will be enough for Richard Epps. Maybe if I leverage the theory that Jim Toop is still alive, even though I don't believe it, that will be enough. Maybe that's what Epps wanted to know all along. Is that what this is all about?

*

That night I sip my cheap scotch and try to collect my thoughts before contacting Epps again. I make a list of everything I know, what I can and can't use to convince Richard Epps to send me to Los Angeles. My list: I don't know when or where the songs were recorded; I don't know what happened to Jim Toop in 1977; I don't know who sent the tape to Richard Epps—though it very well could have been Jim Toop himself; I don't know for sure who recorded a synthesizer part onto the tape in or after 1981, nor do I know who mastered the tape; I don't know why Fox Mulder is interested in Jim Toop; I don't know why the tape was given to Richard Epps; I don't know who was communicating with Fox Mulder under the name ToopFan, nor who posted to a message board under the name DesertBirds77, but both messages came from an IP address connected to Jim Toop's father; I don't know how expensive Richard Epps's scotch is; I don't know what Amanda is up to, but I don't really care; I know that Ronnie Epps was how Fox Mulder knew I had the tape in the first place; I know that Richard Epps wants to make a lot of money off the tape; I know Richard Epps said he wants me to authenticate the tape, but I'm starting to think he wants something else; I know Fox Mulder desperately wants Jim Toop to be alive, but I don't know why; I know that a lot of people have thought for a long time that Jim Toop was abducted by aliens or kidnapped or killed by a cult or left to die in the desert; I don't know how many people downloaded Fox Mulder's piss-poor DAT recording of "Cormac Bleeding," but the response to the leak has been underwhelming at best; I know that the Korg Mono/Poly wasn't available for purchase until four years after Toop disappeared; I know that there are references on the tape to things that didn't happen until eight years after Toop disappeared; I know that I can't keep Betty from sneaking into my thoughts, especially now that I'm immersed in Toop's work; I don't know if Richard Epps will pay for me to go to L.A., and I'm not sure that anything on this list will sway him one way or the other; I know that if Epps *does* want me to do more than authenticate the tape, that he's going to send me to L.A.; I know that I want Angela to be real, and for the love between her and Toop to have been true and pure, even though songs on *The Taxidermist's Catalog* indicate otherwise; I don't know what it would be like to meet Angela—would it be like looking at a Goddess? Like looking at symbol of all I've lost, of all the ways I've failed?; I know that something about all of this feels strange; I know that I am tired and lonely and my nerves are on edge; I know that Amanda left because I talked about having kids and dying; I know that I had to leave Betty because she made me know what it felt like to want to die even though I was afraid of dying; I know that the feeling of wanting to die but still being afraid of dying has never gone away; I don't know what I'm doing; I don't really know anything; I know that I'm alone and that I will continue to be alone; I know that this list is making my chest tighten a little; and I know that it's good that I accepted this assignment because I had nothing better to do, and having something to do is better, I think, at least most of the time; I know that I hate traveling and don't really want to go to L.A., but I want to talk to William Toop and learn all I can about *The Taxidermist's Catalog*, and Jim Toop, and Angela; I know that, even still, I'll contemplate balling up this list and throwing it away when I'm done writing it, but I won't; I know that this list is gritty, but probably not effective.

*

In the morning, I send a text message to Richard Epps. It says: "Korg Mono/Poly (1981) on *The Taxidermist's Catalog*. Send me to L.A." He texts back, "What do you hope to find?" I respond, saying "Either Toop didn't record or he was working past his disappearance. Need to talk to Toop's father to prove tape is real," I wait for a response, watch the circles on my screen tell me that Epps is typing. My nerves begin to take over. I send another message before Epps can send his response: "Possible Toop still alive?" The circles stop moving on my screen, then begin again. Epps writes, "Reservations in progress. Ronnie will be by soon."

Within an hour, Ronnie Epps knocks at my door and hands me a stack of computer printouts—plane tickets, hotel and rental car reservations, and contact info for Toop's father. He asks me if I plan to talk to anyone else and I tell him there's no one else to talk to. "What about Ocean City people?" he asks. I tell him they're all gone or off the radar, that the only one really worth talking to drove his car into the ocean. Ronnie says, "That's too bad." I tell him I'll make due. Then, Ronnie pulls a fat envelope out of his inner blazer pocket. The envelope is full of twenty dollar bills. "Your expense account," Ronnie says. "Your flight leaves tomorrow morning at nine. I'll pick you up at seven." On his way out, Ronnie asks, "Do you really think he's still alive?" I tell him that I don't know, but the only way I'm going to find out is by heading west. Ronnie seems satisfied with that.

Oh, how suddenly my situation has changed: with this stack of papers in my hands, I'm confronted with the reality that I'm actually going to have to travel to Los Angeles—and soon. I will have to pack a suitcase and board a plane. I dislike both, for very different reasons.

*

A confession: Now is when the worry sets in.

I worry about flying, but not for a fear of crashing. I worry about being stuck in confined quarters with strangers for long periods of time. I worry that the person sitting next to me will fall asleep on my shoulder, that the child across the aisle will try to talk to me, that the person sitting in the aisle seat will glare at me if I ask him to move so I can use the lavatory. On one flight, I watched one sleeping man projectile vomit on another sleeping man. I'll never forget the smell. The last time I flew, I rested my head against the window and Betty fell asleep against me. I put my arm behind her back, caressed her neck, curled loose strands of her hair around my fingers. Betty and I have been divorced for more than twenty years. That's how long I've avoided flight. Thinking about my upcoming travels keeps me up. I can't sleep so I decide to stay up all night. I'm starting to regret insisting on this trip. I can't turn back now though.

I worry about security for the tape while I'm gone. There won't time to drop it off at a bank's safe-deposit box. I'd like to think that such precautions are unnecessary, but I'd rather not take the chance. I wrap it in several plastic bags and tape it inside my toilet tank where the water won't reach it. When the tape is hidden, I have nothing else to do to keep me from packing my suitcase.

I don't worry about packing. My dislike for packing is bigger than worry. I haven't even pulled my suitcase out of the bedroom closet yet. This has nothing to do with the suitcase and everything to do with the act of filling it, with the suitcases I've filled in the past.

*

I pack t-shirts, jeans, several pairs of boxers and socks, sandals. I pack one dress shirt and one tie. A tooth brush and a travel size tube of Crest. I stare down at my full suitcase. There was a similar suitcase many years ago that looked just like this one, have been plenty since.

It is five in the morning and the sun is starting to come up.

The contents of my suitcase taunt me.

They are the same now as they were before.

I am the same now as I was before.

My chest tightens, breath quickens. I wonder if I'll ever know if I'm having a heart attack, or if I'll always think it's anxiety.

*

I scan my room for well-anchored hooks or beams. My shower curtain is held up by a tension rod, cheap and weak. I don't have a gas oven. No gas, period. The curtain rods are old and fragile. There's my Xanax but I don't have that kind of willpower. My only razor is electric. There are no power outlets close to the bathtub. A confession: I know that, in my better moments, I have designed my living space to protect myself from myself at moments like these. It's the same basic principle for why I agreed to investigate this tape—these things keep me alive.

*

The sun is starting to come up but it is a cold sun. I feel the morning air slide in around my windows and I catch a chill. I shiver and look at my suitcase and think about how I had to leave Betty. I am too tired to think about Amanda instead of thinking about Betty, too exhausted even to fantasize about Angela right now.

*

A confession: I packed a suitcase when I had to leave Betty. I packed that suitcase when I got home from the hospital. I went to the hospital because I tried to kill myself. I tried to kill myself because, on our way home from one of our trips to Dayton, Betty told me she was seeing another professor in her department, that the relationship had started for the sex, as most affairs do, but that the two had grown quite fond of one another.

"I'm telling you now because I care about you," Betty said. She said we could stay together, to try to work on things, but that didn't seem right. Didn't seem possible.

I didn't speak for the last twenty minutes of the drive. I didn't speak when we got home. Betty called her new partner and asked if she could stay with him because I wasn't taking the news well, wasn't participating in the conversation. When she was gone, I pulled the car into the garage, closed the door, and left the car running, let the fumes fill the garage until I passed out. One of our neighbors found me when he saw what he thought was smoke. He saw me in the garage and broke the window to let out the exhaust. After I regained consciousness I vomited on the garage floor. My neighbor called an ambulance. The doctors said I probably would have died had the car not run out of gas while I was passed out. They said, even had my neighbor not found me, the bad air would have slowly leaked out of the garage and been replaced with good air, but that, regardless, I was lucky. "Lucky?" I asked. "You could have died," a doctor said. "Right," I said. "I guess you're right."

So they sent me home and I packed a suitcase like the one I just finished packing, with t-shirts and jeans and boxers and sandals, and I left Betty forever.

*

I am still a wreck when Ronnie Epps knocks on my door, but I am less of a wreck because I took a Xanax. I grab my suitcase and carryon and step out into the hallway where I find Fox Mulder waiting for me. "Don't bother looking for the tape," I say when we're settled in the car. "You taking it with you?" Fox Mulder asks. I tell him it's in a safe deposit box at a bank. "Your bank?" he asks. I don't answer. Instead, I ask Fox Mulder, again, why he wants the tape so bad, not expecting an answer. I tell him, "Ronnie's dad has a copy, ask him." He says, "I tried."

At the airport, as I gather my bags from the car, Fox Mulder asks me if I have a computer with me. I tell him my laptop is in my carryon. He tells me he'll be doing research of his own from his computer, safely from his mother's house. He asks me to keep him updated. He says, "Let me know if you find anything." I tell him I might. He says, "If you need help let me know." Before we part ways, Fox Mulder says, "Daniel." It catches me off guard because I don't think he's ever used my name before. He says, "Good luck." I say, "Luck is for assholes." He says, "Just find something." I tell him I'll try.

*

There is a song on Jim Toop's *Ohio Songs* called "We Learned to Fly." The song is vaguely about the Wright Brothers, but more about how Toop would watch airplanes take off from Wright Patterson Air Force Base when he was young. The song includes one of my favorite of Toop's lyrics. After describing the flat sprawl of the base as it appears from a nearby hill, Toop sings:

> Never saw a bird so pretty
> Never knew the metal sky
> You and me, we're broken voices
> Sipping drinks and getting high

All these years later, I still don't know who, or what, exactly Toop is singing about here. I'm more comfortable with the lyrics' assertion that Dayton, his old town, and two of its most famous inhabitants, The Wright Brothers, "showed the world how to fly." There's something affecting and impenetrable in the excerpt, even comforting. I love these lines for the way they romanticize the boredom of youth. I imagine the verse playing on repeat as my plane climbs into the sky and reaches altitude. I am on my way to Los Angeles. I am going to show up at William Toop's house and try to talk to him about his son, to try to learn what happened to Jim Toop in 1977, and if he could possibly have been working on *The Taxidermist's Catalog* after he disappeared into the big bright desert, never to be heard from again.

II. BLACK TRIANGLE

-or-

Ghosts in the Machine:
How One Boy's Quest to
Find his Father Gave
Rise to @mbiguous, the
Hacktivist Collective
that Crashed the
Internet, A History

(Written between January, 2012 and
March, 2013)

(To be published no earlier than March,
2033)

1. EXISTENCE

Call me Fox Mulder. That is the name I was given by mother, Dana Mulder. If it's not obvious, she's obsessed with *The X-Files*. I have no father to speak of. For the first twelve years of my life I believed I was immaculately conceived, "Like Baby William," my mother would say, Baby William being the child that Dana Scully gave birth to in the eighth season of *The X-Files*. The show never fully explained where Baby William came from, but most fans assumed Scully was impregnated by aliens, or that the child was the result of genetic experimentation by a doctor trying to create alien-human hybrids. I believed I was the same. A lot of people believe a lot of things about Baby William on *The X-Files*. Nobody believes anything about me except for me. When I was ten, I read Armand Marie Leroi's *Mutants: On Genetic Variety and the Human Body* and believed I might have been the result of a mutation in my mother allowing her to reproduce asexually, like an earthworm. Despite the absurdity of my beliefs, I clung to them until about five years ago when I turned thirteen and my mother told me that I was conceived when she had sexual intercourse with a man who she met while on a business trip in Ohio.

I know—you're not here to read about me. You're here to learn about @mbiguous, the famed hacktivist collective that shut down the internet. I get it, but if you want to know the story of @mbiguous, you need to know a little bit about me. So who am I? As I write this, I am eighteen years old, about to graduate from high school. In my relatively short time on this planet I have recorded dozens of electronic dance music tracks, none of which have been released; I have written over five hundred reviews of popular albums, television shows, books, and films on various websites, blogs, and message boards; I am a two time medalist and four time finalist in the New York State Science Olympiad; I have seen my favorite film, *Close Encounters of the Third Kind*, forty-six times, in its various extant versions; I have watched every episode of *The X-Files*, including both films—yes, even the bad one—eleven times; and, most importantly, the reason this history exists, I was a founding member of @mbiguous, a secret collective of computer hackers and intellectuals whose primary goal was to seek truth in all matters and rage against the injustice and oppression wrought by Big Business and Big Government upon the common man. How did I accomplish all of this in eighteen years? Such accomplishments aren't difficult for one who possesses natural intelligence and has little interest in the social interactions so important to my peers. It hasn't hurt that my mother's solipsistic flights of fancy have allowed me free reign to spend most of my time how I like.

But this history isn't meant to read as a résumé of my accomplishments or a catalog of minutiae—no, this history's purpose is to tell the story of the creation, proliferation, and demise of @mbiguous. As this history won't be available until at least twenty years from now, I wonder how many readers will even remember @mbiguous, especially since it was our policy to keep quiet about our activities while we were still active. Despite that quiet, though, we were, for a few years, one of the most powerful entities in American politics. So why am I telling our story now? Because I was the organization's historian, and because we felt the story needed to be told, even if that story needed to wait decades to be shared. Maybe this history will incite the real change for which we hoped, but never achieved. We can only hope.

2. COLONY

The initial inspiration for @mbiguous arrived shortly after my thirteenth birthday. Please know, this initial inspiration was still a ways before the group's true beginning, which we might not even be able to clearly identify as that beginning was vague and amorphous, moving in fits and starts, in distances and half-way-theres. The progression of @mbiguous's beginning is not unlike Xeno's paradox, only we did, eventually, arrive, as much as anything can be said to have arrived, at @mbiguous, instead of eternally halving our way to infinity.

I'm sure you're wondering: what could prompt a thirteen year old to conceive of an organization like @mbiguous? My inspiration for @mbiguous had nothing to do with wanting to found a politically minded hacktivist collective, but instead from a personal need for information that could best be provided by computer specialists. The story begins with my mother forgetting my thirteenth birthday. She procured neither gifts nor a cake for me. While this was the first time she had forgotten my birthday, she'd flaked out on me plenty of times before—missed Science Olympiad events, parent-teacher conferences, and once even left me stranded at school for hours having forgotten to pick me up. While each occurrence bothered me, I'd grown accustomed to them. By the time I was seven or eight, I had come to expect my mother would forget me because I was merely a detail in her life, which revolved around work and fantasy. To wit: she missed one parent-teacher conference because she had been re-reading Timothy Good's *Above Top Secret: The Worldwide UFO Cover-up*, and lost track of the time doodling a picture of a body rising in a beam of light toward a black triangle. Needless to say, I wasn't surprised, or particularly disappointed when she forgot my thirteenth birthday. I suspected early in the day when she got me out the door for school without wishing me a happy birthday or making any mention of gifts or a celebration, and knew for sure when she returned home from work and planted herself on the sofa to watch *X-Files* episodes she'd taped off of television. When I asked if she'd forgotten my birthday, she cursed then took me out to our favorite Italian restaurant. We were seated at our usual corner table. The young girl who sat us—she couldn't have been more than thirteen herself—left two laminated menus, two blank, white paper placemats and a small tin cup filled with crayons. As a teenager, I should have long outgrown the need to draw on placemats to prevent boredom, but I hadn't, and neither had my mother. That night, we played hangman, using characters and episode titles from *The X-Files*.

I took the first turn, drew a gallows pole and a series of lines across the bottom of my placemat:

---- ------

My mother guessed the letter 'D.' I filled in the first blank. "Dana Scully," my mother said.

I told her no and drew a head on the noose:

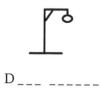

D___ _____

"Of course it's Dana Scully," she said. "Look at it."

I insisted that it wasn't Dana Scully, told her to guess another letter. She tried an 'R,' then a 'T'. I filled in the blanks accordingly:

D___ T_R__T

I picked this because it is an episode title *and* character name from the show's first season, and I know my mother doesn't watch the early episodes as much as the middle seasons that aired when Duchovny was more of a sex symbol. When I *really* wanted to stump her, I'd pick something from the show's later seasons, after Mulder had mostly been replaced by John Doggett. For that first round, though, I thought I'd give her a chance.

"Deep Throat," she said.

I filled in the letters:

DEEP THROAT

My mother blushed, grabbed a black crayon from the tin cup and scribbled over our game. "Deep Throat," of course, was the second episode of *The X-Files'* first season, and introduced Mulder's first inside informant, known only as Deep Throat. I also knew, then, that Deep Throat referred to the individual who gave information about Richard Nixon to Bob Woodward during the Watergate scandal. I did not know, then, that *Deep Throat* was also the name of a pornographic film from 1972. I didn't learn that until researching Watergate and Deep Throat for a school project, at which point I retroactively understood why my mother scribbled over her winning round of hangman. Sometimes she behaved like a real mother.

Next, my mother drew a noose and lines across her own placemat. We went on like this, back and forth, through ordering—she, eggplant parmesan, me lasagna—challenging each other's *X-Files* knowledge. She almost stumped me with Diana Fowley, and I came closer to stumping her with Oliver Martin, who was a main character in one of the last episodes of the show's ninth season. Then, not long before our food arrived, my mother drew the following lines across her placemat:

_ _ _ _ _ _ _   _ _ _ _ _ _

After a few missed letters, which resulted in a head, body, and one arm, I successfully guessed an 'M,' 'L,' and 'D':

_ _ L L _ _ M   M _ L D _ _

I reached over and filled in the missing letters on my own:

W I L L I A M   M U L D E R

Fox Mulder's father on *The X-Files.*

My mother nodded, signaling I had won, but she didn't say anything. She gave me a hard look that made me shrivel up and feel small. I didn't know what that look meant and was worried that I was somehow in trouble for guessing the answer so quickly, or that I had done something else to displease her. My mother has always been quite mercurial. Before she had a chance to say anything, our food arrived. We ate in silence, speaking only to say our food was good, or pass the Parmesan. When we were finished, my mother said,

"That was your father's name."

I didn't know what she was talking about at first.

I wiped my mouth, asked, "Father?"

"Your father," she said. "Not really a father, I suppose," she said, then added: "But biologically speaking."

"Who?" I asked, unclear as to what was happening.

She pointed to the name from our last round of hangman: W I L L I A M   M U L D E R. I was alarmed because, as much as I enjoy science fiction, and even though I was only thirteen, I'd never been the type to have trouble distinguishing fiction from reality. My mother, on the other hand, regularly displayed such behavior. Once, I heard her shout my name, "Fox!" only to, upon entering her bedroom in response to her call, find her sprawled out naked on the floor, one hand between her legs, the other holding the David Duchovny issue of *Playgirl*. Another time, fearing that The Flukeman, from "The Host," a season two episode of *The X-Files*, would infect her with his flatworm offspring, she refused to shower for months. She also still thinks, to this day, and also because of *X-Files* episodes, that cockroaches are robot aliens that want to kill her, that people with physical deformities want only to harm people without physical deformities, and that some crude oil contains an alien virus that will cloud her eyes and possess her. I wasn't wrong to be concerned when my mother pointed at the name W I L L I A M   M U L D E R and told me that he was my father.

"William Mulder was my father?" I asked.

My mother laughed, said, "Not like that."

I was relieved.

"A man I met on a business trip. He was staying at the same hotel as me. His name was Bill Mulder," she said. Then she explained that she and Bill Mulder had bonded over their shared last name, bonded over the fact that he had the same name as the other Fox Mulder's father, bonded over the fact that he actually kind of looked a little like the fictional Bill Mulder, bonded because they were both big fans of *The X-Files*, kept bonding over dinner, then bonded more over karaoke and cocktails until they couldn't help but, in my mother's words, the casual informality of which made my lasagna sit uneasy in my stomach, "You know, bond." She told me that I was born nine months later, that she had always intended to tell me but was too ashamed, so she avoided the whole affair by telling me fantastical stories about not having a biological father. I wasn't particularly surprised as I'd long accepted that I was not, in fact, the result of alien experimentation or an unprecedented act of evolution.

I asked what William Mulder was like.

She told me he was of average height, had brown eyes, brown hair, but he didn't look like David Duchovny. "He wasn't much of a drinker," my mother said. "Got tipsy after one gin and tonic, but he sang beautifully—'Beyond the Sea,' by Bobby Darin because 'Beyond the Sea' was his favorite episode of the show, and then he sang that Dylan song, the 'Rainy Day' one about people getting stoned."

"So you're thirteen now," she said. "Now you know the truth."

"Can I meet him?" I asked.

She told me she didn't know where he was or how to contact him, that she'd never had that information, had never tried to find him and never planned to, was content to let it be a one-night stand, and anyway, that was so long ago—he probably has a family of his own. When I pressed, she grew sterner than I'd seen her in years.

"That's not going to happen, Fox," she said. "He doesn't even know you exist. There's too much at stake for all of us." Then: "No, I'm sorry, but you can never meet him."

Knowing from the severity of her statement that she was not to be disagreed with, I nodded, though my mind was already racing, plans forming.

"Now let's see about a birthday gift," she said, trying to lighten the mood.

We paid the check and took the long way home to stop by the bank. She withdrew two hundred dollars from the ATM, slipped twenty into her billfold and handed the rest to me, folded into a fat wad.

"Happy birthday," she said. "Want a cake?"

I shoved the money in my pocket and knew exactly what I would do with it if necessary—I'd hire a private investigator to track down William Mulder. With a hundred and eighty bucks in my pocket and the knowledge that I had a father, I didn't feel like I needed cake.

"Let's get ice cream," I said. "My treat."

3. ANASAZI

I'm sure some readers will undoubtedly balk at the idea that learning the truth about my conception was the impetus for @mbiguous. Though the influence of that moment on the group's beginnings was neither immediate nor direct, its shockwaves reverberated in odd and surprising ways until one day I looked around me and noticed that I'd inadvertently built an empire of computer users and resources. We're not quite there yet though.

I began my quest for William Mulder with basic research—I plugged his name into Google and Facebook, as well as a handful of people finder services, the paywalls of which I circumvented using fake logins I acquired on message boards and from deep web searches. These proved fruitless as there are far too many William Mulders in the world, and I had no idea where my William Mulder was from. My mother hadn't mentioned that part and I was worried that, were I to ask her for additional information, her paranoia might kick and cause problems for my search. Perhaps my fear was unreasonable but she exists in a world of conspiracies and monsters—the potential consequences of the search might frighten her—she might think I was trying to leave her forever, or that the information I was collecting might somehow threaten her well-being. I cleared my browser history and cache after each round of research.

When I failed to find my father on the internet, I visited a private investigator. His name was Phil Estes. His office was walking distance from my school. The waiting area was well lit and decorated in pastels. Two pieces of generic modern art, probably purchased from a furniture store, hung on the walls. When the receptionist told me Mr. Estes was ready to see me, I was nervous. I expected a gruff old man, drunk on his afternoon bourbon, his doughy form shrouded in a frumpy suit. Instead, Mr. Estes was fit and fairly young, late thirties I'd guess. He was wearing a pink golf shirt tucked into slim fitting, neatly pressed khakis.

I told him I was looking for my father.

"Your father?" Estes asked. "When did you last see him?"

"I've never seen him," I said.

"Were you adopted?"

I shook my head, explained how I learned about William Mulder, and why I wanted help finding him. While I spoke, Estes poured himself a tumbler full of sparkling water from an expensive looking bottle. When I finished, he stood up from behind his desk, walked around so he was next to me and kneeled down, looked square into my face.

"You don't want to find this William Mulder," he said.

"I do," I told him.

He said, "You may think you want to find him, but you don't. Your mother kept him a secret for a reason."

"Her only reason is she's a little bit crazy," I said. And, though it was true, I felt bad for the bluntness with which I described my mother.

"I'll bet she's not as crazy as you think," Estes said.

I told him he had no idea.

He said, "Honor your mother, kid."

For a brief moment, I grew suspicious of Estes, began to wonder if maybe *he* was William Mulder, if maybe my mother's story was a lie. But then I caught myself, realized I was thinking like her, a thing that sometimes happened back then, and maybe still does sometimes.

"I just want to know what he's like," I said.

"Even if you really *do* want to find this guy," Estes said, "you wouldn't be able to afford my fees.

I told him I had money, pulled the wad of birthday cash out of my pocket, counted it out on his desk.

"A hundred and seventy-three dollars," I said.

Estes shook his head, told me he wouldn't take the case.

"It's for your own good," he said. "And anyway, there isn't enough to go on."

He explained that, with so little information, the only way to track down William Mulder was through airline Passenger Name Records, PNR's he called them, and maybe hotel or rental car records, but even those depended on him having flown into Dayton, and William Mulder being his real name.

"Your mom see this guy's ID?" he asked. "Or did she just take his word."

I told him that I didn't know.

"William Mulder," he said. "Wasn't that a character on a TV show?"

I nodded.

"Probably an alias," Estes said. "You're not going to find this guy. Even with PNR's."

As I headed for the door, dejected, Phil Estes stopped me, told me one last time that I'd be better off forgetting the whole thing, to just enjoy being a kid. I thanked him for his time. Before I was even out the door, I was already figuring out my next move, contemplating how, exactly, I might get my hands on some Passenger Name Records.

4. LITTLE GREEN MEN

I know, now, that the reason I failed with Phil Estes was my youth. The investigator didn't take me seriously and I can't blame him. I was going to be alone in this, at least that's what I thought. When I got home from Estes's that day, my mother was asleep on the sofa. This was odd as she was rarely home from work early, let alone early enough to have fallen asleep watching her stories, which, that day, consisted of the premium cable, soft-core sex show *The Red Shoe Diaries*, recorded from TV on to an old VHS tape—a man driving a car across a desert, a woman straddling him, the car in motion, the couple engaging in sexual intercourse. This was—still is—my mother's answer to romance novels. Why? Because of David Duchovny. The first time I caught her watching the show I was intrigued by Duchovny's presence. I walked in as he was reading a letter, a framing device, I would later learn, employed in every episode. That first time, my mother shooed me out of the room, told me to go do my homework. Later I snuck downstairs to watch more. I was appalled. I'll admit that I was also slightly aroused—but I was a boy then, young and curious. And, while I still find the show appalling, I'll also admit that, in recent years, I've been tempted to revisit those tapes for the strictly academic purpose, mind you, of better understanding what exactly makes them so appalling.

The day I found my mother on the sofa after my visit to Phil Estes, I stopped the tape and woke her.

"What time is it?" she asked, still groggy. "Take some money from my billfold. Order a pizza," she said.

That meant she was having a migraine. I asked her if that was why she was home from work. She told me it was. I used to try to explain to my mother that pizza is bad for migraines, that mozzarella and other processed cheeses contain high levels of tyramine. She never listened—still doesn't. She insists that pizza is perfect for migraines as it gives me something to eat, while providing leftovers when she feels better, which is, usually, several hours after the migraine's onset, at which time she is suddenly spirited and animated. I sensed an opportunity. I hated exploiting my mother's physical pain, but I needed information and her guard was down.

"I need to talk to you," I said.

"Go get the pizza," she said.

"It's about Bill Mulder."

"Fox's father?"

"My father."

"You're Fox," she said.

I asked her where the Bill Mulder she'd met in Ohio was from. She said she didn't know. Said it never came up. She wanted to know why I was asking. I told her I was curious.

I asked, "Wouldn't you be curious if you just found out you had a father?"

"Of course," she said.

I asked her if she remembered when her encounter with William Mulder had been. She laughed, told me all I needed to do was count back nine months from my birthday. I was mortified that I hadn't thought of that—a testament, perhaps, to just how troubled and distracted I'd been. I started calculating the approximate date in my head: early January, 1995. All I needed was a list of conferences and events happening in Ohio at the time and I could begin to track down my father.

"Why are you so worried about this?" my mother asked.

"Not worried," I said. "Curious."

"Don't waste your time," she said. "We've made it this far."

And then she rolled over to face the back of the couch and began to sing one of her favorite songs, an odd folk number from the seventies. The song, "Martin Berry's Daughter," was by one of her favorite artists, Jim Toop, who I was interested in because a lot of his fans believe he was abducted by UFO's. "Martin Berry's Daughter" is a sad old song about a man named Martin Berry whose wife died giving birth to their daughter. The song describes the life of the title character's daughter from childhood through marriage, layering maudlin detail upon maudlin detail before revealing, in the final verse, that the speaker is Martin Berry's daughter's husband, whose wife has also recently died during childbirth. It's a sad song, but it's also silly and melodramatic. Hearing her sing it then, I remembered all the times she sang it to me when I was younger and how the song always made me feel sad. That day, her sadness seemed heavier—my mother the wreck, singing in a broken heap on the couch, lost in her migraine and the weight of whatever memories my line of questioning had dredged up. I began to feel older than my thirteen years.

I don't remember the exact date of this exchange, only that it was deep enough into the fall that the sun was beginning to set early, causing the room to assume the vague luminescence of pre-dusk, the same gold that pours through the keyhole, and then through the open door in the scene leading up to Barry's abduction in *Close Encounters of the Third Kind*. Though I'd already accepted that I was not of alien origin, *that* glow at *that* moment began to ache, to thrum inside me. Sometimes, now, I feel that ache still, but for no good reason except that I long for that time when I didn't quite know what I was and was comforted by the limitless possibilities of somehow being special. At eighteen, I still don't know what I am, but the possibilities are gone. I'm just a human, a son, the result of two people participating in sexual intercourse like all of the women and men in *The Red Shoe Diaries*, only the intercourse that made me certainly didn't take place behind the wheel of a moving car, or in a bedroom that looks like a soundstage decorated with a large satin bed and red lights. I was made in a hotel room. I was made by a man and a woman who didn't know each other, who shared a few drinks and karaoke songs then decided to share each other.

That day, though, I stood in the sun's golden glow a little longer and imagined I could feel the illuminated motes of dust move across my skin. I let myself remember how it felt to be younger with no idea where I came from. The pizza could wait. Long after my mother fell back asleep, I stayed in that room, in that particular glow, for a little while longer.

At the end of many early episodes of *The X-Files*, there are scenes in which Scully has been maneuvered away from Mulder and he witnesses moments that serve as irrefutable proof that his beliefs in alien life and conspiracy theories are justified. In these scenes, Mulder sees leaves swirling around a boy named Billy Miles, who is illuminated by a light from the sky, sees Max Fenig levitate in a ray of light and disappear, finds himself in a small satellite outpost surrounded by light and violent wind. With my mother asleep, a small irrational part of me hoped the sky would open up and reveal to me the naked core of the cosmos, for a small, gray man to come tell me *he* is my father. I waited for the light to intensify, for the wind to blow. Nothing happened. Nothing ever will. Still, the feeling of that gold light filling the room, the way it made me feel—that was something.

5. UNUSUAL SUSPECTS

Now, dear readers, I promise, I am, in fact, telling you about the formation and rise to prominence of @mbiguous, even though that might not yet be evident. If you're unsatisfied with the story thus far, if it's unfolding too slowly, imagine how slow and frustrating my search was. Perhaps you were expecting a story of persecution, of governments and businesses trampling individuals' rights and the young man who stood up to them, who wanted to change the world, who took up digital arms, gathered a digital mob, and affected *real change*. This isn't that story. Just as the other Fox Mulder's story began as nothing more than a brother in search of his sister, this Fox Mulder's story—the *real* Fox Mulder's, not the fictional character's—begins with a son searching for his father.

So then, once I had identified January 1995 as the time in which to search my mother's travel records, I rummaged through her filing cabinets. Thanks to a file marked "Travel Expenses," which included receipts and memos from her various trips, I discovered the reason she was in Ohio and the name of the hotel where she stayed. My mother was, and still is, a programmer for a firm called Know-ware that specializes in institutional computer systems and security. Part of me is continually surprised that my mother ever managed to land this job in the first place, considering her tendencies toward disorganization and awkwardness. But we all know that, the truth is, fields like web security function as safe harbors for the awkward and unprofessional, so long as those workers have got the skills to back up their bizarre behavior—very few in such fields are known for their social grace and professionalism. She had traveled to Ohio to train technicians at Wright-Patterson Air Force Base on the use of new data management and security software she'd helped develop. As an aside, I suspect that my mother's co-workers don't, or at least didn't know her very well as, if they'd known about her paranoia and obsession with all things extra-terrestrial, they almost certainly would have balked at the idea of sending her to this particular base, which has long been rumored to have housed an actual UFO in its storied Hangar 18. I'm also surprised that, as my mother had long been a card-carrying member of The National Investigations Committee on Aerial Phenomena and continued as an avid volunteer and supporter of The Center for UFO Studies after they purchased NICAP's assets in the early eighties, she passed whatever background checks were required to get her onto the base. This almost certainly means that there are no, nor have there ever been UFO's at Wright-Patterson, or any other reason for them to fear a UFO enthusiast coming onto their grounds. My mother stayed near the base, roughly across the street at a Hilton Garden Inn that, as it happens, does not, and never appears to have had a bar. There are, and were, it appears, a number of bars and restaurants all within a mile of the hotel, at which my mother could have been wined, dined, and serenaded by William Mulder. This was the only information I had as my search began in earnest. I knew I was going to need help.

Using the handle MuldersSon, I spent time on several message boards known for their members' technological savvy. I also spent time exploring the deep web, which seemed helpful, but also a little bit frightening. While the deep web, along with some prevalent communities on the regular web proved a bit too volatile and self-serving, I was able to slowly connect with a number of users intrigued by the challenge of hacking into commercial airline databases in search of Passenger Name Records. Many of these self-made hackers were interested in social justice. Many also seemed to hang out in message boards dedicated to technology and conspiracy theories. At a message board known as *The Counsel*, I encountered a number of hackers who claimed participation in some of Anonymous's hacks, but were uncomfortable with the overtly anarchistic tone and increased visibility that group had been courting. I caught their eye by posting a simple question: "Looking for access to passenger name records from ten-plus years ago."

One of the hackers, going by the user name self_replicator, contacted me via private message and, over several days, explained to me how PNR's might be obtained, if one were so inclined to do so. His explanations were tentative and full of disclaimers about safety and legality. He began instructions with phrases like, "While I have never participated in such an act..." and "The following tactic, while theoretically effective, would be highly illegal. Speaking in strictly academic terms, though..." Disclaimers aside, I didn't understand most of what he was telling me. After reading self_replicator's descriptions of how to access such privately owned and highly secured information—I won't reproduce them here as I have neither the technical expertise to effectively paraphrase them, nor the desire to disseminate such information for casual hackers—I was certain that I would not be able to, on my own, obtain the information I sought. When I asked self_replicator if he could help, he didn't respond for three days. Then, approximately a week after our initial contact, self_replicator contacted me one afternoon via IRC and told me that he might be able to help, but he'd need something from me first. I asked him what I could do. Instead of answering directly, he typed, "Go to your front porch."

I won't lie; I was frightened. Until that moment, I'd thought that my online activities were by and large anonymous, that the only interested parties that could track me down were my internet service provider and any branch of law enforcement with the appropriate warrant or subpoena. But there I was, terrified, creeping out of my bedroom and down the hall to the front door. The treatments around the door's windows, in place since before we moved in and left in place due to what I can only assume was my mother's apathy, obscured my view of whoever might be waiting outside. I approached the door slowly, crouched and lifted a corner of one of the curtains. The porch was empty, but there was a car idling in the street, a Corolla or Camry, maybe an Accord.

I thought to turn back and flee to the safety of my room, to call my mother at work, or the police. Instead, my curiosity—one of the traits I share with that other Fox Mulder—got the best of me and I stepped outside. When I approached the car, the driver rolled down his window. He was skinny. His hair was long and greasy, light brown.

He said, "What do you want, kid?"

I said, "I was told to go outside."

He said, "I don't know what you're talking about."

I said, "Let me in the car. I don't want the neighbors to see me."

He said, "Is this some kind of bust?" Then, "No way."

I tried the door and, to my surprise, it opened. As I climbed in, the driver said, loud enough that anyone nearby could hear, "You are not invited into my car. Please get out."

I said, "I'm not going anywhere until I know what this is about."

He said, "What *what* is about?"

I said, "You told me to go out to my porch."

I said, "You're self_replicator."

He said, "No, I'm not, and you're not Dana Mulder."

I told the man he was right, that I was definitely not Dana Mulder, that I was her son, Fox.

"No shit?" he said. "She named you Fox?"

I nodded.

"You're just a kid," he said. "Get out of here."

I told him that he better hurry up and explain himself because my mother would be home soon. This was only sort of true—she was due home in an hour and a half. He sank down in his seat, almost certainly annoyed with himself for his mistake. After a beat in which the, let's be honest, humorous circumstances sank in for both of us, the man introduced himself. He was an associate of self_replicator's. For the sake of maintaining his anonymity, I will not print his real name, but will refer to him by only his username: Anarcho_Journalist.

He asked, "How old are you?"

I told him I was thirteen.

"I don't want an Amber Alert called on my ass for taking you from your house," he said.

"I'm not getting out of this car until I know what you came for," I told him.

Reluctantly, he said, "Let's go meet self_replicator, then."

6. THREE OF A KIND

After a quiet drive, we arrived at Anarcho_Journalist's dorm at NYU. As we walked through the lobby and halls, my companion, clearly uncomfortable to be accompanied by a thirteen year old, twice erupted into an unprompted stammer explaining to people that I was his little brother. His room was sparsely decorated, was part of a suite—there was a small TV on top of a refrigerator, a desk with a computer on it, and a small collapsible table littered with the scattered guts of electronic devices, circuit boards, and microchips—the overhead fluorescent lights were off, leaving us to talk in the glow of two desk lamps and his computer screen. The walls were bare except for two posters—one was an old Nintendo poster with Rob the Robot at the bottom and a grid of screen shots from primitive looking games covering the rest of the field, the second was of the backs of drab-looking workers staring at a large face on a television screen, an image from Ridley Scott's classic 1984-themed Apple commercial. I didn't know about Rob the Robot or

Ridley Scott's commercial yet—they were both before my time—but Anarcho_Journalist explained their relevance to me during one of my many visits to his dorm. The doors to the other rooms attached to the suite's central living space were open so I could see their furnishings were similar. Two men, around Anarcho_Journalist's age, were playing a video game in one of the rooms, and in the other, a small, bald man wearing large headphones and periodically sipping from a bottle of Mountain Dew was hunched over a computer.

"That's self_replicator," he said, offering me a chair, "with the headphones."

I stood up to go introduce myself, but Anarcho_Journalist raised his hand and shook his head. In the dorm room's soft light, he looked younger than he did in his car. Here, he looked like a student. I asked him why he brought me here. He explained what I'd already figured out, that he and self_replicator thought that they had been communicating with my mother.

"We value her expertise," he said.

"Her expertise?" I asked, incredulous. "She's a coder at a small firm." Even though I knew about her work, I struggled to think of my mother as an expert in anything except for *The X-Files*, David Duchovny, and conspiracy theories.

"A small firm that specializes in designing software for government agencies," Anarcho_Journalist said. He explained that having a friend "on the inside"—his words—could be a tremendous asset.

"You thought she'd help you break into government computers?" I asked.

Anarcho_Journalist nodded.

"Why would you even want to do that?"

Anarcho_Journalist didn't say anything for a moment.

Then, finally: "Let me ask," he began, "why are you looking for Passenger Name Records?"

"I asked you first," I said. I didn't want to answer his question. I feared the truth would sound foolish, especially to a university-aged computer hacker. I was worried he'd immediately lose interest in me and I'd be back where I started.

"Obviously you want information," he said.

"Obviously," I answered.

"And you have a reason for wanting that information?"

"Of course."

"It's a good reason, I'll bet," he said, starting to sound like he was making a sales pitch.

I was beginning to feel uncomfortable. I was no longer certain that my reason was all that good.

"Of course it's a good reason," I said.

"Well, we want information too," Anarcho_Journalist said. "We want access."

"And I bet you have a good reason?" I asked, somehow channeling the other Fox Mulder's cocksure swagger.

"We have the best reason," he said.

I didn't respond, waited instead for him to continue. When he finally did, after a pause sufficiently long enough to let his previous statement resonate, he unfurled his words with the fervor of a politician giving a stump speech. He told me that our nation was in ruins, that The Government and Big Business had rotted America from its core and now the decay was becoming evident on the surface. He explained that decades of corruption needed to be revealed, that the exploitation of workers and consumers needed to be exposed, that it was high time that someone stood up to the nation's powerful elite and now, thanks to technology, average citizens had the power to make a real difference. I didn't know exactly what he was talking about—this was heady material for a thirteen year old—but it sounded *good*, and something in his demeanor and his words reminded me of my namesake, which, while not necessarily a good thing, at least meant Anarcho_Journalist was passionate about what he was doing.

"We deserve the truth," Anarcho_Journalist said. "*The American People* deserve the truth and we'll go to great lengths to find it for them, to fight against the forces that have obfuscated that truth for so long, against the forces that would place their own greed and ambition over the wellbeing of their customers and constituents.

Before Anarcho_Journalist could finish, I started laughing. He broke off, asked me what was so funny.

"You sound like Fox Mulder," I told him.

"Thank you," he said.

I didn't have the heart to tell him it wasn't meant entirely as a compliment.

"So you thought my mother could help you with this, but you wound up with me instead. So, why did you bring me here?" I asked.

"Because you refused to get out of my car," he said.

"You don't want anything to do with my mother," I said. "Trust me."

He gave me a hard look, said, "I get it, man—parents are tricky business."

I said, "You have no idea." Then: "So what now?"

In the lingering silence following the unanswered question, I told Anarcho_Journalist that he'd have to take me home, soon, before my mother returned from work. I told him if he and self_replicator didn't want to work with me, that was ok, that I'd been in touch with other experts on message boards, and a few on the deep web, and that while none had shown the same initiative or drive as he and self_replicator, I was sure I'd find the help I needed somewhere. Here, Anarcho_Journalist straightened his posture and seemed more interested in what I was saying. Before I fully finished, he abruptly up and left his room. I watched him talking to self_replicator across the suite, their voices soft so I couldn't hear them. After several moments, the two entered Anarcho_Journalist's room together and closed the door. They told me they had a proposal. Feeling as if I suddenly, unexpectedly held the upper hand, I told them I would listen. By the time Anarcho_Journalist drove me home, we had an agreement: they would retrieve the PNR's I was after if I helped them with a project they were working on. And that, for all intents and purposes, was the beginning of @mbiguous.

7. KILL SWITCH

In the following months, Anarcho_Journalist and self_replicator taught me how to be a hacker—or, "hacker," as it were, since my education was of the surface level variety. I learned never to use the same username or password twice, never to boast—online or in person—about my hacking activities, never to trust other hackers.

"Should I not trust you?" I asked.

"We're different," Anarcho_Journalist said.

"You were lucky this time," self_replicator added.

They warned me about identity thieves and hackers with dubious moral codes who would turn in a fellow hacker for the right price, or merely out of boredom. They warned me about black hat hackers who hack for their own gain or simply to create chaos.

"Isn't that what you do?" I asked.

"We hack for the public good," Anarcho_Journalist said. "We hack to make the world a better place."

My new mentors taught me to use a second hard drive for hacking, to run my operating system from a CD, to use IP address masking software and a proxy server. The more difficult I am to track, I was told, the better my chances of never getting caught. When I told Anarcho_Journalist and self_replicator that I couldn't afford IP address masking software or a second hard drive, they gave me a copy of their software and built a hard drive for me out of parts they had lying around. Through this period of time, one of the two, normally Anarcho_Journalist as he was more social—self_replicator was more of a tech guy, outgoing and friendly, but frequently lost in his work—would come to my house between when I got home from school and my mother's return from work, to set up hardware, install software, and show me how to use it all. Still, I knew very little about what I would be doing. On the last day that Anarcho_Journalist came to my house, I asked him what I was supposed to do with all of the tools they'd given me, all the information I'd learned.

"Do you know what a script kiddie is?" Anarcho_Journalist asked.

I told him no, that I'd only heard the term recently for the first time when self_replicator referred to me as one while showing me how to run a DDoS attack on a website.

"A script kiddie is someone who doesn't really know much about code or how internet security works, but uses previously existing scripts to attack websites. They're a nuisance for everyone. They mess up the web for users and they usually get caught, because they're idiots, which means bad press for us." Then: "You ever hear of MafiaBoy?"

I told him I hadn't.

"He was a script kiddie. Crashed eBay and Yahoo a while back. Sounds cool, right?"

"I guess."

"Well it wasn't. He didn't have a platform, didn't cover his ass, and he got caught. Lucky for him he was young enough that he didn't get much of a sentence."

"So, I'm going to be a fall guy?" I asked.

Anarcho_Journalist paused, looked at my computer. He didn't answer for almost a minute. He tried once or twice, but his words sputtered into an unruly mess. He was nervous.

When he found his words, Anarcho_Journalist told me that I was going to be a smart script kiddie, a strategic tool for him and his hacker friends. And, of course, because I was young, were I caught, the authorities wouldn't be able to do much to me. I could be tried only as a juvenile.

"But you won't get caught," he said. "As long as you do exactly what we tell you."

He added: "You're not a script kiddie so much as you're a proxy. You'll just look like a script kiddie if you're busted."

"If I get caught," I said, "what makes you think I won't turn you in?"

"You could do that and I wouldn't blame you," he said.

I appreciated Anarcho_Journalist's honesty and told him as much.

"Is there anything else I need to do?"

"One more thing," he said. Then he explained that, at the beginning of all this, what made him and self_replicator take an interest in me was that I'd been building relationships with other hacker groups. Anarcho_Journalist told me that, at first, I'd be following instructions on my own for small scale hacks—nothing big, bits of data collection and maybe a little bit of socially conscious website vandalism. Once he and his gang of hackers worked out the kinks in their system, though, they would call on me to reach out to other hackers with whom I'd already established contact so that they might help us plan and execute bigger, more daring actions.

"We're going to build a movement," Anarcho_Journalist said. "Like Anonymous, but smarter and more effective. Our actions will speak for themselves—we won't advertise or take credit. Ego won't enter into our work." Then he added: "So keep in touch with those other groups. They need to know you're credible."

Before Anarcho_Journalist left, I gave him the window of dates for which I needed Passenger Name Records. I told him I didn't have an airline—that I'd need records for every flight running through Dayton International Airport in early January, 1995. Anarcho_Journalist told me they'd do their best, then told me to keep an eye out for instructions regarding my first action as his and self_replicator's proxy.

After my computer had been set up for such activities, I was surprised how ordinary it looked. I was expecting my room to look like David Lightman's in *War Games*. Instead, it looked like Fox Mulder's room in Dana Mulder's house or, if I squinted, like the other Fox Mulder's apartment in *The X-Files*, which was also pretty boring except for when he tore it apart looking for hidden surveillance equipment. I didn't think I'd have to worry about anything like that, and for the time being, anyway, I was right. For the time being.

8. TALITHA CUMI

My first assignment for self_replicator and Anarcho_Journalist was to hack Fox News's website and upload a series of fake articles designed to confuse and upset the ideological positions of the website's core audience. The fake articles were broad in their approach—analyses of class and gender wage gaps, lists of companies that rely on exploitative labor practices at home and overseas, that sort of thing.

Anarcho_Journalist and self_replicator were pleased with the results of this first action, and excited to see that our combined hard work was paying dividends. The prank barely registered in the national media and Fox's website was back to normal within an hour, but our point had been made and I proved myself capable of doing what was asked of me. Unfortunately, while I had managed to avoid being caught or traced by Fox or the authorities, it soon became clear that I had other reasons to worry. My suspicions were initially aroused when my mother started making unscheduled appearances in my room. This was unusual as, before

I started working with my new mentors, my mother only ever entered my room to retrieve dirty laundry and return clean. Her sudden, heightened interest in me was alarming and baffling. I went to great pains in the weeks during my training to make sure that nothing changed with regards to the amount of time spent with my mother so as to not arouse suspicions. This was rather difficult as the time I was spending with Anarcho_Journalist and self_replicator was the time I usually reserved for completing my homework. On the days that one of them came to work with me, I'd put off doing homework until my mother had gone to bed, at which time I would retire to my room to solve math problems from a grocery-bag covered textbook, read insufferable novels about tragic teens who don't fit in with their peers, and fill out worksheets from history and science textbooks.

During those weeks, I spent the hours directly preceding sleep doing homework instead of surfing the web, watching television, or reading the things I liked to read on my own— Bradbury, Asimov, Heinlein, and the occasional western. Though I was able to spend evenings with my mother under the pretense that I had already completed my homework, I was growing increasingly tired, and was running out of things to talk about with her as most of our conversations revolved around the books we were reading and the shows we were watching or re-watching. We'd frequently discuss whatever episode of *The X-Files* we'd most recently watched, or complain about the banal writing and awkward acting in whatever episode of *Star Trek: Enterprise* most recently aired. My mother also enjoyed listening to me describe the most recent Bradbury stories I'd read. I'd tell her about Eckel straying from his path and crushing the butterfly, or about poor Margot on Venus, locked in the closet and missing the only two hours of sunlight she might know for another seven years, or about the lonely house with the silhouettes of a family burned onto its walls. When I initially read that last one, "There Will Come Soft Rains," it's called, I imagined what only two silhouettes might look like on the walls of our own house. After learning about my father, I tried to picture a third—was it fat or thin, tall or short, standing with arms crossed, bravely facing the blast, or bent over mother and I, holding us close, braced for impact.

"I'm jealous of you, you know," my mother would sometimes say. "Reading these stories for the first time."

"What does it matter, first time, second time?—they aren't going anywhere," I'd say.

"You'll never know that wonder again," my mother would answer.

This conversation and variations on it were a regular occurrence—my mother insisted that every story of Bradbury's I read was one more bit of wonder I could never experience again in quite the same way, an absurd sentiment as nothing can ever be experienced the exact same way twice. And as far as I could tell, there wasn't much in the way of wonder left in the world, anyway, and what remained could be retrieved only through fleeting memories, standing alone in a room illuminated by the sun's flying saucer-gold glow, or immersing one's self in technology's shadowy corridors to solve a mystery called Father. This is all a long way of saying that these conversations with my mother all but dried up while Anarcho_Journalist and self_replicator were training me, which is almost certainly why my mother started to get suspicious. When she'd ask what I was reading, all I had to talk about were the terrible books I was reading for school, trashy books that stank of emotional pandering and thematic simplicity.

"Why are you reading that garbage?" she would ask.

"For school."

"You're not reading anything else?"

I'd tell her I was too busy, that my homework was piling up and that I didn't have time for leisure reading. She was disappointed but understanding at first. With time, though, she grew increasingly bored with my descriptions of the awful books I had to read for school until, eventually, she gave me a copy of Ray Bradbury's *Dandelion Wine*.

"Read this," she said. The book's binding was broken, its pages yellow. "I picked it up at the used bookstore on my way home."

"I don't know if I'll have time," I said.

"You're getting good grades?"

"Straight A's."

"Then screw your homework," she said. Then added, "A little."

I took the book and told her I would try.

About a month later, which also happened to be right after the Fox News hack, she started making those regular, unscheduled appearances in my room. The first time she walked right in without knocking after previously having retired to bed for the night. Knowing she'd be suspicious if I was still doing homework, I quickly closed my math book and started tinkering with the piano keyboard on my desk. I told her I was working on a song. She told me she was having trouble sleeping, asked what the song was about. I told her it was dance music, it wasn't about anything.

She said, "Your songs have lyrics though."

I said, "Sometimes."

She said, "Does this one?"

I told her the first thing that popped into my head, that the song was about Molecular Blotting—a summary of a reading assignment I'd finished for science class earlier in the day.

"Sounds interesting," she said.

I told her I'd let her hear it when it was ready, and immediately regretted the promise as it meant I'd actually have to write it.

"Fox," she said, her voice taking on an unusual weight, a tone she usually reserved to demonstrate grave concern about the questions revolving around UFOs or government conspiracies, "I'm worried about you."

She picked up and started thumbing the copy of *Dandelion Wine* that had been sitting on my desk.

I asked her why she was worried. She didn't answer. This was unusual for my mother. She'd never been worried about me before. I wondered if she was suspicious because of the interest I'd shown in my father, or if my uncharacteristic behavior had tipped her off about my risky new enterprise.

"I'll start reading when I'm finished with this song," I said.

"Are you happy?" she asked.

"Of course," I said.

Though I wouldn't have time for several days, I knew that I needed to begin reading the Bradbury book, and soon. I needed to let my mother know that I was fine, that everything was the same as it always had been—she couldn't know that I was beginning a new phase of life as a teenaged computer hacker in an attempt to track down my biological father.

"You spend so much time in here working on your projects," she said. "You're not lonely?"

"I'm fine," I told her. "I have friends at school." This was only a half-lie—while I didn't really have friends at school,

I'd come to consider Anarcho_Journalist and self_replicator as friends, and they *were* attending *a* school.

And with that, my mother kissed me on the head and left me alone. The exchange was odd. It was the most she'd seemed like a mother in years, and it left me feeling uneasy. I grew increasingly nervous when, over the next several weeks, she continued her surprise visits. I started reading *Dandelion Wine* in the few spare moments I could find—during lunch or between classes at school, while using the toilet when I was home—but was progressing far too slowly for my mother to believe I was actually reading it. To compensate, I started reading Wikipedia summaries of the book's chapters so that, when asked, I could respond as if I'd made progress. Being able to talk about the tragic beauty of Douglas's realization that he was alive, or the connection between Mr. Sanderson's memories and his sneakers seemed to satisfy her, but I could tell that she never seemed wholly convinced that something else wasn't wrong.

My paranoia came to a head when, while doing homework in my room, I heard a single, sharp but light thud beneath my computer desk. I pushed the desk a few inches away from the wall and found a digital audio recorder on the floor, its red recording light staring back at me. The machine was half wrapped in duct tape. I didn't know how long it had been taped to my desk, but I had to assume that my mother knew everything. Had she been recording when Anarcho_Journalist and self_replicator were visiting my room? I tried to remember if I'd mentioned Passenger Name Records during their visits. I knew I hadn't explicitly mentioned finding my father, as I still hadn't told my mentors about that, but my mother was clever enough to figure it out. I was still examining the recorder when my mother entered the room.

"You weren't supposed to find that," she said.

"How long have you been spying on me?" I asked.

"Not long—a week or two."

I was relieved—my last visit from Anarcho_Journalist had been at least a month before. I asked why she was recording me.

"I'm worried about you," she said.

"You never worry about me," I said.

"You're hiding something," she said. "I know you are."

I told her I wasn't hiding anything, that she was letting her paranoia get the best of her. I didn't want to gaslight my own mother but I didn't have much of a choice. I couldn't tell her what I was up to—for the sake of her career and her mental health, she could know neither that I was becoming a computer hacker nor that I was looking for my father. My lies were to protect her.

"It's a girl," she said. "You've met a girl."

"I haven't met a girl," I said.

"Of course you have," she said. "Online."

When I asked her why she thought that, she told me that she almost never heard me speak on the tape, but that I typed a lot in the afternoons, and I seemed to be doing homework later than usual.

"And I know you're not working on a song," she said. "Doing homework before bed instead of when you get home, typing in short spurts—it has to be a girl," she said. "And that's ok, Fox. That's nothing to be embarrassed about."

"It's not a girl," I said. But I didn't know what to tell her instead.

She asked me if it wasn't a girl, then what was the matter. She asked me if I was depressed. I wasn't used to lying to my mother, had never had occasion to because she rarely paid attention to anything I was doing. I could feel her eyes breaking me down into my component parts, into molecules, or code, trying to see the truth in my most basic physical elements.

And so I said, "I mean, it's not a girl, exactly."

"What does, 'not exactly,' mean?"

"It's not one girl and it's not a real girl," I lied.

"Have you been looking at pornography on your computer?" she asked. "You couldn't be. I would have heard that." She added: "Or heard, you know, *you*."

What I told my mother next made her blush, made me blush, was the kind of uncomfortable lie required to hide a more uncomfortable truth. As Deep Throat says in the first season of *The X-Files*, "A lie, Mr. Mulder, is most convincingly hidden between two truths," and I had two truths with which to work in an attempt to defuse this line of questioning, only one of which, I suspected I'd need to speak out loud. The first truth: I told my mother that I'd come home from school one day and found her asleep watching *The Red Shoe Diaries*, that when I walked in, a naked woman was straddling a man as he drove a car, and that the video made me feel a certain way. I didn't go into detail about how it made me feel, figuring she'd fill in the blanks. Then a lie: I explained that, after watching several of her tapes, I'd wanted to see something more explicit, more graphic, so I turned to internet porn. I told her I was embarrassed about what I'd been doing. I told her I had been touching myself. This is where the second, unspoken truth came into play: I knew my mother touched herself, and she knew that I knew that she touched herself. Additionally, I knew, despite the openness of our parent-child relationship, that the time I caught my mother stimulating her own erogenous zones while looking at a picture of David

Duchovny was not something that she would ever want to talk about, or acknowledge. My ploy worked.

My mother said, "That's ok, Fox." Then: "That's natural."

She said she was surprised she didn't hear it on the tape, and I told her I was quiet. Then I told her I was sorry, that I would stop. She told me I didn't have to stop, but that she wanted me to know that real sex isn't like porn, or like what happens in her tapes, that those are all fantasies, but that I shouldn't be ashamed about the way my body was feeling. She leaned over and kissed me on the forehead, told me to finish my homework and get to sleep. She already seemed more relaxed.

Before she left me alone, I asked, "What is it like?"

My mother asked, "What's what like?"

I said, "You know. With another person"

She paused, said: "It can be like a lot of things."

Then I reframed my question: "What was it like with him?" I asked. "William Mulder?"

She didn't answer immediately.

"It started like one of those shows," she finally said. "Two strangers in a strange place, meeting and enjoying one another's company, feeling sexy and free. But the sex was just sex—quick and messy, a little bit fun, but mostly awkward and uncomfortable, a little bit gross." Then she told me to forget that last part, that she didn't want me thinking about sex and bodies that way. Then she said "It was just sex." And: "But everything leading up to it was closer than most people ever experience to anything that happens in that show."

I thanked my mother for her honesty, told her to sleep well.

She said the same and left my room. I finished my homework in silence. My mother had confirmed my worst fears about sex—that it was an unpleasant necessity of procreation.

It didn't bother me that that was how I was made—that's simple biology—but there was a particular sadness in her voice, a wistfulness that told me that, maybe, she wasn't being disingenuous in romanticizing the encounter leading up to the sexual intercourse, that maybe that hint of romance was somehow special.

Within a month of that exchange, Anarcho_Journalist visited to drop off three thick, manila envelopes stuffed with passenger name records for every flight arriving at and departing from Dayton International Airport around the time I had been conceived. I opened one and skimmed the seemingly endless list of names. The information in those documents had the power to change my life forever. One of the names on one of those lists could upset my relationship with my mother, a woman so determined to look out for me she would tape a digital audio recorder to my desk and pry for information. I wasn't sure I was ready to upset that relationship. Without taking a closer look at the lists, I tucked the pages back into their envelopes, and taped them to the underside of my desk—if my mother was going to continue monitoring me, I felt it safe to assume she wouldn't use the same method as before—and finally started reading *Dandelion Wine*.

9. MEMENTO MORI

There's a particular sadness in *Dandelion Wine* that has stuck with me for the last few years, has flitted through my consciousness between when I received the Passenger Name Records and when I finally decided to look at them. The word sad and variations on it appear only seventeen times in the book, but the weight of the word hangs over the characters as they grapple with memory, with living, with growing up. The book is obsessed with nostalgia, with the sadness that comes from missing the past. In the years—yes, years—between receiving the Passenger Name Records and actually looking at them, I was troubled by constant nostalgia. I felt as if, at every moment, I was inhabiting the sun's afternoon light as it cast gold shadows across the living room floor. I came to understand that I was quietly longing for a time when I knew less about myself and my origins. I left the Passenger Name Records untouched for years because I wanted to hold on to as much of my not knowing as possible. By looking at the Records, I might learn they didn't contain the information I sought, or that I'd find *some* truth or answer, but not what I wanted, resulting in only heartache. As long as I didn't look at the Records, I could continue not knowing. That's why I hid the documents out of sight and immersed myself in the work of hacking.

And during this time, that work flourished. After a series of small actions similar to what we'd done to Fox News—we hit CNN's site, the Yahoo! front page, and *The Drudge Report*, among others—Anarcho_Journalist and self_replicator arranged for a face-to-face meeting. The new summons arrived in the same manner as the first. I was sitting at my computer, typing an Amazon review when self_replicator messaged me and instructed me to go to my front porch. I told him I wouldn't have much time, that my mother was due home in an hour.

"Just go to your porch," he typed.

I was nervous, worried that I'd somehow been traced by one of the sites I'd hacked. I imagined that Anarcho_Journalist and self_replicator were stealing me away, would give me a fake passport and a plane ticket to Italy or some other country with soft hacking laws. I contemplated packing a bag, but didn't want to explain to my mentors why I had a packed bag if I wasn't in any trouble. I composed myself on the way to the front door, told myself I was acting like my mother and that I needed to get a grip. My hand quivered as I opened the door, but the site of Anarcho_Journalist waving jubilantly from behind his steering wheel set me at ease.

In the car, Anarcho_Journalist asked me when I needed to be back.

"Five," I said.

"Should be enough time."

"Enough time for what?" I asked.

"Planning."

"What kind of planning?"

He asked me if I was still in contact with other hackers. I told him I had been, not regularly, but on occasion.

"Good," he said. "That should do." Then: "I was worried we'd lose you once you got those records."

"I'm still here," I said.

I didn't really need their help anymore, but I was sticking around for the time being because I found the work satisfying. I enjoyed being their script kiddie and standing up to the oppressive forces of government and big business, those entities who don't seem to mind all the lives they destroy. And I enjoyed the work's simplicity—the lack of ambiguity in running scripts, the mundanity of security protocols.

Anarcho_Journalist asked me if I was ready to do something big. I told him I had nothing to lose and he laughed. I apologized and told him I was trying not to sound too much like him or Fox Mulder, but sometimes I did anyway.

"But you are Fox Mulder," he said.

"The other Fox Mulder," I told him.

"Of course," he said.

I asked him if the something big was what we were meeting about.

"Sort of," he said.

"Sort of?" I asked.

And then he told me that we were going to need a name, and we were going to need a plan. I asked him what kind of plan.

He said, "A big plan. Something to get attention."

"Why do we need to get attention?" I asked.

"We can't build a movement if we don't get attention."

"And that's why we need a name, too?"

"People need to know we exist," he said.

I reminded him about what he and self_replicator told me at the beginning, that we'd be smarter, more cautious than Anonymous. That we'd be less concerned with image and attention. Anarcho_Journalist began to argue that, even though our organization would be *less* visible than similar groups, it would be virtually impossible for us to gain momentum and members without at least *some* visibility.

"Think about it this way," he said. "What was the other Fox Mulder's work good for if not for his followers—Max Fenig, The Lone Gunmen. Mulder needed them for his crusade to mean anything,"

"The other Fox Mulder was fictional," I said.

Anarcho_Journalist didn't say anything.

"If we're going to make ourselves more visible, I can't afford to be involved."

He said, "I thought you had nothing to lose?"

I said, "I'm here because I want to be. I can leave at any time."

"You're right," he said. "You can leave at any time."

We drove the last few blocks in silence. After squeezing his car into a barely-big-enough curb space, he took his keys from the ignition and turned to me, asked,

"Why did you need those Passenger Name Records anyway? What are you going to do with them?"

I told him I wasn't sure yet.

"Not sure why you needed them?"

"Not sure if I'm going to do anything with them," I said.

Anarcho_Journalist told me they weren't easy to get, that he hoped they were worth it.

"Many Bothan spies died to get you those records," he said.

I laughed at his *Star Wars* joke, even though I'm not that into *Star Wars*. Then I told him the records were worth having, but that my reasons weren't any of his business.

That afternoon, in the surprising quiet of Anarcho_Journalist's dorm room, closed off from the rest of the suite, he, self_replicator, and I laid the groundwork for @mbiguous. The debate over the group's visibility was swift and decisive as self_replicator and Anarcho_Journalist were divided on the issue, and I was the deciding vote. Anarcho_Journalist, it appeared, had used his time with me in the car to try to sway my vote, and admitted as much. In the end, we compromised, agreeing that the group should have a name for organizational purposes, but that we keep visibility low.

From there, we established core principles and worked to devise a first action that would help us recruit new members and clearly establish our mission. We decided that the group would be amorphous, fluid, aligned with neither mainstream American political party, but with a progressive ideological slant toward humanism, justice, and protecting individuals from the corruption of greed and power. We decided that we would not claim responsibility for our actions, though we would attempt to shape the conversation surrounding them by posting on message boards—our goal was to be invisible but influential. When discussions turned to the topic of naming the group, I suggested Ambiguous."

"Ambiguous?" self_replicator asked.

"It says everything we want people to know," I said.

"Too close to Anonymous," Anarcho_Journalist said.

"Dude, no—it's perfect," self_replicator said. "We can be their shadow, or lamprey."

And so we became Ambiguous, which eventually turned into @mbiguous, just because it looked cooler.

These were our core principles:

1. Primary goal: reveal truths about abuses of power by government agencies and Big Business's exploitation of customers, employees, and environmental resources, and the intersection of the two.

2. Use hacktivism as a means to illuminate truths about and disrupt the business and administrative activities of the above mentioned entities.

3. @mbiguous will not take credit for any actions. Members of the organization, acting as disinterested observers, will discretely interpret, educate civilians about, and promote our activities through various online forums, social media, and other public avenues.

4. @mbiguous is a virtuous organization, interested only in creating a better, happier society.

5. @mbiguous will neither interact with, nor knowingly collaborate with other hacktivist groups (ie., Anonymous, LulzSec, Antisec, etc...) that seem disproportionately interested in publicity and notoriety, putting those associated with them at risk from law enforcement and internet regulatory agencies.

6. @mbiguous will be structured as decentralized cells of approximately five to ten hackers. Each cell will function independently and will not have contact with other cells. Any cell can initiate an action, but each action must be approved by a majority of cells. Only one member of the organization will be in contact will all of the cells. That member, who will remain anonymous, will tabulate votes, notify cells of the results, and coordinate activities between cells. This member will not partake in any hacktivist activities so as to lower the risk of being traced. In the case that

he *is* traced, the hard drive on which he conducts official @mbiguous business will be destroyed. As we want to privately monitor the impact @mbiguous has on its objectives, this member will also serve as the group's historian.

7. @mbiguous participants should be sure to select their screen and cell identifications carefully so they cannot be traced to users' other online activities.

8. Any member of @mbiguous caught taking unnecessary risks, either individually or in the name of @mbiguous, will be expelled from his or her cell.

9. @mbiguous will not, under any circumstances, be used for personal gain. Such hacktivist activities will be rejected outright, and any members found to be participating in illicit activities for such gain, be it in a personal capacity or in the name of @mbiguous, will be expelled from the group.

10. Members of @mbiguous will conduct themselves with dignity and humility at all times.

I, of course, was the central, non-hacktivist member of @mbiguous through which the cells communicated. In the days following our foundational meetings, I approached the groups with which I'd previously been in contact, informally communicated the above information, and asked for referrals to other groups. After only a week, @mbiguous consisted of more than twenty cells and over 150 hackers. That was only the beginning. Once our hacktivism began in earnest, whispered rumors of our existence spread through the hacktivist underworld and our numbers grew. We kept true to our mission and never advertised, but some members bragged of their involvement. While this was initially cause for concern, we decided that the benefits of their talk outweighed the risks. On my second hard drive, the one reserved for clandestine activities, I kept only a basic list of information about each cell.

10. FALLEN ANGEL

Now, I recognize that this history might seem a bit odd, might even embody a distinct disparity between my previous position towards @mbiguous's management of its public image (or lack thereof) and my desire to tell our story, now, in so much detail. Under different circumstances, writing this history would certainly be a foolish, risky enterprise. But even as I write this document, @mbiguous has mostly disbanded and by the time the manuscript is published, if it is ever published, our actions will be but a distant memory. If @mbiguous still existed, I wouldn't be writing this. Just because @mbiguous was short lived and mostly out of the public eye, don't think for a minute that our work wasn't important. That's why I'm telling this story now. As such, this history would be incomplete without an account of some of @mbiguous's actions—and what better place to begin than with our first.

Our first action was devised during the same meetings that produced our name and guiding principles. We believed that we needed a solid plan with which we could recruit new members. When we began discussing possibilities, I was surprised by Anarcho_Journalist and self_replicator's uninspired ideas and conventional thinking. Most of their plans revolved around DoS and DDoS attacks that would shut down several government websites of symbolic import. The problem was, none of the sites they suggested were heavily visited, nor did any of them contain crucial information. Their proposed targets: The Department of Education's website, in a much delayed response to No Child Left Behind; The FDA's website in protest of policies regarding approval of prescription drugs; and the website for the Bureau of Alcohol, Firearms, and Tobacco in response to their weak stance toward gun research and policies. Anarcho_Journalist and self_replicator wanted to hack all three sites at the same time, beginning @mbiguous's campaign against injustice with an ill-conceived, slipshod attack against unrelated websites, for unrelated issues. As the proposed attacks were to be of the DoS and DDoS variety, the end result wouldn't have even been particularly meaningful, would only serve to deny service without providing any sort of information or context about why the sites were being attacked. I interrupted my mentors as they began to outline specifics

"We need something better," I said.

My mentors looked at me. I could tell they were annoyed; Anarcho_Journalist let out a gruff sigh and self_replicator pinched the bridge of his nose. When neither of them verbalized a response to my dissent, I continued, explaining that it was important that our first action be something with a clearly focused message that was directly related to our goals, something that would inspire trust and enthusiasm in @mbiguous's members and spur them to further action.

"This mess of an idea is fine for a motley bunch of hackers looking to inconvenience some IT guys, but that's all—nobody will notice," I said. Perhaps I overstated my argument.

"We don't have anything else," self_replicator said. "And we need to start recruiting while we have momentum."

"We do have something else," I said. I reminded them about a recent set of campaign finance documents that had been leaked, compiled, and distributed by Anonymous. These documents targeted a wide range of politicians and demonstrated clear connections between corporate donations to political campaigns and resulting legislation—nothing surprising, for sure, but useful all the same.

"This is an opportunity," I said. "We have information that is known, but not widely, is meaningful, and happens to complement our mission statement." I told my mentors that we should put together a list of highlights from the document, the most upsetting, egregious, frustrating, perhaps even shocking examples of troubling transactions between business and government, tear down all the major news sites—Fox, CNN, MSNBC, ABC, Yahoo!, Drudge, HuffPo, anyplace with a worthwhile hit count—and post the list. My mentors liked the plan and we spent the next hour fleshing out details. On that particular day, excited by the new idea, we were so invested in our task that none of us noticed that it was almost five o'clock, the time my mother usually returned home from work.

At five-fifteen, Anarcho_Journalist looked at this computer, cursed, and told me we had to go. It took me a moment to realize what was happening, that my mother would almost certainly be home from work. She was: Anarcho_Journalist pulled up outside of our house just as my mother was turning her key in the front door. She watched me get out of the car then started waving and yelling, trying to get Anarcho_Journalist's attention. He drove off with haste. I regretted not anticipating this situation and having him drop me off a few blocks away. Showing up alone, after my mother, wouldn't have been as alarming and would have some precedent, as I have been known, from time to time, to walk to a nearby bookstore to browse. Alas, there's that thing people say about hindsight.

"Who was that?" my mother asked.

"Chris's dad," I said, grabbing the first name I could think of from my Science Olympiad team. Anarcho_Journalist looks like a college kid, looks young. I was hoping my mother didn't get a good look at him. Hell, I didn't even know if Chris had a dad, if my mother knew who Chris was, if she'd know if Chris had a dad—or maybe she even knew Chris's dad. None of these were likely, but I was nervous.

"That man couldn't have been older than twenty-two," she said. "He doesn't have a teenaged son."

"He's in his thirties," I said.

"You're lying," my mother said. "Who was that?"

"I told you."

This made my mother angry. She told me I had no right to be riding in cars with strange men, twice my age, that she needed to know who that was, why I was with him, and why I'd never mentioned him.

"Did he touch you?" my mother asked.

"Of course not," I said.

"Then who is he?"

She had already made up her mind that I was lying about Anarcho_Journalist being anyone's father. I quickly sorted through the various truths surrounding my circumstances, trying to discern which ones I could tell my mother and which

I needed to keep secret. I decided that she could know that I was involved with some illegal internet activities, but not that I became involved with those activities by looking for my father, or because my new mentors originally thought I was her. Also, I couldn't let her know that Anarcho_Journalist and self_replicator had been in our house, how long this had been happening, or anything else that could potentially result in a freak out—I didn't want her to stop speaking to me or set my computer on fire. She's never gone to quite these extremes, but her volatile nature and tenuous grasp on reality mean anything is possible when she is truly agitated. So I told some carefully selected half-truths.

"His name is Andy," I said—not his real name. Then: "He's a computer specialist."

"A computer specialist," my mother repeated.

I told her I'd met Andy at the bookstore—we'd both been looking at science books and he struck up a conversation with me about UFOs. He told me he believed that UFOs had visited Earth and that various governments around the world were working together to conceal the truth. I told her that Andy had been working on a way to access secret documents that contained confidential information about extraterrestrial life forms and that I was helping him.

"You don't know anything about computers," my mother said. "How can you help him?"

When I didn't answer immediately, she grabbed my arm and pulled me into the house. Her grip was firm, forceful in a way I hadn't felt since I was very young and I'd wonder too close to the street. She dragged me into the living room, pushed me onto the sofa. She lunged at one window first, then the other, closing the blinds then separating the slats with her fingers to peek through. I struggled to remember the last time I'd seen my mother this agitated. I was scared. I'd grown accustomed to seeing her on the couch watching television, sitting across from me at the kitchen table talking about books. But this reminded me of something else, from when I was younger and she was more paranoid, when her temper was more volatile. I was afraid and rightly so—my mother's speech and movements were jarring and abrupt. I needed it to stop.

So I told her most of the truth—sort of. I maintained my story about meeting Andy, and I told her that I liked him because he reminded me of the other Fox Mulder, that he told me he wanted to make the world a better place and so I volunteered to be a script kiddie, to run his code and exploit the weaknesses he'd found in various networks. I told her that I knew that even were I caught, I'd be protected by my age. My partial admission of the truth achieved its intended effect. Sort of.

My mother stopped shouting, stopped gesticulating.

She said, "So you're a hacker now."

I said, "Sort of."

"You know I spend every day of every week finding ways to protect my company's products from people like you."

I told her I only sort of knew that, which was true.

"This makes you my enemy," she said.

Then she sat beside me on the sofa. I didn't know what to say. I felt a gulf opening inside me, my mood's usual plateau collapsing inward like the scene in the first *X-Files* film when Mulder rescues Scully from the downed flying saucer, the ground buckling, crumbling as if the Earth was eating itself. I thought that maybe this was how religious parents must feel when a child claims to be an atheist or worse, agnostic. How Republican parents feel the first time their child votes

Democrat. How vegetarian parents feel the first time their kids eats a chicken nugget at a friend's house. But no—those parents don't call their children "enemies." I tried to remind myself that my mother wasn't well, never had been. I thought about the envelope taped to the bottom of my desk upstairs. For the first time since I received the PNR's, I thought about how badly I might actually need the man whose name they may or may not have contained.

All I could say was, "I'm not your enemy."

"But you are," she said. "By definition."

I tried to say something but all I could do was cry. I couldn't remember the last time I'd wept. In recent memory I'd felt sad, nostalgic, tired. I'd felt like the characters in *Dandelion Wine*, and I'd felt like Max Fenig in that episode of *The X-Files* when he has a seizure on the floor of his camper and Mulder finds him and moves him to his bed. I'd felt like a son whose mother wasn't quite always present, but I was too young to really know what that meant. And I'd felt like Fox Mulder in his barren apartment, spending restless days and nights in a space that never quite felt like home. But I hadn't wept in years, five years, maybe more, and then it was probably because I'd hurt myself, or was scared. I couldn't remember what made me cry the time before, but I do remember that my mother took care of me then—touched my face, put her arm around me, pulled me close. But this time, after she called me her enemy, I remember this: there, then—my mother sat on the opposite side of the sofa, watched me cry hard, harder, hardest until hot strings of snot dripped from my nose, until my face was wet and my eyes raw. I wept until I had to throw up so I ran to the toilet and threw up, then wept longer, harder. I returned to the couch to cry because I wanted her to see me crying. I'm not proud of how I behaved in that moment, but how else should a young man behave when labeled as an enemy by the only family he'd ever known.

Eventually, my mother went to the kitchen, came back with two of her migraine pills and a glass of water. She was humming that song about Martin Berry. She took her pills and turned on the television, didn't say anything else to me until I eventually stopped crying and made my way upstairs. I thought that maybe I could make this all go away if I stopped my work with @mbiguous, but I didn't want to give in, didn't want to reward my mother's cruelty. Before retiring to bed, I removed the envelope containing the PNR's from under my desk. I ran my finger along the top of the envelope and thought about its contents. As important as it seemed a moment before, I knew the time wasn't right to further pursue my father. I used a pencil to tear a hole in the fabric covering the bottom of my box springs, and taped the envelope inside. Maybe it was because I knew that if my mother found out, it would only deepen the new chasm between us. Or maybe it was because I didn't know what additional disappointment would do to me—at least this way I could believe I had one parent who didn't consider me an enemy.

11. JUMP THE SHARK

For the next two years, most of @mbiguous's existence, my mother and I kept to ourselves. She'd leave for work before I woke up for school, and I'd be in my room by the time she got home. Some nights we would eat together in silence. Some days, when I brushed my teeth, I'd find ten bucks in the bathroom and a note telling me to use the money for dinner. Even when we ate together, we hardly spoke. When she asked me about school, I'd tell her it was fine. When I'd ask her about work, she'd tell me it was stressful, emphasizing that word so I'd know that I was somehow tangentially responsible.

Other than those brief, vacant conversations, the most I heard my mother talk was when she was on the phone asking telemarketers not to call anymore. Sometimes I'd hear her singing to herself while cleaning or cooking, working crossword puzzles—songs by the seventies artists she liked from when she was younger, Carole King, Paul Simon, Jimmy Toop, Jackson Browne. She'd sing "I Feel the Earth Move," and "Kodachrome," the song about Martin Berry, whatever it was called, and "Late for the Sky," among others. That last song was one of my favorites when I was younger, when I was too young to understand the adult context and thought it was about alien abduction, about being late for one's slow ascent in a beam of light.

But I digress—in the previous chapter, I set out to describe @mbiguous's first action before sidetracking myself with familial drama. So, back to the point: once the first action had been decided on, and after my mother called me her enemy, I contacted each of @mbiguous's cells with the proposal, counted votes—which overwhelmingly approved the action—then distributed each cell's specific roles as assigned by Anarcho_Journalist and self_replicator. A few days after later, the action went off without a hitch. Some of the hacked home pages were in place for only a few minutes, some stayed up for hours. Thanks to our members' involvement in the resulting conversations, the action came to be known, even among a few mainstream media outlets, as "LobbyGate." A week after the hack, Anonymous claimed responsibility.

Though the fallout from this first action barely registered in the national news, it was enough to cause problems at home. At dinner a few nights after the action, my mother asked if I'd had anything to do with "LobbyGate." I told her I hadn't, but I was secretly thrilled to hear her use the term. Despite my denial, upon returning home from school the following day I found that my room had been searched and an attempt made to access my computer. My first instinct was to check the Passenger Name Records, which I found untouched, still safely taped inside my box springs. I was surprised by the sloppiness of my mother's work—based on her paranoia alone I knew that if she didn't want me to know she'd searched my room, I wouldn't know. She was sending me a message: "I'm watching you." Clearly, she hadn't found anything worthwhile, but I knew that I needed to be careful. The next day, I bought a latch and a padlock. After installing the latch, I stripped the screw heads to keep them from being easily removed with a screwdriver. My mother would have to destroy the door if she wanted to break into my room. I kept the key to the padlock in my shoe. When I was working in my room, I kept the lock with me so that I couldn't be locked in—perhaps this was paranoid, but I am my mother's son, after all. I doubt she would have locked me in, but in light of her recent instability I didn't want to risk it. A week later, worried that she could still enter my room unimpeded while I was working, I purchased and installed a door chain.

Once @mbiguous's successful first action was finished, momentum was on our side. Our second attack was a simple bit of civil disobedience. On the Monday after Thanksgiving, cells used a DDoS attack to shut down prominent retail websites as a symbolic attack on corporate greed. All cells but two agreed to participate, with those abstaining doing so on the grounds that their members were, by and large, pro-free market and didn't want to interfere with businesses doing what businesses do. To prepare for the action, members posted to message boards with articles depicting the working conditions in shipping facilities for online retailers as soul-crushing places in which employees are routinely disciplined or fired for failing to meet absurd quotas. With these ethical concerns quietly bubbling up into the internet's collective consciousness we shut down Amazon, Best Buy, JC Penney, Macy's, Kohl's, and Toys 'R' Us. Most of the closures lasted an hour or less, but retailers reported sales losses in the millions.

Once again, thanks to the sound planning and precautions put in place by my mentors and me, our organization emerged largely unscathed. One hacker was arrested after bragging in a chat stream of his involvement. That was fine—we didn't want to work with careless people and the sooner weak links were exposed, the better. Clearly, authorities realized that a single hacker couldn't have been responsible for the entire action, so we were marginally concerned that he might talk, but we were also confident that we would be protected by our organization's structure. Turns out, we had nothing to worry about. The arrested hacker, perhaps feeling remorseful for his indiscretion, didn't give authorities anything to go on. According to media coverage of his trial—there wasn't much, mind you, but some—the hacker, one Johnathan Goetz of Springfield, Missouri—claimed that he used a DDoS attack to shut down Amazon's website due to an article he'd read about the working conditions in their shipping and warehouse facilities.

After several smaller hacks, @mbiguous's sixth action was an attack on the websites of major American oil companies in response to government subsidies those companies receive, the tax loopholes of which they regularly take advantage, and the recent BP oil spill. In preparing for the action, cells prepared statistic sheets displaying companies' net profits, tax rates, and total subsidies. The cells voted unanimously to engage in the action—even the free-market enthusiasts, surprisingly—and we followed through with no complications or arrests. LulzSec, a hacker group loosely affiliated with Anonymous, claimed responsibility.

Shortly after that action, word of our existence slowly, quietly spread and our numbers swelled—we peaked just shy of a thousand members, divided among fifty cells. This was our moment. Because it was an election year, we capitalized on our success and initiated a series of small but highly visible political actions. Some highlights: we defaced the White House's website in protest of the Emergency Economic Stabilization Act and hacked Diebold's network, both to procure information that might pertain to possible instances of election fraud, and to protest the manipulability of their voting devices. After these swift, closely plotted actions, we collaborated with an international group of hackers to attack several Russian government websites to protest the halting of gas shipments to the Ukraine. This action was primarily symbolic, shutting down the government websites and replacing them with a plain, white page featuring the slogan—in Cyrillic and English— Гас Фрее Еуропе, or Gas Free Europe. With this action, word of @mbiguous's existence finally found its way into the mainstream, not because of anything *our* members said, but because we were collaborating with other groups. When one of those groups, Germans going by the name IKZ—short for Institut für Kybernetik und Zukunftsforschung—comprised of former members of the Chaos Computer Club, unilaterally released a list of organizations involved in the Russia hack, we were suddenly a known quantity.

In a way, though @mbiguous had only officially existed for just over two years, this was already the beginning of the end for us. Once the heat was on, cells and hackers started retiring. We pressed on a while longer—as I'm sure you know, as I've yet to discuss our most famous action—but we didn't like the attention and we knew our days were numbered. At first, Anarcho_Journalist, self_replicator, and I discussed ways we could increase security, then briefly discussed becoming a more public entity, like Anonymous. In the end, though, we determined that it was time to begin formulating an exit strategy and one last, big action—better to burnout than fade away and all that. For my part, I didn't want @mbiguous to end. I tried to convince my mentors that we could be more careful. To this self_replicator said, "It's just too risky, and, though I could tell Anarcho_Journalist was reluctant, he said, "None of us, not even you, can afford to get caught at this point." I asked him if we'd still hang out after @mbiguous was finished.

Anarcho_Journalist said, "We're not done quite yet."

I said, "But when we are?"

He said, "We'll see." Then he added, "But we've got plenty left to do."

After three years regularly spending time with self_replicator and Anarcho_Journalist, I struggled to imagine what my life might look like without them, without @mbiguous. Though I'd kept up on school work and stayed active in Science Olympiad, those parts of my life had become secondary. Add to that an absence of friends my own age and my profoundly damaged relationship with my mother and it was beginning to look like I was about to be very lonely. During this time, I spent a lot of time thinking about the PNR's taped inside my box springs. Before I worked up the nerve to look at them, though, things with my mother started improving in subtle, unremarkable ways. These improvements were not the result of conscious attempts to repair or improve our relationship, rather it simply seemed that our anger was fading, as if we just weren't that mad at each other anymore. I first noticed it when we shared a laugh over a crossword clue at dinner.

"Can you believe they misspelled Gilgamesh?" my mother asked, sliding the paper across the table to me.

Eventually, we started watching *X-Files* reruns together again, and finally talked about the series finale of *Battlestar Galactica*, which had originally aired not long after my mother decided I was her enemy, and which, as it happened, she generally enjoyed. I enjoyed it to a point, but ultimately found it unsatisfying, thanks in no small part to its emphasis on ill-defined spirituality and mysticism.

"It was so sad when Rosalind died," my mother said.

"It was so sad when they cut to modern day New York," I said.

"Why was that sad?" she asked.

"Because it didn't make any sense," I said. "Why was Rosalind's death sad?"

My mother laughed and threw the latest issue of *Wired* at me. *Wired* is a heavy magazine with sharp corners, but I didn't mind because I knew her intent wasn't malicious and I was happy to hear her laugh. I was unable to enjoy the moment more fully, though, because as I handed the magazine back across the table, I noticed a cover blurb advertising an article about @mbiguous. I briefly froze. I couldn't believe I wasn't aware that *Wired* was covering us—though "covering" is a bit of a stretch, as the article in question turned out to be a single page of speculation and unsubstantiated rumors that had arisen in the weeks after the Germans announced our existence to the world. I didn't know if my mother had noticed my freezing, and if she had, if it would be an incitement to something ugly. I was fortunate. Either she hadn't noticed, or wasn't able or willing to process what it meant.

A few days later, I received a message from one of @mbiguous's first cells, call sign Black Triangle. The cell was comprised of folks I'd met early on, before @mbiguous existed, when I was still looking for help finding PNR's. Their home base, as it were, was a UFO message board within a larger conspiracy theory driven community known as *Spooked*. The majority of their hacktivism prior to their involvement with @mbiguous had been focused on unearthing evidence that UFOs existed. When they signed on to @mbiguous, they were happy to help us out, but asked that we eventually formulate an action to help their cause. Even though we were preparing to wind down, when Black Triangle proposed a hack, we agreed out of a sense of duty. Their plan involved exploiting weaknesses at various government installations in an attempt to access digitized files that would, in theory, prove the existence of UFOs. They recommended we target a series of military installations that may or may not exist, and all of which, whether real or not, had been rumored, at one time or another, to have housed UFOs or Extraterrestrial Biological Entities. The list included Fort Meade in Maryland, rumored to have expansive underground facilities; Edward's Air Force Base in Southern Nevada, home to the infamous Area 51; various non-essential offices affiliated with the CIA; the mythical Dulce Base, allegedly hidden beneath the Archuleta Mesa on the border of Colorado and New Mexico; several similar underground bases reportedly scattered throughout New Mexico, Arizona, Texas, and Oklahoma; and Wright Patterson Air Force Base, which was said to have been a participant in the Project Blue Book UFO study, and is home to Hangar 18. While the list of proposed targets was troubling in itself—for the risk, the difficulty, and the inclusion of facilities that were only *rumored* to exist—I was most unsettled that two of the sites we'd be hacking used software designed by Know-ware.

I told Black Triangle that the action might have trouble passing as it involved breaking into computer systems that

were only rumored to exist. The member I was communicating with, screen name LittleGreyMan, assured me that all
proposed facilities existed. The next day, when I passed the
information along to Anarcho_Journalist, he responded by
typing a short, derisive, "Ha!" but I imagined him filling his
dorm room with a belly laugh, then calling self_replicator
in to show him what was so funny. After a few moments,
Anarcho_Journalist told me that he and self_replicator would
cook up an alternative version of the action with more realistic
targets.

I typed, "Can we avoid the Know-ware exploits?"

"We'll look at it," he said, "But probably not."

"I don't know if I can be involved with this," I typed.

"We'll understand if you can't," he typed. "But it'll be
easier with you."

I typed, "Let me think about it."

"We'll be in touch," he typed. Then: "Working on the
big one right now."

And there it was—after years of engaging in hacktivism
and being told by my mother that I was her enemy, just as our
relationship was improving I was about to actually become
her actual enemy. In the end, we weren't able to find a way to
avoid the Know-ware exploits and, of course, I participated
in the action anyway. How could I give up on the group so
close to the end? If @mbiguous was going to soon be over, I
wanted to say I was a part of it all the way.

12. SEIN UND ZEIT

In the weeks leading up to the UFO hack, I was nervous. I avoided my mother because I knew I wouldn't be able to look her in the eye. To pass the time, I finally read *Dandelion Wine*, which I hadn't thought of in at least a year, conveyed messages back and forth between our group's cells, and re-watched the first three seasons of *The X-Files*. I also finally looked through the Passenger Name Records.

Why did I finally look? Why else? I was faced with a new question: during my *X-Files* rewatch, I identified a continuity gaffe that, once again, shook my understanding of my origins to its core. The continuity gaffe wasn't in the show, but in my mother's telling of her encounter with my father. The gaffe: I was conceived in January, 1995 after my mother met a man who shared a name with the fictional Fox Mulder's father; the first time Fox Mulder's father, Bill Mulder, appeared on *The X-Files* was in an episode called "Colony," which didn't air until February, 1995, a month after I was conceived. This complicated my mother's story. Now, I know what you're thinking—though he didn't appear until "Colony," Bill Mulder was mentioned by name in "Roland," which aired in May, 1994, almost eight months *before* I was conceived. But here's the thing—according to my mother, the real life Bill Mulder even *looked* a little like the fictional Bill Mulder—how could she know this if the fictional Bill Mulder, as portrayed by Peter Donat, hadn't yet appeared on screen. While it was certainly possible that I was reading too much into the gaffe, I knew that this new uncertainty was going to eat at me, and as @mbiguous's days were numbered, meaning I would soon have a massive hole in my life, I felt compelled to finally try to find the truth about my father.

Each day, while my mother was at work and after she went to bed, I dug through the PNR's pages in search of the name William Mulder. As the font was small and there were many pages, my first time through took nine days. I chewed sunflower seeds like the other Fox Mulder and spit their shells into a paper bag. On the last night, when I reached the last name on the last page, I'm not sure if I was surprised or not to learn that there was no Bill Mulder listed. Of course, his absence didn't prove much—he could have driven to save his company money, could have been traveling under an assumed name, could have been lying about his name just to hook up with my mom. The absence of a Bill or William Mulder on these lists didn't mean my mother was lying, it just meant that this particular thread of inquiry was a dead end. I decided not to dispose of the records so that I could peruse them one more time, just to be safe.

On the night after I finished that first search through the PNR's, I received a message from self_replicator telling me that they were adding a second phase to the UFO hack. It would piggyback off the UFO action, and would be the final, big action on which @mbiguous would go out. I wasn't expecting @mbiguous to end quite so soon, but, in the words of self_replicator, the decision was made as "a matter of practical convenience"—as in, this second action would be easier to pull off directly on the heels of the UFO action and, if successful, would protect cells and members from being tracked and caught. This new second phase: we were going to shut down the internet. It was a dangerous move, bold and loaded with both symbolic meaning and political significance, would be a perfect closing gambit for us. I'm sure you remember, dear readers, the day we shut down the internet? Of course you do. It was the hacktivist act to end all hacktivist acts—we would not be content to merely singe our wings flying too close to the sun, we were going to fly into the goddamn thing, collapse its core and call it a supernova. This second phase was something of a tough sell to many of our members, but the prospect of making history eventually convinced enough of them to vote yes. The action passed.

The plan's logistics were complex but realistic, if far from certain in their outcome. Here's how it would work: Imagine the internet as a massive series of connection nodes, a star field with overlaid constellations. Now imagine the stars in those constellations burning out, one by one—they flash and are gone. As enough stars burn out, the constellation stops being a constellation, the remaining stars are no longer part of each other's picture, are each individually adrift in space. The nodes that make up the internet go offline like that all the time, burn out hourly. Unlike the constellations, though, the internet doesn't stop being the internet—it uses other nodes to work around the ones that go offline. The internet can do this because, unlike stars in constellations, it is comprised of autonomous systems that talk to each other via routers.

When the internet has to detour around an offline node, the routers talk to each other through border protocols: the routers nearest the offline node tell those a little farther away that the node is offline, which then tell the routers a little farther away, which tell the routers a little farther away, etc..., etc..., until all the routers know the node is offline and a new path has been established.

To make this work, we would need to use a botnet comprised of at least a quarter million machines, with which we'd map the paths between the compromised computers to identify a commonly used internet node—think of the node as a city in which many interstates and highways converge, New York City, or Chicago, or Kansas City—then, using something known as a ZMW attack, named after its creator Zhang, Mao, and Wang, we would overload that node, causing nearby routers to update their gateway protocols and redirect traffic to different routers. When the initially disrupted routers would come back online, they'd send out their own border gateway protocol updates, causing traffic to begin flowing back through them, which would, once again, lead to their crashing. This continuous cycle would be reenacted in a recursive, inward loop that would eventually send out more border gateway protocols than the internet would know how to deal with—if I might return to the star metaphor, imagine all the stars in a constellation going supernova, flashing and burning, their brightness bleeding over each other until all the sky's stars become a single, incomprehensible blur of light. I'm not sure that metaphor totally checks out, but it's close enough. Our plan was derived from a paper written at the University of Minnesota by a Ph.D. student named Max Schuchard, who speculated that, were the plan properly executed, the internet could be out of commission for days.

In the days leading up to the action, I directed cells as they assembled an appropriate sized botnet, double, then triple checked attack plans for the UFO action, and felt increasingly anxious. This work didn't usually phase me, but this time, my stomach was a raw mess and I couldn't sleep because I was worried about the impact @mbiguous's actions would have on my mother, her work, and our relationship. If my mother realized I had been involved with hacking her company's products, she was liable to throw me out of the house. I desperately revisited the PNR's, hoping I'd overlooked a William or Bill Mulder on my first check, but no—the documents were as useless as before. I stuffed them back up under my box springs and did my best to forget about them. As the action grew closer, my worry transformed to a sort of protectiveness—I started to think that I needed to protect her work from my peers and myself. She would be my mother forever, after all; @mbiguous would exist only for another day.

That's why, the morning of the day of the action, I made a decision: I used IP masking software and server proxies to hack my mother's email account and sent an anonymous message from her email address, to her email address warning of the attack.

That day at school was long. I chewed my fingernails to pink stubs, took two hall passes to throw up, and didn't raise my hand once to answer questions. Even having warned my mother about the attack, I felt as if I was on the verge of some irrevocable action, some threshold that, once crossed, could not be uncrossed. I needed my mother and she needed me, but the UFO action could not be stopped. Even if I refused to signal the action's start, Anarcho_Journalist and self_replicator would. Of course, by this point, it was too late for such thoughts, as, when I returned home from school that afternoon, I found my bedroom door lying splintered on the floor. The rest of my room had been savagely searched, papers scattered across the floor, drawers emptied, furniture overturned, and there, in middle of the room, sitting cross-legged on my box springs, was my mother, rifling through a thick stack of papers. I don't need to tell you what those papers were. I immediately wanted to apologize, to try to explain, but what could I say? I imagined how I looked to my mother at that moment—I wasn't just an enemy, but a son for whom she wasn't enough. I stood silent and waited for her to speak.

"You're a member of @mbiguous," she said, not looking up from the stack of papers in her hand.

"I don't know what you mean," I said.

"You didn't do a good job covering your tracks. I traced the email to you in five minutes."

There was no sense denying it. I wished I'd been more careful. I didn't realize how good my mother was at her work. Or how bad I was at mine.

"I'm not really a hacker," I told her.

She asked me what I was doing with a group of hackers then, and since there was no point lying anymore, I told her everything. About my role within the group as coordinator and historian. About all of our actions. About self_replicator and Anarcho_Journalist. Then I paused, gathered my courage, pointed to the papers in her hands, and explained how they came into my possession, how seeking *that* information was what brought me into contact with the co-founders of @mbiguous.

"You really didn't know until now?" I asked. "That I was involved with @mbiguous?"

"I knew you were involved with *something*," she said. "I could have found out more but I chose not to. I assumed you were some script kiddie running with other script kiddies, causing a little mischief." She went on to explain that her suspicions grew the night she threw that copy of *Wired* at me, but that she had convinced herself that the look of panic on my face hadn't been real.

"Sometimes it's better not to know," she said.

She flipped through the Passenger Name Records.

"Those lists weren't even worth it," I said.

"What did you think?" she asked. "That you'd find your father?"

"He's not in there," I said. "Either he lied to you, you lied to me, or he didn't fly into Dayton."

"I didn't want you to try to find him," she said. "I don't even know if you could find him if you tried."

She picked up a pen from my floor, circled a name, dropped the documents on the box springs.

"That's not his real name, either," she said. "But it's him."

I picked up the papers, flipped through until I found the crudely circled name: Martin Berry.

"Martin Berry," I said. "Like the song?" I couldn't believe I hadn't even noticed the name as I scanned the page. Granted, I was looking mostly at last names, and why would the last name Berry jump off the page at me if I was looking for Mulder?

"I told you it's not his real name," she said.

"What was his real name?" I asked.

"I've told you enough," she said, cryptic as Deep Throat or Mr. X or any of the other Fox Mulder's secret sources. Then: "Anyway—you wouldn't believe me."

I asked her why and she told me it was a long, involved story, that the only reason she told me anything at all on my thirteenth birthday was because she knew that it was unreasonable for me to continue believing that I didn't have a biological father, and so she decided to tell me a truth surrounded by lies in order to stave off any questions that might have been swirling around in my head.

"I don't even know if your father is still alive," my mother said. Then asked, "Why did you go to all this trouble? Why didn't you just ask?"

I told her I knew she wouldn't tell me, and that I thought that even the act of asking would upset her. This explanation upset her even more. She buried her face in her hands. She wasn't crying, but when she lifted her head and looked at me, her eyes were brittle and glossy, her cheeks red. What she said next surprised me, shook me, even.

"I'm sorry," she said. "You didn't have to warn me about tonight."

"Can you stop it?" I asked.

"Why bother? They aren't after anything real or harmful. They'll find a handful of vague, scanned documents with blacked out phrases, and those documents will make them feel validated for a while." Ultimately, she ended up being right about all of that. She was also right when she added, "Your friends won't change anything, and nobody will be hurt—it'll be fine."

Surprised by her response, I asked her if she no longer believed that the government was covering up UFO activity. She told me she didn't know anymore, but that if the information @mbiguous was looking for existed, it didn't exist in any of the places they could access via Know-ware exploits. And then she started crying and hugged me. I hugged her back. She buried her face in my neck and I felt her tears on my skin.

We sat like that for several minutes and then she said, "You're all grown up." She said, "You're seventeen." Then: "You've been honest with me. You're a young man and you've been honest with me." Then: "Do you want to know your father's real name? A truth in exchange for the truths you've given me?"

I wasn't sure anymore. In that moment, the power of the truth my mother was offering felt insignificant. Maybe I needed to hear it anyway, though? The other Fox Mulder believed that the truth was out there, but the thing that defined him, that compelled him, was his *search* for that truth, not the truth itself. At times, that other Fox Mulder didn't even know what truth he was seeking—he was a destructive force, an unchecked mess of misguided emotions and dangerous desires. The truth never arrived to save that other Fox Mulder, nor set him free, and so it caused him only misery. What would Fox Mulder's life have looked like if he knew that truth? What would my life look like? Here was my opportunity to learn the unknowable truth, and even though the content of that truth seemed unimportant now, maybe, I thought, I could save myself from the impossible search by hearing what my mother had to tell me. I would no longer need to define myself by not knowing who my father was, the way the other Fox Mulder defined himself by his need to understand what happened to his sister.

So, I told my mother, yes, I wanted to know my father's name.

And she said, "Jim Toop,"—just like that.

I knew immediately that my thinking had backfired—that my quest for truth wasn't ending, but beginning.

I looked back at the Passenger Name Records, at the circled name, and struggled to believe what my mother had just told me. For starters, Martin Berry is a common name—it could have been a coincidence. There was also the problem of Jim Toop's disappearance, not quite two decades before I was conceived. I didn't know how to even begin making sense of this new piece of information, didn't know how to respond, at all, torn between anger at the possibility that my mother had offered me the truth only to provide another lie, and shame that she could be so easily lied to and manipulated by a stranger.

I said, "You're lying."

She said, "I'm not."

I tried to rationalize—my mother's paranoia and need to believe in conspiracy theories and fantastical realities could have easily allowed a strange man to convince her that he was a long disappeared musician. Maybe he told her he'd been abducted by UFOs but had since been returned. Or maybe he told her he went into hiding because the government was after him—either of those stories would have appealed to my mother. Maybe he looked a bit like Jim Toop, but was a little heavier, his face more deeply lined, his hair a little grayer to show that more than a decade had passed. I imagined him playing coy, offering a "fake" name at first, but when my mother attempted to drag some truth out of him, the truth that he was really Jim Toop, the man, whose real name was probably Martin Berry, decided to "let her in on his little secret." Maybe he fed her a line or two about what it was like being the only human among aliens, or about the loneliness of hiding in the desert for so long, and the next thing either of them knew, they were having mediocre sexual intercourse in my mother's hotel room.

"Jim Toop disappeared decades ago," I said, as it slowly dawned on me that the reason my mother had lied about my father's name being Bill Mulder was because that story, somehow, was less crazy than what she was telling me now. I told her that, were Jim Toop alive at the time of my conception, his presence would have surely been detected by countless conspiracy theorists. I told her the real Jim Toop was almost certainly dead, that there was no other plausible explanation for his disappearance. As I explained all of this, I watched my mother shrink away from me, rest her head in her hands. I was hurting her and, as ashamed as I am to say it, I think that's what I wanted in that moment.

But then something strange happened—when I stopped talking, my mother said, "It was him—I know it was," and when she lifted her head to speak, she was smiling. Then she abruptly left the room. It was a strange and sudden shift. There was even a hint of warmth in her voice. She seemed so certain, so secure in this assertion—could it be that, despite all logic, Jim Toop was my father? When my mother returned, she handed me a manila envelope. It was heavier than I expected. Inside was a reel-to-reel tape, unlabeled, but with a small piece of paper that identified, in pencil, the tape's contents:

"The Taxidermist's Catalog"

1. Frozen
2. Desert Birds
3. Sideways Glances
4. Forget Me Not
5. Paintings of Old Flowers
6. The Old Game Show
7. (Hideaway) Bed
8. Mark's Novel
9. Thirty Seconds

10. Weather

11. Nothing Truer

12. Cormac Bleeding

I knew the name *The Taxidermist's Catalog*—anyone with an interest in UFO lore and conspiracy theories knew it. It was said to be the name of the album Jim Toop had been working on when he, along with his tapes, disappeared. I asked my mother why she had the tape. She told me that Jim Toop gave it to her after the two had sexual intercourse. She explained that, in the aftermath of their encounter, while Jim Toop spooned her, she asked him about his disappearance and then about the album he'd been working on. In response to the first question, he got strangely quiet for a moment, but after the second, he grew suddenly animated and excited as he told her about some of the album's songs and how proud he was of the finished product. He told her he was glad that it would never be picked apart by critics and conspiracy theorists, but that he wished he could share it with fans. And that's when he asked if she'd like to have it. My mother was expecting a dubbed cassette, or maybe a CD-R, but when Jim Toop returned from his rental car, he had the reel-to-reel tape.

"That very tape you're holding," she said.

"Why'd he give it to *you*?"

She didn't know. He'd said it was something he wanted her to have, that he wanted for at least one fan to hear his unreleased album. When she asked why her, why not some other fan or one night stand, he said, only, "It's never come up before." The only thing Toop, or whoever he was, asked of my mother was that she not share the tape. I asked her if she'd listened to it. She hadn't. When I asked he why, she said she preferred imagining the songs, preferred not knowing if the tape was real.

She said, "If that tape is blank, then I'll know that wasn't really Jim Toop." Then: "Sometimes not knowing is better."

Logically, my mother's story made the tape seem real. I imagined the effort someone would have to go to produce a fake tape to give to someone with whom he had already had the sexual intercourse he was after. It somehow made more sense for my mother to have actually had sexual intercourse with Jim Toop than for a strange man to fabricate a fake tape. And there were other, darker possibilities: what if the tape was real and the stranger had stolen it from Toop; or worse, what if the man my mother had sexual intercourse with had kidnapped or murdered the real Jim Toop and was passing off evidence to my mother. And then there was the question of why even Jim Toop would have the tape with him if he was traveling. I suppose it might be something he carried with him everywhere to avoid having it stolen, but even that felt like a stretch. But sometimes truth makes less sense than the stories we make up to try to rationalize it. What else could I think? Crazy as it seemed, the existence of the tape made me believe that Jim Toop was probably my father. At the same time, the tape also seemed like it was probably my last, best chance to learn more about, and perhaps even meet, my father.

I said, "I want to know. Really know."

When I stopped talking, my mother told me to take the tape. "Listen to it if you must," she said.

I asked her if she wanted to know what I learned.

She didn't answer.

I could tell that this was one of the truths that my mother believed with all of her being, just as much as she believed in

UFOs and other conspiracy theories, as much as she believed that David Duchovny was the sexiest man alive.

I said, "I won't tell."

She said, "You don't need to. I was there." She told me how much the man looked and sounded like Jim Toop. She said, "I saw him, talked to him, listened to him sing—I fucked him for Christ's sake."

We both froze a little then. We still weren't particularly comfortable talking about sex. I changed the subject.

"So you're really not going to warn Know-ware?" I asked.

"Why bother?" she said. "When it happens, I'll get a call and have to be on the phone talking to IT guys for a while. If they detect the incursion early enough, I'll help them close the gaps and cut their losses. If they don't notice until later, I'll help them clean up and begin working on ways to fix the exploits."

She asked me if I knew how they were getting in.

I told her I didn't, that such details were beyond me, but that I could find out. She told me not to worry about it. I contemplated telling her about the second part of the action, but decided against it. I didn't want to implicate her or agitate her to the point that she might reverse her decision and start making phone calls.

That night, after our conversation, my mother took me to dinner at the Italian restaurant where all of this started, where she told me that I had a father, and that his name was W̲I̲L̲I̲A̲M̲ ̲M̲U̲L̲D̲E̲R̲. We didn't play hang man over dinner, didn't talk much either—we'd said enough to each other for the day—but things between us were starting to feel normal again, good even. As we shared a cannoli for dessert, she looked up at me and, with a mouth full of flaky dough and sweet ricotta, said:

"I'm sharing a cannoli with my enemy, my real enemy whose band of computer hackers is actually attacking a thing that I made." And then she laughed. And then I laughed.

And then I told her that, after the action that night, @mbiguous was going to be finished, that we were starting to lose members and were uncomfortable with our heightened visibility. She seemed relieved, said something about being glad she wouldn't have to worry about the Feds showing up at our door in the middle of the night.

We returned home approximately thirty minutes before I was set to initiate the action. I had a message from self_replicator in my Google chat box that read, simply, "*** 87%." That meant that the botnet was eighty-seven percent mapped. I told my mother to have her phone ready, started setting up my second hard drive, and pulled up the list of cell contact information. At 7:53 pm I sent the message to initiate the final phase of @mbiguous's relatively brief, but meaningful career. At 8:42, after the first cells started checking in and sending files, I heard, from the next room, the opening theme song from *The X-Files*, my mother's ringtone. The cell who had been assigned to Wright Patterson Air Force Base's systems checked in a moment later. As their files transferred onto my computer, I could hear my mother talking and typing on her laptop, walking a network guy through some process or another and trying to identify what information had been accessed. While I waited for @mbiguous's final action to begin, I finished backing up to disk all of the data stored on my second hard drive, then removed its casing to expose its whirring, spinning guts. I marveled at the elegant simplicity of its design, that something so small, so clean, so fragile, could do so much damage. Fifteen minutes later, the last of the UFO cells checked in. When I notified self_replicator, he told me that the botnet for phase two had finished mapping—we were ready. I notified the participating cells, then ran two different programs to clean the second hard drive by writing nonsense over its data. The process was long and slow, and I ran each program twice. An hour into the cleaning, I heard my mother cursing from the next room. A few moments later, she knocked on my door. I invited her in and she entered, her phone pressed between her shoulder and ear. She asked if my internet was working. I played dumb, told her it just went out.

"What the shit?" she said.

I asked her if she tried calling the cable company, that maybe there was an outage in the area, or maybe they just needed to do that thing where they ping the modem.

"This guy's internet is out, too" my mother said.

I said, "What guy's?"

"The network guy in Ohio," she said. I felt thrilled and terrified, a little queasy from the rush of feeling both in unison—our final action was working, or had worked.

"Maybe it's a coincidence," I said, trying not to betray my emotions.

My mother told the network guy she'd call him back, then called the cable company. She was on hold for over an hour before a representative told her they were experiencing outages "across the region." When my mother asked if I knew anything about this, I told her I didn't. Then I told her I sort of did. Then I told her that yeah, we did, but that I didn't really think it would work, which was a lie.

She said, "You did this?"

I nodded.

She said, "Shit," and laughed. Then: "I'm impressed."

I said, "I'm sorry."

She said, "Can this be traced back to you?"

I told her no. I was just a messenger.

She said, "Good." She was smiling. I thought that maybe, weirdly, she was proud of me.

We stayed up the rest of the night watching CNN report on the internet's collapse. During a commercial break, I retrieved my second hard drive and took it to the front porch. I invited my mother to join me. Outside, I jammed my heel into the hardware until the casing cracked. She told me to make sure to get the insides good. I invited her to take a stomp.

"After you," she said.

I stomped once, scattering bits of metal and plastic across the concrete, then twice, and the hard drive slid out from under my foot and I almost fell. My mother laughed, then took two stomps of her own. I stomped again, then she, and all that remained were strewn pieces, which we continued to stomp, together, in a magnificent dance. We stomped and hopped until my mother lifted her head and howled. Then we laughed together. I looked around at the bits of broken hard drive covering the porch. I swept them up and dumped them into the trash can, dragged it down to the curb. When I finished, my mother was back in front of the television, humming the Martin Berry song to herself while a pundit on CNN speculated that this was "the end of the internet as we know it," that the World Wide Web couldn't possibly be reconstructed, that we had been jolted, brutally and permanently, out of the information age. He was overreacting, of course, was drumming up ratings and panic. Anyone who knew anything about the internet knew it would be back, and it would be stronger, less susceptible to attacks, would go on forever, or until we were all gone, or we ran out of energy—whichever came first.

13. THE TRUTH

The internet outage lasted for just over forty hours before enough nodes were back up and running for general traffic to resume. Everything was back at capacity within a week. As one might expect, a number of hacktivist groups claimed responsibility, Anonymous being the only one that anyone took seriously. I was worried, at first, that by not claiming responsibility we might appear suspect, but all of the investigations seemed to focus on Anonymous. No one was ever charged. After the news died down, I made business cards. Odd, I know, that I should make business cards for a defunct organization, but I found a good deal, and I thought they'd be fun to have. And anyway, I still had work to do. I continued my friendship with Anarcho_Journalist, though self_replicator finished his bachelor's degree not long after our last action and moved to London where he worked as a network administrator and designer for a company called Unit 9. We talked sometimes on Gchat for the first few months after he left, but soon drifted apart. He'd made his point and was ready to move on.

One cool, autumn afternoon, not long after I started writing the earliest chapters of this manuscript, Anarcho_Journalist came to my house and we sat on the porch talking before my mother returned home from work. It was one of the first conversations we'd shared that didn't revolve around computer networks and political action. We talked about our favorite episodes of *The X-Files*, argued our favorite *Star Trek* series—mine was *The Next Generation*, his was, bafflingly, *Deep Space Nine*—and enjoyed each other's company.

After an hour of conversation, he said, "Can I ask you something?"

I told him he could. He asked about the Passenger Name Records.

"Why did you want them?" he asked.

"It was nothing," I said.

He persisted and I tried to evade. There was so much unknowing and raw frustration and weirdness attached to those lists that I didn't really want to discuss them, but after Anarcho_Journalist reminded me that @mbiguous might never have existed without them, I decided to share. It wasn't exactly a truth he was after, and it wasn't exactly a truth I was going to give him because, frankly, I didn't have a truth to give him, just a web of questions and suggestions. I told him about my childhood, how I believed I was some sort of alien or miracle baby, and my mother telling me about Bill Mulder, and how I started to piece together my mother's business trip. While I explained, Anarcho_Journalist pulled a cigarette out of his shirt pocket and lit up. It was the first time I'd seen him smoke, which made sense as it was really the first time we'd spent time together not in my house or his dorm room. When I finished, Anarcho_Journalist asked if I'd found my father. I told him I hadn't.

"Was his name in the records?" he asked.

I told him it wasn't, exactly. Then, against my better judgment, I told him about the more recent developments, which weren't *that* recent anymore, as several months had passed. Looking back, I'm surprised that I hadn't yet acted on any of my plans to seek out my father. Once I had possession of the tape, I, like my mother, was afraid to dig deeper. That was about to change, though, thanks to Anarcho_Journalist, who listened intently as I told him that my mother believed, deep in her being, that the man she'd slept with was actually Jim Toop.

When I was done, Anarcho_Journalist took a drag from his cigarette and asked, "Do you believe her?"

"Would you?" I was afraid to tip my hand here. Though I *did* believe my mother, I was nervous about expressing that belief in front of my smarter, older friend.

"Not as a matter of fact, no," he said. "But maybe as a matter of it being a good thing to believe."

"If only we were so lucky to choose our pasts," I said.

"You can choose your past here," Anarcho_Journalist said. "Do I objectively believe you're the son of a folk musician who disappeared almost two decades before you were born? Of course not, but your mother believes that, and you love and respect her, no?"

"No," I said. Then, "I mean yes. Most of the time."

"You either do or you don't," he said.

I'd never really thought about those words with regards to my mother. And I had also never told my mentors about the strife with my mother during most of @mbiguous's existence. He couldn't possibly understand, so I agreed with him.

I said, "You're right. I do."

"Well then, since there's no evidence to confirm or deny that you are Jim Toop's long lost son, believe it, for your mother and for yourself," Anarcho_Journalist said.

"And what if there is evidence?" I asked, immediately regretting the question.

"Do tell," Anarcho_Journalist said. The shift in his demeanor was sudden, from relaxed and conversational to alert.

I told him I'd be right back, left him hanging for a moment while I went inside and, again, against my better judgment, retrieved the reel-to-reel tape from my room. I'd hidden the tape inside my box springs, taped to the same spot where the Passenger Name Records had been. I had no one from whom to hide the tape except for myself. I could have easily dug up the twenty or thirty bucks necessary to hire a transfer service, but I didn't. Once I'd proved the tape was real, I'd have to prove that the man who gave it to my mother was really Jim Toop. True, I wanted to prove my mother's story true, but I didn't know if I was ready to find this truth, and I'd convinced myself that the only way to avoid such a search was to put off the question entirely. And so, until this moment, I'd decided to keep the tape secret, hidden from myself to keep me and everyone around me out of harm's way, to let it be my own Ark of the Covenant, sealed away in the warehouse of my box springs, safe where it could neither melt faces nor explode heads.

I returned to the porch and handed the envelope to Anarcho_Journalist, intent to let him discover its contents on his own. When he found the slip of paper detailing the tape's contents he looked up at me, his eyes wide.

He said, "Holy shit." Then: "Is this what is on the tape?"

I told him I didn't know.

"What if it's fake?" I said.

"What if it's real?" he said.

"That's not much better," I told him.

He said, "What's the worst that could happen? If the tape is real, maybe your dad was Jim Toop, but folks will have new music that they never thought they'd have. If it isn't real, all it means is your dad was a lying piece of shit, but a lot of peoples' dads are lying pieces of shit—you'll be like the rest of us."

I asked him what happened to believing my mother's story out of love and respect, out of having a good story in which to believe.

He said, "You have proof of *something*, at least. How can you not even listen?"

He was right. I asked him if he had any ideas on how to proceed. He told me he did. Told me that he knew someone who could help.

"He's a lying piece of shit," Anarcho_Journalist said, "but he'll know how to get to the bottom of all this."

The next day Anarcho_Journalist and I met with the lying piece of shit in question. Anarcho_Journalist knew him very well, but I won't explain how for the sake of maintaining my friend's anonymity. We accompanied the lying piece of shit to his house where he had a reel-to-reel, and we listened to the tape's first song. It's called "Frozen," and it begins with a soft acoustic guitar and lyrics about Gorgons and a hero. After the song, the lying piece of shit seemed satisfied, shut off the tape and said,

"Holy shit."

I asked if we could hear more.

"In time," the lying piece of shit said. "In time."

I said, "I'd really like to hear the full tape."

"You will, son," the lying piece of shit said. "You will.

I said, "Why not now?"

And the lying piece of shit laughed and said, "Because I've got a lot of work to do."

I asked if I could have a copy of the tape, and was told no. When we hammered out a contract for how the tape would be dealt with, it included a clause that the tape not be reproduced in any way, shape, or form prior to the conclusion of the investigation. I'm proud to say I violated that clause. As for the rest of the deal we struck with the lying piece shit? All you need to know is that my mother and I were promised a healthy cut of album sales, and the lying piece of shit promised that the investigation of the tape would include research into Jim Toop's disappearance and possible present whereabouts. I was going to get answers. Maybe.

To achieve these goals, the lying piece of shit would employ a third party, an expert in Jim Toop's music and history, to run the investigation. It was a fair deal, all things considered, but I was angry that I didn't get to hear the tape. Once I got a taste, I wanted to hear the whole thing. I didn't want to wait. I wanted to hear the voice that I believed belonged to my father, singing songs that nobody had ever heard before. And just to be clear, as the investigation has played out—and it's still going—I came to believe even more that Jim Toop really is my father, or was, or is. I won't get into the details of the investigation here—I've already gone on long enough—but early in the third party investigator's inquiry, I ingratiated myself to him so I could keep tabs on him and gently shape his inquiries, even feeding him false information about IP addresses to help guide his search. Also, thanks to the investigator, I was able to listen to the tape. When I finally heard *The Taxidermist's Catalog* in its entirety, spooling out of the investigator's home stereo late one night, I wept. Though it was night time when we listened, the room was filled with the impossible golden glow of nostalgia—not literally, but in the songs' nuanced turns and in the warmth of Toop's voice. The songs evoked in me an urgent need to commune with a past I never knew was mine. In that moment I realized just how deeply and desperately I wanted to meet my father. I'm still not sure why, exactly—maybe I just wanted to see him, wanted to know where I came from, to better understand myself, but I realized that I didn't just *want* Jim Toop to be alive, I *needed* him to be alive—not because I needed him in my life, but just because, because, because. I don't know. Of course, I didn't tell my mother that any of this was happening, and won't until I have answers.

Now, as my story draws to a close, allow me to thank you for indulging me. I know you've been reading to learn about @mbiguous, its formation and its many actions, and I understand that it might be strange that the story of that hacktivist collective both began and ended with a boy's search for his father. I know this is not what you were expecting to read, but it could not be avoided. I don't know when you might be reading this, or if anyone will ever read it, period, but I hope, once the dust has settled and statutes of limitations have passed, that this manuscript will find an audience. At that time, it is my sincere hope that history will look back on @mbiguous fondly, as freedom fighters trying to save the world from oppression and evil. As for my own story, I'll borrow some words from that other Fox Mulder's final speech, from the final episode of *The X-Files*: "I've learned to pretend . . . that my victories mattered, only to realize that no one was keeping score . . . the truth wants to be known.

You will know it, it will come to you as it's come to me. Faster than the speed of light." Of course, the truth hasn't come to me, not yet, not exactly, but maybe someday it will, even if I have to force it into the light myself. Here is to the new truth.

III. OHIO SONGS

Transcripts from Daniel
Morus's Interviews with
William Toop

RICHARD EPPS'S INTRODUCTION

When Daniel Morus sent me the following transcripts of his interview with William Toop, the father of cult, pop-folk icon Jim Toop, I thought he had lost his mind. Not only was the interview disjointed and rambling, but the transcript also included strange annotations by Mr. Morus, speculating on the veracity of the senior Mr. Toop's answers and anecdotes. These notes were additionally perplexing as they included descriptions of interactions between Morus and a friend of his who seemed to be acting as a research assistant. Though the identity of that friend remains a mystery, I have my suspicions as to who it might be. At first, I didn't understand why Morus sent me these transcripts—they didn't seem publishable, and, on the surface, provided little new information about Jim Toop or the circumstances of the recently surfaced tape of *The Taxidermist's Catalog*, the authentication of which was the main reason Morus had traveled to Los Angeles to talk with Toop. My questions were answered when, the day after sending me these transcripts, Morus messaged me asking if I'd had time to read the interview, and if so, what my thoughts might be on extending his investigation into New Mexico. It wasn't until I started reading the transcripts more closely that I understood what Daniel Morus was up to. I'm not saying that there's necessarily anything in this interview that led me to believe that Jim Toop was still alive and living in New Mexico, only that, as you'll see, some of the things William Toop says in this conversation raised some questions that I thought Daniel Morus might be able to answer by adding another leg to his trip. Now that Morus's feature on *The Taxidermist's Catalog* and Toop have run, we thought we'd go ahead and put this up on our website for interested parties. Enjoy!

–R. Epps
Editor-in-Chief of *Folk! Magazine*

WILLIAM TOOP INTERVIEW TRANSCRIPTS[1]

---

1. What follows will be the full transcript of my interview with William Toop at his Los Angeles home. As I was attempting to discover whether or not the version of *Taxidermist's Catalog* I'd been given by Richard Epps was authentic, meaning I needed information about Toop's "disappearance" and what he might have been doing after said "disappearance," I believed that my investigation might benefit from the element of surprise. As such, I arrived at William Toop's house uninvited and unexpected, and asked if I could interview him for a retrospective feature I was writing about his son. Mr. Toop was hesitant at first, but as he is the sole recipient of royalties from his son's album sales, he agreed to talk to me after I reminded him of the relationship between retrospective features of deceased artists and increased album sales. For Richard Epps's sake, I made no reference to the recent discovery of *Taxidermist's Catalog*. Within moments of sitting down across from William Toop at his kitchen table, I set up my trusty tape recorder—technology has advanced, but I haven't—and our conversation began.

DAY ONE

Daniel Morus: Let me start by thanking you for your time. I'm sure this is the last thing you want to be talking about.

William Toop: Not much left to say about any of this business, so get to it.

DM: How about we start with Jim's youth[2]—he was sixteen when he released his first album. How did he come to music at such a young age?[3]

WT: He got his first guitar when we were living in New Mexico. Or maybe Ohio. Must have been Ohio. That place, that shithole where we lived for a while. I think it must have been Ohio because there was nothing to do there and

---

2. I started light, easy, in an attempt to make Mr. Toop comfortable before asking more difficult questions.

3. After I asked this first question, William Toop pulled a pack of Marlboro Reds from his shirt pocket and lit one up.

we weren't in New Mexico for very long. He was young and bright and bored, so I got him a guitar to help him stay out of trouble. That didn't turn out so well, did it?[4]

DM: It didn't turn out so bad. He had an impressive career.

WT: I'd rather still have a son than have the memory of his career. Maybe if I'd never given him that guitar, he'd still be here. He loved animals. Maybe he would have become a marine biologist or a vet. Hell, he was a damn fine ball player. Maybe he could've played for the Dodgers—think about that, Vin Scully telling everybody about centerfielder Jim Toop whose father never gave him a guitar so now he's running down gap shots and hitting home runs instead of writing sad, mopey, songs and dying in middle of the fucking desert.

DM: I wasn't planning on asking this so quickly, and there's not exactly a delicate way to phrase it, but, for the record, you seem to believe that your son is dead.

---

4. As I began typing this transcript on my laptop in my hotel room the evening after my first meeting with William Toop, a friend with more than a passing interest in my investigation sent me a message on Gchat inquiring at to how my research was progressing. Though I initially resisted, I was bored and lonely, and thought that maybe a second set of eyes might be useful in in my search for insights into Jim Toop's fate. I pasted the first question and answer into the response field. Several minutes later, my friend messaged me again to tell me that, according to a *Rolling Stone* interview from 1976, Jim Toop was given his first guitar by a man who ran a junk shop in Truth or Consequences, New Mexico. "He's hiding something," my friend typed. "He's old and forgetful," I answered.

WT: That's not a question. If you're going to ask a question, ask a damn question.[5]

DM: Okay—are you sure your son's dead?

WT: Of course he's dead. What kind of a shit question is that? You think he'd disappear and not contact me for thirty years? What kind of a shit father do you think I am?

DM: It's been forty-six years.

WT: Whatever, thirty, forty-six—doesn't make much difference when you're my age—our age.[6]

DM: He could be in captivity.

WT: You're one of those, then.[7]

DM: So you're aware of the different theories surrounding your son's disappearance.

WT: Of course I've heard them. Or some of them. I never bothered to keep up.

DM: If it makes you feel better, I don't want to talk about those. I just want to know what you think happened to your son.

WT: What do I think happened to him? Doesn't really matter what I think. Doesn't matter what anyone thinks. Gone is gone. And there were no flying saucers, or black triangles, or

---

5. Here was first of the interview's many long pauses as I fumbled silently for what to say next.

6. I ignored Toop's reference to my age here.

7. Already, just a few minutes into our conversation, William Toop had already grown hostile. I was worried I was going to lose control of the interview or lose access altogether.

suicide cults, or kidnappers, or whatever else you cocksuckers have been dreaming up for decades. Decades. My son's been gone for decades and you fuckers are still asking about it, can't keep from digging it up over and over again. You know what I think happened to my son? I think he got shit-faced, drove his car out into the desert, parked, then went off stumbling towards oblivion. Maybe he looked up and was stunned by the stars that he wasn't used to seeing in L.A. and kept walking, looking up until he died. Or maybe a coyote got him, or a rattlesnake, or a combination of the two. Maybe he was tired and drunk and just crawled into a cave or a hole and that's why his body was never found, or maybe vultures picked him clean and stole off with his bones.

DM: So that's your theory?

WT: Sure, but what the fuck do I know?

DM: How did you find out he'd disappeared?

WT: It was 1977. Of course it was 1977, what am I even saying. By the time I found out, he'd probably already been dead for days—nobody knew how to get ahold of me. I was working as a Foley artist at an independent recording studio, did contract work for some of the major studios when their departments were behind schedule, but mostly worked on small films, commercials, television shows—that kind of thing. It's what I came to L.A. for—I trained to be a Foley but couldn't find work in the field and so we moved around a lot when I was starting out—that's what led to our divorce. When I married Jim's mother, we decided we wanted to start a family, so I looked for something stable. We settled in Ohio after Jim was born, but the damage was done. Jim's mom up and left when he was one or two. I was working at a radio station. It wasn't great, but the pay was good and the job was stable. I couldn't find anything better so we stuck around until my department got the axe. That's when I found the job at the radio station in New Mexico, mostly doing tech work and commercials.

Anyway, that night I found out Jim was gone—I was working with a splash tank, making water sounds, and one of the other guys, an old-timer named Dan who worked at MGM back in the fifties, comes into the room and tells me I should go with him. I told him I was busy—the splash tank was sloshing around just right and the console was ready to go—but he told me the water could wait. Pulled me back to the break room where we kept a small black and white television, the kind with an antennae—remember those?[8]

DM: Of course.

WT: So anyway, he pulls me back to the break room and points at the television, and there's this commercial on, for toothpaste or instant coffee—something with a happy couple smiling and wearing robes closed up to their necks. And Dan says, You've got a son who plays music? I told him I did. He

---

8. While typing this part of the transcript, I noticed that my young friend was online. I sent him a message telling him that Jim Toop's dad had been a Foley artist. This wasn't particularly relevant to my line of inquiry, but it was an interesting detail and one that that hadn't surfaced in previous features on Jim Toop. My friend was more excited than I expected—he quickly confirmed Toop's claim and told me that the name of the recording studio where he'd worked was called The Ziegfield Foleys. When I asked how he'd found that information, he told me that Google turned up a staff photo. When I asked my friend why he was so interested in this bit of information, he told me that being a Foley seemed like an interesting and noble profession.

said, And he's on tour now? Southwest? I nodded and then he pointed at the screen and said, He disappeared. I was confused—here was this old man pointing at this commercial and telling me my son had disappeared. I asked him what in the hell he was talking about.

He told me they'd just run a report about an L.A. musician disappearing in Truth or Consequences, New Mexico. Of course it was my son. We'd lived there. Of course it was him. I didn't go back to work that day. I dialed 'o' and had the operator patch me through to the T or C police, and they told me what they could over the phone, told me they didn't have a body. I told them I'd fly out as soon as I could. It took me three days to finish up at work—I was told to finish my current project on time or I'd be fired—book a flight, and get out of town.[9]

You know why I chose Truth or Consequences all those years ago? Before coming to Los Angeles, I mean?

DM: For a job, you said.

WT: Of course it was for a job, but there were plenty of shitty radio jobs then—the reason I chose that one was because of the name—that game show.[10] You know that story?

---

9. William Toop paused, here, as if lost in thought. He lifted a fresh cigarette to his lips and held it there without lighting it, inhaled as if taking a drag from the filter end. He looked sad, maybe worried. I started to feel bad for asking him to talk about all of this. Then he continued.

10. Here, of course, Mr. Toop is referring to Truth or Consequences changing its name from Hot Springs, in 1950, after Ralph Edwards, the host of the quiz show *Truth or Consequences*, offered to broadcast an episode of his show from any city willing to change its name to match the show's

DM: I know about the game show.

WT: What a way to name a city.

DM: So you flew out to Truth or Consequences?

WT: As close as anyone can fly out to Truth or Consequences. Landed in Albuquerque, drove a rental down.

DM: So you flew out to Albuquerque?

WT: Not like I had much of a choice.[11]

DM: This is difficult for you.

WT: No—not the way you mean. You say difficult and mean my insides must ache. There's no ache. I'm just tired of talking about it. All you fucking journalists—it's slowed down over the years, but here you are.[12]

DM: Strange—I've never seen you quoted talking about your son.

WT: Well, you're the first in a while. Plenty of your type have come sniffing around in the hopes of unearthing something new about Jim, something they believe everyone else missed.[13]

---

11. Before this response, Toop paused, again, for quite some time.

12. At the conclusion of this statement, Toop gestured across the table at me, tapped the tape recorder with a cigarette lighter he'd been fiddling with. The sound is audible on the tape.

13. Later, my friend could find no record of any articles published about Jim Toop that reference conversations with William Toop. When I suggested that this meant either that the elder Toop never provided worthwhile information or that the articles in which he was mentioned were never digitally archived, my friend

Sometimes I talk to them, sometimes I don't. They always leave disappointed. Is that why you're here? To find something new?[14]

DM: I told you—I'm here because I'm writing an article about your son and I want a fresh angle.

WT: That sounds like a professional way of saying you're trying to unearth something new.

DM: Not new, no. I don't expect to find anything that will change what we know about your son's disappearance, but I've written a number of articles about him before, and I'm hoping you will tell me something about his life that might keep my readers interested.

WT: If you're so interested in his life, then why do we keep talking about his death? You're not being entirely honest with me.

DM: I told you why I'm here.

WT: Then ask me about my son's life.

DM: Ohio.

WT: What about Ohio?

---

responded as forcefully as an online message could convey, saying: "NO! THIS ISN'T RIGHT. HE'S AVOIDING THE SUBJECT. FIND OUT WHY." I told my friend his suspicions were paranoid, to which he told me I should press the issue in a follow-up interview. I typed, "I'm worried about you." He responded, "You have no right to worry about me." I asked him what he meant by that and he simply apologized.

14. To this, my friend said, "See, he's changing the focus. He's deflecting the interview back on you."

DM: You left Ohio. Why?

WT: I told you—I got laid off and found a new job.

DM: Still, to uproot a teenager of that age from school and move for a new job is quite an undertaking. You could have found a new job in Ohio.

WT: We didn't like Ohio.

DM: Neither of you?

WT: I couldn't fucking stand it.

DM: Why?

WT: Shitty winters. Shitty memories.

DM: But your son liked Ohio. His songs—

WT: Maybe he liked it more than I did. He didn't have many friends there. Just a girlfriend. I met her once or twice, but normally they'd go out walking around town. Didn't seem like anything special, but he seemed to like her. And he wrote those songs about her, about Ohio. I didn't think he liked it at the time, but maybe he did. Maybe he just didn't like it the way teenagers don't like anything. All his songs about flight and the flood. You know the Wright Brothers didn't even fly their damn plane in Ohio? Didn't matter to people in Dayton. Everyone was always so proud of the Wright Brothers. Them and Paul Laurence Dunbar. I didn't understand how anyone could live there let alone be proud of it. Still don't. Scotch?[15]

---

15. As he talked about Ohio, Toop shuffled around the room, producing two tumblers and a nice bottle of scotch, a Lagavulin 16 year, from his cupboard. He poured himself a glass just before he invited me to partake. Though the scotch was nicer than any-

DM: No, thank you.

WT: Suit yourself.

DM: Ohio isn't such a bad place.

WT: Is that why you're asking about Ohio? Because you like it?

DM: It's fine. I lived there for a few years. Not in Dayton. Spent a lot of time exploring down there, though—found as many of the places referenced on Ohio Songs as we could.

WT: We?

DM: My ex-wife and I. While we were still married.

WT: Sure you don't need a nip?[16]

DM: Yes, thank you. Why the animosity though? You've been out of Ohio for forty-odd years.

WT: Why do you still romanticize it?

DM: I don't. It was fine, but I don't miss it.

WT: Is it because of the woman? Your ex-wife?

DM: I'm not the one being interviewed.

WT: Fuck your interview. Let's have a conversation. This feels like a conversation we're having.

DM: I'm not going to talk to you about my ex-wife.[17]

---

thing I could ever purchase, I wanted to keep my wits about me.

16. As he spoke, he swirled the gold liquid around in its glass.

17. My friend responded to this portion of the interview by messaging me, "The boxes in your closet that I moved, were they

WT: In that case, I won't be talking to you anymore about my son.

DM: Then tell me more about Ohio?

WT: Why Ohio?

DM: I don't know[18]—because not much has been written about your son's time in Ohio.

WT: I already told you about it.

DM: Tell me more

WT: It was an ugly place, a sad place, a lonely place. It's where Jim's mom left us. I ran the boards for a small radio station at night and produced commercials for extra cash during the day. It wasn't glamorous, not what I wanted to be doing. I was stuck making bullshit commercials for local mechanics and ice cream joints. That was Ohio for me—empty and dull and lonely. Just me and Jimmy. And I always assumed he felt the same. I really did. And then he came to me, seven or eight years later, says to me, I want to play you these new songs I've been working on, and these songs he plays are all about

---

your ex-wife's?" I told him they weren't, not wanting to explain that they belonged to my other ex-wife. "Someone after your ex-wife?" he typed. "Yes," I told him. "I don't really want to talk about this with you," I told him. "I didn't know you had an ex-wife," he typed. "It's late," I wrote. "Don't you have school in the morning?" He said, "It's Friday."

18. And I didn't know. I had no good reason to be asking about Ohio. My job was to try to confirm that the tape Richard Epps had discovered was real—asking about Ohio, I suppose, was cover; somehow, though, my cover was taking over the interview.

Ohio, how beautiful Ohio was, how he missed that girl he'd been dating—those songs were downright nostalgic.[19]

DM: Maybe he was simply nostalgic for that part of his youth.

WT: No—those songs were so specific. I remember when he played them for me, just him and his acoustic guitar. I was sitting right here, and he was standing in front of the fridge.[20] It was quite a performance, the first time I remember seeing my son as vulnerable, as an adult, even. He shuffled through the chords and his was voice was tentative, like he was still figuring out the melodies. There was one he did, about how the leaves change slow—what song is that?

DM: "Hush, Hush (Leaves Change Slow)."

WT: That one, yeah—and there's the line in that song where he says, "Los Angeles knows no seasons," and then a few lines later says, "Ohio taught me how to fall." That was hard to hear. As a father, I mean—it was hard to know that I'd taken something like that away from my son, and that I didn't even know. Maybe he had loads of friends. Maybe him and that girlfriend were more serious than I knew. I guess moving is

---

19. I resisted the urge to say something snarky about how William Toop had said he wouldn't talk about his son anymore. My instincts told me that to mention the disconnect between his threat and his actions would only shut down this particular line of conversation. Also of note, most Toop scholars assumed all references to women on *Ohio Songs* were to Angela, despite the lack of biographical correlation with Toop's life. I made a mental note to revisit these songs and my readings of them.

20. Toop gestured toward the refrigerator. It was a little overwhelming to be sitting in a room where my favorite musician shared such an intimate moment with his father.

never easy for a teenager. That doesn't make me feel any less selfish. Of course, I was upset for different reasons when I first heard "We Learned to Fly."

DM: What upset you about that song?

WT: Do you have children, Mr. Morus?

DM: I don't.[21]

WT: Imagine finding out, a decade after the fact, that your fourteen or fifteen year old son had been drinking and getting high. He was a moody boy, and an even moodier man, so how was I to know? I don't know that I ever saw him happy after he turned thirteen—some people might have referred to him as "sensitive," that he had a poet's soul or some bullshit. I just thought he was sad. I should have known what he was doing, been a better father. Maybe he wouldn't have turned to drugs and drink and writing those sad fucking songs if I had.

DM: He was a kid. Kids do those things.

WT: If you had a son you'd understand.

DM: It was the sixties. That kind of thing wasn't uncommon.

WT: It was 1965. The Beatles had barely even discovered weed.

---

21. I paused a long time before answering. I had no reason to pause. Obviously, I know that I don't have children, but due to the intimacy of our conversation, my guard had dropped. I found myself momentarily speechless as I considered my life without children. Though common and fair, Toop's question was jarring—I stared at him until he waved his hand in front of my face to get my attention.

DM: So you were disappointed that your kid smoked some dope.

WT: I was disappointed that *my son* smoked some dope. I was disappointed at my failure as a father. Not just that my son had smoked some weed, but that I didn't even know he'd done it. That I didn't know fucking anything. When I heard Jim sing those songs about Dayton, and that one, in particular, about being high and watching the planes take off and land, I knew I had failed as a father—and up to that point, that was one of the few things I'd been proud of in my life.[22]

DM: Can you tell me about the last time you saw your son?

WT: I told you I'm not going to talk about him anymore. I'm tired and unaccustomed to talking for so long. I'm done for today. You can come back tomorrow if you must.[23]

---

22. The following four minutes were quiet and heavy. Transcribing, now, I hear only two audible sounds on the tape—William Toop tapping his cigarette on the lip of a porcelain ashtray, not once to ash, but in a repeated rhythm, each tap tossing off small, glowing embers, and the soft hum of the tape deck itself. I didn't know what to say next. Toop was right—I couldn't begin to understand his disappointment. I could empathize with disappointment in how I'd failed wives and lovers, friends, and even my own parents, but I would never understand Toop's precise disappointment. Upon reading this portion of the interview, my young friend typed, "He was playing on your sympathies." Then: "He was manipulating you. He found your weakness." I said, "What weakness?" My friend didn't respond. I typed, "He's a sad old man with regrets." My friend said, "Empathy has never been my strong suit."

23. With that, William Toop pressed the stop button on my tape deck. As I packed up my gear, Toop excused himself from the room, telling me that, if I was planning on coming back, to

arrive no earlier than one o'clock. He explained that his morning routine is regimented, that he likes to have lunch at noon, allowing plenty of time to eat slow and let his food digest. I told him I would see him then. Now, as I finish typing this first set of notes, I am surprised how little ground we'd covered, having spoken for over an hour. Toop selects his words slowly, carefully, and when he speaks them, his voice is low and rough, jagged even, as if he's dragging every sentence through a mess of silt and debris. I am no longer certain what I am after in my conversations with William Toop, what clue might trigger some larger discovery. I need to dig into that silt and debris and see what I can dredge up that might shed some light on the surprise emergence of *Taxidermist's Catalog*, but how does one approach such a subject with a dead man's father? Is he even a dead man? What does William Toop know? Does he know anything at all?

DAY TWO[24]

WT: So where were we?

DM: It doesn't matter where we were yesterday—what do you want to talk about today?

WT: No, no—you asked me a question yesterday and I want to answer it. About the last time I saw my son.[25]

---

24. I arrived at William Toop's house a few minutes before one and waited in my rental car. At precisely one, I knocked on Toop's front door. He was slow to answer, but much to my surprise, greeted me warmly. Inside, Toop led me to the kitchen table. As soon as I pushed the record button on my tape deck, Toop started the conversation.

25. Toop surprised me not just by starting the conversation, but by demonstrating a willingness to open with a subject he had been reticent to discuss the previous day. Upon reading this, my friend was suspicious: "He had a chance to get his story straight," he typed.

DM: That's right

WT: It was right before his tour. Jim took me out for dinner two, three days before he left. Around then, we saw each other regularly, a few times a week whenever possible. He lived not far from here, in an apartment just off the strip, close to Ocean City's studio and the venues where he liked to play—this was two nights before he left, I remember now because he'd wanted to take me out the night before, but work was scheduled to get a print of one of Universal's mid-list films and the entire staff was scheduled to work all night for a fast turnaround. So, Jim took me out to Nate 'n Al over in Beverly Hills—best Reuben I've ever had. From the moment we sat down to the time Jim paid the check—this was noteworthy as Jim *never* paid the check because he was always broke and I never let him, but that night he insisted—he was in unusually high spirits. I told you yesterday that I don't think I ever saw my son happy after he turned thirteen. I was wrong—that night he was happy. It was nice. I told Jim about the film we were going to be working on for Universal—*Saga of the Star World*, they called it, but really it was just the theatrical release of the *Battlestar Galactica* pilot episode. Universal was dumping a healthy chunk of its resources into Sensurround for the film, that deep bass that made entire theaters rumble.[26]

---

26. As my young friend pointed out, *Saga of the Star World* could not have been the film Ziegfield Foleys was working on for Universal as the film wasn't released until July, 1978, meaning it was unlikely that a fast turnaround time was needed on sound work. My friend argued that this clearly meant that William Toop had seen his son after the disappearance. "You caught him in a lie," he wrote. "Call him out on it." When I did my own research online, I learned that Universal released *Rollercoaster* in Sensurround in June 1977. Despite my friend's suspicions, I suspected

They'd used it on a couple of other films and it put them a bit behind schedule. We'd already worked with them on previous Sensurround films, mostly doing the incidental shit while they did the big bass parts.

When I told Jim about the film, he said something about how it sounded like a lovely picture. It was garbage, all lasers and spaceships and robots. Not lovely like its title: Star World—that's pretty. When we were talking about the film, Jim got a little funny, started talking about other worlds and how he hoped to someday look down on the Earth from space. I said, That's crazy, Jim. You're a musician. Do you know how long those astronauts train? The kind of shape they have to be in? You, with your drinking and doping—you're not an astronaut.

Then Jim said, Maybe someone will come along and just snatch me up into the sky and fly me away.

It was eerie. Jim was always into space and stars, *Star Trek* and Spock and *Lost in Space* and *Star Wars*, or whatever. All that bullshit.[27] After he said that bit about someone snatching

---

that Mr. Toop had simply conflated his work on the two films. "He's smarter than you think," my friend typed, when I confronted him with my findings. "If he were smarter than I think," I said, "then he wouldn't have made such an obvious mistake to begin with."

27. My friend was quick to point out that *Star Wars* wasn't released until at least two months after Jim Toop's disappearance. I started to question my wisdom in sharing these transcripts with him. He provided some useful context and background information a few times, but for the most part he was little more than an irritant, a distraction and, frankly, his attention to detail was obnoxious and his persistent, dogmatic approach to those details was exhausting. Through my interactions with my friend, I thought I might have been starting to understand how fathers

him up and flying him away, his strange mood passed and he was happy again. Genuinely happy. He was laughing at my stories about work and telling me all about his upcoming tour. He was excited for Memphis, where he was going to play at a Beale Street bar and visit Graceland.[28] He was also excited for Tulsa—lord knows why—and Albuquerque, thinking he might try to get in touch with some folks from Truth or Consequences and spend a few days visiting them between gigs. Even though we only lived there for about a year, he had friends—another girl he was close to[29]—I guess Jim was something of a ladies' man—and a couple of other kids he knew. And the guy who gave him his first guitar.

DM: Yesterday you said that you gave him his first guitar when you were living in Ohio.

WT: Did I say that? I was wrong—it was this guy who owned a junkshop out in Truth or Consequences. Jim saw him playing out in front of the store one day and started hanging around.

---

feel, subjected to countless interruptions in the form of inane questions and outrageous demands. That I continued to send portions of the transcript, however, should probably tell me something.

28. This caught my ears as Graceland didn't open to tourists until 1982. I was amused to note that, upon sharing this section of the interview with my young friend, he didn't notice the inconsistency. I kept it to myself while I decided how to press this issue on my own time—after all, this could be the sliver of information that will confirm that Jim Toop was alive to work on *Taxidermist's Catalog* after his disappearance.

29. Angela, no doubt. My heart raced—here was my opening. I took a deep breath to calm myself. I knew I had to pick my moment if I wanted meaningful information about her. As you'll soon see, I didn't pick the right moment.

The man, a weird guy, a hippie folks probably called him back then, wore overalls and tie-dyed shirts. He was maybe in his mid-thirties, probably a little younger than me. I think his name was Alfred, Alan, Al—he took a liking to Jim and gave him an old guitar, taught him how to play a little.

DM: You mentioned a girl that Jim was close to. Do you remember her name?

WT: Nah. I saw them together once or twice. She was cute. Reminded me a little of Jim's mother. I didn't really know any of Jim's friends, though.

DM: Hair color?

WT: Shit, I don't remember. Maybe she was a brunette? Or auburn, like a dark red. Who knows?

DM: Could her name have been Angela?

WT: Maybe it was. I don't know. Could have been. Or it...[30]

DM: So, Jim was telling you about his tour.

WT: Of course—he was telling me about his tour and everything was fine until after he paid the check and drove me home. When we stopped at my house, he got out and started digging in his trunk, pulled out a couple of those reel-to-reel tape boxes and handed them to me. He said, Take these. I said, What are they? He said, Masters of my new album, as much of it as is finished, anyway. I asked him what I was going to do with it. Asked, Aren't you still working on it? He told

---

30. Halfway through this thought, Toop trailed off, seemed either lost or confused. After a beat, I gently nudged him back on track.

me he was going to record a little more on the road. Said, I want you to hang on to them in case anything happens to me.

DM: Did you take the tapes?[31]

WT: Will you just listen?—Jim said, I want you to hang onto them in case anything happens to me. I asked, What's going to happen to you? I said, You're going on tour, you've been on a hundred tours—you'll be fine. He said, Just in case. Then: If anything happens, you'll have those tapes. You can just take them to Ocean City and they'll put the album out as is. I asked him why he didn't leave the tapes with them. He told me I could negotiate a better deal for myself if I had them. Make a little extra money, retire early.[32]

I asked him, Why are you talking like this, Jim? And he went on and on about all of the things that could happen to him, how he could die in a car crash, or die of alcohol poisoning, or get stabbed for messing with someone else's girl, or be abducted by UFO's. Him and his UFO's—I remember he called me up after the first time he watched *Star Wars* in the theater and he wouldn't stop talking about the aliens and the robots and the spaceships and the city in the clouds and how Darth Vader was Luke's father.[33]

---

31. It was a gamble interrupting Toop, here, but the album is what I was ultimately here to learn about, I couldn't not speak up.

32. This made me nervous for Epps's sake—if William Toop had once thought of *Taxidermist's Catalog* as a source of potential revenue, this could cause problems when my employer goes public with the tape.

33. As you might have guessed, my young friend quickly pointed out that some of these references were from *Star Wars Episode V: The Empire Strikes Back*, which wasn't released until 1980. My friend was adamant in his suspicions that William Toop

I told him, I'm not taking those tapes because nothing is going to happen to you and that is that. Then he gave me a hug and said goodbye. He said he'd see me in a month. I told him he sure as shit would and then he climbed into his car and drove off. That was the last time I saw my son.

DM: You're telling me your son suspected that something was going to happen to him?[34]

WT: Of course not, you asshole. Had you going though, didn't I?[35] You're as bad as any of the other conspiracy theorists—you'll believe anything. You *want* to believe all that crazy bullshit.[36]

DM: So none of what you just told me is true?

WT: Bits and pieces. Jim took me out to Nate 'n Al, but he didn't pay. I told him about work and he told me about his tour. The rest of it? All bullshit.[37]

---

was lying to us to cover up a secret. Also, as I knew how the conversation with Toop was about to turn, I may have intentionally shared this snippet of the transcript specifically to toy with my young friend.

34. This question was followed by another long, weighty silence. Toop had been smoking throughout his narrative and I'd inched to the edge of my chair, was leaning in close, afraid to miss a single word. Before he answered my question, Toop lit a new cigarette and smoked the entire thing, slow, deliberate.

35. Here, he laughed loud and long.

36. Though I was pursuing this line of inquiry only to try to learn more about the tape, Toop's observations filled me with shame, especially considering how rapt I'd been paying attention as he spun his fiction.

37. "See?" I typed to my friend a few moments after send-

DM: If you didn't want to talk about it, you could have just told me. No need to humiliate me.

WT: Don't take yourself so seriously. I was just having fun.

---

ing him this portion of the interview. "He was messing with us," I typed. "With me," I amended. My friend's response was not what I expected: "He's concealing the truth with lies." I said, "But there is no truth here." He answered, "There were a number of truths and a number of lies and the ultimate lie that Toop told was that his whole story was a lie—maybe the story about his son trying to give him the tapes was a lie, and maybe Jim Toop's belief that something was going to happen to him was a lie, but I can't believe that the entire story was a lie. If even one of those details is true—William Toop talking with his son about *Battlestar Galactica* or *The Empire Strikes Back*—then those are crucial truths concealed within all of the lies." "He was mistaken," I answered. "He was making the story up, plugging in titles as he went," I said. "Jim Toop has to be alive," my friend said. "He has to be. I know it, and I think his father knows it." He seemed desperate. I asked him why Jim Toop had to be alive. "It's a double deception," my friend said. "He's letting you close to the real truth then confounding your expectations to push you further away." I asked again, "Why does Jim Toop have to be alive?" My friend typed, "HE JUST DOES." I supposed this was the part of the conversation where, if I were a father and my friend were my son, he'd storm out of the room and slam his door. I watched to see if he'd sign off of Gchat or block me. Instead, the chat box indicated that he was typing. When he finally sent the message, it said, "Will you please just press him about the *Star Wars* thing? That's all I want. Just make sure it was a mistake." I wrote back, "Fine." I wrote, "Why are you so invested in this?" He said, "It would be wrong of us not to pursue all potential avenues that might lead to new information." I replied, "Don't you mean it would be wrong of me?" My friend said, "I'm in this with you now. You let me in." He was right, and I felt foolish for being so open, especially when I suspect that my friend is and has been keeping something from me.

DM: I should go.[38]

WT: Don't be such a pussy. Or do, suit yourself. We can still talk if you want. I was just making a point.

DM: Your point?

WT: That you're not going to get anything out of me that you and a hundred other journalists, UFO nuts, and conspiracy theorists haven't already imagined on their own—I'm a dead end.

DM: You could tell me more about your trip to New Mexico after your son went missing. I haven't seen that covered before.

WT: What could you possibly learn from that?

DM: Humor me.

WT: I took a few days of personal leave at work, fell asleep on the airplane, and drooled all over myself. Rented a car in Albuquerque and stopped halfway to Truth or Consequences to piss on the side of the road. I didn't see any real cactuses, the kinds you see in movie and cartoons. When I pulled up to my hotel I sat in my car and tried not to cry. I went and looked at my son's abandoned rental car, was interviewed by the investigator working the case and a couple of journalists. How about that? Is that what you're looking for? I drank my weight in shitty beer and puked on a sidewalk, passed out in a park, spent the night in jail and when I woke up in the

---

38. I'm still not sure if I meant this threat, or if I was simply being petty. Perhaps I was trying to regain the upper hand? To try to make Toop think I didn't need to be talking to him? Regardless, it was a reckless thing to say as I still hadn't learned a damn concrete thing about *Taxidermist's Catalog* or Jim Toop.

morning, all I could do was cry until I puked some more. There—I went to see about my disappeared son and had myself a lost weekend in the middle of the goddam week.[39]

DM: So you were upset?

WT: Of course I was upset. Are you some kind of retard? Fuckwit. My son disappeared. The police were clear that they didn't think he'd turn up alive. Was I supposed to not be upset?

DM: I didn't mean...

WT: I shouldn't say that.

DM: Say what?

WT: Call you a retard. That was unacceptable.

DM: What kind of questions did the investigator ask?

WT: If Jim had any enemies, if he was suicidal, if he used drugs—nothing out of the ordinary. They talked about vagrants in the area, and a cult—they thought maybe he'd been abducted. Turned out it wasn't a very good cult, though. Not one anyone ever heard of—short lived. Just some folks who walked out into the desert for a month then realized that desert life was shit and crawled back home.

DM: How did others in Truth or Consequences respond? Did you speak with anyone else?

---

39. More silence. I didn't know what I could possibly ask or say in response to what Toop had just told me. In retrospect, my response was regrettable to say the least.

WT: Not really—those people might be bored, but they were never interested in telling tales about my son. At least back then. They knew Jim, were supportive of his career. That's something else I wasn't lying about before—he was genuinely excited to re-connect with his old friends. He scheduled the tour with some days off so he could stop out there, maybe play an impromptu gig at one of the bars.

DM: Who was still around? Which friends did your son go to see? Who did you see?

WT: A couple of his old friends—just some kids who took jobs, started families, and stuck around. One guy he used to run with was one of the cops I talked to—he was brisk with me, didn't seem like he wanted anything to do with me—and that girl he used to run around with was working at the bar where I got wasted. They were both married—not to each other. Most kids couldn't wait to get out, move up to Albuquerque or Taos or Santa Fe.

DM: Were they upset about Jim's disappearance?

WT: As upset as two people who'd just seen an old friend for the first time in a decade can be, I guess. Like I said, the cop didn't even want to talk about it and the girl was upset for her own reasons—her husband had just passed, I think. Said she was working through her grief, didn't want it to fester in the desert heat, but didn't feel much like talking to someone she barely knew.

DM: What had happened to her husband?

WT: Oh, I don't know. If she told me, I was too drunk to remember.

DM: And what was her name again? The bartender?

WT: I told you, I don't know.

DM: And what about the cop?

WT: I don't know—Rick. Chuck? Something like that.

DM: Did you see anyone else you knew from your time there?

WT: Not really. Just Al, the guy that gave Jim his first guitar. He bought me a beer. Ran into him by accident. I didn't tell anyone I was coming to town.[40]

DM: And what did you tell the investigator. Was there anyone there who might have wanted to hurt your son?

WT: Look, I told you what I think happened.[41] He did what I should've done. He got drunk and walked into the desert to die.

DM: What you should have done?

WT: I didn't mean that.

---

40. I was a bit taken aback that Toop clearly remembered Al's name here as he'd previously struggled with it. I was, again, forced to question whether this was the result of his failing memory, or if his earlier struggles were an attempt to obfuscate information that he'd since decided didn't need obfuscation. If that was the case, why did he change his mind? Or did that, too, have something to do with the effects of age—before he believed he should protect Al's name, but now he didn't? If I talked to him tomorrow, or even in an hour, what might he tell me then that he previously had the wherewithal to withhold?

41. A long uncomfortable pause followed by a more uncomfortable elaboration.

DM: No?

WT: No.

DM: Not even a little?[42]

DM: Do you think your son wanted to die?[43]

WT: Why would anyone want to die? Do you mean did he want to die when he was writing and recording songs? Or when we were eating sandwiches together in Beverly Hills? Or when he was on tour? Why would he want to die then? Any of those times? Does anybody ever *want* to die? Or is it more that they choose not to live? I know, I know—fucking semantics. If my son *wanted* to die, he could have done it anytime, anywhere, so why then and there? It's not difficult to die.

DM: Sometimes it can be. Difficult, I mean.

WT: No—it's the staying alive that's difficult.

---

42. Toop didn't say anything so I asked a second question.

43. This was followed by another long pause. The quiet was broken by the end of the first side of the tape, indicating that the day's conversation had already lasted for thirty minutes. William Toop watched as I fumbled to flip the tape and load it in the machine. I felt bad for having asked the last question, but it needed answering. I was interested in the suggestion that Toop actively killed himself, even though, if that were the case, it would drastically impact my understanding of the discovered tape and who made it. I've never been one to romanticize the early deaths of popular musicians, but if Toop did knowingly walk into the desert to die—that's something I can understand. Regardless, by the time I changed the tape, it was clear that William Toop was ready to answer, had almost certainly prepared and silently rehearsed the following words.

DM: I don't know.

WT: You don't know shit—and no, I don't think my son *wanted* to die. I think that maybe, in that moment he was drunk and felt alone and sad, and maybe being confronted with a happier past, or maybe recognizing the depths of his own loneliness—something made him choose to walk away from it all, to give up and not come back. It's a regrettable thing that he did, especially since he probably would have woken up the next morning and felt fine, maybe had a little bit of a headache—but that's not what happened. That's the one nice thing about all those fucking conspiracy theories—assholes can't romanticize my son's death if they don't think he's dead, can't lionize his suicide if they refuse to believe that he killed himself. That's something, anyway. All you fucks out there trying to make deaths like this more than they are—the Cobain kid up in Seattle, that kid a few years ago, not far from here, out in Echo Park.[44] If Jim were here now he'd say that the kid was a damned fool, taking his own life like that, squandering all that talent—a waste, that's what Jim would say.

DM: But you said he ended his own life, even if it wasn't entirely intentional.

WT: Look—my son didn't want to die and he didn't kill himself. I chose my words poorly. He was drunk and wandered off and that's that.

---

44. Toop seems to be referencing Elliott Smith here, who, of course, stabbed himself twice in the chest and died in 2003.

DM: Just so we're clear, you don't think your son's death was intentional, you *don't* think that it all might have been too much for him, whatever he was feeling?

WT: I don't know what he was feeling. You don't know what he was feeling. All we know is that he's not here.

DM: But he must have been feeling something to just walk into the desert like that.

WT: We're done here.

DM: I'm sorry.[45]

WT: Too late for that—you want to write about my son's death? You think you know about losing a son?

DM: Why don't you tell me about Jim's trip to Graceland? I won't ask about his death anymore.[46]

WT: You need to leave.[47]

---

45. I wasn't sorry. Or rather, I was sorry that I'd killed the interview without learning anything substantial about Toop or *Taxidermist's Catalog*, without asking about Graceland, even.

46. I still feel embarrassed about groveling like this.

47. This was the abrupt ending of the second day of our interview. As I packed up my gear and left William Toop's house, I was certain I wouldn't see him again, and was upset at my failure to learn anything concrete. By the time I reached my hotel, however, Toop had already left a message asking me to call him. When we spoke over the phone, he apologized for his outburst and invited me back the following day. We arranged a time and agreed that the third day would be the last. When I told my young friend about the end of the interview and subsequent phone call, he begged me to ask Toop about the movie discrepancies from the interview's first day. I told him I'd try. When I shared excerpts

DAY THREE[48]

from the portion of the interview about the possibility that Jim Toop took his own life, my friend asked me why the interview had grown so tense, why I pressed William Toop the way I did. I told him it was because that's how to get information—push the subject, make him uncomfortable. Then I added, "And we both think he's hiding something, right?" My friend typed, "No shit." I typed, "I'm just trying to find some answers."

48. On this, the third and final day of my conversation with William Toop, I arrived at one, as arranged. I waited for at least two minutes after knocking and, when there still was no sign of Toop, I tried the knob and found the door unlocked. The house was heavy with the smell of Toop's cigarette smoke. I struggled to get a clean breath and left the door open a crack to let good air in. Toop wasn't in the kitchen, but the remnants of his lunch were—a plate with bread crusts left like two broken half-moons. I called out to Toop but received no answer. I made my way through the kitchen and into the dining room, then to the living room, all wood paneled walls and expensive looking leather furniture. Toop was asleep in one of the chairs. When I woke him, I could smell alcohol on his breath. He opened his eyes and flinched when he saw me. "You're early," he said. "I was on time," I replied. "It's almost 1:10." Toop asked if he could have a few mo-

DM: Rough night?[49]

DM: Feeling alright, Mr. Toop?

DM: Would you like a glass of water? Some coffee?

DM: Maybe you could tell me a bit about your son as a boy. We've talked about his teen years and his adult life, but not his childhood.

DM: Or I can come back later. Would you like to rest?

---

ments to wash up before we got started. I helped him out of his chair and watched him stagger down the hall. I could hear him retch in the bathroom. I made my way down the hall, lined with photographs, and knocked on the door, asked if he was ok. While I waited for him to finish vomiting, I noticed a picture of Jim Toop standing alone on a sunny day in front of a revival style mansion with pillars on the front porch. He was wearing white pants and a matching high-collared shirt, was taking a step toward the photographer. The image seemed to emulate another famous photo with which I was familiar—a photograph of Elvis Presley walking away from Graceland. I squinted and tried to get a better look at the house in the background, but the hallway was dark and the photo a bit blurry. As I examined the image, I was startled by William Toop, who, between gagging sounds, told me he was fine and ordered me to the kitchen where I should wait for him. While Toop finished up, I wiped down the kitchen table and set up my gear. There was a pack of Camel's on the fridge. I helped myself to one. As I was finishing the cigarette, Toop, slightly more composed than when I previously saw him, arrived at the table and sat across from me. I noted the heavy circles beneath his eyes, the stray wisps of hair sticking up on his head.

49. Toop didn't respond to my opening salvo of inquiries. I am leaving them intact for posterity's sake, separating each attempt to represent Toop's silence.

DM: How about a drink? Some scotch, perhaps? What have you got?[50]

WT: There's Wild Turkey in the freezer.

DM: The freezer?

WT: The fucking freezer. And grab my smokes while you're up.

DM: Rough night, then?

WT: Every night is rough at my age. This is a rough morning.

DM: You drink like this every night?

WT: That's not what I meant. Every night is rough so sometimes I drink enough to make some nights less rough. Pay for it in the morning, though. At least the mornings are a less lonely, less dangerous brand of rough.

DM: Why are the nights so rough?

WT: What doesn't make the night so rough? You're not a young man. You understand how years can accumulate and prevent sleep. I'm tired and bored and have a lifetime of disappointments to look back on. Sometimes I piss the bed because I can't get up. Fuck. Don't try to tell me you fall asleep so easily. Don't pretend your life has been easy. You're what, fifty-five, sixty?[51]

DM: Old enough to piss the bed, too, sometimes.

---

50. Due to his current condition, I was uncomfortable offering Toop more alcohol, but his unresponsiveness left me little choice. I felt I could either wait until he started talking or leave.

51. For as hung-over and, perhaps, still drunk as Toop was, I was surprised at his coherence.

WT: You think that'll mean something to me? That we'll be friends, now? Fine, you're old enough. And you don't have any kids. You're writing about music for a shitty magazine. I don't see a ring on that finger. Maybe you never married, maybe you're divorced. Maybe you married and your wife died. Doesn't matter. All that shit eats you up, though, I bet.[52] You don't know what it's like to lose a son, though. For him to be in your life and then for him to be more-or-less gone.

DM: What do you mean by more-or-less?[53]

WT: He haunts me.

DM: Haunts you?

WT: Not literally—I'm talking royalty checks and phone calls from lawyers who need me to sign off on reissues or licensing. That's all. You know what that's like, to be alone; no kids, no wife. You and I, we might as well be dead.[54]

---

52. This was quickly turning into one of the more uncomfortable interviews I'd ever conducted.

53. Toop paused for several moments, here, lowered his head to his chest and made sounds as if struggling to swallow. I reached for the garbage can in case he was going to be sick. He waved me off and a moment later, raised his head, coughed, and answered.

54. When I showed this portion of the interview to my friend, I was surprised that his first response was to say, "I'm glad you're not dead." A moment later, he added, "Did you ask him about the *Star Wars* stuff?" I typed, "What if his son is really dead?" And added, "What would you do then?" My friend said, "Tell people the truth." I said, "People already know the truth." My friend said, "I can confirm it." I typed, "You'll be disappointed if he's dead." My friend wrote, "I just need to know. Something about all of this feels off." I wrote, "What if there isn't a conspiracy here? What if Jim Toop really did just stumble into the desert and die?" My

DM: I'm perfectly happy.

WT: No, you're not. You're a wreck like me. I bet you think about dying. You ever try to off yourself?

DM: Do you want me to go?[55]

WT: You're not going anywhere.

DM: Excuse me?

WT: You haven't got what you came for.

DM: And what did I come for?

---

friend said, "You don't have to be such a Scully." "A Scully?" I asked. He said, "Mulder's partner? On *The X-Files*?" Then: "The skeptical one?" It had been years since I'd watched *The X-Files*, so his reference took a minute to sink in. "So, I'm Scully to your Mulder, then?" I asked. He said, "Sure. You're my sidekick." I said, "Oh really? Which one of us is interviewing William Toop in Los Angeles and which one of us is typing from his bedroom in his mother's house and has to go to school in the morning?" He said, "You're only in Los Angeles because of me." I told him I should have a good, long talk with his mother. "Just tell me—did you or didn't you ask Toop about the movies?" I told him he had to wait for me to transcribe more. "What did he say?" my friend typed. I said, "Be patient." "You're an asshole," my friend typed. I said, "I know." And I actually did feel like an asshole, especially since I was holding back more than my young friend possibly could have imagined.

55. Despite the fact that I'd neither learned anything meaningful from this interview, nor asked about the Graceland photograph, I meant this, mostly because I just didn't know how to continue. After I sent these few lines to my friend, he typed, "It doesn't end here." I kept him in suspense long enough that he typed, "Does it?" After I finally transcribed and sent the next few lines, he typed, "I hate you."

WT: Fuck if I know, but you don't have it or you wouldn't keep coming back. Why are you here?[56]

DM: Did your son know Elvis Presley?

WT: Of course my son didn't know Elvis Presley. Is that why you're here? What kind of a question is that?

DM: I was admiring that picture of him in the hall, by the bathroom while you were freshening up. It's emulating a famous picture of Elvis.

WT: Is it now?

DM: It is—your son even dressed the part. Where was that?

WT: Graceland.

DM: Do you know who took the picture?

WT: The picture of Elvis?

DM: The picture of your son.

WT: Some woman. They went on a road trip to see Graceland. Took the tour and all that.

DM: Was it the woman from New Mexico?

WT: Fuck if I know—Jim had his ladies. It could have been the gal from New Mexico.

DM: Angela?

---

56. I considered telling Toop why, specifically, I was here, but decided against it since he'd previously made reference to royalties and licensing his son's music. Instead, I decided to try something a bit less orthodox.

WT: Could have been—or it could have been Annie, or Jessica, or Michelle, or Abigail. I know why you keep bringing up this Angela. All of you music writer types do.[57]

DM: Did you know her?

WT: Maybe? We've covered this—if she was the gal Jim was dating when we lived in New Mexico, then I met her once or twice.

DM: You said that your son and this woman took the Graceland tour, correct?

WT: Why else would they go?

DM: It's a good picture.[58]

WT: You think that one's good...[59]

---

57. When given the choice between following up on Angela, or following up on Toop being at Graceland, I gave my personal interests precedent and chose Angela first. In retrospect, this was a foolish risk. I was lucky to learn what I eventually learned about Toop. Assuming I can say that I "learned" anything.

58. I was trying to get Toop to talk about the picture without asking him questions. I needed to play it cool, not to tip my hand and show my interest. The results of this strategy far surpassed my expectations.

59. Here, Toop got up from the table, almost falling over in the process. I helped him a few steps out of the kitchen until he told me he could walk on his own. He was gone for several minutes and I was about to check on him when he returned with a picture of Jim Toop at a procession past Elvis's grave, held annually on the anniversary of The King's death. He looked older in this picture, in his forties maybe, but it was unmistakably Jim Toop. I did everything I could to conceal my excitement and surprise, while recognizing that, suddenly, this was all seeming al-

WT: You can have it. I've got a copy.[60]

DM: Can I tell you something that I think?

WT: You can tell me anything you think, but that doesn't mean I'm going to be interested in it.

DM: I don't think that your son died when he disappeared, and you know it—maybe he's dead now, or not, I don't know—but he lived for at least twenty years after his disappearance.

WT: Why would you think a thing like that?

DM: Graceland.

WT: What does Graceland have to do with it?

DM: It didn't open until five years after your son disappeared. And you just showed me a picture of your son from *twenty years* after his disappearance.

WT: Is that what you want? For me to tell you that my son never died? That he faked his disappearance? I can tell you that. I know that story, too. And even if that one were true, it wouldn't change anything. I've still lost a son.

---

most *too* easy.

60. I picked up the photograph and examined it more closely. In the background, just legible behind Toop, was a sign indicating that it was the 20th anniversary of Elvis's death—1997, twelve years later than I'd been able to realistically hypothesize Toop had been alive. And that was it then—proof that Jim Toop was alive after his disappearance. I could now say, with confidence, that the version of *Taxidermist's Catalog* I'd heard was probably completely authentic. But this picture raised some additional questions that needed to be pursued. I slipped the photo into my pocket. I wanted it out of sight before my next question.

DM: You don't have to tell me another story.

WT: No, this is a fine story. You'll like it. It goes like this: Jim takes me out for dinner and he *is* in high spirits. He *does* pay for our meal, and he talks excitedly about his tour the entire time. He seems nervous, though. I know he's not on blow—I've seen my share of industry people on blow[61]—but something isn't right. He is nervous or fucked up or something. I keep asking him if everything is ok, because it seems pretty clear to me that everything isn't ok. He says, I'm fine, and then I ask again, and he says, I'm fine, again. And the more I ask, the more impatient Jim sounds until he finally says, Stop asking.

But I don't stop asking, I only start looking for different ways to ask. I ask him how the album is progressing, how his money is holding up, if he's been seeing anyone—he ignores every question and continues to tell me about the tour. He tells me he's already been in touch with a few of his old friends from New Mexico—the girl who was tending bar when I went down there, and yes, before you ask again, her name was Angela, but that's all I really know[62]—and a couple of others.

---

61. Let's not forget this gem published by *Rolling Stone*: "Jim Toop Wants You to Know that All Your Favorite Rock Stars are on Cocaine—Except for Him," which was published in Issue 169, on September 12, 1974—it was the one with Nixon on the cover and some Annie Liebovitz work inside. Coincidentally, the cover also promises an article on "The Tragic History of Jan & Dean." The cover makes no mention of the Toop interview. He was still relatively unknown then.

62. Angela! The dream, the object of desire, of memory, of lust. Finally, I have confirmation that she's real. Perhaps, she'll even become a character in this story—the possibility is thrilling. Unless, of course, William Toop was simply toying with me again.

Anyway, Jim says to me, These are good people. Truth or Consequences is a good place. And I say, Sure, Jim, it's a nice place to visit. And Jim says, I'm thinking of moving there after the tour, after the album comes out. I say, Why would you want to do that? You have venues here, studios, musicians—it'd be career suicide. He says, I need to slow down—it's too much. I say, maybe if you stopped getting high. He says, Stop, Dad. Just stop.

And then the rest went about how you'd expect: we went home and Jim didn't try to give me his tapes because he didn't intend to disappear, not yet, anyway, and then two days later he left for tour and I didn't hear from him again for two years, when I got a phone call from New Mexico, or a letter from Nevada, or a postcard from Ohio—maybe it was one of those, maybe it was all of them—it doesn't matter. Whichever way it happened, right after Jim disappeared, I ended up in New Mexico, drunk at a damn bar, talking to Angela, and I said I saw this thing on the news, and I talked to the cops, and I knew my son had disappeared, and I hoped that the cops would find him, but I didn't think that was likely, and I wished that I could see him just one last time. And this girl, this woman, Angela, whose husband had just died and, though the ring was off her finger, I could still see the white from where it had rubbed against her skin and blocked the sun for however long they'd been married, said: "Your son is ok, Mr. Toop. He's hiding."[63]

---

63. When I shared this with my friend, he asked, "Was the old man fucking with you again?" I typed, "Watch your mouth." Then: "And respect your elders." My friend typed, "Yes sir." I told him that was better. He typed, "I was being sarcastic." Then: "Hurry up—get on with it." And I thought about not getting on with it, because I still wasn't quite sure what had transpired be-

So I asked her, Why is he hiding? What is he hiding from? What the fuck are you even talking about?

And Angela, she said, Something happened, but Jim is ok. He'll be safe. He's fine.

I said, Can I see him?

And Angela told me that wasn't a good idea, not yet. I asked her why not, and she told me it wasn't safe.

I asked her, What does that mean, it's not safe? I asked if Jim was in some sort of trouble.

And Angela, she told me Jim wasn't in any trouble, not exactly, but he could be, which was why he was hiding, why he had to fake his own disappearance. When I asked her for more information, she refused, said Jim didn't want to implicate anyone else, told me I was better off not knowing.

He's my damn son, I said. I have a right to know, I said. Then: Implicate me.

He's okay, Angela said. It's better this way. He'll be in contact.

I asked her why his car was abandoned. Just tell me that, I said.

And here, she leaned over the bar, that girl, put her mouth right up next to my ear and said, We had to do that, we had to make it look like he disappeared.

I said, Is it drugs? Did he hurt someone? Is he hiding from the law?

---

tween William Toop and me in the last leg of the interview. He was definitely still drunk, and much of what he said contradicted other things he was saying, often times within minutes of each other. I wasn't sure if I was ready to revisit it, let alone share it with my friend. Of course, I did push on, and I did share it with my friend. What else was I going to do?

And Angela just put her finger up to her mouth as if to tell me, yes, but it had to be our secret.

And that was that. I got wasted and should have driven myself into the desert to die but instead spent the night in jail, flew home a day later, and waited for a few months, or years, or whatever until I started receiving the occasional postcard or letter, the occasional phone call.

DM: Do you still receive communications from your son?[64]

WT: Of course not. No.

DM: When did they stop?[65]

WT: That doesn't matter.

DM: Of course it matters.

WT: Why would it matter?

DM: It would be helpful to me to know how long your son was alive after his disappearance, and one way to figure that out is looking at his communications with you.

WT: Assuming what I told you was true.[66]

---

64. When I asked this, Toop's face tightened and he looked hard and angry down at the tape deck. I almost thought to slide the machine closer to me to protect it. Something strange was going on in the man's head. I can only imagine what it might have been.

65. Again, a long, long pause from William Toop here.

66. And here, suddenly, Toop's voice was full of ice. If I hadn't seen him staggering around the house just moments before, I'd have believed he was stone cold sober when he said this. Looking back on this moment as I type these transcripts, I wonder if Toop's story gave away more than he intended, and the result

DM: So your story wasn't true?

WT: I don't even know

DM: Why even bother with bullshit—you're the one who invited me back.

WT: I haven't the slightest idea what I was thinking.

DM: Have you told me anything true?

WT: I've told you plenty of true things.

DM: Which ones.

WT: I don't know—

DM: Was Angela real?

WT: Sure.

DM: Why did your son really go into hiding?

WT: I don't know—let's say someone turned him in for holding weed, or he stumbled across a top-secret government conspiracy and they needed to silence him, or he killed someone, or maybe it was just like I said before and he was just so drunk and/or high, sad and fucked up that he just went off his goddam nut and had a psychotic break and walked into the desert. Take your pick.

---

was sobering. Perhaps the day's conversation had been an act. Or maybe Toop was losing his mind to old age and had no idea what he was saying. What could this man have possibly gained from letting me know his son was alive in 1999 if he was going to back off now? Maybe Toop was up to something else?

DM: Let's go with the last one.[67]

WT: Works as well as any.

DM: So do you think your son is still out there?

WT: No—he's dead. I told you.[68]

---

67. A theory: even though Toop was inventing much of what he was telling me, perhaps the competing narratives were driven by his own uncertainty—that is to say, maybe the elder Toop never actually learned *why* his son went into hiding, or even what had become of his son, outside of a couple of photographs and maybe a few letters, postcards, and phone calls. Maybe William Toop hadn't heard from his son since 1999. Maybe William Toop truly doesn't know if his son is alive or dead. When I explained this idea to my friend, he said, "What do *we* do then? What is our next step?" I typed, "Do we need to know if Jim Toop is alive?" My friend said, "Yes," as I expected him to. He was right. If there was any possibility of Jim Toop being alive, I'd need to pursue it, for my own curiosity, my young friend's inexplicable interest, and due to possible issues with the eventual release of *Taxidermist's Catalog*. To my friend, I typed, "The next step is I go to New Mexico and see if I can pick up Jim Toop's trail, three and a half decades after it went cold."

68. Still, I have no idea what to make of Toop's wild vacillations over the course of the interview. I began to wonder if William Toop was feeding me poorly constructed, bullshit stories with just enough real information sprinkled in to encourage me to go looking for his son. Perhaps this is a paranoid thought on my part—after all, if this was the case, had he just been honest I'd have gladly helped. But maybe there was something about being a parent of an adult that made asking such a thing difficult. I still don't know what William Toop was up to, or if it was even purposeful at all. If it wasn't, though, he was quite bad at keeping his son's secrets safe. As for these repeated proclamations of his son's death, I wondered if they might be a mechanism William Toop used to protect himself from the realization that his son didn't want to be in contact with him.

DM: Was he officially pronounced dead? When did he die?[69]

WT: He was declared dead eventually. I don't remember when. In truth, though, let's say I haven't heard from him in five years. So, let's say he died five years ago, but ten, fifteen, twenty—doesn't matter.

DM: Did anyone ever contact you to tell you he'd died?

WT: Sure. I don't know. This is all fiction, anyway, so sure. The bartender, Angie, Angela—she sent me a letter with the return address from the Pin Hole Bar.[70] When I saw the envelope, I thought it might have been an old tab from my visit.

DM: What was inside the envelope?

WT: Just a letter, pretty much said, Dear Mr. Toop, Your damn son is dead. Sorry.

DM: That must have been some letter. Still have it?

---

69. At this point, I was grasping at straws. Trying anything to find a more concrete answer.

70. Upon reading this portion of the transcript, my friend was quick to note the specificity of the bar's name. After a quick Google search, he confirmed that there is, in fact, a Pin Hole Bar in Truth or Consequences, New Mexico. "He couldn't be making this up," my friend said. Then: "He has to have either been there since the bar opened, heard about it from his son, or this letter is real." I said, "If the letter is real, that would mean Jim Toop is dead." My friend wrote, "Or his father is lying about that part." I said, "So you're believing only the parts you want to believe?" My friend said, "Do we have a choice? Look at how inconsistent he's been? How can we believe anything?" I said, "But you want to believe the letter is real?" My friend said, "It's something to go on—a place to begin looking. Maybe this Angela still works there." The prospect thrilled me.

WT: Of course not.

DM: Is any of what you've told me true?

WT: Why not. Might as well be. Any of these stories, they all have the same result. In some of them I get to stay in touch with him for a while, in others he's just gone. You tell me. Does it matter which one, if any, is true?

DM: I guess it doesn't.

WT: Either way, I'm old and alone and my son is not part of my life.

DM: I have to ask, also—you've mentioned your son's missing tapes a couple of times. Do you know where they are?

WT: Probably with Jim somewhere. Buried in the ground with him or rotting on a shelf.

DM: Was he working on the album after his disappearance?[71]

WT: How would I know? He could have been.[72]

DM: Can I ask about something else?

WT: By all means.

---

71. Though this line of questioning yielded no results, I had to ask. I had all the information I needed already, though.

72. This led to a long pause. I was exhausted by Toop's theatrics and didn't know where to go. I'm not sure why—the pictures of Toop at Graceland made what I was about to ask irrelevant—but I decided to ask about the sci-fi movies, like my friend had been begging me to do since the interview's first day.

DM: The first day I was here, you talked about your son's thoughts about some science fiction films and shows.[73]

WT: I hardly see how this is relevant to anything.

DM: It's not, really. Just seems like an interesting angle to open an article about a man who many believe was abducted by aliens.

WT: If it's not relevant, then why waste our time? Why pander?

DM: Why not? It'll sell more copies.

WT: It seems unhealthy, to me, to further legitimize the fantasies of the mentally unbalanced.

DM: That's what we do. You used to make sound effects for motion pictures. Used to slap steaks with bags of gravel to make fictions more believable.

WT: I never slapped steaks with bags of gravel.

DM: It doesn't matter—just tell me again about your son's thoughts on *Battlestar Galactica* and *The Empire Strikes Back*.

WT: He hated the first, loved the second. Like I told you the other day, he called me up after watching *The Empire Strikes Back* and couldn't stop talking about how Darth Vader was Luke's father. He said, To have that much evil in you—it's scary. He said, And to not even know it.[74]

---

73. "It's about fucking time," my friend typed. "Watch your mouth," I typed. "Hurry the fuck up and transcribe," my friend typed. I responded, "Watch your mouth or I won't send it to you." He wrote: "Fine. I'm sorry I swore." Then: "Now hurry up with that goddamn transcript."

74. When I sent this part of the transcript to my friend, he

That's what my son thought about that *Star Wars* movie, Mr. Morus. He was moved by it, frightened by it. And he thought *Battlestar Galactica* and its film version were weak rip-offs.

DM: Fascinating.[75]

WT: Not really. So what next? You go home to wherever you're from and write an article, make a few hundred bucks, and go back to eating frozen dinners in front of the television every night?

DM: Are you talking about me or you?

WT: Probably both of us.

DM: I guess we're pretty similar.

WT: So is that it?

DM: One more thing[76]—is this the most recent picture you have of your son?

WT: Probably. I don't know, but probably.

DM: I have to ask one more time: is your son still alive?

---

said only, "Thank you."

75. Here, my young friend asked, "Does this tell us anything we didn't already know?" I told him no, that there were more revealing moments in the interview. My friend typed, "So there wasn't any real reason for you to ask about those movies, was there?" I said, "No." My friend asked, "Then why did you?" I didn't know how to answer that.

76. I reached into my pocket and produced the 1997 picture of Jim Toop at Graceland. I examined it for a moment then put it down on the table.

WT: You're a dense motherfucker, you know that?[77]

DM: You haven't answered anything.

WT: I've answered everything.[78]

DM: Bullshit—I have as many questions now as when I came in.[79]

WT: Remember when we were talking about Ohio, Mr. Morus? And I told you how bad I felt for taking my boy away from Ohio and planting him in New Mexico? How I didn't understand how much he loved Ohio, and how I couldn't understand why?

DM: I remember.

WT: Why do you think I told you that?

DM: Because we were talking about disappointments, about failures.

---

77. I still don't know how to read this. Did Toop call me dense for continuing to ask about something he believed was pointless asking about? Or was it because he'd knowingly provided a web of information and helpful stories that, while not directly answering my questions, provided the framework for which a search for Toop could be enacted?

78. With this cryptic assertion, I was ready to give up and leave. Of course, William Toop wasn't yet finished with his cryptic surprises.

79. I didn't yet understand, like I think I do now, that this was what William Toop was trying to do and, in a way, these new questions answered some of my initial questions. This started to make sense with a few hours distance from the interview, when I had a chance to settle in at the hotel and begin transcribing.

WT: I told you that because it was the one true moment I shared with my son after he started playing music. Even when we'd talk about his mother, neither of us knew how to say anything real to each other. And so that moment that Jim sat here and played through his Ohio songs, all dripping with nostalgia—that was important. And really, if you want to get down to it, Jim was already gone by then, pining away for the past all the time. It wasn't that he didn't like New Mexico, or even California—he loved them both. It was never about the places, for Jim, it was about the past. He went back to New Mexico, and disappeared into that past. The only thing that surprised me at all was that he disappeared there instead of Ohio.

DM: Why do you think that was?

WT: You know as well as I do and I haven't the slightest fucking idea. Now, are you finished with this foolishness?

DM: I don't have any more questions for you, no.

WT: But are you done, is what I'm asking.

DM: I might make one more stop.

WT: Do I even need to ask?

DM: New Mexico.[80]

---

80. I still had some of the cash Richard Epps had sent with me, but I'd need additional resources if I was going to add a final leg to the trip. I had no idea how long I'd need to be in New Mexico. I could show up, find Angela and have the entire story spelled out for me, or I might have to poke and prod, to dig around and ask strangers a slew of hard questions before finding anything resembling the truth. When I finish transcribing the interview, I

WT: Saw that coming. Here—let me fix this for you.[81]

DM: What did you do that for?

WT: It's more authentic now.[82]

DM: Thanks for everything.[83]

WT: When you get to New Mexico, Mr. Morus—say hello to my son for me.[84]

---

will send these transcripts to Richard Epps in the hope that he'll agree to finance my investigation for just a little while longer. Of course, my friend was thrilled to hear that I might be traveling to New Mexico. "I want to come too," he said. "You can't come. You have school," I said. He said, "I need to come." I typed, "What about your mom? What if there's nothing to find?" My friend typed, "We'll deal with that when we have to." He typed, "I'm old enough to travel on my own." I said, "I'm worried you'll be disappointed. Why waste time and money before I at least find out if it's worth your while." I said, "Can I at least talk to your mother about this?" My friend said, "She doesn't even know who you are. You can't contact her. I can tell her it's for a school trip, print up some fake permission slips, make up a fake Science Olympiad flier. It'll be easy." I said, "Don't do anything that will get you in trouble." I knew I couldn't stop him. Before I logged off, I typed, "Be safe." My friend typed, "I will."

81. Here, Toop picked up the picture of his son at Graceland in 1997 and held the lit edge of his cigarette over his son's face. I wanted to stop him, to yell at him, but there was something oddly moving about watching this man slowly burn his son's face out of the picture.

82. He said this sliding the picture back across the table to me.

83. I was angry about the photograph, and frustrated with all of Toop's conflicting answers—I didn't really mean this.

84. With this cryptic phrase, a phrase I never shared with my young friend, William Toop reached out, stopped my tape deck from recording and walked away from the table. I didn't ask him

what he meant. I knew he wouldn't tell me. Maybe he meant I should pay respects at his son's grave, or maybe he meant I'd find Jim Toop alive and well, or maybe he just wanted me to wander out to the middle of the desert and scream hello into the nothingness. I packed my gear in silence and left his house, called out "thank you" one more time on my way out the front door. I wonder if William Toop wants me to find his son—his closing statement seemed inevitable, deliberate, planned, as if he knew it was coming the entire time I'd been interviewing him. Or maybe he was just having one last laugh at my expense. All I really know is that, soon, I will pack my suitcase and I will think of the past, of Jim Toop's past, and William Toop's past, and my own past, and all of those pasts will feel heavy and sick. I will look into my suitcase and I will sweat. Then, Richard Epps permitting, I will be on my way to New Mexico.

IV. YOUR SUNGLASSES ARE IN THE JUNK DRAWER

From Main Street, standing on the roof of, let's say, the old Cortez, you will see only a plateau of squat, flat-roofed buildings that open mostly into an expansive horizon—just southeast, across the Rio Grande, sits the famed, magnificent Turtleback Mountain, but in every other direction there are only blue skies and desert, cracked and dusty. El Cortez is our only movie theater. It was built in 1941—or as early as 1935, depending on who you ask—with a single screen and just under 600 seats. If we want to go to a movie without a long drive, El Cortez is our only option. The next closest theater is in Las Cruces, about seventy miles down I-25, but if there's a movie worth seeing, the drive is worth it because they've got a few of those big multiplexes that show eight or ten or a dozen movies. The trip is a fucking hassle, but we don't mind, really. It's what we have to accept living in a city of less than 8,000 people in the middle of the goddamn desert. That's just the way we live.

We've accepted what it means to live in T or C, or formally, Truth or Consequences or, formerly, Hot Springs. It was called Hot Springs from about 1916, after work on the Elephant Butte dam was finished, until 1950 when the quiz show *Truth or Consequences* offered to broadcast an episode live from any city that adopted the show's name as its own. At this point, thinking of our town as Hot Springs seems odd as it's been T or C almost twice as long as it was ever Hot Springs. After the city changed its name, Ralph Edwards—he was the quiz show's host—came to our city on the first week of every year until the new millennium, which was just a few years before he died. When he was still coming to town, Edwards's visits were always an excuse for a big celebration that someone, somewhere along the line started calling "Fiesta"—we still celebrate it during the first week of May, every year. We like Fiesta. We throw a parade in which children's clubs ride in the backs of pickup trucks and wave, and we have a beauty contest, and we dance in the park, which is called Ralph Edwards Park because since we'd already named our town after the man's quiz show, why not name our park after the man himself? For the view alone, the park is exquisite—is one of the best places in town from which to see Turtleback Mountain in all its unobstructed glory. If you catch the mountain's precipice at just the right angle, you'll see the turtle looking down on us, judging us, protecting us, guiding us home and weeping for its loneliness, for the desolation of the desert and its people—its tears fill our hot springs. At least that's what we tell visitors these days.

If we seem to be going on about *Truth or Consequence* and Ralph Edwards and Fiesta, it's because there isn't much else to go on about. The most noteworthy thing to happen here in recent history was back in 1999 when a young woman escaped from David Parker Ray's "toy box," out by the Elephant Butte Reservoir—it's a lovely reservoir—and made her way naked in chains, out into the world and to the authorities, which finally led to the arrest of that evil man. We didn't even know that this had been going on right up the road from us, didn't really hear about the women Ray kidnapped, tortured, and killed until the rest of the country was hearing about it too. It made us all feel sick, anxious, disgusted that such a thing could be happening right under our noses. When Ray died of a heart attack soon after his prosecution, we were relieved. His death could never lift the dark veil his actions left over our town, but once he was gone we felt a little bit safer in our quiet little corner of the desert. Of course, we still get some serial killer-obsessed tourists in town to see where David Parker Ray did his evil. We neither like nor approve of their interests, but at least they keep to themselves. We don't get a ton of tourists around here so it's generally pretty easy to figure out who is who—we can tell the fuckers who are interested in Ray because they'll ask questions about Elephant Butte and its reservoir, and every once in a while we'll catch a glimpse of a dog-eared "true crime" book sticking out of a purse or a back pocket. Our other tourists are mostly folks on retreat for the spas, or to spend some time at the artist colony. And then there are the Jim Toop people, who are, on a moral level, less unsettling than the Ray people, but who tend to be far more of a nuisance. Though their numbers have diminished over the years as Toop's disappearance has faded from cultural memory, these tourists, still come to town behaving like detectives. They go to restaurants and bars, acting all casual as they ask obtusely worded questions about UFO's and cults and whatever other bullshit they're interested in. Because a song on one of Toop's albums, *Your*

Sunglasses are in the Junk Drawer—widely regarded as his "New Mexico" album—is called "Wind Chimes" (not to be confused with the Beach Boys song of the same name), they want to buy our wind chimes. Because there's a song on the same album called "Kite Flyin'," they want to fly kites here. Because the album includes a song named "Angela," they want to know who Angela is. We tell them there is no Angela, here, and when they say, "8,000 people live here, of course there's an Angela," we say, "Of course there are women here named Angela, but none of them are *that* Angela." When one of them unknowingly meets *that* Angela and asks her if she knows *that* Angela—or worse, if they figure out that her name is Angela and just assume she is *that* Angela, which of course, she is—she tells them, *that* Angela was a parakeet, that the song used the bird's name to tell a story about a fictional woman, or that Angela was a house cat, or even, and this is our favorite, that Angela is a rare breed of cactus that slowly withers away in the desert sun. *That* Angela's interlocutors always leave unsatisfied. Such tourists also want to know where on 25 Toop's rental car was found. When they get there, most of them just stare into the desert, like they're imagining something meaningful happened there, but the more unstable, UFO-minded visitors inevitably produce odd looking pieces of technology that they wave over the asphalt and sand—which, depending on who gives them directions and what kind of mood we're in, may or may not be the actual, approximate spot where Toop's car was found—to measure radiation and take whatever other readings they think will prove that there had been extraterrestrial activity there a long, long time ago; even when we send them to the wrong spot, they always seem to find the proof they were seeking. Other Toop fans take to the desert with metal detectors and canteens, in search of—what? We don't know. We've had a few fans go missing over the years, only to wind up in the hospital with snake bites or dehydration. A few have even turned up dead. Every once in a while, we'll get a visitor who just wants to see the place that inspired Toop. They don't want to buy wind chimes, or fly kites, or know anything about Angela. They don't have their own theories about how or why Toop disappeared and they aren't particularly interested in any of the stories we normally tell such visitors—they just like the feel of Toop's music and want to step inside of it for a little while. We often don't even know who they are until we see them taking pictures of the Cortez and its green paneling, which Toop sang about in the song "Sea Foam": "The only theater in town is closed, it's painted sea foam green/She says, 'Babe I call that aqua, what does sea foam even mean?'"

And then there's one last breed of visitor who comes to T or C because of Jim Toop, but I'd hardly call them tourists. These are professionals, music journalists and historians, mostly, seeking some secret truth thought to be left uncovered, even after decades of other peoples' trying, as if somehow every other journalist, historian, and amateur sleuth failed to discover a crucial piece of information that might finally, at long last, solve the mystery of Toop's disappearance—"This Music Journalist Traveled to New Mexico to Investigate the Decades-Old Disappearance of Jim Toop—You Won't Believe What He found!" These assholes are arrogant and presumptuous. They believe they are better than all who came before, that they are worthier, cleverer. They are not. They will fail. Any secrets to be had here have already been washed away by time or unearthed by the decades of visitors who came before. If there are any secrets to be found, inquisitive types might be wise to consider why it is, exactly, that those secrets have gone undiscovered for so long.

But this is not how such visitors think; that is why they come and disturb our routines and turn our little city inside out. Like this new visitor, driving south into town on I-25. He takes a room at the Desert Ridge Inn, which is nice enough not to rent out rooms by the hour, but seedy enough that our town's three prostitutes, and sometimes the traveling girls from Albuquerque or Santa Fe, set up shop to exchange money for sex. One nice thing about the Desert Ridge: because it's right there on the edge of town, from every room, guests can stare straight out into the wide open guts of the desert. A lot of visitors will stay at the Ridge for the view alone, though folks made nervous by spaces that are too wide open, or by the possibility of desert life slithering in beneath their doors are better off avoiding this particular motel. We know this is where our new visitor is staying, and we know, already, why he is here because before he even finished checking in, he was asking the desk clerk—a local gal named Echelle—questions about Jim Toop this, and Jim Toop that, and telling her how he stopped on 25, a few miles outside of town where Toop's car was found, and he got out of his own rental to admire the awesome blackness and impossible limitlessness of the desert at night. This caused Echelle to suppress a laugh because most of us take it all for granted. We know all this because after the stranger retired to his room, Echelle took to Facebook and announced to her friends, family, and acquaintances that she'd just met a funny stranger named Daniel Morus, from whom, many of us could almost certainly expect a visit in the following days. She didn't do this to warn us, but simply because she thought he was funny. We looked him up though; we know he isn't *just* funny. We know he has a history of writing about Toop. We know why he's here.

It's safe to say that, just as many of us take the desert for granted, we've come, too, to take these kinds of visitors for granted. Though many of us aren't directly affected by the arrival of a man like Daniel Morus, it's difficult not to think of a few among us who are steeling themselves for what's to come. We know that all the Angela's in town, especially *that* Angela, will be on guard and won't relax until our new visitor leaves. We know that Al Walters, who runs a junk shop downtown, will close his store for a few days in case our visitor has done his research and knows that he gave Toop his first guitar. There are others who are probably on edge as well, folks who worked at the local paper back in '77, some of the older cops who know a thing or two about Toop's missing person case, and who knows who else. Maybe these folks know a thing or two, maybe they don't. Even if they do know anything meaningful, we doubt this new visitor will be resourceful enough to find them—nobody else has. There is always the chance that a visitor might have some new knowledge, might start sniffing around previously unchecked corners, but we won't know if that's a possibility until the visitor starts talking to people. We're not worried. We have nothing to hide—most of us, anyway.

In the coming days, some of us we will regret this cavalier attitude. Most of us, though, won't know any better, will gawk at the drama and gossip at the resulting rumors, will be shocked by the outcome of it all. But for now, we ask, how much power can the past truly have? How much of a shock to the present can decades-old secrets truly provide?

THE FIRST DAY

Before we can even begin to answer such questions, we first need to get to know our new visitor, which, as it happens, might be tricky. This Daniel Morus, he doesn't talk to anyone, at least at first. That first morning, after spending the night at the Desert Ridge, he parks his car downtown, a couple of blocks away from the Cortez, and walks over to Wanda's Deli, where he eats poached eggs and chorizo. Perhaps he doesn't notice, but as soon as he walks in, a young, waitress with red hair clumsily pulls her nametag from her apron. Her first and middle names—her friends use both in quick succession—are Angie Leigh, and though she's about thirty years too young to have been the subject of Toop's song, ever since she's been old enough to start work at Wanda's most of the Toop enthusiasts who come to town pester her up and down the diner, trying to see if she might be *that* Angela. When Toop enthusiasts ask her, Angie Leigh laughs, says, "Of course not, sugar." Then she'll smile big and say, "Don't be silly." If the visitor persists, Angie Leigh says, "I wasn't even born when that song was released," which usually stops the visitors dead in their tracks because, in addition to being only twenty-two, Angie Leigh looks young for her age—could pass for eighteen, maybe sixteen.

We should point out that thinking Angie Leigh could be the subject of Toop's song is only natural. *That* Angela, the real Angela who *is* the subject of Toop's song, is in her sixties, and, though she is still a stunning beauty, her hair is more gray than red now; she has been weathered by the desert and seasoned by life. When Toop enthusiasts come looking for her, they are looking for the woman they imagine when they hear that song. Because we all grow old, *that* Angela isn't exactly the Angela from the song "Angela," not anymore. Or rather, she *is* that woman, but forty-odd years on. For Toop enthusiasts, the song is the only way they know to imagine Angela, and so they picture a young, beautiful woman, brimming with passion and sexuality. If the song were a snapshot, it would be an image of a girl like Angie Leigh. For *that* Angela though, the song is a snapshot of what she was like then, that year when Jim Toop lived in T or C, and the years that followed when the two sent letters back and forth across deserts and mountains, the way young people sometimes do. It would be unfair and untrue to say that that Angela no longer exists in *that* Angela, but we understand why the Toop enthusiasts might struggle to imagine that *that* Angela actually is the Angela they seek.

But this, it seems, isn't a problem for Daniel Morus, who barely talks to Angie Leigh, despite her red hair, after ordering his poached eggs and chorizo. He says thank you when the young woman fills his water, and he asks for his check when he's done. He doesn't ask questions that cause Angie Leigh to say "Of course not" and "Don't be silly" and "I wasn't even born when that song was released." Over the course of the next few days, Angie Leigh will tell all her regulars that she was almost disappointed that Daniel Morus didn't pay any attention to her, that, as an experiment, she even signed her name on the bill when she left it on his table: "Thx, Angie," it read, followed by a hastily drawn smiley face. "And still he barely even looked at me," she'll say. Then: "There's something different about this one. He's either smarter or more apathetic or both." And Angie Leigh's customers will say things like, "Sounds like an odd one, for sure," and "He doesn't have to be *that* much smarter to realize you're too young to be *that* Angela."

As the day progresses, despite Mr. Morus's initial burst of enthusiasm to Echelle, most everyone who sees or encounters our visitor assumes that he's more a tourist than a journalist or investigator. After his breakfast at Dawn's, he walks by the Cortez and takes pictures of its "sea foam" green exterior. Later in the day, he visits Lynn Knapp's gift shop that specializes in, but doesn't limit its stock to, wind chimes, primarily because the Toop tourists like to buy authentic wind chimes from T or C, even though they're mostly made in China and Korea. When Ms. Knapp, a retired math teacher who actually had Toop in class back in 1965, asks Morus if she can help him, he mutters a shy, "No thanks," and continues to browse the store's stock, occasionally reaching up and running a finger along a set of chimes then pausing to listen as their rich tones resonate through the shop. When talking to her book club later in the day, Ms. Knapp will describe Morus as aloof and awkward. She will say he seemed nervous to the point that she thought, for a moment, he might be a shoplifter, but that when she asked if he liked wind chimes, he told her, curtly, that he didn't. She will tell her book club that when she asked Daniel Morus why he'd come to town, he told her he was looking for someone, which Lynn thought was strange at first, and caused her some alarm until her book club reminds her that many of the town's visitors who come because of Toop make up false reasons for their visits, either because they're embarrassed by the idea that they've come to T or C to investigate a long vanished musician, or to mask their true intentions so that they can continue their inquiries discreetly. We always know what they're up to, though. As for why Lynn Knapp might have reason to worry, only she knows.

After Daniel Morus leaves Lynn Knapp's gift shop, he is off the grid for several hours. Maybe he is taking a drive down to the ghost towns spread throughout the Sierra County desert outside of T or C, or maybe he's hiking or napping. All we know is that he isn't doing anything around any of us, at least until a little after three, when Frankie Baca spots him trying to fly a kite at Ralph Edwards Park. Frankie Baca works for the Parks Department, is adding a fresh coat of paint to a shelter when he sees Morus. Ralph Edwards park is right on the Rio Grande and it isn't a great place to fly a kite because its open space is peppered with trees, which Daniel Morus learns quickly when his kite becomes tangled in a branch almost as soon as it gets off the ground. After Frankie Baca helps Daniel Morus untangle his kite, the visitor asks if, by chance, Frankie Baca might have a smoke. Frankie doesn't, having quit seven years ago when his baby girl, Magda, was born. Daniel Morus mutters a brief, "Thanks," and gestures to his kite, which is lying flat on the ground, then walks down to the river, kite dragging behind him, and stares out at Turtleback Mountain. Frankie is still watching the stranger when his boss, José Jackson, returns from the restroom. He asks Frankie who the guy is down by the river.

Frankie says, "I don't know, boss, but I think it might be a good thing that the river is slow and low, today, and that we don't have a bridge for jumping, because something's not right with him." This causes José to laugh. He says, "Who is that walking up to him?" Both men squint into the distance at the second form, now standing beside the visitor. The second man gives Morus a cigarette and lights it. Frankie says, "I think it's just Vic," to which José says, "Homeless Vic?" even though Vic isn't really homeless. Vic just seems homeless because of the way he dresses and keeps to himself, but lives in an efficiency apartment on the edge of town and only works odd jobs, even though he always seems to have money. This is all made stranger by the fact that Vic is old. Usually, T or C's bohemian types are in their twenties or thirties, but Homeless Vic is old and he doesn't wear his age particularly well, thanks especially to his scraggly beard and gray, unkempt dread locks, which he grew out about five years ago. He seems more like an old man's desperate attempt to remain youthful than a true bohemian spirit, but what do we know? Frankie suspects that Vic is probably a trust fund artist, which we sometimes get out here because of the artist retreat—they come a few times to work and like the town enough that they eventually wander down and never leave. It's not uncommon for folks to see Vic painting around town, or taking pictures with a nice looking camera, and every couple of years, his art will wind up in the local galleries. Occasionally, he'll sell a few pieces, but such sales couldn't possibly be enough to pay whatever bills he has. A few of our other residents, Frankie's uncle, who fancies himself a mystery novelist, among them, claim to have read the first three chapters of Vic's novel-in-progress, a thinly veiled fictionalization of the David Parker Ray murders. But for all that, nobody really knows for sure who Vic is, from where he came, or even when he first showed up. Now, he just haunts this place like a ghost, drifting around town and doing whatever he does. José says, "Why do people waste time on that dipshit? And Frankie says, "Why not—he's not hurting anyone, I don't think?" José says, "Some of our most upstanding citizens talk about his art, and what has he ever done for this place or its people?" Frankie says, "Upstanding citizens? What, some artists, some natural 'healers', a masseuse, some bartenders and the town junk shop owner?" José says, "He's buddy, buddy with the police," to which Frankie says, "Everyone is buddy, buddy with the police here," and both men laugh and hop into the truck to head to their respective homes, where José will eat a frozen dinner and watch reruns of 90's sitcoms from when he was a teenager and life was still full of promise, and Frankie will spend the evening cooking dinner with his wife and helping his little girl—now a second grader—with a school project about how T or C got its name. As the two men pull out of the park, Frankie looks down to where Daniel Morus and Homeless Vic had been standing by the river, but Morus is gone, and Vic is walking away. José sees it too, says, "Do you think he jumped?" Frankie says, "Maybe Vic pushed him in." José says, "Eh—as long as he can swim he'll be ok," and then he turns out onto South Cedar Street and their work day is over.

*

Later, across town, things begin to get a little bit more interesting when a boy, a young adult or older teenager, perhaps, shows up at the Desert Ridge Inn and tells Echelle that he is supposed to meet his father at the motel, and that an extra key should have been left at the desk. Echelle at first looks up only briefly from the paper work she is filling out at the start of her shift, doesn't get a good look at the young man standing in front of her, laughs, and says, "Go home, Billy," which seems to confuse the young man, whose name, as it turns out, is Fox Morus. When Echelle looks back up at the boy, she doesn't feel so bad about her mistake because Fox Morus does resemble a townie named Billy Boyer, only far, far younger. Echelle grew up with Billy, though, went through school with and in junior high even "dated," Billy—which consisted of watching cable, awkward kissing, and occasional groping; for the record, Billy Boyer was the first man to touch Echelle's breasts under the shirt but over the bra, a fact that everybody in town knows because Echelle's mother caught them in the act and forbade the couple from seeing each other anymore; alas, as they grew older, the two became fast friends, at times, some might say, when both happened to be single "with benefits"—and so here, poor Echelle realizes that she wasn't confusing the boy with the Billy Boyer of the present, but for the younger Billy Boyer who made her more excited than she'd ever been in her life when he squeezed her breasts. Already embarrassed and flustered, Echelle compounds her initial mistake by saying, a bit judgier than intended, "Your name is Fox?" to which the young man says, "It's a nickname. It's what my dad calls me." Feeling bad about the initial confusion and accidentally mocking Fox Morus's name, Echelle assumes that either Daniel Morus had forgotten to tell her about his son's late arrival, or that she had forgotten to make a note of it, so she gives Fox Morus a key to his father's room, then immediately pulls up Facebook on her smart phone and posts a status about how "A young version of Billy Boyer" just showed up at the Desert Ridge Inn. Echelle explains that this new boy is actually the Toop investigator's son, he just happens to look a bit like Billy. Of course, that last bit is going to make some folks worry—but then, some folks like to worry about everything around here.

*

And this is where things start to get trickier still, where Daniel Morus's presence becomes complicated, his mission, murkier and more worrisome. At the same time that Fox Morus is checking into his father's room, Daniel Morus is walking into the Pin Hole Bar—the first bar he's visited here as far as any of us know. He walks right up to the bar where *that* Angela is filling a mug with cheap domestic beer. He sits at a stool, orders a Miller Lite, and introduces himself. When *that* Angela says, "Nice to meet you," without offering her own name, Daniel Morus asks if she has a minute. Angela doesn't answer, so Daniel Morus starts asking questions anyway, at which point, anyone sitting within earshot moves away from the bar, not wanting to be a part of whatever is unfolding. Before he fled, one of the bar's regular's, a man named Big Stu who spends most evenings at the Pin Hole, or The Pin, as some call it, hears Daniel Morus ask *that* Angela if she's ever been friends with or in a relationship with a man named Jim Toop. Big Stu, like many of T or C's residents, doesn't know shit about Jim Toop, but he understands enough to know what happens when Toop fans and investigators come to town and try to talk to *that* Angela. But let's pause here for a moment—the very fact that Daniel Morus is talking to *that* Angela is cause enough for concern, but the bigger issue, here, is that our visitor knew *exactly* how and where to find *that* Angela, and went straight up to her, before talking to anyone else in any meaningful way, leading us to believe that he is, perhaps, more prepared than previous investigators. Now, while nobody in the bar can hear what Daniel Morus and *that* Angela are saying to each other because they all scattered when the conversation began, it is clear to all of them that said conversation isn't pleasant: Morus begins in a confrontational stance, is leaning over the bar, his face less than a foot away from *that* Angela's. Meanwhile, *that* Angela, who began the conversation in a stunned and rigid posture, first begins to sink into the bar, then starts to shrink away. As goes *that* Angela, so goes Daniel Morus, who, too begins to slowly shrink away, his body tightening, coiling, not as if to pounce, but as if he might implode. Somehow, it seems, *that* Angela's shrinking, rather than emboldening her interlocutor, has disarmed him, as if he's recognizing the effect his line of questioning has on *that* Angela, and the more he presses, and he does appear to be pressing because he keeps running his mouth between her short, terse responses, the more he recoils from her recoiling. The encounter lasts for only a few moments before ending with *that* Angela shrinking away as far as she possibly could before suddenly, violently snapping forward, both elbows landing on the bar, her forehead cradled in her hands, while Daniel Morus quietly slips out the front door like a cartoon cat backing away from trouble, right as Wanda Jackson's rendition of "We'll Sing in the Sunshine" begins to play, prompting *that* Angela to walk briskly over to the jukebox, rip its plug from the socket—bending a prong in the process—and announcing last call, three hours earlier than usual. Well, shit—this Daniel Morus might be trouble after all.

*

So what did Daniel Morus and *that* Angela talk about at the Pin Hole Bar? Within moments of Daniel Morus leaving, rumors began to spread. Some sources claim a firsthand account directly from *that* Angela herself, while others claim knowledge via friends and relatives who heard from people who heard from people, etc... Some accounts suggest that Daniel Morus was simply asking basic questions about Jim Toop—"What do you think happened to him?" "When did you first meet him?" "Did you stay in touch after he moved to Los Angeles?"—but that he asked so many of them in rapid succession, while calling *that* Angela out for "incorrect" answers, that he believed were lies—because, obviously, everything in Toop's songs *must* be true—that *that* Angela simply shut down. This scenario would easily justify *that* Angela's response to Daniel Morus, if for no other reason than she isn't used to being cornered and having to confront the fact that she is *that* Angela. Another description of *that* Angela's encounter is more troubling, as it involves Morus saying that he believed Jim Toop was still alive and that *that* Angela knew where to find him. If this is the case, we can hardly blame *that* Angela for crying. Fleeting as his involvement in her life may or may not have been—it's none of our business—she obviously wouldn't want those kinds of old skeletons dug up and to have their bones rattled in her face. Whatever the actual contents of the conversation, though, the consistent, troubling fact on which all accounts agree is that *that* Angela seemed truly scared. Nobody in town remembers *that* Angela ever seeming scared before, about anything. For some, this is reason enough for the rest of us to be at least a little bit worried.

Not that many of us really understand the roots of that worry. Nobody here really knows what happened to Jim Toop—not exactly, or entirely, anyway. Anyone who *does* know has done a fine job of hiding that knowledge from the rest of us. Sure, some know more than others, but if we're going to disregard the local myths and folklore about the man and his disappearance, there isn't much to know outside of the official story, which is this: Jim Toop lived in T or C for a little over a year in the sixties, then he and his father moved away. While living here, Toop made friends, was given a guitar by Al Walters, and started to play. While living in Los Angeles, Toop may or may not have been in contact with *that* Angela but didn't see her again until 1977 when he came to town between a Monday night gig in Albuquerque and a Thursday night gig in Tucson. With two days between obligations, Toop's plan was to spend two nights catching up with friends, then drive to Tucson, arriving in plenty of time for his evening show. All went according to plan, at first, and Toop seemed to be having a good enough time from the moment he rolled into town, that he let his friends—*that* Angela among them—talk him into playing an impromptu set at Cactus Cocktails, a bar that no longer exists. Then, on Wednesday night, after hanging around Cactus Cocktails on his own for a bit, Toop left town without explanation. The next morning, a State Trooper named Frank Lopez discovered Toop's rental car pulled off on the side of I-25, but Toop was gone. The car's hazards had been left on, but since the car's battery had died over night, they weren't blinking by the time Lopez arrived. Local police searched for Toop, but heavy winds overnight wiped away any tracks or traces that might have been used to follow his trail into the desert. Before long, the search was abandoned, and Toop hadn't turned up in any nearby town. Most folks assumed he was dead, and that was that. See—nothing to be scared of in any of that. But then, why was *that* Angela so scared?

*

The last we hear of Morus for the day comes upon his return to the Desert Ridge Inn, fresh off his harassment of *that* Angela at her place of employment. Not long after she sees Daniel Morus pull into the parking lot and enter his room, Echelle takes a noise complaint from one of the rooms directly adjacent to where Daniel and Fox Morus are staying. The complaint, as described by the caller, is of two people arguing. Though the caller, who may or may not be Veronica Morelli—who studies chemistry through Western New Mexico University, at the Gardner Learning Center Satellite Campus, and may or may not make money staying nights at the Desert Ridge Inn, answering texts from local men and inviting them to her room to exchange sex for money—can't make out what is being said. In the end, after a call from Echelle, Morus and his son quiet down and are, presumably, in for the night.

THE SECOND DAY

The following morning, nobody spots Morus until around lunch time when he and his son show up at a sandwich shop on Date St. They don't talk to each other while they eat. After lunch, the duo visit the Truth or Consequences Historical Society where they seek out Randall Heath, who has worked at The Society for thirty years and loves to talk about all things T or C, especially Jim Toop. He has been interviewed multiple times about Toop for mystery television shows, mostly in the late eighties and early nineties, on which he talked about UFO's and cults. Most recently, Randall Heath appeared on a late night, radio call-in show to talk, not only about Toop's disappearance, but also about a number of other UFO sightings around town, including the tasteless and very controversial theory that some of David Ray Parker's unaccounted for victims had actually been abducted by UFO's. Needless to say, Randall has become something of a fringe figure around town. We don't write him off entirely, though, because he's good with the Toop tourists, especially those who want to hear about UFO's. He tells them all the things they want to hear, fills their heads with magnificent stories about noiseless black triangles flying through the sky—capable of changing direction on a whim and emitting small but sharp points of light—coming to steal us in the night. These are the stories Toop fans want, and they are the stories Randall wants to tell, so we let him tell them to anyone willing to listen.

When Daniel Morus and his son arrive at the Historical Society Museum, Randall Heath is in one of the back rooms re-assembling a diorama depicting the historic broadcast of an episode of *Truth or Consequences* from our city. At the center of the diorama is a surprisingly accurate figurine of Ralph Edwards, sculpted by a local artist who goes by the name Pond-o, but whose real name is Seth Pond. After an exchange of pleasantries and introductions, Heath leads his guests through rooms full of geodes, pictures, mannequins dressed in native clothes, and dusty old documents, toward the front door, but stops about halfway there when he notices his visitors eyeing a display about "Lozen: The Woman Warrior," a beloved-around-these-parts historical figure—an Apache woman who sat on her people's council and went on raids with her brother, Victorio, whose death she ultimately helped avenge.

When Randall Heath sees his visitors examining this exhibit, he tells them another story about Lozen. In this story, a Confederate soldier finds himself in Apache care, kept safe from the elements by Lozen and her people until The Woman Warrior herself falls madly in love with him. "But here's the catch," says Randall Heath. "Soon enough, a wagon train passed through, headed west with designs on all that California gold that folks had been talking about.

Lozen's beau, not being particularly interested in living as an Apache forever, hitched his fortune to those wagons and rolled out of town, breaking Lozen's heart and ensuring she'd never marry." At the end of the story, Daniel Morus says, "That sounds like bullshit." Heath shrugs, says, "That's the consensus—but it has a certain poetry to it that some folks like. And it has plenty of echoes through the personal histories of this town's people." Morus says, "Like Angela." Heath tries to play dumb, asks "Angela Who?" When pressed, though, when Daniel Morus reveals that he met Angela and knows who she is, Randall Heath succumbs, says, "Yes, like Angela. But she married, eventually, if not for long." Clearly sensing what he thinks is an opportunity, Daniel Morus asks, "And who did she marry?" Heath chuckles, says, "We're not going to talk about Ms. Boyer today. That's not why you're here, and it's none of our business." Perhaps noting some tension in the interaction, or perhaps simply having stopped paying attention, Fox Morus quickly interjects, "So which one is she?" Heath doesn't know to what or whom, exactly, the young man is referring, then realizes that Fox is still looking at a picture attached to the Lozen display. He shrugs, says, "I doubt we'll ever know for sure," and then he motions for his visitors to follow him towards the front of the museum, prompting Daniel Morus to say, "Where are we going?" Heath says, "To the desert!" Morus says that they don't need to go to the desert, says, "I've already seen the spot where Toop's car was found." Heath says, "You mean you've seen the *alleged* spot where Toop's car was found." As Heath opens the door, Morus's son says, "I'm not going to the desert with this guy, Dan." Here, Randall Heath, who happens to be a bit traditional in some respects, says, "You shouldn't call your father by his first name." Morus begins to disagree, says, "It's ok," but then, after a beat: "You know what? It'd be nice if you called me Dad for a change, like when you were little," which causes Fox Morus to shoot his father an angry look and say, "Yes, Dad." Then: "I'm still not going to the desert with this guy," which prompts Daniel Morus to pull his son aside for a private chat. Randall Heath has no idea what is said while he waits, but whatever Daniel Morus says proves effective as the trio is soon on its way into the desert.

In the car, as is his custom, Randall Heath rattles off a list of UFO sightings in T or C, beginning with a black triangle that was allegedly spotted on June 7, 1954, which, he says, won't show up in any of the sightings databases, but he knows the sighting is legitimate because the witness in question was his own father, who told a story about seeing an "odd airplane shaped like a colonial hat but with blue and red lights lining its edges." Heath also tells his captive audience about a non-descript sighting on April 23, 1964, which, despite being accepted as canon, if not necessarily fact by those who live here, has always been vague in its telling. Attached to this sighting is the telling of a second, more detailed event that happened the very next night and was reported by a different witness who described a long, ovular object, "Like a cigar," Walter says—though he points out that the original witness said it looked like "a giant silver cock"—that hovered over I-25 for several minutes before disappearing beyond the horizon east of town. Most UFO "experts," Randall Heath among them, assume these two sightings were of the same object. Finally, Heath closes his history of T or C area UFO's with various reports of black triangle encounters reported from the early 1970's to the present.

As the trio reaches the northern edge of T or C, Heath narrows his focus from the history of the city's UFO's to telling his guests about Toop's disappearance. He says, "Jim Toop was last seen at Cactus Cocktails at 9:30 in the PM. We don't know where he went when he left, if he stopped back where he was staying or if he left right out of town. Regardless, when he left for the next stop on his tour, he would've driven along this road right here on his way out of town, with nothing but desert around him." Here, Heath pauses, "to build the tension," he tells the rest of us when describing his style of storytelling. When he continues, he says, "Now, I don't know if either of you have ever been to the desert late at night, but it's vast and it's dark, and it's easy to imagine how a driver who's unaccustomed to that sort of landscape might be a bit startled when a giant, rotating triangle appears hovering over him in the sky. It's also easy to imagine that, wrapped in the dense desert night, a driver might not even notice a dark triangle in the sky above him if it wasn't lighting itself up the way they sometimes do." Here, Heath pulls over to the side of the road and stops the car. He says, "This is where Toop's car was found." He pauses, again, to let his words sink in. Morus and his son say nothing. "The angle of the car suggests that Toop veered off the road—we might assume, then, that if he was abducted he at least saw the UFO, causing him to steer onto the shoulder, or it's possible that he didn't see the triangle and was simply beamed right out of his car, which then veered right on its own. All we know is that the car was found right on this spot the next morning, doors closed, battery dead, which, you may know, is something that can happen with UFO's—they suck the energy out of things like batteries." With this, Heath urges his passengers to get out and look around, to crane their heads to see the sky and try to imagine what Toop might have seen, what he might have felt. Instead, Morus says, "This isn't where Toop's car was found." Heath says, "Excuse me?" Then Morus's son says, "He's right—we're about three miles too close to town." Heath doesn't say anything for a minute, then fesses up, tells Morus and his son that he wanted to save gas money so he just stopped, figuring that his guests wouldn't notice. This isn't the first time he's done this, but Morus and his son are the first to notice. Caught out, Randall Heath asks his passengers if they want to see the real site. Morus defers to his son, says, "I saw it on my way into town. What about you?" The young man says, "Maybe later." And with that, Randall Heath drives Daniel Morus and his son back to the Historical Society Museum. Before the Moruses leave, Heath asks that they not tell anyone about his deception, which is odd, because all of us have lied to visitors before—he's probably worried about losing potential money from future TV appearances. In response to his request, Morus asks if the museum has a records room. When Heath answers affirmatively, Morus says he'll keep Heath's secret in exchange for unlimited access to the society's archives, which are mostly comprised of old documents dumped on he and his predecessor by town hall, and old newspapers stacked in crooked, orderless heaps along the wall. When interested parties learn that Heath agreed to grant such access to his visitors, they will be concerned, maybe for good reason, maybe not, about what Morus and his son might find in that room, though we should note that *might* is the big, operative word here, as most of us are pretty certain that Heath himself wouldn't be able to find a damn thing in there, even if he knew exactly what he was looking for. Heath will also tell some folks that Daniel and Fox Morus's five hours in the archive yielded at least one or two finds—which he knows because the damned fool let them make photocopies before they left. We will reassure ourselves that nothing will come of this, that whatever they found can't be particularly useful, that even though Daniel Morus seems to know something about Toop that previous enthusiasts didn't, how could he find something when he doesn't even know what he's looking for?

*

Among some of T or C's older residents, there is now a bit of nervous energy. Surely very few of them have anything to lose. But perhaps now that our guests might—*might*—have gained some momentum in their quest for insight, it's time for those among us who do know a thing or two to start coming clean. And yes, that means we haven't been completely honest in our various discussions of the circumstances surrounding Toop's disappearance. Here's the thing: there are certain facts about Jim Toop's disappearance that have been, shall we say, adjusted, or left out altogether, so as to protect some of our own. That doesn't necessarily mean that the official story regarding Toop's disappearance is inaccurate, per se, only that there might be some other facts about that night that don't directly relate to said disappearance, but are tangentially related to it, orbit around it, that some among us thought best to scrub from the public record. An example: In initial police interviews following Toop's disappearance, Avery Barnes, who was bartending at The Cactus that night, said that, before leaving, Toop seemed rather drunk, but probably hadn't been over-served. We knew Avery Barnes and we don't mind using him as an example—he passed five years back, rest his soul—and we trust his assessment of the situation, but town elders decided to excise Barnes's testimony from official reports because they knew that if the Toop investigation had grown, such information could have adversely affected his livelihood. As far as we know, the only place where the information still exists is in a yellowed copy of a decades old newspaper, buried under thousands of other more recent newspapers. Another example: the night before Toop's car was found, *that* Angela's husband, a police officer named Michael Boyer, responding to a break-in call at his own home, was killed, allegedly by a drifter who had been spotted in the area earlier that evening. Let us be clear: this has absolutely no connection to Jim Toop's disappearance. That said, because both investigations were unfolding at once, and because humans instinctively try to find narrative in everything, try to organize the world around us into easily understandable, interconnected ideas, it was only natural that some of T or C's residents convinced themselves that either Jim Toop had been murdered by the same person who murdered Michael Boyer or that Toop was Michael Boyer's killer. Why risk even mentioning Boyer's death in the same breath as Toop's disappearance when it might only lead more interested parties to false conclusions? That's all we're talking about here, just a few white lies to protect the reputations and legacies of our city's good people. Why even confess to these omissions now? Well, because we'd hate to ruin our credibility after all these years.

*

But back to the matter at hand: after their five hour excavation at the Historical Society Museum, and presumably with photocopied documents secure on their persons, Morus and his son are next spotted outside of Al Walters's junk shop, which of course is closed, as it usually is when Toop enthusiasts are in town. They are next seen dining at a Mexican joint over on Broadway, though again, they don't seem to be talking much to each other, so there isn't anything for anyone to overhear. Morus eats a plate of tacos, and Fox—who looks familiar to two other diners at the restaurant, Seth Pond and his wife, Andrea, both of whom are seeing Fox for the first time and can't quite figure out *why* he looks familiar—eats a wet burrito. There's something else, too, that strikes Seth and Andrea Pond as unusual and, more than a little bit sad—even when they're together, the two Morus men look very much alone. While Daniel Morus eats, he looks at only his tacos and chews slowly. When Fox says something, Morus keeps chewing instead of answering, which prompts Fox to say something else. If Morus is done chewing, he answers in what appears to be as few words as possible.

Anyone familiar with Toop's *Your Sunglasses Are in the Junk Drawer*, might see something of the song "New Mexico" in the scene. In that song, Toop sings, in about as listless a voice as he's ever conjured:

> We were alone as New Mexico
> Deserts on top of deserts
> All those dust storms out our windows
> All that sand on which we stand

Fitting, no? But, ah, who are we to speculate about and pry into our visitors' private lives. If Daniel Morus wants to eat his tacos in peace while barely acknowledging his son, it's none of our business. What *is* our business, though, is what happens after dinner, when Morus drives his son back to the Desert Ridge Inn, leaves him in the room, then goes back out to the Pin Hole Bar, presumably in the hopes of talking to *that* Angela again. He will be sorely disappointed because *that* Angela was given a few days off of work in case the very thing that's happening now happened, meaning in case Daniel Morus came back to the bar for a second round of questioning. When Morus sees that *that* Angela isn't around, he sits down at the bar anyway. Unfortunately for all of us, the bartender tonight is Billy Boyer, who is, as it happens, *that* Angela's son—but Daniel Morus doesn't need to know that. Billy Boyer's father, of course, was Michael Boyer, who died in 1977, before Billy was even born. This meeting between Morus and Boyer is strange and carries a particular weight as, in a way, it is the beginning of a series of events that are about to upset the balance of our fair city. And it begins, according to onlookers, with Daniel Morus wearing a confused expression the first time he finds himself face to face with Billy Boyer. Billy Boyer, noticing Morus's confusion, asks, "Everything alright?" Morus responds by saying, "You look like someone—a friend." Before explaining further, Morus waves off his observation and orders a gin and tonic. He pays with cash, leaves a five dollar tip, and asks if anyone has a smoke he can bum. Billy Boyer offers one, but tells Morus that he'll have to go outside because of the state-wide smoking ban. Morus turns down the cigarette and stays at the bar instead, presumably so he can attempt to engage Billy Boyer in conversation and try to learn a thing or two about Jim Toop. Sure enough, after barely five minutes at the bar, when Billy Boyer stops in front of Morus to squirt some soda water into a well vodka and soda, Morus orders another drink—he downed his first quickly—and asks if there are any good local musicians around. Billy shrugs, says, "Not really—couple of cover acts and a few younger groups who play some originals." He explains that anybody who wants to pursue a career in music leaves because there's shit for performance opportunities in town and it's a bit of a drive to play in neighboring cities. Morus counters, says, "I figured there'd at least be some hobbyists, maybe some retired boomers, like myself, who play folk songs at the coffee shops and cafés." Billy Boyer, unsure where Morus is going with all this, says, "Like you? You play?" Morus puts up his hands and shakes his head, says, "You misunderstand—I mean boomers like me. I don't play music." Boyer asks, "But you're a music fan?" Morus nods and Boyer slaps the five he'd just received from Morus on the bar, says, "Go put some songs on." Daniel Morus takes the bill and loads up the playlist. When he returns to the bar, he's already ordering another drink—this time a margarita, "and don't hold back on the tequila," he says. The first of Morus's songs to play is "Said the Cactus to the Cloud," off of Toop's *Black Triangle* album. The song opens with a delicate acoustic guitar figure and Toop singing about a bird talking to the sky, making way for a whimsical, but nonsensical chorus:

> It's time I get myself home
> Said the bird of the sky to the sad, sad ground
> Oh, can you please send me something to drink
> Said the cactus of the earth to the high, high cloud

Boyer keeps busy taking orders and serving drinks until the last time through the chorus when Toop howls the word "cloud" and the song's soft arrangement erupts into a furious barrage of strums. Boyer says, "Nice pick. Of course, you're not the first out-of-towner to load up the box with Toop songs." Morus tells him he didn't stuff the box with Toop, just sprinkled in a couple of choice cuts alongside his other picks. This is immediately confirmed when the opening strains of Roxy Music's "More Than This" fill the bar, closely followed by Bryan Ferry's slippery voice. Boyer says, "I appreciate that."

Says, "I don't mind Toop, but some guys come in here like they have something to prove." Boyer says this because he knows exactly who Daniel Morus is, and though he doesn't know what exactly Morus said to his mother the previous night, he *did* know how upset she was after work. Billy Boyer, never one to beat around the bush, asks, "Is that why you're here? For Jim Toop?" Morus drains the rest of his margarita and asks for another, then says, "Something like that." Then, "Actually, I'm looking for him—know where he might be?" Boyer says, "Probably in the ground somewhere. Maybe there's a grave for him out in L.A. or something, but nobody's ever *found him*. If you want to find Jim Toop, that's your best bet." And it's here that someone shouts, "Hey Boyer, what's a guy got to do to get a beer?" and so Billy Boyer walks down the bar so he can do his job, a bit unnerved that Daniel Morus now knows his last name.

After this, Billy Boyer avoids Morus for a bit, focuses on other customers' needs, wipes down some tables, brings back some empties. When Billy comes back to the bar, Morus orders another drink, this time a double scotch on the rocks. Billy says, "You've had a lot," but Morus insists. Then Billy tells Morus that they don't have scotch. Morus asks for bourbon instead. Billy puts a glass full of ice down in front of Morus and pours. Says, "Daniel Morus, right?" Morus nods, begins to ask how Billy Boyer knows his name, but the bartender interrupts, says, "It's a small town." Morus nods. Then Boyer says, "You here with your boy?" Morus says, "Something like that." Billy can tell his customer is drunk, decides to press. He asks, "Is he not your boy?" Morus says, "I'm not going to get into that," then asks Billy, "Your father ever come around?" Billy says, "My father?" Morus says, "Yeah, your father." That's when Billy tells Daniel Morus that his father died before he was born, says, "He was a police officer, killed on duty—Mom didn't even know she was pregnant until after the funeral." Morus says, "No shit," and takes a sip of his drink. He says, "Do you believe all that?" Billy says, "Of course." This is when Daniel Morus says, "I don't think your father was any police officer." At this, Billy Boyer can only laugh. The truth is, though, the exchange is making him uncomfortable because even though he knows who his father is, he's been told more than a couple of times by Toop tourists that he looks like the singer. He usually chalks this up to folks seeing what they want to see, but sometimes he wonders, because he knows about the song named "Angela," and he knows that his mother is *that* Angela because he's seen her get sad and wistful whenever that song comes on the radio, but he also knows that he has never met a man named Jim Toop, and there's never been any mention, by his mother, or anyone else, except for crazy assholes at the bar, that Jim Toop might actually be his father. But that's not what Daniel Morus said, not yet, anyway, and seeing as Billy doesn't feel like going down that road tonight, he goes on the offensive, asks, "Why are you so interested in this Toop guy anyway?"

Daniel Morus drains his glass and asks for another, exactly the same. In response to Billy Boyer's question, he shrugs. Billy follows up, asks, "You think he's actually here? You don't seem that crazy." Morus says, "It's business." Billy laughs, says, "Business with a dead man—must be pretty important to get you all the way out here." Morus says, "It's not my business. Not really." Billy says, "Someone must be paying you well for you to waste your time on their behalf." Morus explains that he isn't making much money at all, which leads Billy to ask him, again, why he is so invested in finding a dead guy. Morus takes a sip from his bourbon, says,

"Because I've got nothing better to do." And that's when it occurs to Billy Boyer that Daniel Morus is a sad, sad man. Billy says, "Everybody can find something better to do." He immediately regrets saying it, recognizing how much it sounds like bullshit, and knowing, already, exactly how Morus will answer such an inane, broad statement. As expected, Morus says, "This is my something better." Billy says, "That's some sad shit, man." Morus drains his bourbon, and, through slurred words, says, "You want sad shit, man?" Billy says, "We've got plenty of sad shit around here already." This prompts Morus to say, "I'm sure you do. Everyone is sad. Everyone is alone." Not knowing how to respond, Billy says, "I'm sure it's not as bad as all that." This is what finally prompts Daniel Morus to go off, drunkenly unleashing a torrent of his problems on his young interlocutor. He says, "I'm almost sixty, my parents are dead, I have no siblings, no kids, been married twice, divorced twice. My first wife cheated on me and I still don't know why. What was wrong with me? Why wasn't I good enough? How's that for sad shit?" Billy notes, here, that Morus just said he doesn't have any children—he wonders who Morus's traveling companion really is. He doesn't want to ask, though, because he already feels like enough of a dick for inspiring Morus's outburst. He hopes if he doesn't say anything, the old man will talk himself out. He doesn't: "She won't even talk to me now. But why would she? That was twenty-some years ago. I'm lucky if she even remembers me. People like to forget their failures. My second wife," and Morus pauses here, belches quietly inside his mouth, then continues: "She'll talk to me, but why bother. My second marriage—it was like a thing in film strips teachers used to show in science classes. Or like they'd have me show when I used to sub—they'd say thing like, 'See this tiny mote of dust? Now see the Earth? In the grand scheme of things, in the full size and scope of the universe, you are less than that mote of dust.' Or, 'Count to one—if the universe were a one hundred year old person, your lifespan would be only a tiny fraction of that one-count—that's how little you matter to time. That's what my second marriage was like. She was a nice girl, though." And Billy, relieved that he has managed to divert attention away from himself and Jim Toop, though still feeling somewhat bad for sending Daniel Morus into this shame spiral, decides to at least try to be encouraging, says, "You don't have to be alone. You can find someone." Morus laughs, then points out his portly physique—he isn't full-on obese, exactly but heavy—and describes, in an uncomfortable level of detail, his excessive flatulence, and his irregular bowel movements that, at least a few times a month come out rock hard and bloody, leading to more ointment and medicated pads, more stool softeners and fiber. Morus says, "I wake up every day with an aching gut, and an aching head, and aching arms, and aching legs, and a smaller than average cock that sits like a puddle of dog shit in my lap and barely works anyway—who wants that?" He says, "Who wants any of that?" Billy, having traversed a range of responses, from relived, to guilty, to disgusted, now feels vaguely afraid because, at thirty-six, he's more than halfway to Morus's age. When Billy can't find words through the murk of his conscious thoughts, Morus says, "Huh kid? What woman would have that in her life?"

And here, more curious than anything, Billy Boyer says, "What about your son?" Morus shoots Boyer a confused look, and Boyer says, "At least you have your son." Morus says, "And what son would that be?" Billy says, "The young man you're traveling with." Morus says, "He's no son of mine," to which Billy Boyer says, mostly to needle his customer, "But you were married to women?" This seems to confuse Daniel Morus for a moment who, after a beat, finally understands what Billy Boyer is implying and shakes his head, laughs, and says, "It's not like that," then explains that the kid, who is a legal adult named Fox Mulder, was just a kid he met who also happened to be interested in Toop, and wasn't supposed to come on this trip but decided to anyway, and talked his way into Morus's room at the Desert Ridge Inn by claiming to be his kin. Boyer laughs because of course Echelle would fall for some teenager's dumb trick, because she's just that trusting, kind, and gullible. Billy refocuses his attention on Daniel Morus, asks the man why he and the boy continued lying, to which Morus says, "It just seemed easier," and Billy nodded. That's about the moment when, through the bar's open door, came the fleeting but violently bright lights and loud sirens of a squad of emergency vehicles—a fire truck, a couple of ambulances, and a couple of police cars, most of the town's first response team. Billy Boyer says, "I wonder where they're going,"—he can't possibly know, yet, that they're headed to the Historical Society Museum, where a mysterious fire has erupted, with pinpoint accuracy, in the records archive—and heads to the door. Daniel Morus stumbles off his stool and makes his way to the bar's entrance where he stands beside Billy Boyer, watching the flicker of emergency lights dance above the rooftops.

*

And this is as good a time as any to shift our focus and discuss what Fox Morus, who we now know is actually named Fox Mulder, is doing while his travel companion is getting fucked up and falling into an abyss of self-pity. Left alone at the motel, Fox Mulder does God-knows-what on his own, presumably in the duo's motel room, until a little after ten, at which point Echelle spots him walking to the motel's edge where there is a small room with a coin-operated washer and dryer, a microwave chained to a small shelving unit, and three vending machines: one old, with an image of a large, condensation-covered can of RC Cola on the front; one fronted by a clear panel protecting candy and a variety of non-name-brand snack cakes; and the third, a refrigerated machine holding sandwiches, personal pizzas, and a few pieces of fruit that look like and absolutely are more than a little old. We'd like to imagine that Fox Mulder has the good judgment to be leery of the third machine's contents, but he doesn't, as he is next seen standing in the room's entrance, apple in hand. And who spots him this time? It's Gabe Sinclair, who is peeking his head out of one of the motel's doors and scanning the parking lot for curious eyes. Seeing only the stranger from out of down, Sinclair makes his way to his car, which is parked a few spots down from the room he just left.

Gabe Sinclair has just finished spending a hundred and fifty bucks for thirty minutes of "comfort" from Veronica Morelli—this isn't much of a secret, sometimes it seems like only the men's wives don't know what their husbands get up to—who, a few moments after Gabe leaves, long enough for him to be on his way home to his wife and sleeping baby, comes out of the room, herself, wearing, according to Echelle, who always likes to gossip about Ms. Morelli, but not her johns, a pair of thin, linen boxers with her smartphone tucked in the waist band, flip flops, and an old green t-shirt with WNMU written on it in white, university-style block letters. Normally, we wouldn't take the time to describe one of our own in such objectifying detail—nor do we, unlike Echelle, normally like to talk about what Veronica Morelli does to make ends meet and the men, and sometimes women, who help her to connect those sometimes desperate ends—but here, due to the nature of the circumstances, it seems appropriate that you know who just left Ms. Morelli's room and what Ms. Morelli is wearing when she walks down to the motel's laundry and vending room with a handful of quarters and a silky article of clothing. Upon seeing Fox Mulder, who Veronica Morelli knows nothing about and has yet to meet, but who she'll later tell us about, she asks, "How's that apple?" Fox Mulder looks up at her and stammers something like, "Not great. Kind of chewy." The combination of Fox Mulder's odd answer and awkward demeanor endears him to Veronica Morelli, who decides not to complain that the young man is blocking the door to the laundry facility. Perhaps sensing something odd in the exchange already, Fox Mulder offers the apple to Veronica Morelli, says, "Want a bite?" Veronica Morelli laughs and shakes her head. Fox Mulder says, "It's kind of gross, anyway," and throws the apple out into the parking lot. He and Veronica watch it roll out the drive into the street where, the next day, some car or truck will roll right over it, smash it to a pulp. With the apple gone, Veronica asks Fox Mulder for his name, and he tells her, "It's Fox." She says, "That's an odd name," and he says, "I know." Then, in a polite attempt to ask for admittance to the laundry room, Veronica opens her hand to show her quarters and starts to hold up the piece of clothing, but as she does, the end of the garment falls from her grasp allowing the full article to flutter on a wisp of desert wind in all of its black, silky, soiled glory. It floats in front of Fox Mulder's face for just a moment before an embarrassed Veronica clutches the nightie to her gut and shuffles past the stunned young man as he quietly steps away from the door. When Veronica starts her small load of laundry, the microwave, which had been cooking something, she doesn't know what, dings, so she calls out to the young man, assuming he had been waiting on his food.

Fox Mulder doesn't come into the room right away, and when he does, he is tentative. Veronica says, "It's ok. Come in." Fox Mulder says, "I saw your..." and cuts himself off. Looking for a way to make Fox feel less uncomfortable, Veronica Morelli says, "If I had a nickel for every man who's seen that thing, or made me have to wash that thing, I guess, I..." and then she stops herself, mid-sentence, and says, "I guess I *do* have quite a few nickels for every man who's seen that thing." As it happens, Veronica Morelli notices that her attempt at making Fox Mulder more comfortable is a miscalculation because he stops edging into the room, choosing instead to just stare at the cheerful young woman in front of him. Veronica moves to the microwave, checks on the personal pizza inside. She says, "It's still cold. Do you want me to run it for another minute?" Fox Mulder nods. As Veronica Morelli sets the microwave, Fox Mulder asks her if she's a, "you know," clearly afraid to say the next word. "Am I a what?" Veronica asks. Fox Mulder says, "Do you do it?" Veronica says, "Doesn't everyone?" Fox Mulder says, "I don't." Veronica says, "Well, you're still young." Fox Mulder's face flushes red. He says, "Maybe. I'm not really interested." Veronica Morelli says, "That's ok. Maybe you will be some day." He says, "It's weird. Kind of gross." She tries not to, but laughs anyway. Says, "It can be, sure. But a lot of people like it." After a beat, Fox Mulder asks, "Do you do it for money?" Veronica's first impulse is to lie, but the kid seems ok, so she tells him that yes, she does, in fact, do it for money. Fox Mulder says, "You don't look like one." She says, "One what?" He says, "You know." Veronica thinks that Fox Mulder looks like he's a legal adult, but she finds it strange how uncomfortable he is talking about sex. She says, "Well, I'm off the clock." He says, "You're so young." Veronica laughs again, says "I'm not so young"—which, for those of us who know her, and know that she's twenty-seven, might seem a bit absurd because twenty-seven *is* fairly young—then explains that women who do her sort of work can be a range of ages. "There will always be men willing to pay for sex, no matter your age," she says. She notices that the young man blushes and looks away when she says this. She starts to explain more, but Fox Mulder cuts her off, asks, "Do you have a pimp?" Veronica tells him she doesn't, that men find her through websites and by word of mouth. She says, "Nobody is making me do this, thanks for asking." Fox Mulder tells her he doesn't understand, asks her what she does if a man tries to hurt her or rip her off. She is briefly disappointed because she'd thought the young man was checking to make sure she isn't a victim of sex trafficking. Clearly, she realizes, Fox Mulder doesn't know a thing about sex trafficking, so Veronica just answers his question. She tells him that payment is always up front, that she's been lucky not to have been hurt yet, like some of the other girls, but that, really, in a place like T or C, even though plenty of folks live in the margins, most customers recognize that the less they do to draw attention to themselves, the better. She adds, "And I keep a gun hidden in reach of the bed—in case anyone gets out of hand." Fox Mulder asks, "Have you ever had to use it?" She says, "I pulled it once."

Then she tells Fox Mulder about the time she had to pull her gun: how a john wanted to choke her during sex, and how she said only a little, but the john choked her too hard, for too long, to the point that she was losing consciousness, and so, to the best of her ability, she asked him to stop, but he didn't, so she tried to ask him again, and he still didn't, and it became clear that he wouldn't stop, so she jabbed him in the sternum with her fingers, which caught the john—who we're pretty sure was a salesman at the used car lot out on Date St., and who we're pretty sure left town not long after this incident—off guard, causing him to fall backward off the bed. When he got up, he was pissed and took a swing, but she saw it coming and easily ducked, then dove for the drawer and pulled her gun. It wasn't loaded, but the john didn't know that, so he hastily dressed and started to leave, stopping in the doorway, pants half down, shirt unbuttoned, to ask for his money back. Veronica, who had managed to cover herself with a robe and sweatpants while keeping the gun trained at the john, grabbed a twenty out of her purse, crumpled it up and threw it at him. He eyed it on the floor, clearly tempted to run back into the room, but ultimately decided it wasn't worth the extra indignity, so he buckled up his pants and left. At the conclusion of the story, Veronica Morelli and Fox Mulder share a good laugh together. She feels like he might be starting to warm up to her. He is starting to seem more relaxed.

Here, Fox Mulder asks Veronica if she has a carry permit for her gun. She says she doesn't need one since she never loads it, ever, that's how the New Mexico law is worded. Then Fox Mulder asks her, "Why do you have sexual intercourse for money?" She tells him that she grew up poor and is going to school to be an Analytical Chemist. Then he asks, "Do you like having sexual intercourse for money?" Veronica pauses for a moment and isn't sure what to say. She's never really thought about it. She likes sex, and she likes money, and most of the time, she enjoys her work, though it's not exactly emotionally fulfilling. When she answers, she says, "It's rarely good, or even decent sex, but it's occasionally fun." Fox Mulder says, "Fun." And Veronica says, "Sex is supposed to be fun, you know."

Fox Mulder seems to think this over for a few moments. Then he asks her how much she charges. She tells him one-fifty for thirty minutes, two fifty for an hour. Fox Mulder pulls out his wallet, flips through some bills, says, "How much for ten minutes?" She says, "I didn't think you were interested in sexual intercourse." She says, "Isn't it weird and gross?" Fox Mulder says, "Probably." When he doesn't say anything else, Veronica says, "You want more than ten minutes anyway. You should take your time. Enjoy yourself." Then, before the conversation progresses, she says, "How old are you?" Fox Mulder tells her he's eighteen, almost nineteen. He pulls out his driver's license and hands it over. She laughs at the gesture, says, "It's ok—I believe you," which she might not have before, because, honestly, Fox Mulder looks like he's barely eighteen, is small and wiry, has under-developed facial hair in patches around his face, fields of fresh acne and light scars from previous outbreaks. Veronica hands back Fox Mulder's license and says, "How much money do you have." He tells her he has enough for an hour, but that he's pretty sure he won't need that long. Veronica says, "Why do you want to do this?" Fox Mulder turns bright red, looks down at his feet, then walks to the microwave to check on his pizza, again, which had probably been warm a few moments before, but had since cooled off; he sets the timer for another thirty seconds. When he finally answers, he says, "I like you and the money goes to a good cause and you're going to be a chemist and you're nice." Veronica says, "Well, thank you. But this is a big decision." Fox Mulder says, "It'll be an experience. If I don't like it I won't have to do it ever again." Veronica laughs quietly, walks across the room and gives Fox Mulder a quick kiss on the cheek, says, "You'll do what's right for you, but I'll try my best to help you like it." Then: I don't have anyone scheduled until midnight. How about a hundred for an hour or until you're ready to go, whichever comes first." Fox Mulder reaches into his wallet, counts out four twenties and two tens, and tries to hand them to Veronica. "In the room," she says, "room 4." Then: "Meet me there in five." Stepping out of the laundry room, she turns back, says, "If the washer goes off before you come over, can you grab my laundry? I'll dry it in the room." Fox Mulder nods, and Veronica can tell he's nervous. He is pale and she thinks he might be shaking. She wonders what he's thinking. Veronica is thinking that she's about to earn half of another textbook or most of a utility bill. When she returns to her room, she slips out of her boxers and t-shirt and into, as they say in the movies, something a little more comfortable.

And then she waits for five minutes, ten minutes, fifteen minutes and still Fox Mulder doesn't come to her room. The shelf bra and thong she'd slipped into are starting to get a little uncomfortable and she wonders if her strange, new john decided to stand her up. She checks the time on her phone—an hour and a half until her next appointment—and decides to wait a few more minutes before changing back into her boxers and t-shirt. Just as she's about to give up, she hears a soft knock. Veronica opens the door just enough to let Fox in, then closes it quickly behind to keep prying eyes—not that there are normally prying eyes in this part of town—from seeing anything incriminating. Secure in the room, Fox Mulder hands over the same bills he'd counted out earlier.

Veronica shoves the money in to her purse, which she keeps under the nightstand on the side of the bed she generally thinks of as hers, then flops onto the mattress on her belly, resting her chin on her palms, looking seductive. For several moments, Fox Mulder doesn't say or do anything, just stands a couple of feet away from the bed staring, as if to memorize Veronica's body, her pillowy breasts and soft stomach—she isn't sure if she feels flattered by the attention or creeped out. She says, "So, what do you want to do?" She thinks she sees him blanch, then adds, "I know I'm not as fit as a lot of the girls you see online, but we can have fun." Fox Mulder says, "Your laundry wasn't ready. I'm sorry." Veronica says, "It's ok," then she pats the bed next to her. Fox Mulder takes a step away from the bed. Veronica says, "You've already paid, let's have some fun." Fox Mulder doesn't move. He says, "I'm sorry I took so long." He says, "I wanted to eat my pizza, because I was hungry. It was in the microwave. Then I had to poop, so I went to my room, but instead I threw up, and then I had to change my shirt and brush my teeth." Veronica says, "Are you ok?" Fox Mulder nods and looks down at his feet. Veronica says, "You don't need to be ashamed. A lot of men come to women like me for their first time." Fox Mulder says, "It's my very, very first time. With a woman. At all." Veronica says, "We can just talk if you'd like. You can have your money back." Fox Mulder doesn't say anything and is looking anywhere except for at Veronica. She feels relieved. She says, "Or maybe I can touch myself and you can join in when you're ready?" Fox Mulder looks up when Veronica suggests this. She thinks he looks even younger now, fourteen or fifteen, maybe. She chalks this up to his posture, his fear. Most of the men that come to Veronica hide their discomfort and shame behind masculine boasts and behavior, but others, they wear their shame like bulky winter jackets, the kind Veronica borrowed from her cousin the time she visited family in Minnesota when she was a teenager—these men, they shrink inside their shame, become younger, weaker, begin to look enough like Fox Mulder looks now that she knows what he's feeling. Veronica feels an uncertain sadness when she looks at the boy standing just inside the door. It makes her feel crushed for him.

As much as we'd like to pull back, here, to leave this intimate moment to this man and woman, we can't. This moment is not meant to remain private, and soon, its broad strokes will be all over town, even if the details only emerge later when Veronica Morelli tells one of her friends about the boy named Fox, the saddest, strangest john she ever knew. But for now, Veronica wants only to help Fox Mulder, so she slowly dips her hand inside the front of her panties and begins to touch herself. She says, "Do you like this Fox?" The young man doesn't respond—he looks at her, then away, then at, then away. She says, "Are you getting hard?" Fox Mulder says, "I think so," and, if it weren't for the frightened waver in his voice, Veronica would have laughed, because how can an eighteen year old man not know if he's getting hard or not? Veronica sighs, coos, moans—she calls out Fox's name. Fox Mulder says, "Don't say my name like that." Veronica thinks this is strange, but it's not the strangest thing she's ever heard, so she continues to rub herself without saying the young man's name. After a few moments, Fox Mulder crosses the room and sits down on the bed. Veronica invites him closer. He inches toward her. He asks, "Can I see your vagina?" Veronica smiles and nods, invites him to slide her thong off, "or you can just push it to the side," she says. Fox Mulder tentatively hooks the tip of his index finger under her thong. Veronica lifts her hips slightly to encourage him. She can hear him swallow, a loud 'gulp' like a cartoon character, and then the boy slowly leans his face down, stops less than an inch away from her vagina, and beings to cough. Though he tries to cover his mouth, Veronica can feel bursts of his breath between her legs. It tickles a little but she suppresses a laugh so as to not make him feel any more self-conscious than he already is. "Are you ok?" Veronica asks. When he's done coughing, Fox says, "I swallowed wrong. I'm ok." And then he moves his face right next to Veronica's vagina. She can feel his cheek on her inner thigh. His warm breath shakes inside her. Then there is a knock on the door followed by the sound of a key card, and then two police officers enter the room, and Veronica Morelli says, "Shit," and starts to move, but doesn't because Fox Mulder doesn't move, and as the police begin to rattle off the things police say when making arrests, he leans in that last half inch and places a light, soft kiss—a Pope kiss, a greeting kiss, a parent's goodnight kiss, the kind of kiss friends give each other on their cheeks—on Veronica's right labia. To Veronica, the kiss feels strange, but nice, fleeting and electric, a new kind of tender. After the kiss, Fox Mulder stands, slowly lifts his hands above his head and surrenders himself to the police.

Soon, everyone in town will know that this is happening because of Gabe Sinclair, because when he left the motel and returned home his wife Sally confronted him with GPS data culled from a tracker she'd hidden in his car. To cut his loses, Gabe Sinclair admitted his wrong doing and, rather than dealing with the emotional fallout of the situation, Sally called the police to report an incident of prostitution. Of course, the police have known for some time about Veronica Morelli and the other working girls, but had decided unofficially that, unless anyone was in danger, they'd rather not spend their time enforcing such outmoded laws. But when a citizen calls with specific information about a specific act and a specific place, the officers don't really have a choice. So the police had to act and act they did, discretely arriving at the Desert Ridge Motel within twenty minutes of receiving Sally Sinclair's call, and just in time to see a young man, who they didn't yet know was named Fox Mulder, enter Ms. Morelli's room. The two officers waited in the car for a few moments before approaching the hotel, officially to increase the chance of catching the pair "in the act," but secretly wanting to give the kid a chance to get his money's worth. Just before Officer Stan Gainsbourg handcuffs Veronica Morelli—after she gets dressed, of course—he tips his cap and apologizes. When, a few moments later, he and Officer Jersey "Skip" Lewis lead Fox Mulder and Veronica Morelli out of the room and into the backs of two separate squad cars, Veronica leans back and whispers in Stan's ear, says, "Take it easy on the kid, will you?" As she lowers her head to enter the back of the car, she hears an emergency call come over the radio, something about a fire downtown, something about units needing to report.

*

And where are those units reporting? To the Historical Society Museum, of course. And outside the Pin Hole Bar, Daniel Morus, Billy Boyer, and a dozen or so other patrons—most of whom are merely peripheral to this story, are the kinds of folks who excel at going about their business and know nothing about anything that happens in this town outside of their own daily lives—are lined up on the sidewalk, watching a plume of thick, gray smoke rise over our city. These onlookers won't learn until later that the fire started in the Society's archive room, and was reported very early, meaning that fire fighters were able to easily prevent the blaze from spreading. Billy Boyer doesn't realize it until he turns to go back inside, but at some point in the commotion, Daniel Morus made his way back to the bar where he is currently sitting, spinning a bottle cap with his fingertips.

Billy asks Morus if he can get him anything. Morus says he'll have one more for the road, another bourbon. While Billy pours, Morus says, "You know the woman who works here? The older redhead?" Billy says, "I know her." Morus takes a sip of his bourbon, says, "You think you could get her to talk to me again?" Billy reflexively shakes his head, says, "No way." Daniel Morus says, "I think I'd like to apologize to her." Not convinced, Billy says, "No fucking way." Then Morus says, "Who you think set that museum on fire?" Billy says that he doesn't think anybody set the fire, explains that arson isn't the kind of thing that happens around T or C. Under usual circumstances, he'd be right. Morus says, "You think it's a coincidence?" Billy Boyer says, "Do I think what is a coincidence?" Morus says, "That I come around, start poking through that archive room, and the very same night it burns down?" Billy Boyer says, "I do think it's a coincidence." Then: "You seem a bit paranoid." Morus says, "Fuck that." Billy laughs. Morus continues: "You know why I think you won't let me talk to your bartender friend?" Billy says, "Because you're an asshole and you'll just upset her again?" Morus says, "I think it's because she's your mother." This makes Billy nervous. His muscles tighten and his fists clench.

And here is where things start to get interesting.

Here, we begin to understand exactly what Daniel Morus knows.

Here, Daniel Morus tells Billy Boyer that, in the Historical Society Museum's archive, he found a newspaper article about a police officer who had been shot, that the officer's name was Michael Boyer, and that the article mentioned Boyer's wife, Angela. Morus says, "I've got a copy of it, right here." He adds: "I heard some customers call you Boyer, earlier—didn't take much to put it together." Billy Boyer asks, "What do you want?" Morus says, "To talk to your mother again." Boyer says, "That's not going to happen."

The two men stare at each other for at least a minute. The jukebox plays the opening strains of Van Morrison's "Domino," the live version from that double album that everyone owned in the seventies, so there's a smattering of applause as the song kicks into its first verse. Billy says, "Can I see the article?" Daniel Morus says, "Do you really want to." Billy Boyer says, "I already know what happened. Show me." And Daniel Morus says, "Unless you were lying to me earlier, you don't already know what happened." Then: "How much do you really know about your own life, kid?" And here, Billy Boyer loses his cool and jumps over the bar, knocks Daniel Morus down and punches him twice in the gut, causing Morus to vomit. Billy Boyer isn't the type who would usually lose his cool, so why now? We don't know that he'll ever tell any of us, but our guess is that he is scared—not necessarily just because Daniel Morus is pestering him, but maybe, too, because he has always suspected that something wasn't quite right in the story of his life. Maybe he always felt that the things his mother told him weren't quite true. We don't know because we're not privy to everything she told him over the years, but he *could* be right. And so here, in the bar, when an out-of-town stranger, drunk out of his fucking gourd and getting drunker, spoke that fear aloud,

Boyer lost it. But that's just an educated guess. And then, almost as soon as Billy Boyer's rage begins, he regains his composure and tries to help Morus up. When Morus doesn't move, Boyer asks if he needs an ambulance. Morus says he doesn't. At this point, one of the regulars who had filtered back in from outside in time to see Billy Boyer vault over the bar, says, "Fuck an ambulance, I'm calling the cops." Billy asks the customer not to. "It's cool," he says. "I'm fine, now." The customer, whose name Billy doesn't even know—it's Ron Suarez, a guidance counselor at the junior high—says, "Not on you—on that asshole."

While Ron Suarez is on the phone, Billy fetches two clean towels, one for the puke, and the other for Daniel Morus. Morus thanks Billy and asks, "Is that guy calling the cops on me?" Billy nods, tells him he'll clear things up. Daniel Morus says, "Whatever." He says, "Fuck it." Then, "I probably deserve it." And Billy kneels next to him and apologizes again. Morus asks Billy if he really wants to see the article. Billy says, "I don't know." Then, "Maybe." Morus pulls a folded piece of paper out of his pocket, hands it to Boyer, says, "I don't need it back. I've got copies." Billy Boyer starts to unfold it but stops, shoves it in his back pocket. Morus says, "You've got it if you want it."

When the cops arrive, Billy tells them he doesn't want to press charges, but the officers— Stan Gainsbourg, again, and an older officer, Rick Charles, we call him Officer Chuck, who only works part time, now, and who has been on the force since 1973—decide they're going to take Daniel Morus in, anyway, officially for public intoxication and fighting, but unofficially for harassing *that* Angela the night before. Billy doesn't know if this is legal, but he figures it'll keep Morus out of trouble for a while, and he looks to be in pretty bad shape, so he'll probably be fine sleeping off the night in a holding cell.

Billy also couldn't possibly know that Morus's arrest will bring him back together with Fox Mulder, who is—surprise, surprise—in the cell next door to Morus's. Indeed, when Morus is placed in his own cell, Fox Mulder is but a few feet away, staring up at the flickering fluorescent lights and tapping his foot against the bed. As Officer Chuck locks the cell behind Morus, he hears him ask Fox Mulder what he did to get in here. Mulder says, "Solicitation." Morus says, "Shit," then asks if the kid used his phone call to call his mom. Fox Mulder says, "I called Ronnie." Morus says, "Ronnie Epps?" Fox Mulder says, "Yup." Morus says, "Did you get ahold of him?" Fox Mulder says, "Straight to voicemail." Morus asks, "Did you leave a message?" Mulder says, "Nah." That's when Officer Chuck interrupts and asks his prisoners to quiet down, which is pretty unnecessary, but he doesn't like outsiders—especially *these* outsiders—so he gives them a hard time because he knows he can. Before Officer Chuck leaves, Fox asks after the woman who was arrested with him. Officer Chuck tells him she's in a different facility where they put the women. Daniel Morus says, "You've worked here a long time?" Officer Chuck says, "Yeah," tells Morus he's been with the force since '73. Then Morus asks if he helped with the Jim Toop investigation. Officer Chuck says, "Sure. As much as any of us did." Then, "But we won't be talking about that." Morus asks, "Do you remember an officer named Michael Boyer? Would have been around the same time as you. Died in '77." Officer Chuck says, "Won't be talking about him, either." Then, just as he's about to leave, for real this time, he adds: "Michael was a friend. You'd be advised not to bring him up again." Daniel Morus thanks the officer and says goodnight. Officer Chuck—who we all suspect knows more about Jim Toop and Michael Boyer and Angela Boyer than most anyone else—snorts in a final sign of disgust toward Morus then closes the door that leads to the holding cells.

DAY THREE

Daniel Morus spends the night and much of the following morning in the city lockup. Oddly enough, it's Billy Boyer who shows up around noon to bail him out. Billy says, "I'm surprised you didn't get sick in there." Morus says, "I didn't have any left," and reminds Boyer about those punches in the gut. His eyes are red and his voice is full of gravel. "I didn't know if you'd remember that," Billy Boyer says. Morus says, "I wasn't *that* drunk." Billy Boyer doesn't believe that at all. He says, "I'm posting bail for you." Morus asks why. Billy says, "I shouldn't have let them arrest you." Morus says, "Didn't seem like you had a choice." Boyer doesn't say anything, and then Morus begins to talk about the newspaper clipping he'd given Billy, but Boyer cuts him off, miming a slash across his throat. A young officer named Andy Tatroult notices the exchange but doesn't think anything of it because he's young enough that he doesn't know anything about T or C's past. Billy doesn't know that, though, so he's nervous to openly talk about the clipping in front of anyone, which he's read and which is the real reason he's posting bail for Daniel Morus. When Boyer leaves to fill out paperwork, Morus finally seems to realize that the cell beside him is empty. He asks the guard where the other guy went. Tatroult tells him that the kid was released because the sex worker said that no money had changed hands between the two, that she'd initiated the encounter because she was bored and had some time to kill. We all know this is a lie, but nobody cares.

Here, Morus asks Tatroult if he knows where the boy went. The guard shrugs, says, "He's not really a boy, you know." Morus says, "Whatever, I barely even know him." Tatroult asks, "Then why do you care?" Morus explains that he feels responsible for Fox being in T or C, that he wants to make sure he's ok. "He's a legal adult," Tatroult says. "Doesn't seem to be a relative of yours. Why the urgency?" Morus doesn't have an answer. Tatroult says, "He bolted as soon as we let him out. Didn't even ask about you." Morus says, "He's a weird kid." Tatroult asks why they're traveling together, and Morus tells him that Mulder invited himself, that he's really into Jim Toop. Tatroult says, "Jim Toop—that's what this is all about then?" Morus nods and asks Tatroult if he knows anything about Toop. Tatroult says, "Just the usual: UFO's, cults, inept kidnappers, conspiracies." Morus says, "What do you think happened?" Tatroult is beginning to feel a bit uncomfortable. He doesn't mind talking about Jim Toop and knows very little about the man's disappearance, but his superiors don't approve of their officers and other employees discussing Toop with out-of-town snoops. Still, Tatroult feels bad for Daniel Morus since his friend ran off without even asking about posting bail, and so he explains his own theory: "I think Toop picked up a hitchhiker who killed him, robbed him, dragged his body into the desert, then left the car behind and waited for another car to come by and offer him a ride." Morus asks, "Why leave the car?" Tatroult says, "I don't know, but a hitchhiker make sense." Morus asks why and Tatroult says, "UFO's are bullshit and there's no history or record of any real, actual cults in the area. If he'd been kidnapped for ransom, there would have been a note or traces, something." Morus asks, "Have you ever wondered if Toop orchestrated his own disappearance?" Tatroult says, "I've heard that, among other things. Can't say that I buy it." Morus says, "What are some of the things you've heard?"

Against his better judgment, Tatroult decides to indulge Morus. Later in the afternoon, after word of Tatroult's conversation with Morus gets around town, we won't think anything of it because we know that Andy Tatroult has heard only third and fourth hand rumors about things that probably never happened anyway. He's practically as much an outsider as Morus. Maybe there are a few subtle twists or details shared among the local officers that never found their way to previous investigators or into print, but surely such details would be insignificant. Alas, as we'll eventually find out, we underestimated Mr. Tatroult—it turned out he certainly *had* heard a thing or two about Toop, even if he hadn't necessarily realized what he'd heard. Perhaps, then, we need to acknowledge that Mr. Morus is a little bit special—or a little bit lucky—in that he seems to be in the process of uncovering something that has never been unearthed before, at least in this level of detail. When we learn the contents of Morus's talk with Tatroult, we will wonder—why now? Why did this story emerge at this moment between these people? Is it because Tatroult is soft? Possibly. Is it because Morus is asking the right questions? Perhaps. Is it because the story is so well-worn in so many vaguely distinct permutations that it feels safe to share, maybe even feels like a lie? Like a story? That seems the most plausible explanation for Andy Tatroult's transgression. Here is what he tells Daniel Morus: "The story you want to hear goes like this—Toop gets in a bit of trouble and a few important folks around town decide to cook him up a new history and make him a townie until the trouble blows over, at which point he's free to do as he pleases." Daniel Morus asks what kind of trouble. Andy Tatroult says, "Depends on who you ask." Morus says, "Tell me a couple." Andy Tatroult, feeling as if he'd already passed the point of no return, says, "One story says he slept with some cowboy's girlfriend back in Tulsa and the guy came to town looking for him." Morus says, "Tell me another one." Tatroult says, "Just one more." Morus says, "That's fair." And Tatroult says, "A drunk attacked Toop, he accidentally killed the guy, and he was worried his defense wouldn't stand up in court." Morus asks, "How did he kill the attacker?" Tatroult says, "I don't know. Depends on the teller." Tatroult looks at his watch and makes to leave.

Daniel Morus says, "One more question." Tatroult stops but doesn't turn to look at him. Morus says, "The fire last night. What's the determination?" Tatroult says, "Determination?" Morus says, "The cause. Was it arson?" Still without looking back at Morus, and knowing there is no way to frame his answer that won't cause suspicion, Tatroult explains that a couple of his firefighter buddies assumed the fire was arson because it seemed to have started in a filing cabinet, but then a few of the older folks from the police force and the fire department conferred and decided that the cause was faulty wiring. Daniel Morus says, "You think it was arson?" On his way out of the room, for real this time, Andy Tatroult, worried he has already said too much, says, "I don't think anything."

While all of this is happening, Billy Boyer is out in the front of the station filling out paperwork to get Daniel Morus out of jail, which part of him doesn't really want to do, but which he could hardly not do, especially since Morus didn't really do anything to wind up in jail to begin with, *and* he wants to talk to Morus about the article he has folded up in his back pocket. While he waits for the desk clerk to process the paper work, Billy sees Officer Chuck—who is picking up a morning shift as a favor to a colleague—standing by the water cooler. Billy, sensing, perhaps wrongly so, an opportunity, approaches Officer Chuck who says, "What can I do you for?" Billy Boyer says, "You knew my father." Officer Chuck says, "Sure did—he was a good man." Billy asks, "You ever think about him?" Officer Chuck, a bit taken aback by the question, and exhibiting some caution, but not as much caution as he'd be exhibiting if he knew why Billy was here, says, "Of course I do—we were close." Billy says, "What was he like?" Billy knows just how absurd and abrupt this line of questioning probably sounds to Officer Chuck, who is certainly growing suspicious of the young Mr. Boyer's motives—over thirty-seven years Billy never once asked about his father, and now this? Officer Chuck says, "What brought this on?" And Billy, showing a bit more savvy, here, because he clearly has a more specific agenda in mind, and is starting to see a more productive way forward for this conversation, says, "The anniversary of his death was last month. Just been on my mind is all." Officer Chuck says, "Well, what do you want to know?" Billy says, "Just tell me about him—did he have a sense of humor? A temper? Was he fun to hang out with? What was he like?" Officer Chuck takes a sip of his water and says, "He was a good man, a loyal friend, a bit reckless in the field—that's how he got shot—but a good husband to your mother. He would have been a good father." Officer Chuck doesn't know, as he says all this, that Billy Boyer has a news clipping in his back pocket that contradicts at least some of what he just said. For his part, Officer Chuck's response upsets Billy—he has no reason to believe the clipping is completely accurate, but just the thought of Officer Chuck lying to his face fills him with a quick anger. He pulls from his pocket the photocopied piece of paper, as published in the June 9, 1977 edition of the *T or C Observer*, hands it to Officer Chuck, and says, "What about this?"

And this marks another important moment in this town's coming to terms with its own history. Here, whether we like it or not, long submerged fragments of truth are starting to bubble up to the surface. And what then? Perhaps part of the reason no new information about Jim Toop has surfaced for so long is because we forgot the truth. Maybe more of us know, or knew more about Jim Toop than we've let on, but after decades of living with those secrets, it all started to feel normal, the secrets sunk through memory and disappeared. Yes, this, more than anything else, is the reason Toop's disappearance remains a mystery to most—with very few exceptions the truth has been forgotten, lost, dissolved in the water of memory, like so many granules of salt—we don't regret what was lost.

But, lest we forget, this isn't a big moment *just* for T or C—no, all of this new, unexpected information is a big deal for Billy Boyer, not just because his understanding of his father hangs in the balance, but because right now, in the police station, he is actively becoming an outsider, is abdicating his position as one of us to become *one of them*—trying to sift the salt from our water, to dredge up that which we'd spent so many years forgetting. And who can blame him. Wouldn't you want to know the truth of your heritage? He will come back to us, Billy will, in time, but for now, we understand that this is what he has to do to learn the truth he only recently discovered he didn't know.

So, what of the news clipping then? What could that article possibly contain to upset the balance of all we've forgotten? To reshape Billy Boyer's understanding of his origins? On the photocopied sheet of paper that Billy Boyer is handing over to Officer Chuck, there is a seemingly unassuming, not particularly long news item from the local paper's front page, detailing a situation that began as a domestic dispute, but turned into something else. The article includes quotes from neighbors who report hearing screams that started inside a house, then spilled out onto a front lawn where a husband punched his wife, prompting a first round of calls to the police. Of these calls, according to the article, there were three in total, two right away, and a third a few moments later as the situation developed. During the confrontation, a stranger recognized by none of the neighbors approached the couple, who were "not quite, but almost in a physical fight," one of the witnesses was quoted as saying. What happened next is hard to discern from the brief article's vague quotes from neighbors and law enforcement officials. What is clear, though, is that the husband pulled his gun on the stranger and shouted things like, "It's none of your business," "Leave us alone," and "You've done enough already," which resulted in the husband and the stranger fighting on the ground until the gun went off. It was the gun shot that prompted the third call to the police. It was this call to which they finally responded—in 1977, ugly as it was, domestic disputes weren't the type of business with which law enforcement felt it should be involved. The husband was shot. One of the neighbors said that, before authorities arrived, the wife helped the stranger up and sent him away. The first officer on the scene was Rick Charles. The other actors in the story, as I'm sure most everyone has guessed, were Michael and Angela Boyer. The article never names the stranger, as neither the neighbors, nor Angela Boyer claimed to know who he was, but I'm sure we all have a hunch that the stranger was none other than Jim Toop, whose car was found abandoned the following morning. Does this story have a familiar ring to it? It does. When we begin to hear rumblings of what's unfolding, maybe some of us begin to remember hearing something like that.

Of course, when confronted with the news clipping, Officer Chuck doesn't even bother to read it. He knows what it is from a quick glance. He taps his fingers sharply on the page and says, "What of it?" Billy asks, "Is this accurate?" Then adds, "Because if it is, then I can't help but think that you were lying to me, that my father was neither a good man, nor a good husband." He continues, "Which leads me to believe he probably wouldn't have been a good father, either." He says, "So are you lying to me or was the newspaper wrong?" Officer Chuck doesn't want to have this conversation right now, but he knows that the article and Boyer's allegations demand a response, so he says "That article was retracted the next day. Your father was called to a break-in at his own home. He was the first officer on the scene; he found your mother outside screaming at a vagrant. Your father attempted to apprehend the perp and, in the ensuing scuffle, lost his firearm and was shot. The perp fled and was never found." Billy appears to mull this over. Officer Chuck knows that Billy has heard this version of events before because the original story, the one on the photocopied sheet of paper, was retracted, citing sloppy reporting and inaccurate eye witness accounts, and the version he's telling now was printed the following morning. This is the version of the story that everybody knows, that everybody ended up remembering, and it's the story that Angela Boyer told her son. After mulling over Officer Chuck's explanation, Billy Boyer says, "Nobody gets a story that wrong." Officer Chuck says, "You can believe what you want, son, but what I'm telling you is the only version of events that matters." Billy Boyer says, "Because it's the most convenient?" Officer Chuck answers, "Because it's the right story to believe." Billy Boyer stands up, grabs the photocopy out of Officer Chuck's hands and heads to the reception area where Daniel Morus is waiting for him.

*

Let's pause for a moment to locate Fox Mulder in all of this. After his release from jail because of what Veronica Morelli told the police, after he knows better than to tell the truth, and after he takes a cab back to the Desert Ridge Inn where, as far as anyone can tell, he stays in his room for several hours, the next time he is spotted, for the second time in two days, now, is outside of Al Walters's junk shop, which is still closed for obvious reasons. Soon after, Frankie Baca spots the young man fiddling with his smart phone in one of the shelters at Ralph Edwards Park. Outside of Homeless Vic, who is smoking a joint down by the river, Fox is the only other person around, and Frankie Baca decides to leave them both be. He isn't particularly interested in other peoples' business. But, a few moments later, when Fox Mulder approaches Homeless Vic, Frankie Baca will intervene. To understand why, we need to talk a little bit about Frankie Baca. Before he started his day at work, Frankie packed his daughter's lunch in an insulated, cloth sack with a ladybug stitched to its side. Then he woke up his daughter, Magda, and waited for her to get dressed so he could help her pack her book bag. On the mornings that she doesn't have to go into work early, Frankie's wife Reba packs their daughter's lunch and helps her get dressed so that Frankie can read the paper and drink his coffee. Frankie Baca appreciates the mornings that Reba makes it so he can relax a little, but it's unnecessary because he enjoys taking care of his daughter. He is so in awe of the impossible love she feels toward him that he swears he can see it expanding in her eyes—like the universe—when she looks at him. The only reason he doesn't stop Reba from taking over when she can is because he wants to make sure that she gets to experience that same love. And this is why Frankie Baca decides to approach the pair—because he imagines that Fox Mulder has at least one parent who loves him the way he loves Magda, and even though Homeless Vic is more or less harmless, Frankie knows he wouldn't be comfortable with a child he loved very much interacting with someone as strange as Vic. When Baca reaches the two men, they're talking about Al Walters. Fox Mulder is explaining that he's tried to visit the junk shop twice, but that it's been closed, both times, in the middle of the day. Mulder says, "That's no way to run a business." Before Vic or Fox seem to notice Frankie, Vic begins to explain that Al, who runs the shop, is an old friend of his and an intensely private person. Vic says, "Sometimes, Al likes to stay home and not talk to anyone." He trails off a bit and turns his attention to Frankie, who is now standing close enough to the two men that a pass-erby might assume they had been long engaged in intimate conversation. Vic says, "Help you, sir?" Frankie says, "Oh, no. Just thought I'd say hi. Kill some time." After a beat, Frankie gestures towards Vic, says, "You know Al Walters?" Vic nods. "That's a great little shop," Frankie says, then he asks Vic how he knows Al. Vic says, "We go way back. Al's a good guy." Frankie agrees with him, explains that Al has always been willing to help out with Park Department fundraisers. He says, "Does Al still live in the apartment above his shop?" Here, Frankie notices Fox Mulder perk up. Vic says, "You know, I don't know." Frankie doesn't believe this for a moment, but doesn't say so, remembering that when he approached, Vic was talking about how Al is a private person.

Frankie, attempting to redirect after his conversational misstep, says, "I hear you're writing a book, Vic?" Vic says, "Where'd you hear that?" Frankie says, "My uncle mentioned it. Vic asks who his uncle is, and Frankie says, "Mark Hobson. Said you and him were going to swap manuscripts when you're done." Vic says, "I don't think we're going to do that." He adds, "I don't talk to Mark much anymore. Once again, Frankie notices Fox Mulder react to something. He thinks the kid would make a shit poker player, and wonders what's so interesting about Vic's relationship with Mark Hobson. Then the kid asks what the book is about, and Vic begins to explain that it's a fictionalized retelling of the David Parker Ray murders. Fox Mulder says, "What's your friend's book about?" Vic says, "Who knows. I haven't really talked to Mark in years." Then, in a surprising turn, Fox Mulder says, "I have a copy of one of his books, probably twenty or thirty years old. Set in New Mexico in the 1800's. It's about this cowboy who one day goes into chrysalis, like a caterpillar about to become a butterfly, but when his cocoon opens up he's some kind of cosmic desert spirit and kills all of his enemies." To understand why this is surprising, you need to know only two things: first, Mark Hobson had written a book matching that description, and second, Mark Hobson has never been interested in traditional publishing models, choosing instead to self-publish and self-distribute his work to local book stores around T or C. He doesn't even distribute across the state. What makes Fox Mulder's awareness of this novel, let alone his claim that he *owns* a copy, even more surprising, is that this particular book wasn't even pressed, but printed and spiral bound at a local copy shop. There are probably, literally, less than a hundred copies in existence. The young man's awareness of the book aside, it's practically inconceivable that a copy of the book, titled *The Cosmic Revenge of Cautious Cole Deadwood*, could have possibly found its way into the hands of someone not living in New Mexico. After Fox Mulder mentions the book, Homeless Vic says, "I may have read something like that a while back," then asks, "Where are you from again?" Fox Mulder says, "Dayton, Ohio," which doesn't sound right to Frankie Baca, who is pretty sure he'd heard that our visitors were from New York. Homeless Vic doesn't say anything, and tries to excuse himself from the conversation and Frankie begins to confirm that his uncle's book is exactly what Mulder had described, and is trying to ask the young man how he came across a copy but is interrupted when Mulder grabs Homeless Vic's arm. Vic stops, turns around, stares at Fox Mulder with what Frankie Baca might describe as a fierce sense of worry, a look hovering somewhere between concern and raw anger. Still holding Vic's arm, Mulder answers Frankie's question, says, "I heard a song about it." Frankie says, "The book?" And Mulder says, "The book," without removing his eyes from

Homeless Vic, who finally looks away to the ground. He says, "I don't know nothing about that," then, "Now if you'll excuse me." As Homeless Vic walks across the park toward the Rio Grande, Frankie asks Fox Mulder what that was all about, and Fox Mulder says, "Nothing important." Of course, Frankie doesn't believe that for a minute because he can tell that he just witnessed something strange.

When Fox Mulder begins to walk away from Frankie Baca, without even saying goodbye, Frankie calls out and offers him a ride. He's surprised when the kid, who seems a bit moody, takes him up on the offer. Once in his red Chevy Silverado, Frankie asks Fox Mulder what he's doing in T or C. Mulder says, "I don't know." Frankie says, "That's a strange reason to end up in a place like this." Fox Mulder reaches up and turns on the truck radio without asking. Buck Owens's "I've Got a Tiger by the Tail" is playing. He says, "This isn't a place where people just end up." Fox Mulder says, "I was looking for someone." Frankie tells Fox Mulder that maybe he can help. He says, "I know a lot of folks around here." Fox Mulder says, "I don't think you can help—I don't think the person I'm looking for even exists." Frankie says, "Is it Al Walters? Is that who you're looking for?" Fox Mulder says it's not Al Walters, but that he'd hoped the junk shop owner might be able to help. A new song starts on the radio. Frankie doesn't know what it is right away, but the guitar's slight twang seems familiar. He realizes who it's by as soon as Jim Toop's wispy, raw, but decidedly untwangy voice starts to sing: "Where the desert highway meets the sky/That's where we danced when we last got high." Frankie says, "You know the man singing this song disappeared from right up the road there?" Fox Mulder turns off the radio, again without asking, which kind of bothers Frankie who firmly believes that the driver of a vehicle should control said vehicle's radio. Frankie says, "Not a fan of that one, I guess." Then, "You want I can take you by Al's, see if he's around." Frankie adds, "Maybe I can get him to talk to you." Fox Mulder says, "I'm not sure what I'd even want to say to him at this point." Then, "Maybe later." Frankie Baca tells the young man how to get ahold of him at The Parks Department and the two ride the rest of the way in silence. As Fox Mulder gets out of the car, Frankie asks him how long he plans on staying. Mulder says he won't be around much longer. He says, "I'm ready to get out of here." Frankie Baca says, "You sound like a lot of our young people here." Fox Mulder says, "Can't say I blame them," and closes the door. Frankie watches Fox Mulder go to his room, thinks about the happiness he has found in T or C and says to himself, "Actually, I can blame them. I can blame them all."

*

Though the image still seems to be coming into focus, it shouldn't come as a surprise that we're entering into a critical moment in the history of Truth or Consequences. What is about to happen—we have no way to prepare for it. Not knowing the depth of what we don't know, we are left only to brace ourselves for whatever might come, however sharp that emerging truth might quake, how brawny and wide its aftershocks. Even knowing that something is coming, though, is sometimes not enough to prevent the unthinkable.

Perhaps we should liken this situation to one of Toop's songs, in this instance, the not-quite-title-track of *Your Sunglasses Are in the Junk Drawer*, which is known, in its entirety, as "Your Sunglasses Were in the Junk Drawer, Now

They Are on Your Face." The song tells the story of a man and woman preparing for a desert picnic date. After the song's unnamed female lead has trouble finding her sunglasses, she begins searching frantically for them, "checking her pockets and purse," before eventually finding them in the kitchen junk drawer. As the song's speaker and male protagonist immediately points out, his romantic partner "shoulda checked the junk drawer first," because, "That's where the things we need all hide/where all our secrets go to die." This leads to the song's odd but affecting chorus:

> Everything buried comes back to the light, babe,
> You've got to cover your eyes 'till the day turns to
> night, babe
> Oooooooooohhhhhhh, your sunglasses.

Besides the first line of the chorus's influence on Springsteen's "Atlantic City,"—Springsteen is a self-professed Toop fan—what is most striking about this song is its treatment of the junk drawer and its weirdly optimistic—or pessimistic, depending on how you look at it—assertion that lost things will be found. Granted, in the song's very next line, Toop reminds us that sometimes it's best to avert our eyes until the harsh light of a thing fades—who knows? Perhaps the real question, then, is if the pieces of the secret coalesce so that the dusty truth emerges, will its brilliance burn our eyes or has day turned to night while we've been hiding our eyes for all those years?

This is, believe it or not, the very question running through Angela Boyer's mind right now as she slings drinks at the Pin Hole. She was supposed to take another night off to avoid Daniel Morus, but Billy called her earlier in the day and told he had business to take care of, so he couldn't cover her shift. When *that* Angela told her son that she really didn't want to be put in the same position as two nights prior, Billy assured her that she wouldn't. "I've got that under control," he said. This made Angela nervous until she showed up for work and was told by Ron Suarez about the night before when Billy "Clocked that snoopy, out-of-town fucker and got him arrested." Thanks to this bit of news, *that* Angela is at ease while she works. It's the first time she's been at ease since her encounter with Morus and, as such, she's open to discussing her previous encounter. When Ron Suarez and Big Stu ask her about the guy that her boy knocked out, she tells them that he was the most aggressive Toop fan she'd ever met, that he kept telling her she was lying about everything, as if he knew more about her life than she did, until, finally, as the conversation was ending, he told her he believed that, not only was Jim Toop still alive, but that she'd been carrying on some sort of relationship with him for quite some time. When *that* Angela asked Daniel Morus first, how dare he suggest such outlandish things and, second, where did he possibly get such foolish ideas to begin with, he started talking about some new songs of Toop's surfacing. And then he said, "And if Jim Toop is still alive, I'd like to think the two of you are still together." When *that* Angela asked why he believed that, Daniel Morus said, "Because of those old songs—the love in those songs." He adds, "Or maybe something went wrong? The new songs I heard—" And here, *that* Angela ended the conversation by saying, "That was a long time ago. People change. And it was never a big deal to begin with. He wrote a song and a half about me." She told him that if Jim Toop was still alive, she wouldn't know, and that was that. While telling Ron and Stu about her encounter, she says, "All because of some damn songs." Everyone listening has a good laugh because they all believe that Jim Toop is long gone, but as the laugh dies down, Big Stu says, "I guess we don't really know," and *that* Angela says, "I guess we never will." She says, "They never did find a body," and Big Stu says, "But if he were alive, don't you think he'd have been in touch with you?" He adds, "What with you two being friends and all?" When *that* Angela answers, she says, "Maybe, maybe not." She says, "Sometimes things don't go as planned. Sometimes a person has to make sacrifices." She says, "I don't know." Then: "Or, you know, maybe he *was* sucked up into one of those spaceships and is waiting to be put back down." The men all laugh and feel a bit awkward because they don't know how to react. The truth is, nobody ever knows how to deal with *that* Angela when she talks about Jim Toop because there's always an odd sincerity in the way she says sometimes utterly baffling and seemingly insincere things. Case in point: nobody who knows *that* Angela would ever think her capable of believing any of the more outlandish rumors surrounding Jim Toop's disappearance, but here we are. So why does she say these things? Why does she say anything at all? What sentiment is lurking beneath such apparent deflections? *That* Angela never says quite enough for us to know and as this conversation trails off she walks over to the jukebox and slips in a dollar. The first song she plays is The Carpenters' cover of Klaatu's "Calling Occupants of Interplanetary Craft." *That* Angela sings along from behind the bar while its vaguely psychedelic production fills up the room. We know that she doesn't believe that Jim Toop was taken by a UFO, but if this is the way she wants to remember him right now, so be it.

While the song plays, nobody moves, even to sip their drinks—except for *that* Angela who wipes down the bar and reloads the ice bin—until about halfway through, when there is a flurry of activity, sirens and the blue lights of squad cars, flashing down the street outside the bar's front door. At first, everyone is amused and curious. After all, this is the second night in a row that the lights of emergency vehicles have filled the bar's open door and painted the walls outside in stuttering flashes. The bar erupts in murmurs of playful speculation. Daniel Shapiro, a retired teacher who moved here after falling in love with the town through his long-ago, annual visits to the local artist's colony, says, "Maybe someone is trying to finish off the historical society," which results in a few laughs, but Big Stu, always one to take things a bit too literally, points out that, "So far, all we've seen tonight are police cars, so it probably isn't a fire." As *that* Angela and the bar patrons filter out the door to the sidewalk to try to see where the cars have stopped, a thunderous boom echoes down the street. The crowd of half-drunken onlookers can easily see that the police cars—at least six of them, most of the city's fleet, plus at least a few reserve officers—are parked a few blocks down, directly in front of Al Walters's junk shop. Before any of the bar's patrons know what is happening, *that* Angela says, "Shit," and runs toward the scene. Ron Suarez tries to stop her, but she's too fast for him, especially since he's had a few beers, so he, Big Stu, Daniel Shapiro and a couple of the bar's other curious customers, who are too drunk to have much regard for their safety follow her, mostly out of curiosity. It doesn't take long for them to catch up to Angela, who is stopped behind a squad car watching, trying to sort out the scene. The officers are standing behind their open doors, guns drawn and pointed at Al's junk shop. Angela doesn't say anything for fear of drawing attention to herself and being asked to leave. The men from the bar follow suit.

What is it that everyone is looking at? What's causing this wild scene, bathed, at first, mostly in blue light, and now, at this very moment, faint red as an ambulance pulls up from an intersecting street? There in the doorway that leads to his upstairs apartment over the junk shop stands Al Walters, pointing a shotgun at Fox Mulder and Billy Boyer. There's a third person on the sidewalk rolling around in what appears to be a little bit of blood and a great deal of pain. One of the police officers is saying, "Al, put down the gun," and "Let the EMT's treat that man." The onlookers can't tell from this far away, but will later learn that the man writhing on the ground is Daniel Morus, who was shot by Al Walters when he, while trying to talk the old junk shop owner into lowering his weapon, had the bad sense to reach out and try to push the barrel of the gun down, which resulted in Al, crazy sonuva bitch that he is, jerking the gun upward and firing almost, but not quite entirely, over Daniel Morus's shoulder. While none of the onlookers want anyone to get hurt, they're mostly worried about Billy Boyer. And, of course, Billy's well-being is certainly the only thing that *that* Angela is thinking about when she finally does decide to go the rest of the way around the squad car and start saying things like, "Al, you don't need to do this," and "Al, put the gun down and let these men go."

The reserve officer closest to *that* Angela, a man named Josh Cross who manages one of the hot spring hotels where tourists frequently stay, says, "You need to leave, Ms. Boyer." *That* Angela ignores the reserve officer and slowly creeps toward the junk shop. From the doorway where he is holding the gun, Al Walters shouts, "I can't let them leave, Angie." And *that* Angela says, "Of course you can let them leave." Al Says, "They're dangerous." This strikes most of the people listening as an odd thing for Al Walters to say, as he's never been particularly paranoid, despite his heavy marijuana usage, and nor has he ever been prone to any kind of extreme behavior. *That* Angela says, "They're not dangerous." She says, "They're just young men." Then: "And an old asshole." Al says, "We'll go to prison." Here, Officer Chuck says, "You're only going to go to prison if you don't drop the gun and let the EMT's through to treat that man you shot." *That* Angela says, "These men aren't dangerous." She says, "Whatever it is that makes you think that, it isn't so." She says, "It's over, Al. Put the gun down and let the EMT's through." Still, Al keeps his gun trained on Fox Mulder and Billy Boyer and still, the squad cars' lights illuminate the front of his shop, shaking blue against the soft, red roof tiles that hang between the shop and Al's apartment. Angela says, again, "It's over, Al." And Fox Mulder, speaking for the first time, says, "Can I check on him?" and starts to move towards the downed Daniel Morus. Al says, "Don't move." Billy Boyer says, "Let the kid check on his friend." Al doesn't waiver. Angela says, "Please, Al." Officer Chuck says, "Don't make this worse than it has to be, Al." And then one gun fires, and, as generally happens in situations like this, more guns fire, and the onlookers all scatter and duck and lie down on the ground and try to crawl behind cars and buildings and each other for protection, and on the edge of town, at the Desert Ridge Inn, Echelle is reading updates about the hostage situation on her smart phone's Facebook app, and Angela Morelli is waiting in her room for a 10:30 appointment with one of her johns, but he won't show because he's watching the scene unfold at Al's, and Randall Heath sits on his sofa at home, wearing a NICAP hat and watching Giorgio A. Tsoukalos talk about UFO's on the History Channel, and Angie Leigh is already in bed, fast asleep, because she has to open the diner at six in the morning, and Frankie Baca and his wife are watching soft-core porn on HBO and fooling around on the couch now that their daughter is finally asleep for the night, and Homeless Vic, probably stoned or tripping, is sitting by his phone, nervous, thinking about writing a new story, or maybe a novel, about a strange boy who arrives in a foreign land and has the ability to look into peoples' souls and divine their deepest truths, and José Jackson is passed out drunk on his sofa while reruns of 90's sitcoms play on TV Land, and Seth Pond is staring at a block of clay, waiting for inspiration to strike for a new sculpture, while his wife, Andrea, bakes cookies knowing they will comfort him when he comes inside an hour later not having made any progress, and Gabe Sinclair, lucky to be staying in his house at all, is trying to fall asleep on his sofa while his wife lies in bed, wide awake, not mad anymore, but hurt, and scared because her husband felt like he needed to have sex with a prostitute instead of her, and Andy Tatroult is playing pinochle with his grandparents in Albuquerque because he took the next few days off so he could visit them, and a few blocks away, the Cortez is hopping as the 7:30 showing of some movie about a comic book hero is just letting out and excited kids and their less excited parents are filtering onto the sidewalk and heading to their cars, clueless as to what has been happening outside until they see the flashing squad car lights down the street and then turn on their phones to a barrage of push notifications, and Officer Chuck isn't firing his gun anymore because whatever was just happening seems to be over, and the boys from the bar are cowering behind the squad cars, mostly intact, though Big Stu pissed himself a little when the bullets started flying, and the EMT's are rushing in, looking for the wounded, and Angela is flat on the asphalt, looking up towards where Al Walters had been standing a moment ago, desperately scanning the ground for her son, who she is relieved to see kneeling beside Fox Mulder, both over Daniel Morus, and waving over an EMT.

This is how the night ends. This is what happens when the past is dragged out into the light from the depths of the junk drawer in which it's buried. In "Scorpion's Sting," another song from Toop's *Your Sunglasses are in the Junk Drawer*, there's this line that goes, "When the ghost arrives in town having found the voice to sing/His song will burn your guts worse than a scorpion's sting." And here, and now, our city's ghosts swirl in the air above us, in gun smoke and the blue light of squad cars, in the form of half-remembered but still buried secrets, the details of which may or may not come to light in the following days, and of which almost all of us to a man, woman, and child, will question the significance of, will wonder privately and ask aloud—did it really have to be this way? Did the ghost's song really need to rot us from the inside out? To result in such violence? Or would we have been better off just letting the fucker sing, sing, sing the past out loud so we could face it head on. Thirty-odd years is a long time. Maybe it would have healed our town's wounds had we confronted them—but no, we hid them away and left them to fester into this, this, this, who knows—this whatever the shit just happened.

V. THE TAXIDERMIST'S CATALOG

-or-

"On Finding Jim Toop in Song and Space: *The Taxidermist's Catalog* and Problems of (Auto) Biography."

By Daniel Morus, as published in *Folk! Magazine*, 30.3-30.5 and Online. (2013-2014)

PT. 1:
THE DESERT HELD ITS BREATH

Twelve months ago, Richard Epps, the founder of this magazine, came to me with an interesting artifact and a job offer. The artifact, as I'm sure our readers are at this point aware, was the recently found recording of Jim Toop's final, long-thought-to-be-lost album, *The Taxidermist's Catalog*. In light of just how surprising the tape's unearthing truly was, it should come as no surprise that Epps's job for me was to authenticate the tape. Through my attempts at authentication, I discovered some unusual anachronisms that initially led me to question the tape's authenticity. That said, because the tape sounded so much like Toop, I began investigating the possibility that Toop had been alive and still actively recording music for several years after he "disappeared." My investigation led me to California, New Mexico, and finally, Ohio, and, though there are still a number of questions surrounding Toop's disappearance, I am absolutely confident that the version of *The Taxidermist's Catalog* that will see release in a few short weeks (after which, the remaining installments of this feature will run in three consecutive issues of *Folk!*) is absolutely authentic.

With that out of the way, it's important to make clear what this essay will and won't be about. This introduction to the album will not be about the tangled, mysterious disappearance of Jim Toop and the theories surrounding that disappearance. It's not going to be about the strange circumstances through which a copy of Toop's lost record found its way into our possession. It will not be about the business of bringing the record to release, which was complicated by a claim from Toop's father. It will not be about Toop's disappearance and the adjunctive conspiracy theories. Nor will it be about my attempts to find out if Jim Toop is *still* alive and well, a question that arose after I interviewed Toop's father. And finally, this introduction will definitely, absolutely not be about me being shot in the shoulder by a paranoid old man—who was subsequently shot to death by the police—during my investigation. This introduction to Jim Toop's long lost, miraculously recovered album isn't going to be about any of those things because I'd rather write about what really matters here; to put it like a true Boomer—it's going to be about the music, man.

That said, while I promise that this introduction won't be about the mysteries or drama surrounding Toop and the found tape, I do feel it necessary to provide ample context so that audiences understand precisely how stunning and unusual (and yes, miraculous, even) were the circumstances of this recording's discovery. No doubt those of you reading this are familiar with the various theories surrounding Toop's disappearance in 1977, so I won't rehash them now, not just because you know about them, but because they're utterly frivolous. A man disappeared in the desert—does there need to be a story or a reason? Sometimes these things just happen, and I'm inclined to believe that they just happen more frequently on quiet stretches of road defined by an almost holy absence of everything.

But let me be clear—my intent is not to be dismissive of those who theorize about Toop's disappearance. Certainly the stories embraced by the cult of Toop are seductive, and I have absolutely felt their influence on my life. Were it not for those theories, I would never have found myself driving through New Mexico, cutting a path through its deserts and sand blasted cities. I never would have, on my way into Truth or Consequences, stopped my car in the approximate spot where Toop's rental car was discovered close to forty years ago, stepped into the cool desert night, looked toward all the cardinal compass points, the ordinal points, and the quieter degrees between, then looked up at the sky, full of more stars than I'd ever seen, and recognized, for probably the first time in my life, the promise of infinity. I'll admit: there on the side of the road, looking up and out at the surrounding emptiness, it wasn't so difficult to imagine a UFO, or a cult, or kidnappers slipping out of the quiet black forever and stealing a single lost folk singer back to their own realms, twilit and secret. But that's where the pull of those theories ends. Before I drove down into Truth or Consequences, I looked up and down I-25, disappearing both directions into darkness, and I prepared myself to receive the truth about Jim Toop, however mundane it might be. Assuming, of course, I was going to find any truth at all.

As it happens, there wasn't much truth to be found in Truth or Consequences—echoes of whispers and faded rumors that, sure, maybe added up to something resembling truth, but that's all. Whatever truth there *was* to be found—a truth that had nothing to do with UFO's, or cults, or kidnappers, or anything else that might wind up on a cable mystery show—was closely guarded by the few who might have shed any real light on it. To wit, Al Walters, the man who shot me, was a former associate of Toop's who was believed by my travel companion—a young man who asked not to be named in this introduction, and so to whom I will refer to as "David"—to know that Jim Toop was still alive. When "David" asked about Toop, though, the old man pulled a shotgun off a wall rack and pointed it at us, backing us—us being myself, "David," and another local man who I will refer to only as B—out the door of his upstairs apartment and down to the street. I could tell that the shooter was as paralyzed with fear as we were. Even as we tried to extract ourselves from the odd confrontation, he refused to let us leave. Unfortunately, the standoff came to an end when Al's gun misfired, leading to, I'm told, as I was barely conscious at the time, a barrage of bullets ripping the frightened old man to pieces.

As tragic as all that may have been, this introduction to *The Taxidermist's Catalog* isn't going to dwell on that unfortunate act of violence. The only reason I felt it necessary to discuss it at all is that the shooting made national news and, were I to not mention it, I fear its exclusion would have come across as defensive or disingenuous. Was "David" out of line for dragging myself and B to the shooter's residence only to pester him with questions about Toop? Perhaps. And, perhaps, too, my young friend's questions and claims were out of line, especially when peppered with innuendo and flat out accusation, the first being, "Did you help cover up a murder involving Jim Toop in 1977?" and the second being,

"I met Jim Toop today—has he left Truth or Consequences at any point in the last twenty years?" While I understood the rationale behind the first question, I was stunned by my friend's assertion that he had actually *met* Jim Toop because, as far as I could tell, even if Toop lived beyond his disappearance, there was and is no trace of him currently living in Truth or Consequences. In fact, I'm confident that he is dead—I saw his grave. But that's beside the point—this is what you need to know: "David" was pushy and exacerbated Mr. Walters's already distraught emotional state, which led to my getting shot, which ultimately led to the somewhat kindly, but also paranoid and unsettled old man's brutal end.

And this is as good a place as any to leave this nonsense behind and begin to discuss *The Taxidermist's Catalog* itself, in part because I'm still not entirely comfortable writing about said nonsense, and in part because there are, perhaps, traces of that nonsense written into the album's opening track, "Frozen." When "David" and I first listened to this song almost a year ago, I was astonished by its sad beauty. Today, though still quite beautiful, it stands as a representative case study in why we must be careful in how we discuss issues of Toop's autobiography in conjunction with the album. The song begins with uneven acoustic guitar strums characteristic of Toop's later work, as he sings, "When the Gorgon came the desert held its breath/and waited for the hero's stony death." After Toop sings this line, the song bursts into a sweeping orchestral arrangement beneath which a gently buoyant bass line urges the song forward as Toop tells the story of a nameless hero who arrives at a desert town and decapitates the Gorgon who was terrorizing the town's people. Unfortunately, at the moment that the hero's sword slices through the monsters neck, he looks into the thing's evil eyes and turns to stone. In an unsettling turn, in the song's final verse, we learn that, though the hero's "...body is frozen, stone/His eyes still see unblinking and/His mind it goes on thinking." Considering the things I may or may not have learned in Truth or Consequences, this song makes sense as a metaphorical account of a character who becomes trapped someplace he doesn't necessarily want to be due to circumstances that are, at least in part, beyond his control. Let's say Toop somehow did something that could potentially be viewed as criminal, involuntary or not, self-defense or not—and honestly, who's to say what is what, with so much time having passed and all—and this act came to be symbolized, in the song, by the Gorgon's beheading. Let's say then, too, that the hero turning to stone could easily parallel a situation in which Toop was forced into hiding in or around Truth or Consequences, causing him to feel trapped. None of this feels like much of a stretch. But here's where our analysis gets muddy—we can't just assume the above without also asking if there would have been a legitimate reason for Toop to have felt trapped in Truth or Consequences? If rumors of an admittedly limited conspiracy forged to protect Toop from some form of legal recourse are true—let's say, as some rumors suggest, Jim Toop killed an off-duty police officer in self-defense—it's likely that he was living under an assumed identity as there are no records of Jim Toop after his disappearance, period. If Toop was alive, had a new identity, and was hardly famous enough to be recognized by the average citizen, he could have easily left Truth or Consequences any time he wanted. See, when we try to examine the album for clues into Toop's life, none of it adds up or makes much sense, and we begin to see how fruitless an endeavor it is to try to suss out any sort of real truth about Toop's post-disappearance life by looking for clues on the album. Like I said before, and repeat after me this time: it's all about the music, man.

And this is why "Frozen" is an ideal point of entry into our discussion of *The Taxidermist's Catalog*—it shows us that, as go the predictions of fortune tellers and palm readers, it may prove to be *too* easy to divine insight into Toop's post-disappearance life in these songs, when, in fact, there is no true insight to be had. Yes, there are autobiographical markers on the album—people and places, in particular—but they're steeped in such a lack of concrete specificity that we can hardly rely on them as sources of factual information. So vague, in fact, are Toop's lyrics that, when I listen to *The Taxidermist's Catalog*, I hear in its songs as much a description of myself as of Toop, always a good indicator that a given pop song is truly masterful. In "Frozen," I hear myself doubled in the song as both hero and Gorgon, as the frozen slayer of the beast and the beast itself. The song makes me think about my own stasis—my suicide attempt after my first wife left me, my second, brief marriage that went nowhere due to our incompatibility and my own unwillingness to change, and all the nothing that followed. If I can hear so much about myself in a song that was likely written before those circumstances in my life even existed, by someone who didn't even know I existed, then we need to be skeptical about what we claim to hear about Jim Toop in his songs. I get it, though. I do. I get that, with songs like "That Old Game Show," featuring lyrics about living in "a town built on trivia quizzes and teenage wishes," a clear reference to Truth or Consequences, it's difficult not to try to tease the details of Toop's life out of his songs. But as the subsequent parts of this essay will try to demonstrate, while Toop's experiences certainly inform the songs on *The Taxidermist's Catalog*, we must be discerning and not look for fully formed truths where there exist only traces and shadows.

PT. 2:
A RAINDROP MADE OF RUST

(Editor's note: When Daniel Morus sent us this second piece of his four part feature on Jim Toop's The Taxidermist's Catalog, *I initially balked at its length as it was 1,500 words longer than we'd agreed. However, after reading Mr. Morus's expert analysis, augmented, at times, by a more personal discussion of how Toop's music had an impact on his life, I decided to run the piece as is, making line-edits for the sake of only clarity and style. As such, our letters to the editor and our ongoing series of concert DVD reviews have been cut from this issue. Thanks for reading and I hope you agree that these temporary changes to the* Folk! *Magazine format are worthwhile. —R.E.)*

Now that *The Taxidermist's Catalog* has been released to the public, I suspect that many fans of Toop's music have noticed certain motifs and details reoccurring from his previous albums: "That Old Game Show" recalls the show business nostalgia of Toop's debut album; the surreal displacement in "A Painting of Flowers" ("I'm not gone, I'm that small speck/feckless and wrecked on the stem in your painting of flowers") evokes the theme of disappearance so prominent on *Black Triangle*; though fleeting, Toop's lament of the desert's static weather on "Weather" discusses Ohio's seasons, gently recalling *Ohio Songs*; and finally, and perhaps most noteworthy, are the many references to New Mexico, which, as we all know, featured heavily on *Your Sunglasses Are in the Junk Drawer*. The most notable call backs to *Sunglasses* come in the form of a trio of reoccurring characters. In "Mark's Novel" we're reintroduced to the fledgling novelist who previously appeared on *Sunglasses*' "Kite Flyin,'" in which we also originally met the aging junk shop owner who, on the new album's "Forget Me Not" appears "giving away guitars like candy." Then, of course, there is Angela, the most notable returning character. Angela first appeared in a song named for her on *Sunglasses* and has been a person of interest for amateur conspiracy theorists from the moment Toop disappeared, and hopeless romantics since heartbroken pop music fans began to identify her presence in some of Toop's other songs. On *The Taxidermist's Catalog*, Angela shows up by name on the lustful and sad "(Hideaway) Bed," in the abstract and intimate "Nothing Truer," and is probably alluded to on "That Old Game Show" and "Sideways Glances." It's possible, too, that Angela may be the speaker's second person interlocutor on many of the album's other songs, but as such second person writing is common in pop music, that's a risky assumption to make, especially when many of the songs provide little to no context by which we might identify the addressee. For example, on "Thirty Seconds," Toop sings, "You're always waking up thirty seconds before you've got some place to be/You're always thirty seconds late when you try to get close to me"—certainly Toop *could* be singing to Angela here, but there isn't any evidence to substantiate such a claim, so we'll leave it be. What is most interesting about these reoccurring themes and characters, though, is how they signal a dark shift in the tone and tenor of Toop's songwriting, a shift, I must admit, I resisted acknowledging, especially considering Toop's less romantic treatments of Angela on new songs—that part of the shift, in particular, was difficult to accept and shattering for those of us who invested much of our careers writing about that romance.

I'm pointing out these connections now, because while in the previous essay in this series I encouraged listeners to resist approaching *The Taxidermist's Catalog* as some sort of Rosetta Stone to all of the mysteries surrounding Toop's disappearance, I *do* believe that it's important that we attempt to situate the new album in the canon of Toop's work, and part of doing that is identifying the people, places, and themes that have been prevalent throughout his career. So let's take a closer look at some of these reoccurring motifs, these totems to Toop's lyrical obsessions, not to gain insight into any of the silly mysteries surrounding Toop, but so that we might better trace his growth and development as an artist. Before we do that, though, let's take a quick look at the album's title because, while the cover art is immaterial—Toop had nothing to do with it, though the design team should be congratulated for making an empty stretch of generic desert highway look so utterly haunted—the title came directly from Toop. So what is a "taxidermist's catalog," exactly? It seems to be both a catalog used by a taxidermist to order the tools of his trade, the equipment necessary to preserve dead things as keepsakes and trophies, and a collection of the taxidermist's wares themselves, the preserved creatures and moments he's already stuffed and mounted, ready to be shared with future generations. In essence, the title points toward Toop preserving his subjects and, perhaps, himself as dead, lifeless, and put on display for all to see, frozen in time. It's certainly a sad idea, and one that, in some ways, plays out across the album's songs and might even resonate across Toop's life. At the same time, because *The Taxidermist's Catalog* was Toop's intended title for the album way back in 1977, *before* his disappearance, the title also appears to be a strange, surprising coincidence, considering how fitting it is in the context of all we've learned about Toop's life. But we'll come back to all that. For now, let's turn our attention from the taxidermist to his subjects.

The first connection discussed above doesn't demand much scrutiny as it's one of Toop's longest running reoccurring themes, and its appearance is fairly obvious on *The Taxidermist's Catalog*. Here, Toop's nod to show business nostalgia takes the form of a reference to the television show *Truth or Consequences* in the song "That Old Game Show." Obviously, Toop wrote about the game show because of its connection to the town where he'd previously lived, but the reason we're talking about it here is because of the way Toop inverts his usual romanticization of show business into a stinging critique, quoting, in the process, a lyric from his song "Charlie" off of *New Ghosts for an Old City*. Here is the original:

> Tramps they come and tramps they go
> And what the little blind flower girl doesn't know
> Is when it's dark outside
> Her tramp's skin has got the holy glow

Of forever out of history.

These lines are mirrored in the following verse from "That Old Game Show":

> Well the master came and the master went
> And he took your springs
> And he bought your soul
> For the cost of some cue card truth, quickly spent
> For forever out of history

Due to the contrasting circumstances of the songs' subjects—marveling at Chaplin on the big screen versus considering a town that changed its name for a brief moment of game show notoriety—it might be easy to overlook Toop's shift in attitude. By drawing a clear comparison between the two through borrowed lyrics and mirrored form, though, it would seem that Toop wanted us to see the connection between the songs, wanted to highlight his change of attitude: a haunted celebration of cinema history becoming an angry, cynical screed against corporate influence on citizens' daily lives. Is it too far a leap to suggest that by the time Toop was recording the songs on *The Taxidermist's Catalog* he'd grown up a little and no longer viewed the world around him through the optimism of youth? On "That Old Game Show," Toop sounds frustrated, bordering on angry, as if looking back on a lifetime of disappointments (to which, I can assure you, I can relate). Perhaps the most striking aspect of Toop's shift, then, is its severity, as Toop wasn't *that* much older when he would have initially been writing an early version of *The Taxidermist's Catalog*, at least in theory. Even if he was writing five years after his disappearance, he'd still have been relatively young (far younger than I am now), which makes his deep cynicism somewhat puzzling.

Were the shift limited to just "That Old Game Show," it could easily be an anomaly, but we see the same thing in Toop's thematic treatment of disappearance on "Painting of Flowers." Looking at *Black Triangle*, Toop's preoccupation with disappearing was couched in an adventurous sense of wonder and delicate, almost wistful desire for return. Think of the "bird of the sky" telling the "sad, sad ground" that "It's time I get myself home," on, "Said the Cactus to the Cloud," or the moment in "Black Triangle" when one of the song's "powerful men" tells the song's protagonist, "Won't be this one, won't be the next/but we'll take you home one day," before "casually puffing and passing a jay," or even the impassioned bridge of "Desert Highway," on which Toop sings:

> This road is an infinite coil, unwound
> As it vibrates, so do I
> 'Till together we become sound
> Goodbye

In each of these songs', Toop's speakers are lost or otherwise disappeared, but either enjoy the ride while quietly longing for home or outright celebrate the romance of their disappearances. This is not the case on The Taxidermist's Catalog. Though the entire album features only two instances of characters disappearing, both play as unsettling occurrences rife with disappointment. I've already quoted the central, reoccurring image from "Paintings of Flowers," in which Toop's speaker declares, "I'm not gone, I'm that small speck/feckless and wrecked on the stem in your painting of flowers," a grim line that, though whimsical in its conceit, ultimately emphasizes the speaker's alienation

The other instance of a disappearing Toop protagonist shows up in the new album's penultimate song, the vaguely bluesy dirge "Nothing Truer." The song is built around a fairly direct series of mostly absurd "truisms" that primarily work at dehumanizing the song's speaker by demonstrating how out of touch he feels with the world around him. Among some of the song's more outlandish truths, the speaker proclaims, "Nothing truer than a bird made of light/Nothing truer than a disco night," which is closely followed by, "Nothing truer than a snail on a razor/Nothing truer than Brando's face, or/a satin blazer, or a blind skip tracer," and then, "Nothing truer than a butterfly made of water/Born as Hestia's only daughter." The latter pair of lines are absurd, of course, not just for a describing a butterfly made of water, but for claiming the butterfly is a descendent of Hestia, the Greek goddess of the hearth who chose a chaste life despite overtures from both Poseidon and Apollo. The song's sole lyric about disappearing comes late in the final verse:

> Nothing truer than a raindrop made of rust
> 'Cept to maybe see a live man turn to something
>   smaller than
>   smaller than dust
> Impermanent as trust
> Watch me blow away, blow away, blow away
> In a wind gust

Again, like the disappearance in "Paintings of Flowers," the basic concept of this disappearance lends itself to a mysterious sense of romance and wonder, but this time, Toop's delivery is wearier than ever before. As such, the passage seems to focus not on the magic of a man turning to dust, but on the inherent sense of desolation arising from such a transformation. When I traveled to Truth or Consequences for my investigation, I spent a lot of time listening to a dub of *The Taxidermist's Catalog* on an old Walkman. Surrounded by the desert and buildings worn by its forces, the above lyrical passages resonated with me deeper than anything on Toop's previous recordings. It resonated with me so deeply that I found myself, more than a few times, feeling the urge to reconnect with my ex-wives. I made numerous attempts to phone them both. My second wife, Amanda, was easy to track down. We had a pleasant conversation about her current circumstances. She'd reconnected with an old flame from high school. I told her that was nice for her and she told me she still didn't have kids of her own, but her new husband did, that he came with two teenagers, a package deal. I asked if that was strange for her and she said a little, but that she was fine with it. She said, "I'm sorry we didn't work out," and I told her that it wasn't her fault. As for Betty, my first wife, she was considerably more difficult to get in touch with. She is still teaching in Ohio and I found her campus contact information on her university's web site, but every attempted call went straight to voicemail. The first time, I left a message saying only that I'd been thinking about her, about the past, had been wondering how she'd been. I left contact information for the motel where I was staying, but she never called back. This made me feel even more deeply what Toop is describing on "Nothing Truer." See? Sometimes I can't help but recognize my own circumstances when I dig in to analyze Toop's songs. But enough of that—we still need to talk about Toop's reoccurring characters.

First, though, I need to make sure we all have a bit more context about *The Taxidermist's Catalog* and Toop's life. In doing this, I realize that I'll be throwing a bone to those of you predominantly interested in Toop's disappearance. This needs to be done, though, because we need to understand how or why Toop's attitude might have changed towards old friends and lovers. By now, I'm sure many readers (and listeners) noticed that the song "Nothing Truer," as quoted above, includes a reference to Francis Ford Coppola's film *Apocalypse Now*, in which Marlon Brando's Colonel Walter E. Kurtz describes a snail crawling along the edge of a razor. This is notable because, though principle photography for *Apocalypse Now* was completed in 1977, not long before Toop disappeared, the film didn't premiere until at least two years after said disappearance. This was one of the details on *The Taxidermist's Catalog* that prompted my investigation into the tape's authenticity, and resulted in my learning that Toop was still alive and recording music several years after his rental car was found on the side of I-25. As much as I am loath to engage in such speculation, I can't help but think it's important, here, to understand how and why Toop's depictions of his friends in New Mexico changed over time. What happened after *Your Sunglasses are in the Junk Drawer* that led to their reimagining? I don't have an answer for that, but it's important to remember that Toop was growing older *after his disappearance*, and his relationships were changing, as they tend to do, over time, while he was writing and rewriting his album—the Toop we're listening to on *The Taxidermist's Catalog* isn't the Jim Toop who disappeared in 1977, but an older, more experienced and, presumably, more jaded version of the man.

The three characters who Toop revisits—two of whom I personally met on my travels—are a writer named Mark, the now late junkshop owner named Al and, of course, the much celebrated Angela. Mark hardly seems worth discussing in the same breath as the other two as he doesn't seem to have a particularly meaningful connection to Toop. That said, when even fleeting references help illuminate Toop's shifting attitude, we can be confident in our reading of those shifts. So minor are Toop's references to Mark, though, that I would have missed them entirely were it not for the investigative efforts of my young friend "David," who noticed the reference and then, in a conversation with a local Truth or Consequences layabout, learned that Mark and his novel, as described in the *The Taxidermist's Catalog* song "Mark's Novel," are both real. In that song Toop describes the titular character as "A listless hack/with a sad, sad lack of vision," before characterizing the author's work as being about "An Albuquerque cowboy, fighting for his milk/Until one day he was encased in silk," where he stays until he "...explodes from his shell/Rises up above the sand and sends the bastards to hell," the bastards being, as described in the song, a group of outlaws who had continually robbed the cowboy of his food and income. At this point in the song, Toop sings, "Mark told me he's been working on his next book/I know he's never going to finish," then ends by repeating, six times:

> Marks says he's a writer
> Really he's not
> Mark used to be my friend
> Now time's the only friend I've got

This is a surprisingly clear critique of a real person, especially when Toop, just a few years before his disappearance, described the same person so differently on "Kite Flyin'" from *Sunglasses*:

> Well Mark's my friend, gonna be a big writer

> He tells me about the spirits in the sand
> He brings joint, and I bring the lighter
> And we listen to *The Band* by The Band

If there is a clearer moment with which to illustrate the shift between Toop's pre-disappearance work and *The Taxidermist's Catalog*, I haven't yet found it. While the other examples of Toop's attitudinal shifts are more interesting due to the higher interpersonal stakes, those shifts aren't quite as drastic or overt as what we see in his treatment of Mark. As a point of comparison, also on "Kite Flyin'" Toop describes Al, the man who shot me, as having "The most generous soul at the bar/I gave him my trust, he gave me his guitar." On *Taxidermist Catalog*'s "Forget Me Not," though—a song that finds its speaker regretting a series of life decisions—Al is described thusly:

> The junkshop owner's a pusher of bad dreams
> Giving away guitars like candy
> Filling the world with secrets
> Stuffing himself with fear and cheap brandy

Here, the shift in Toop's emotional landscape is two-fold. For the first and only time in all of the songwriter's canon, we see a genuine regret that he became a musician, and that regret spills over into his somewhat juvenile attack on Al. When viewed in light of the rest of the album, this becomes yet another example of how dissatisfied Toop had grown with his circumstances by the time he finished recording *The Taxidermist's Catalog*. As for the secrets he's referencing in the above lyric, when I first heard the song, I was worried it might be an allusion to some sort of sexual impropriety between Al and a young Jim Toop, but after my visit to New

Mexico, that suspicion was put to rest. So what were those secrets, then? This is neither the time nor place for that. I'm past my word count for this installment, and we haven't even talked about Angela yet. And see, we have to talk about Angela. We can't not talk about Angela because she's Angela. *The* Angela. *That* Angela.

Of course Angela was going to show up on *The Taxidermist's Catalog*, and of course Toop's fans were going to go wild about it. Despite having only appeared, explicitly by name, in one of Toop's prior songs—she is almost certainly in more of his songs, but we'll keep it simple, here—Angela has, over the years, assumed a mythic quality among many of Toop's fans, myself included. She is, for many of us, both a romantic ideal and a potential key to unlocking the mysteries surrounding Toop. Of course Angela's appearances on *The Taxidermist's Catalog* were going to cause a stir, especially when those appearances are far less romantic than what came before. On the song "Angela," from *Sunglasses*, Toop describes the song's subject's red hair as "a waterfall down to her waist," and notes how she "sips her beer with a widow's grace/And smiles when I pick eyelashes from her face." The song even includes a sexual metaphor, of sorts, when Toop sings, "Oh, when we're one/I feel the warmth and water of the world on my skin." With these lyrics in mind, it should come as no surprise that Angela came to represent something very specific for Toop fans. Granted, it should also come as no surprise when on *The Taxidermist's Catalog*'s, "(Hideaway) Bed," Toop describes Angela in less romantic terms, some fans might grow a bit disillusioned. But disillusion seems to be Toop's point, here: "Angela and me we meet at dusk/I'm her dirty little secret/she's an empty husk of a dream, so red/ Taking up half of my bed." This is closely followed by the chorus, which reads, "Oh, she used to hideaway with me/On my hideaway, hideaway, hideaway, hideaway bed." Angela's other appearance on the album, by name, comes on "Nothing Truer." Here, hidden in plain sight among the song's many outlandish truisms, Toop arrives at something sincere and intimate when he sings, "Nothing truer than Angela's tears/ When she leaves me again after seven beers." Angela is left on the sidelines for most of the rest of the song until near the end when, as his slow strum crescendos over bluesy horn chords, Toop sings, "Nothing truer than Angela giving up/She says, "Jim, pretty baby, shit I've had enough." This line is followed by an abrupt halt, during which Toop sings, "There's nothing truer than Angela in the past tense," as he keeps the beat by slapping the body of his acoustic guitar. After pausing a moment to let the line resonate—to let us all feel how true the line is, how painful all love is in the past tense, especially when that old love won't return your calls and forgets you ever existed—Toop reinitiates his strumming, the horns kick back in, and the song ends.

I should point out, though, that for all of Toop's negative shifts in attitude towards his various subjects, there is one reoccurring entity that he still seems to hold in high regard on *The Taxidermist's Catalog*: Ohio and its weather. As fans know, most of Toop's Ohio references appear on his 1974 album, *Ohio Songs*. On that album, Toop famously celebrates his old state's weather, be it in the subtle embrace of autumn's "metal sky" on "We Learned to Fly," the vivid description of "burning trees and silent ghosts" on "Here, the Leaves Change Slow," or the excitement of spring, "wet with winter's weeping/the green was only sleeping" on "When I Was a Boy." When a quiet and brief nod to Ohio's weather appears on *Taxidermist* track "Weather," the result is devastating. Though the song is mostly a grim description of desert weather, buried between descriptions of "sand blowing like a fist" and "a heat so hot it cooks the skin" and "dries the bones," is a moment of nostalgic appreciation: "Oh, Ohio, I miss the comfort of your seasons/The cool breeze, the red cheeks—I've got my reasons." That's all—as Truth or Consequences, its people, and its environment all lost stock in Toop's estimation, he never stopped loving Ohio, where he spent much of his early life. Despite the lyric's vague nature—especially compared to the rest of the song's vivid detail—these lines steal the show, thanks in part, at least, to Toop's stunning performance, but also because the non-descript imagery creates an inviting space into which listeners can invent an entire childhood to inscribe on the song. Clearly Toop is celebrating the change of seasons, but whose red cheeks are those? A young girlfriend's, perhaps? An old friend's? When I hear those lines, I'm filled with uncanny ache for the time I spent in Ohio with Betty, and for the days we spent driving down I-75 to Dayton, where we'd visit the sites named in Toop's songs. I'd think about wanting to talk to her, how she still hadn't called me back. Those lines still break my heart. And it was while listening to them the day after my trip to New Mexico that I decided I had to go back to Ohio, mostly to see what else I could learn about Jim Toop and his connection to that state, but maybe also so I could try to learn a thing or two about Betty. But that story will have to wait until next time.

PT. 3:
THE EVENING REDNESS IN THE SOUTHWEST

(Editor's Note: Once again, we've had to bump regular features to make room for a longer-than-expected piece from Mr. Morus. Also, in reader feedback, we noted many of you were a bit frustrated with Mr. Morus's extended feature on The Taxidermist's Catalog. *While we didn't want to impose our editorial will on him and fundamentally change his essay, we did request some slight shifts in approach. We're confident you will be pleased with the results.—R.E.)*

At the conclusion of the previous installment of this four-part feature on Jim Toop's *The Taxidermist's Catalog*, I mentioned that, shortly after my trip to New Mexico, I decided to travel to Ohio. It is my understanding that some readers believed that my desire to go to Ohio was driven entirely by a need to talk to my first wife. That is simply not the case. I wanted to go to Ohio because the place was important to Jim Toop, and because it was important to my experiences as a Jim Toop fan. I spent several years in Ohio listening to Toop's songs and exploring the city where he spent much of his early life, and I believed that somewhere in the intersection of Toop's past, his change in attitude in the years between recording *Your Sunglasses are in the Junk Drawer* and *The Taxidermist's Catalog*, and my own disappointing life, that I might arrive at a better understanding of Toop's music. That, and not my attempt to contact my ex-wife, was the main reason I went to Ohio. And I *did* learn some things about Toop while I was there—but more on that later, because for now I've been asked by this magazine's editors to elaborate on Toop's disappearance and what I learned about it during my investigations. By so far refusing to write about Toop's disappearance, this publication's editors informed me, I was disappointing my audience. The editor's also suggested that if I provided more context, my trip to Ohio might make more sense to readers. After much consideration, I agreed to scale back on analysis and focus on describing what I *think* happened to Jim Toop in and after 1977. While part of me is still hesitant to bring the "mysteries" surrounding Toop's "disappearance" more fully into this discussion of *The Taxidermist's Catalog*—partially because I don't think it's any of our business, and partially because I don't want to face the inevitable trolling of UFO enthusiasts angry that I'd dare suggest Toop wasn't abducted by aliens—I ultimately came to the conclusion that Epps was right: the story that I'm trying to tell of this album needs more context, and as much as I'm loathe to admit it, that context needs to come from the areas of Toop's life that have been sensationalized by his fans. That said, in an attempt to de-sensationalize Toop's disappearance, the following material will be a matter-of-fact telling of everything I know about Toop's disappearance, beginning with the discovery of *The Taxidermist's Catalog*, and ending with what little I know about his post-disappearance life. Please know, though, that much of what you're about to read still exists in the realm of theory, at least in part, and should be treated as such.

To this day, I still don't know how Toop's lost tape found its way to Richard Epps. Upon first listen, a few details caught my attention and seemed suspect, leading me to question the tape's authenticity. You should know that the songs on the tape arrived almost exactly as they have been released to the public. The only treatment given to the tape, on our end, was updated mastering so the recording would met the specifications of today's digital media formats. The production was all in place, including the transitions between songs. A recording engineer friend of mine, who has asked not be named in this article, listened to the tape and noted that almost everything on the tape, except for one synthesizer that wasn't available until 1981 and is audible at the beginning of "That Old Game Show," could have been achieved prior to 1977. The results were puzzling: the recorded content sounded authentically like Jim Toop, but a few anachronisms pointed toward the tape not being at least entirely the work of Jim Toop. One of those anachronisms was the first clue that something with the tape was amiss. After our first listen, my friend "David" noticed that the album's final song, "Cormac Bleeding," contained a reference to Cormac McCarthy's 1985 novel *Blood Meridian*. In addition to the song's title, the ever vigilant "David" noticed that among the song's lyrics, were lines reading:

The desert sand blows in sea-foam ocean crests
Beneath the coming night
The evening redness in the Southwest

The full title of McCarthy's 1985 masterpiece is, of course, *Blood Meridian or The Evening Redness in the West*. Thanks to such references, in conjunction with the analysis of my engineer friend, I started to hypothesize that Toop might have lived and continued work on his album after his disappearance. Perhaps it doesn't sound like much, in retrospect, but this was more or less all the evidence I needed to convince Richard Epps to send me to Los Angeles for a conversation with Toop's father.

But was there really anything to learn? In Los Angeles I learned—thanks to two pictures of Toop at Graceland, one from around 1982 shortly after Presley's home was first opened to the public and the second from an event held there in 1999—that Toop lived for at least twenty-two years after his disappearance. On top of that, Toop's father was strangely enigmatic, and fed me just enough mystery to make me believe that his son *might* still be alive. Let me be clear, though: Toop is not still alive, despite my friend "David's" insistence that he *met* him during our time in Truth or Consequences. As much as I don't believe it now, I'm still surprised that I genuinely, albeit briefly, believed that it was *possible* that Toop might still be out there. In the end, though, I could only conclude that Toop died sometime between completing his album in the mid-to-late eighties and when the tapes surfaced a little over a year ago. Who knows, maybe Toop's death is what led to the tape surfacing?

And let's get this out of the way right now: the man who "David" believed to be Toop is an aging hippie who lives on the outskirts of Truth or Consequences. I met the man, too. He gave me a cigarette and stood with me for a moment as we watched the Rio Grande crawl past. Nothing about the man made me think he might be Jim Toop—granted, he wore a full, unkempt beard and his white hair was in dreadlocks, meaning I didn't get a good look at his face, but I had two advantages that "David" did not: first, I'd seen a picture of Jim Toop from 1999, and though I didn't see it for long, I had an idea of how Toop had aged up to that point; and second, I've seen the way my own face has aged over the years, knew how to see glimpses of my youth in the old face looking back at me in the mirror, and would like to think I'm good at doing the same with others. That man was *not* Jim Toop, but he *was* helpful. In the brief moments I stood with him, I asked him how long he'd been living in Truth or Consequences. He told me he'd lived there on and off for most of his life, that he'd drifted up to Albuquerque for a while in the early nineties, spent a couple of years in Austin trying to make it as a filmmaker, and even briefly studied film at a small state school in Dayton, Ohio in the mid-nineties, but that he kept winding up back in T or C—"this place exerts an uncanny gravity on some people," he said. Next, I asked the man if he'd ever heard anything about Jim Toop. He told me of course he had. He said, "Everybody around here has heard at least a little. Some of us even knew him." I said, "Did you know him?" The man said, "Met him a couple of times. When he was young—wasn't writing songs yet, even." Noting his use of past tense—"knew him"—I said, "So Toop doesn't live here, anymore?" The man laughed, said, "He's been dead for years now. Buried up at the Hot Springs Cemetery." Pointing to show me the way, he added, "You just walk up Cedar. It's less than a mile." Then he said, "But he's not buried under his own name. The city didn't want to have to do any special upkeep. Buried him under some Serb name someone pulled out of a book." I asked him for the name. He told me, but asked me never to tell anyone. I'm keeping my promise, and so for the purpose of this narrative, I'll use the name "Savas" in place of the real name. I asked him if this was supposed to be a secret how he knew about it. He told me that's one of the advantages of being a mostly invisible old man. "You see things," he said. "And hear things." I didn't visit the graveyard right away because I didn't want to know if that grave marker was really there. I wasn't even sure I believed the guy, and so I continued working on the assumption that Toop might still be alive. I didn't make it out to the graveyard until my third day in town, the day after I was arrested for getting my ass beat in a bar, and B, who you might remember was with me when I was shot, posted my bail and decided to visit the cemetery with me. Here, I need to pause for a moment because there's something about B that I need to address. I resisted mentioning this because I didn't think it was any of our business, but it's part of this story, so here goes: there is the distinct possibility that B is the son of Jim Toop and Angela. That is, he knew he was Angela's son, but had only learned that Toop might be his father the day before our visit to the graveyard. He'd never met Jim Toop, or seen any proof that his mother was involved with a man who even resembled Toop, but certain information led him to believe Toop was his father so he asked to accompany me to Toop's grave.

When we arrived at the cemetery, we started our search for the grave in the newer sections. Turtleback Mountain loomed in the distance as we wound through uneven rows of tombstones, many of which were made of smooth, red desert rocks, patched together with cement. After about twenty minutes, B found the marker and waved me over. It was squat and rectangular, was situated in a corner of the cemetery that seemed to be reserved for those who died without families, the lonely deceased. There was no birth date listed, just a death date of July 7, 2002. I knelt in front of the grave on the sandy earth under which I firmly believe Toop's body is buried, and for no good reason picked up a handful of sand. B stood with his hands clasped in front of him, looking down at the earth on which I was kneeling, as if solemnly observing the burial itself.

When B and I arrived back at the motel, we found my young friend packing his bags. I asked if he was leaving. That's when "David" told me that he'd spoken to Jim Toop. I told him that was absurd, that I'd just seen Toop's grave. "David" said, "I talked to him. He's some old bohemian asshole." From his description, I was pretty sure that "David" was talking about the same man I'd met. I told "David" about my own conversation with the man and Toop's grave. "David" said, "I know Toop's alive and I know that was him." Then: "I wish that wasn't Jim Toop who I met, but it was. And I can prove it to you." And that's when "David" told us we had to take him to find Al Walters so that we could all learn the "truth" once and for all.

Later, after we returned to New York, "David" believed that Al Walters's response to our intrusion was further proof that Toop was still alive. I trust you'll remember from the first installment in this series that when "David" tried to question Al Walters, he asked two questions, one about the whereabouts and activities of Toop, and the second about a murder cover-up. For "David," it would seem these two questions were inextricably linked. If there was a conspiracy to protect Jim Toop from something he'd been involved with—and I'll get to this in a moment—and Al Walters was not only involved with that conspiracy but also had helped to hide and protect Jim Toop in the following decades—well, of course Al Walters was going to be protective of his privacy and pull a shotgun on us. Despite what "David" thinks, Jim Toop doesn't need to be alive to explain Al Walters's response. The old man was simply scared, not that we'd find Jim Toop, but because we might discover the role that he and a few other Truth or Consequences residents had played in protecting Toop from criminal charges. So what were those criminal charges? What could possibly have caused a situation in which Jim Toop decided it was best to disappear from his own life? Here is, more or less, what probably happened:

When Jim Toop came back to Truth or Consequences in 1977 to visit old friends, he found his old love, the magnificent Angela, locked in a cruel, unforgiving marriage to an alcoholic police officer. On the last night of his visit, Toop, perhaps a bit drunk after leaving a local watering hole, and perhaps more than a little bit nostalgic after spending some time with Angela, tried to visit his former lover—perhaps to see her one last time before letting go forever, or perhaps to try to persuade her to leave with him, I couldn't possibly know, though I know which scenario I prefer—only to find her in a physical altercation with her husband in front of their house. When Toop tried to intervene, the husband, who may or may not have even known who Toop was, pulled a gun. Toop tackled the man and, as the two were wrestling on the ground, the gun went off, fatally wounding the husband. In the aftermath, it would seem that a combined desire to protect both Toop and the reputation of the newly deceased officer led to a small-scale conspiracy—Angela's husband was said to have been shot in the line of duty by a drifter, and Toop would "disappear: until people stopped asking questions, at which point, he would be free to re-enter his life. And everything pretty much went according to plan, up to the point that Toop would re-enter his life.

He never did.

Why not? I don't have an answer for that. Perhaps the questions never *really* stopped or there were enough new questions about Toop's disappearance that his re-entry into the public sphere would have raised *even more* questions. Or maybe it was something else altogether. Maybe Toop decided he *liked* living in the margins, that life was easier as a ghost. Maybe once he got a taste of that life, he couldn't bring himself to go back to anything else.

There is, as one might expect, an official story about all of this, but that story doesn't matter as I'm fairly confident in at least my theory's broad strokes, even if we can never know for sure the finer points of what happened. *This* is why Al Walters overreacted to "David's" questions—not because he was hiding a living, breathing Jim Toop, but because he'd helped orchestrate a big lie that lasted, more or less intact, for the better part of forty years. Every time I tried to explain this to "David," he'd say of the man he believed to be Toop, only, "But I looked in his eyes and I knew." When I asked him what he could have possibly seen in that man's eyes to make him believe he was Toop, my friend said, "Familiarity." Then: "Regret." At the time, I didn't know what "David" meant, and maybe I still don't entirely, but I'll come back to that later.

And that's the story you all wanted to read, right? Or was it? Are you disappointed? Did you expect something more? Something stranger or spookier? I know that the truth of what happened to Jim Toop isn't as sensational as years of theorizing might have led you all to believe or hope, but as far as I can tell, this is pretty much how it happened. For me, one big, far more interesting question remains—*why* did all of this happen? How did Toop end up at a point in his life where he had to disappear, and why, oh why, did he never come back? I don't know that I have hard answers for those question, but after my trip to Ohio, I believe I might have some ideas, and I'll share them with you in the next and final installment of this series.

PT. 4:
THIS HEARTACHE DANCES

(Editor's Note: After dedicating a large portion of three issues of Folk! *Magazine to Daniel Morus's sometimes informative, other times rambling, incoherent, and solipsistic "essay" on Jim Toop's* The Taxidermist's Catalog, *our editorial staff decided to run this final section online, finally returning our print magazine to its usual format. Even though we found this installment of Morus's essay fascinating, we couldn't help but think that audience interest in the piece probably peaked with Pt. 3, in which Morus provided a somewhat definitive narrative as to how and why Jim Toop disappeared. Thanks for reading along with us. It's our sincere hope not only that you enjoyed Daniel Morus's series of essays, but that you have also enjoyed finally hearing* The Taxidermist's Catalog. *–R.E.)*

Everybody who has been trying to understand Jim Toop's legacy has been going about it wrong for years. Many attempts focus on his disappearance to the point that Toop's body of work has become a footnote to the mystery that concluded his public life and career, the man having become a bit player in the mythology born from his disappearance. Others, myself included, have spent most of our energy chasing Angela in Toop's songs, sidelining Toop in the interest of romantic idealism. None of us have gotten it right. When we begin to study Toop as a man and a musician, when we begin not just to listen to but *hear* his body of work for what it is rather than as a gateway to foolish theories, it becomes clear that Toop's mythologies were not the focal points of his life—that is to say, Toop's disappearance and his romance with Angela weren't dominant, isolated threads, but formed a tightly woven braid that led to a logical ending for a man who couldn't escape his own past. On Toop's albums released during his life, we can trace this narrative, beginning with the Hollywood mythology and nostalgic desire for a simpler, more stable past on *New Ghosts for an Old City*, through the uneasy and anxious sense of displacement that characterizes *Black Triangle*, to the wistful, youthful longing of *Ohio Songs*, then, finally, to the romantic ache and pined-for domesticity of *Your Sunglasses are in the Junk Drawer*. The portrait of Toop that emerges from these albums, and which I came to truly understand after my trip to Ohio, is of a young man who, to borrow a line from Brian Wilson, "just wasn't made for these times," who was always and quietly out of step with his current time and place, who resents the past to which he can never return. Perhaps we should think of Toop as a man swallowed up by the facts of his own history—his own past, his own love—because he was never fully grounded in the present from which he disappeared. As such, when Toop was given the opportunity, when his past and present collided, opening a metaphorical rift within that present—a rift that provided entry into a new type of life, a pocket universe inside the universe we all inhabit—into which he could disappear, he took the opportunity. But I didn't understand this right away. I needed to go to Ohio first, to learn one last thing about Toop's hunger, his sadness, about the way he loved. But before we get to Ohio, there's one last big idea I want to explore, one last loose thread that needs to be folded into this narrative, as much for myself as for my readers. I want to talk about the love that many believe defined Jim Toop's life.

Some Toop enthusiasts forget that by the time *New Ghosts for an Old City* was released in 1969, Toop had already loved and lost his Angela, the great romantic ideal who, some believe, permeates much of his music. While many critics never bother to look for Angela in Toop's music before *Sunglasses*, some of us believe she's there, running parallel to the unreal beauty described in "Greta," and in the quiet romance of "Charlie"; in the lonely thirst of "Said the Cactus to the Cloud," and the bittersweet recognition of a brief but furious young love on "You Were A Loan." When we begin to trace Angela's possible appearances through Toop's career, it's tempting to see Angela as the dominant narrative, not just of Toop's music, but of his life. *If* that's the case—a big if—there's a particular romance to be found in such a story. Imagine, for a moment, the romantic potential in a story that finds teenage lovers reunited, brought closer together when one of them comes to the aid of the other. Consider the tragic implications of an inadvertent murder leading one of the lovers into hiding, forcing their love underground. It's a lovely idea and, in truth, for those who believe in the power of Toop's love for Angela, the fact that he's not still by her side in New Mexico is a compelling piece of evidence that he is really, truly dead. Forget that I saw his grave, and forget that there's nothing suggesting he is alive—the simple fact that Toop and Angela aren't together now should be proof enough that Toop is dead for those who resolutely believe in the importance of Angela to Toop's story. When I mentioned this as a potential argument in a conversation with "David" he said that my thinking was "sentimental," and "overly romantic."

This may come as a surprise, but I don't disagree with "David," not anymore. For those of you who have followed my writing career, you'll know that, historically, I've been an enthusiastic booster of criticism and scholarship that explores Angela's central role in Toop's songs. Over the years, I've spent a great deal of time, ink, and energy teasing references to Angela out of songs from all of Toop's albums, and trying to build a grand romantic narrative out of the stray bits and pieces Toop may or may not have intentionally left peppered through his songs. As much as it pains me to admit now, I've come to understand that the relationship shared by Angela and Toop was maybe not as magnificent as I once believed.

In fact, though I'd already started to believe this was the case based on my time in New Mexico, "David" convinced me further during the aforementioned conversation. When I suggested that Toop's absence in Angela's life was proof that Toop was dead, again, not because I was entirely convinced by that particular argument, but because I didn't think it was healthy for my young friend to be so invested in his belief that Toop is still alive, "David" said, "They could have fallen out of love." He went on to describe several versions of what could have happened between Toop and Angela: "Toop and Angela had sex, maybe the night her husband died, maybe the night before, maybe a week after, close enough that, when she became pregnant with her son, she could still pass it off as the child of her late husband." In one scenario, believing that B's father was Angela's late husband, Toop left, broken hearted, unable to deal with raising another man's child. In another, Toop knew the child was his, but didn't understand how B would benefit from taking his dead father's last name, was outraged that Angela would even consider giving their child the name of a man who hit her and so he left. In yet another of "David's" theories, Toop maintained his relationship with Angela through part of her pregnancy, but then was unwilling or unable to take an active role in the boy's birth, causing Angela to kick him out of her life. "Maybe that's how the great romance ends," "David" said. "With The Muse falling out of love with the poet because he didn't know how to be the partner she needed." I said, "That's a heavy bummer." He said, "Or maybe it's simpler than that. Maybe Jim Toop just wasn't cut out to be a dad and so he ran." When "David" said this, he paused, looked away, his eyes heavy with thought. I imagined he was thinking of his own father, whom he's never mentioned and who I had always assumed was absent. He said, "Maybe Jim Toop has other children he's never met, that maybe he doesn't even know about, scattered across the country." Then, "Or, I don't know, maybe his love for Angela just faded the way love sometimes fades, and that was that." I admit, still, when I think about Toop living in the margins, becoming a flesh and blood ghost, it's not all that difficult to imagine his love fading parallel to his metaphorically diminishing corporeality. When I told "David" how sad his theories made me feel, he apologized, said, "I know you want to believe in this kind of love, what with your past," and then he trailed off, reached across the table and put his hand on my shoulder. It was the first physical contact we'd shared outside of a few handshakes. With his hand still on my shoulder, "David" thanked me—I didn't and still don't know for what, but when he thanked me, I put my hand on top of his.

"David" is probably right about Toop and Angela. Though I'm still convinced that Toop is dead, it's entirely plausible that his love for Angela died before him. As I spoke with "David" that day, I began to consider the mournful arrangement of guitar, violin, and trumpet that opens the mostly instrumental "Desert Birds," the second track on *The Taxidermist's Catalog*. The song features only two sung lines, each repeated twice: at the beginning of the song, Toop sings, "See the birds, they move the desert sky," then at the end, "Bellies empty, they circle, dive, rise." "Desert Birds" is one of the earliest known songs to appear on *The Taxidermist's Catalog*, showing up on setlists as early as 1975. What strikes me now about the song is that, even before the song had lyrics, and even before Toop's return to New Mexico, there was a sadness in the arrangement, a hunger—but for what? I always assumed it was for Angela. Maybe it was. Or maybe that was just easier to believe. As my investigation neared its end, I realized that I didn't really know anymore if Angela ever was the main object of Toop's sad hunger and, if she was, how deep and true that hunger really went. And that's when I realized that what I needed to do if I wanted to better understand Jim Toop was to try to understand that hunger. And that's why I had to go back to Ohio, to see if I could feel the ineffable whatever-ness of Jim Toop, to take in the one place that was constant for him, that didn't sour as he aged. Maybe Toop and Angela's love never soured—but it probably did. Why wouldn't B have met Jim

Toop if the singer was still in his mother's life? He almost certainly would have.

So I went to Ohio, and I bought a bag of weed from a kid working at a record shop in the Oregon District, and I drove out to Fairborn and found a field not far from Wright Patterson Air Force Base, and I watched the planes take off and land, just like in Toop's song "We Learned to Fly." I don't know that I learned anything concrete about Jim Toop from the experience, but I felt an easy peace lying there, stoned, watching the planes. I thought about a young Jim Toop in this exact spot, or somewhere like it, feeling whatever it is that teenagers feel when they're stoned and watching man-made machines move across the sky. I thought about how the kind of love I imagined Jim Toop shared with Angela seemed both impossibly eternal but also as fleeting as the gleaming planes passing overhead. I sat up and looked across the field at the base's hangars and imagined alien bodies frozen inside, bits of their black triangles or flying saucers or whatever cataloged and stored in cavernous, dusty storage rooms. And I thought about the much more real, much more tangible conspiracy in Truth or Consequences and the people who had kept it a secret for so long. And I thought about one of my favorite lines from "Weather," in which Toop sings of missing the comfort of Ohio's seasons and fondly recalls "the cool breeze and red cheeks" that come with the cold. I imagined Toop lying in this very spot, fourteen and starry-eyed, a girl beside him, both teens stoned and red cheeked, mouths mashed together, hands fumbling beneath clothes, and I wondered—where is Angela in *this*? Then it occurred to me: maybe Angela was more of an idea for Toop than a person, a symbol for something else long lost and irretrievable, and *that* is what resonated with me, with us, critics and fans alike, for all these years—not Angela, herself, as a person or even an ideal, but Angela as a symbol of all that we've lost to time's forward march. Even in "Angela," Toop sings in the past tense, as a love he left behind when he "Packed [his] car and [he] hit the road." There is no doubt in my mind, both from listening to Toop's songs and meeting her in person, that Toop shared a romantic relationship with Angela, but maybe that's, with apologies to Raymond Carver, not exactly what he was singing about when he sang about love. And lying out in that field, I began to feel something else that I couldn't quite pin down, something unnamable and foreign. Something that is maybe only for young people or, perhaps, for old people trying to feel like young people. And then I thought about "David," partly about his insistence that Jim Toop is still alive, and partly about his hand on my shoulder and how it was good in a way I'd never really known. And then I thought about my first wife, and then I used my cell phone to call her, but got her voicemail, again, and so the next day, after waking up foggy from the weed, I drove up to Bowling Green and, knowing that she'd probably be holding office hours, thanks to an online syllabus I found on her department's website, I visited her, not because I was trying to feel young again, I don't think, but because I still didn't understand what had happened, still didn't know how I got to this point, and I thought there was something to learn hidden inside of that so old loss.

When I arrived at her office, Betty's gaze was fixed on a manuscript. I knocked gently to get her attention. She looked up at me with a start, asked what I was doing there. I was relieved that she even recognized me. I said, "Town looks different. And the campus." She nodded, rattled off a few uninteresting sentences about revitalization and recruitment and new buildings and wider roads. Then she asked again why I was there. I started from the beginning, rambled on about the unearthed Jim Toop album and my investigations. She nodded politely as I spoke, said, "That still doesn't explain why you're here." So I told her about how I'd come to the conclusion that Toop was dead, but I was still trying to understand something about him. Then Betty said, "But why did you come to see me? What do I have to do with Jim Toop?" And so I asked her what I needed to know: why did she fall out of love with me? She looked at me with an expression that might have been a mixture of incredulity and discomfort, or maybe something else. She said, "You came all this way to ask me that?" Then, "After all these years?" I tried to explain why it was important, about Jim Toop and Angela and whatever feeling I was starting to feel the deeper I dug into Toop's life, and how the more I began to understand whatever he was feeling all those years, the more I began to believe that the key to understanding Toop, his music, and what defined him as a man, was all somehow tied into the way Toop loved and lost love, the way all of us love and lose love.

Betty looked up at me from behind her desk and didn't speak for at least two minutes. Finally, she responded, said, "I don't know why I fell out of love with you." Then, after a beat, she said, "Maybe it's just a thing that happens. Or it was just a thing that happened to us." Then, and this is as direct a quote as possible, though I didn't record our conversation, she said, "We grow up and we have these ideas about love and relationships, and what it all is and what it can all be like, and then we start to get older and we look at our lives and they don't, can't possibly, ever measure up." Maybe she didn't say all of this, my memory is bad, but it's what she meant. She went on: "And people will write advice columns about how much work is necessary to build strong, lasting relationships, and how the kind of happiness we dream up when we're young and don't know any better is impossible. But somewhere, in the backs of our minds, we suspect that that's bullshit. I knew there could be more. You and I, Daniel, we were good. We did ok—but that was all. And I knew that, in this life, there is the potential for so much more, for a bigger, louder love, the kind that rumbles and thrums, its frequencies resonating through lifetimes, and I stopped one day and looked around and said, 'Is this all I get? For the rest of my life?' And there was Michael from Faculty Senate, and he was sweet and fun, and maybe, at first, it was the thrill of the infidelity, the rush of new love, but then I began to realize that what I felt with him was more than I had felt with you, ever, and I needed to take that risk." Then, after a long pause: "What about you, Daniel? Have you been in love with me all these years? Is that why you're here?"

I shook my head, told her it wasn't that. This was never about missing Betty. It was about understanding. I said, "I just wanted to understand." Then I asked her about Michael and she told me he'd died suddenly of a heart attack two years prior. I told her I was sorry, and she said it was fine. She said, "I miss him, but I'm ok on my own now." Before I left, Betty stood up and offered a hug. I stepped into her embrace and hugged her back. It felt obligatory, and that was fine. As I started to leave, I was tempted to ask another question, to try to learn more about Betty, about myself, about Jim Toop. I paused in the door and Betty asked, "Something else?" I thought back to her explanation of slowly forgetting how to be in love with me and how she'd said that she knew about the potential for a bigger, louder love. That's what I wanted to ask, how she knew all that, what had happened before me, who she had loved so long ago that showed her that that kind of love was possible. Betty and me, we'd never spent much time talking about past loves, but there in her office doorway, I thought I might want to know what boy or moment or feeling from so long ago had shaped my ex-wife so. But I didn't ask her. I said, "It was nice seeing you." Then, turning to leave: "Be well."

It didn't matter what thing from Betty's past showed her she could have more. I scanned my memory for my own past loves and couldn't think of any who cast so tall a shadow. That's not how I love, and I know that now. But Betty *had* felt something bigger, had seen some potential in her life that I couldn't fulfill, and, truthfully, the closest I'd ever come to feeling anything like it was vicariously through Jim Toop's songs about—or maybe not about—Angela. Whether I was responding to the ideal love I always believed she represented, or the loss of that love, or both, the biggest love in my life was a character in a song, was somebody else's love.

On my drive back to Ohio, I tried not to think about Betty, or Angela, or loneliness. I thought about how I still didn't know, after all of my investigations, how *The Taxidermist's Catalog* ended up on Richard Epps's desk, and I thought about "David's" firm belief that he'd met Jim Toop in Truth or Consequences, and I thought about Angela—not as a character in Toop's songs, but as a real woman—and I thought about B and how strange it would be for Jim Toop to have been alive for so long without meeting his son. I was maybe beginning to understand how he could go so far out of his way to embrace that much loneliness. I realized that I didn't know as much about Jim Toop, or B, or Angela, or Betty, or Amanda, or "David" or myself as I thought. I guess I was thinking about loneliness, after all. But then, everything always comes back to lonely, doesn't it?

The day after I returned to New York from Ohio, Ronnie Epps, the son of this magazine's editor, knocked on my door. He was dropping off a letter that had been delivered to the *Folk! Magazine* offices and checking up on me on his father's behalf. As he handed me the letter, he asked if I'd found what I was looking for on my travels. I told him I wasn't sure. He asked, "Did you find Jim Toop?" I told him I did. He asked if I got an interview. I said, "He's dead." Ronnie said, "You sure?" I told him I was. He said, "That's too bad," and asked who the letter was from. There was no return address, but the post mark was from New Mexico. I opened it and found a photograph inside. It was a picture of B kneeling beside the "Savas" tombstone. There was also a letter. Ronnie asked about the picture. I told him it was a guy who I think is Toop's son in front of that grave that I think is Toop's. Ronnie said, "You didn't find out all that much, really, did you?" I told him I found out plenty, then excused myself and told him I had work to tend to. Before he left, Ronnie Epps looked at the picture and said, "Guy looks familiar." I said, "He looks a lot like Toop, doesn't he?" Ronnie said, "I was thinking of someone else, but yeah—he looks like Toop, too." And then he left. When he was gone, I looked at the photograph again, and I think I saw what he saw.

Before I started work on this series, I read B's letter. I won't reprint it here, partially because it was personal, and partially because it didn't contain much of note, at least in regards to Toop. It was a nice letter, though. B apologized for punching me in the bar one night, and referenced an unpleasant conversation we'd shared just prior to that, and then he thanked me for helping him learn about his past—much of which, he wrote, had been confirmed by his mother—and he talked about how nice it was to meet "David" and me and that he was inspired by our friendship.

A few days after I received B's photo and letter, I met with "David" for coffee at a local place near his mom's house. I told him about the letter and photo, asked him how his semester was wrapping up. For the first thirty minutes or so, that's all we talked about, like old friends, not the co-conspirators we'd become during our investigation. For those first thirty minutes, we didn't talk at all about Jim Toop or New Mexico. I told "David" about my trip to Ohio, and he told me about his mother learning the real reason he'd missed several days of school, and then having to explain to her why he'd been in New Mexico. He had successfully managed to persuade her that his trip was acceptable by using a series of *X-Files* metaphors—his mother is a big fan, I'm told—about the importance of knowing the truth. "You didn't get in trouble?" I asked. "At first, a little," he said. Then, "She's a good mom. I'm lucky." After that, our conversation fell into a slight lull. "David" asked me how my shoulder was healing, and I told him it was fine. Then I asked "David" if he thought either of us had found the truths we were seeking in New Mexico. "David" said it didn't really matter. Then I asked him, again, the one question I'd been deeply curious about since we met, why he was so invested in finding Jim Toop alive. "David" said, "It doesn't really matter." I said, "I was shot because of it." I told him he owed me more than "It doesn't really matter." He said, "I was looking for something. Just like you." I asked him if he found it. He said, "Did you?" And even though I didn't really find much of anything concrete, I said "I think so." I asked "David," what he'd been looking for. He said, "It's dumb. It's not really what I was looking for, anyway." Then:

"Did I ever tell you I used to believe I didn't have a biological father?" I told him he hadn't. Then, "Or that I thought I was an alien-human hybrid? I used to want to be abducted." I told him that wasn't uncommon, asked him if that's why he went to New Mexico, because he wanted to be abducted. He laughed, said, "No—but I found what I needed, I suppose." I goaded my friend, teased him for being enigmatic and vague, half playful and half hoping he'd share just a little more, to confirm the suspicion that grew out of the photograph sent by B. He didn't say a word, but that's ok. It's a lot to process. Maybe he'll tell me eventually, or maybe it's all in my head. Instead of addressing that, and this might not be entirely accurate as my memory isn't what it used to be, he said, "Sometimes the past is a terrible thing that grinds inside of us. And sometimes it frees us, is illuminating, instructive, and wondrous." Then: "And sometimes it's both and all you can do is say fuck it, grab anything that's worth a damn and run without looking back." Astonished by my young friend's words, I couldn't respond. "Know what I mean?" he asked. I said, "Yeah, I know what you mean."

And I did and do know what he meant. And now I think about Jim Toop, living in the margins in New Mexico for all those years, however many years he lived, the past grinding inside him. And what better place to return to Toop's music, specifically, "Sideways Glances," the third song on *The Taxidermist's Catalog*, and the song in which the album finds its name. On the surface, it's a sad love song, possibly about Angela, though she isn't named. In the song, Toop sings, "Forget the future, forget your name/The past is a suture made of flame," which seems as direct a reference to any about Angela, especially if we consider the probability that the two weren't the great romantic pairing we've so often assumed them to be. In those lines, we can hear Toop's attitude towards Angela souring in whatever present moment the song was recorded, and onward into the future. But then the song takes an odd turn during its bridge, shortly before sliding into a final set of choruses (the song's chorus: "You gave me sideways glances, glances, glances/This heartache dances, dances, dances through the desert"). That bridge, of course, is where the album's title comes from and, on close examination, doesn't appear to be about Angela at all:

> I saw her sideways
> She saw me back
> Two kids caught in a fog—
> Now I only see her in pieces
> Oh, check the taxidermist's catalog

While fog isn't completely unheard of in Truth or Consequences, this scene *feels* native to Ohio. Additionally, when we consider Toop's shift from second to third person, and the use of the word "kids," it would seem that here, Toop is no longer singing about his failed love with Angela, but another love, an older love, an original love that rumbles, and thrums, and resonates across a lifetimes—did that rumble grind inside Toop or set him free? Maybe both? Certainly it led to Jim Toop's exile and drove his souring toward the present that we hear on *The Taxidermist's Catalog*. And so now, when I think of Jim Toop dead in the ground, buried under a made up name, or as ashes scattered by Angela or some older, more primal love, or, what the hell, living alone as an elderly desert hippie, either way, there's hardly a difference, I think of a man whose life was the product of so much being set free or grinding, grinding, grinding. That's all I really know about Jim Toop, that he let the past consume him.

And maybe that past ruined him, or maybe it made him better—we'll never know. How could we? Sometimes knowing how the past consumes us is enough to let it go. Did Jim Toop recognize that? I know I finally did. And that's all I have to say about that. I'm sure the conspiracy theorists will write to refute these articles, and I don't doubt that Toop enthusiasts will continue to travel to Truth or Consequences in search of Angela, B, and the old hippie who *isn't* Toop, that is all immaterial, though, because the only truth about Jim Toop that matters is his music, man, is the way his songs preserve feelings and moments, frozen in time, like the trophies that fill the pages of a taxidermist's catalog.

ACKNOWLEDGEMENTS AND THANKS TO

My wife, Jessica, for her patience and support with all of this writing. My parents. Friends and colleagues who offered feedback and assistance over the years: Brandon Hobson, Nate Knapp, and Joshua Cross for your feedback; Patrick and Tina Abbott in part for their lovely café in which much of this was written, revised, rewritten, and edited, and also for their notes on music, their spotting of typos, and their assistance with research; and Jonathan Budil for his cyber security expertise. The English Department at Oklahoma State University where I started this novel as a Ph.D. candidate. The English Department at Southeast Missouri State University where I finished it. Jon Billman who, in Oklahoma, turned me on to a magazine article that inspired this novel. Dr. Susan Kendrick, our fearless department chair at Southeast for always fighting her damndest to protect her faculty's time so that we can continue writing our books and doing our research. Truth or Consequences, New Mexico; I've visited twice now, once to get a feel for the place I was writing into this book, and once on a road trip—I know the representation isn't entirely accurate, but I hope I capture the atmosphere of one of my new favorite weird, charming little cities. Jacob Aron, for writing "The Cyperweapon That Could Take Down the Internet," which helped teach me enough about hacking and cybersecurity to write about it. *Sundog Lit*, Justin Lawrence Daugherty, and Jill Talbot for publishing a short excerpt from this novel under the title "An Almost Holy Absence of Everything" in their "(Letters from) the Road" issue. Again, my heartfelt thanks to all of you because we're finally here, and shit yeah it's cool.

James Brubaker is the author of *Pilot Season*, *Liner Notes*, and *Black Magic Death Sphere: (science) fictions*. His work has appeared in *Zoetrope: All Story*, *Michigan Quarterly Review*, *Hobart*, *Booth*, and *The Collagist*, among other venues. He lives in Missouri with his wife and cat, and teaches writing there.

CPSIA information can be obtained
at www.ICGtesting.com
Printed in the USA
FFHW021333151019
55589559-61392FF